MORE HOPES AND DREAMS

1950. After her marriage went badly wrong, Dolly Taylor returned to Rotherhithe from America. She is now helping her best friend, Penny, to walk again after she contracted polio. Not able to have children of her own, Dolly envies Penny for having a beautiful baby daughter, Gail. Penny's husband, Reg, has set up his own business as a builder, and offers Dolly a job in the office. Tony, who was engaged to Dolly before the war, also works for Reg, and is still pursuing his childhood sweetheart. Although Dolly lives in close-knit Wood Street, with friends and family around her, will she ever find happiness there?

MORE HOPES AND DREAMS

MORE HOPES AND DREAMS

by

Dee Williams

Magna Large Print Books
Long Preston, North Yorkshire,
BD23 4ND, England.

British Library Cataloguing in Publication Data.

A catalogue record of this book is
available from the British Library

ISBN   978-0-7505-4416-0

First published in Great Britain 2016 by Shadenet Publishing

Published in Large Print 2017 by arrangement with
Dee Williams

Magna Large Print is an imprint of Library Magna Books Ltd.

Printed and bound in Great Britain by
T.J. (International) Ltd., Cornwall, PL28 8RW

Thank you to Sue Shade, for all her hard work in helping me to self-publish this novel.

Thank you to my granddaughter, Samantha, for producing this lovely cover, and to her and her sister, Emma, for being such patient models.

I also wish to thank all those kind people who have been asking when will there be a new book. Well, here it is. I hope you like it.

This is for my family who are always there when I need them. So thank you, Carol, Gez, Emma, Samantha, and Oscar – my new grandson-in-law, welcome to the family. I love you all and wish you a long and loving, happy future.

INTRODUCTION TO
MORE HOPES AND DREAMS

Many times, I have been asked to write a sequel to *Hopes and Dreams*. It seems that my readers would like to know what happened to Dolly after she returned home from America to find her best friend, Penny, who'd had a baby, confined to a wheelchair after contracting polio. They would love to hear about the ups and downs the two friends have when they get together again.

Dolly Taylor lives at 20 Wood Street with her father, Jim, and mother, Grace. Before the war, she was engaged to Tony Marchant, who still lives at 98 Wood Street with his widowed mother. However, Dolly fell in love with Joe Walters, a GI, and married him in May 1944. She eventually joined him in America on 6 May 1946, returning to England shortly before Christmas 1949, after her marriage failed.

Shortly after getting married, Dolly had been caught in the Woolworths' rocket attack. As a result, she lost her unborn baby and could not have any more children.

Penny Watts married Reg Smith. They now live at 2 Wood Street, with Reg's mother, Ivy, also a widow.

Penny has two younger brothers: Billy, seventeen, and Jack, twenty, who is away on National Service. Penny's daughter, Gail, was born in November 1949.

Reg is now running his own building business with the help of his gratuity money. He employs Dolly's father, Jim; Penny's brother, Billy, as an apprentice; Tony, and Dolly who works in the office.

Chapter 1

January 1950

'Hello, love,' said Grace when her daughter walked into the kitchen. 'How was your first day at work?'

'Not too bad,' said Dolly, putting her handbag on the table. She looked in the mirror that hung over the fireplace and, after taking off her hat, gently fluffed up the back of her hair. 'It's freezing out there.'

'What was it like in your office?'

Dolly laughed. 'Not exactly The Ritz. I'm in a wooden hut on site.'

'Is it very cold in there?'

'Reg brought me in a paraffin stove, so I've got something to warm me hands on, and I am able to make a cup of tea. It's all right till someone opens the door.'

'Let's hope the weather gets better soon, although it's got a few months to go yet.'

'I hope so too, for Reg's sake. He can't do a lot of outside work in this weather. It's a good job there's still a lot of people that want their bomb-damaged rooms decorated.'

'That's those poor devils who can get their landlords to pay for it,' said her mother.

When Dolly had returned to England, she was surprised to find that so many things were still

15

rationed or in short supply. She thought about all the lovely clothes for sale in America, and those wonderful nylon stockings; she was pleased she'd brought a few pairs back with her.

Grace looked at her daughter. She was so thrilled to have her home again after her years in America. She glanced at the official-looking letter leaning against the clock on the mantelpiece. With a bit of luck, Dolly would be able to start putting her life back together again. It was a new year and the beginning of a new decade. Hopefully, it would be better than the last ten years. 'So, what did you have to do today?'

'Just find out where everything's kept. Mind you, it's going to take a bit of time to get a lot of the stuff sorted. Reg certainly needs someone to put everything in order. There are piles of paper and invoices everywhere. He's very untidy.'

'Well, he has been rather busy what with starting his own business, and there's Penny and the new baby to worry about. I reckon he's been wonderful.'

'So do I...' Dolly had also been staring at the mantelpiece. 'Is that for me?'

Her mother nodded.

Dolly took the letter and, turning it over, said, 'It's from America.'

'I could see that.'

As she sat at the table and slowly opened the envelope, a tear trickled down her cheek.

'You all right, love?' asked Grace, putting an arm round her daughter's shoulder.

Dolly nodded and wiped the tear away. 'It's from Joe's solicitor. It says Joe's divorcing me on

16

the grounds of desertion.'

'You were expecting that.'

'I know. But this makes it very final.'

Dolly knew that the past six years were now well and truly over, but she would never forget the good times she'd had being a bride and going to America. It had been a wonderful experience, but it was now time to put her marriage to Joe behind her. It wouldn't be long now until her divorce papers came through.

'I'll pour out the tea,' said her mother.

'Thanks. I'll pop in and see Penny afterwards.'

'OK, love. I expect your father will be home early tonight, so you know roughly what time dinner will be on the table. Don't be too late. Remember, his darts night has been changed because of New Year's Day.'

Dolly smiled. 'I'll only be a little while.' She was pleased that her dad was also working with Reg. That meant, apart from his pension, there was some money coming in, and it gave him something to do.

After she'd finished her cup of tea, Dolly said, 'See you in a bit.' She picked up her hat and, pulling her coat collar up over her ears, hurried along to number two, where Penny lived with her husband, Reg, and his mother, Ivy Smith.

She didn't bother to knock on the front door; she just pulled the key through the letter box and, like everyone else, walked in. 'It's only me,' she said, pushing open the kitchen door.

'Hello there, Dolly, love,' said Ivy. 'How was your first day working with that son of mine?'

Dolly smiled. 'Fine. Where's Pen?'

17

'Just putting Gail down. You can pop in if you like.'

'Thanks.'

'Would you like a cup of tea?'

'No, thanks. I've just had one.'

Dolly went along to the front room that had been converted for Penny's wheelchair. She gently pushed open the door and stood there for a moment taking in the lovely scene.

Penny was leaning over her baby's cot and gently stroking her daughter's tiny face. 'Who's a good girl for her mum, then?' she cooed.

Dolly swallowed hard. 'Hi, Pen,' she whispered.

'Dolly, come on in and look at your lovely god-daughter.'

'Hello there, my little beauty,' said Dolly, gently stroking baby Gail's cheek. Turning to Penny, she said, 'And how are you, my old mate?'

'I'm fine. What sort of a day have you had working with my husband? I hope he's looking after you.'

Dolly smiled. 'He's been great. Mind you, his office is in a mess.'

'I know, and I'm thrilled that you're going to sort it all out for him.'

'So am I. I just hope I'll be able to cope.'

'Give it time.'

Dolly sat on the bed. 'I got a letter from Joe's solicitor today.'

'And what did he have to say?'

Penny knew how things had been for Dolly after she had gone to America as a GI bride.

'He's divorcing me.'

'You knew that was on the cards.'

18

'I know, but it's still a bit of a shock when you see it in official writing.'

'Dolly, I'm so sorry things didn't work out for you and Joe.'

'So am I.'

'Now you can move on and pick up your life again. Do you still have a soft spot for him?'

Dolly nodded. 'I really did love him, Pen.'

'I know you did, but that part of your life is over now. Look at me; I've had to learn to adapt. Believe me, it's been bloody hard at times.'

Dolly threw her arms round her best friend. Silently, they both shed a few tears.

'God,' Penny began, 'who'd have thought all those years ago when we were in the shelter worrying whether we would live to see the next day, that you would have been married and back from America, and I'd be stuck in a wheelchair and not able to take my daughter out in her pram.'

Dolly wiped the tears from her face. 'You will push your daughter's pram one day, and I shall be here helping you every step of the way.'

'I hope so. Oh, I do so hope so.' Penny also brushed her tears away. 'Reg said he was pleased that you were going to work for him. He knew he needed help, but didn't fancy anybody coming in that he didn't know. He's not used to being the boss and was worried that someone might take advantage of him.'

Dolly laughed. 'Can you honestly see anyone taking advantage of Reg?'

'No, not really. But he didn't want that Meg Windsor coming in. She's like her mother – a bit of a blather-mouth. One day, before you knew it,

19

everything about his business would be up and down the street.'

'Did Tony want her to work for Reg then?'

'Good God, no! Tony's worried to death that she's gonna whisk him up the aisle. Thank goodness you're back to put that idea right out of her mind.'

Dolly knew that Meg had a soft spot for Tony, even when she and Tony were engaged at the beginning of the war. As with so many couples, her and Tony's engagement had been a hurried affair. They had grown up together and had been going out for years, but when he was called up for National Service, they wanted to make it official.

'I told you,' said Dolly, 'I'm not getting married again.'

'I know, but that's what you say now. Give it time.'

Dolly wasn't going to get into that argument. 'I have to go. Dad will be home in a minute, and Mum will have the dinner on the table. I'll pop in later, if you like.'

'I'd like that.'

Dolly kissed her fingers and put them on Gail's tiny face. She then kissed Penny's cheek. 'See you later.'

Penny sat and watched her friend walk away. What wouldn't she give to be able to walk again? Nobody knew how hard it was to adjust to sitting all day and feeling so helpless. Her baby stirred.

'What is going to happen to us, my darling,' she said, gently stroking her daughter's soft cheek. 'Will I be able to take you to school one day and take you shopping?' Tears slid down Penny's cheek. 'Will you want a crippled mother?'

'All right, Dad?' asked Dolly as she walked into the kitchen.

'I'm fine, but what about you? Your mother told me that Joe's solicitor will be sending you divorce papers.'

'I was expecting them, but it's still a bit of a shock.'

'Well, that part of your life is well and truly over, so you must try to start again. After all, you are still very young.'

Dolly smiled. She loved her dad and knew he was happy to have her back in England. He was heartbroken when she married Joe and went to America, but as he said, that was behind her now and she had to start her life all over again. Although, she knew she would never forget Joe. After all, he had been a special part of her life.

'So how was your day working with Reg?' asked her father.

'I didn't see a lot of him. He just showed me the office and more or less said to get on with it. There's plenty of filing and putting things in order. But I think I shall enjoy doing that, being on my own and looking after his business affairs.'

'That's good,' said her mother as she put the dinner on the table, 'Sorry, the meat's a bit sparse. Who'd have thought that all these years after the war ended, things would still be on ration? A shilling's worth of meat doesn't go far.'

'You do a grand job, Grace,' said Jim.

'It must have been wonderful to see all that

food in America,' said Grace, sitting next to her daughter.

'Yes it was. Those Yanks didn't know what the war was all about. They couldn't believe it when I told them how little we had to manage on. The shops are stacked with stuff we haven't even heard about. And you should see all the different varieties of food.'

'Well, it is a big country,' said Jim. 'And they don't have to import goods like we do.'

'I know.' Dolly knew her father was thinking of the time he was in the Merchant Navy and how lucky he'd been, and the ships he'd seen sunk when they crossed the Atlantic bringing supplies here. She also thought about her own journey from New York to Deansville. It had taken two days. 'I think the thing I enjoyed most about America was the bathroom, and not having to go outside in the cold to the lav.'

'Now, that's something I'd really like,' said her mother, 'a lav inside. That must be the height of luxury.' Grace was pleased her daughter was now talking about her life in America. Was she beginning to accept that it was over?

Later that evening, Dolly was sitting with Penny. It was getting late when Reg came home.

'How did you get on today?' he asked Dolly, after he'd kissed his wife and checked up on his sleeping daughter.

'Fine.'

'Good. I'll pop in tomorrow to see if you need anything.'

'OK. Look, I'll be off now. See you tomorrow, Reg, and you, Pen.' Dolly kissed Penny and left them alone.

'So how did it go today?' Reg asked Penny.

'Same as usual. Bathed Gail with the help of your mum, of course. Struggled to the lav. Did the veg. And that about sums up my day.'

'I'm sorry, love. I wish there was something I could do to make things better for you.' Reg held his wife close. He could almost feel her frustration.

'I'll be all right. It's just that I'm having a bad day.'

'When you're ready, I'll pop you into bed and massage your legs.'

'I'd like that.'

It was a crisp, cold night as Dolly walked back home. She thought of how she and Penny had laughed and talked about the good times they'd had. All their lives they had been friends, but now both of their lives had changed dramatically, and they couldn't turn back the clock. What would the new year of this new decade have in store for them?

She thought about the sad, but happy feeling she'd had when she held Gail at her christening. It had been such a privilege to be her godmother, and she would do everything she could to make that darling baby as happy as possible, as she was going to have a lot of hurdles to overcome in the future. Dolly wished she had been there for Penny when she was first struck down with the deadly illness. Polio had affected so many people. To be pregnant must have been a double blow. Gail had to be born by Caesarean delivery, and Penny was terrified her baby would also have the virus, but thank God, so far, everything was fine. Penny had told Dolly that she was one of the lucky ones, as only her legs were affected. She had been so worried about going into an iron lung.

Dolly's mind wandered back to her own baby. If only they hadn't gone shopping on the day that the rocket had fallen on Woolworths. If only her baby had lived – how different things might have been. What if there had been another baby? She probably would still be in America, and she and Joe would still be together. There were a lot of 'what ifs' in her and her best friend's life. Dolly got angry with herself. She couldn't change things. She was back home now, and determined to help Penny as much as she could. Penny deserved every happiness.

That night in bed, the moon shone through the curtains as Dolly snuggled down and tried to sleep. Today, she had been working for Reg. She had been nervous, not only about the job, but also about seeing Tony, as he too now worked for Reg. After everything that had happened, she really thought he would have settled down and married Meg, but after the christening, he had told her that he didn't love Meg. He'd been hoping that Dolly would come back into his life, as he still loved her. He had been full of hope. Deep down, she still had feelings for Tony, but knew that she couldn't rush into another relationship, even though they had been engaged once, many years ago. Although he'd been her first love, could she love him as much as she had loved Joe? She promised herself that she would never hurt Tony again.

Chapter 2

It was the following Friday when Tony walked into the office.

'This is nice and cosy.' He held his hands over the stove. 'So how's my best girl, then?'

'Tony, I'm not your girl,' said Dolly, pleased that she worked alone and didn't have anyone else around to hear this conversation, otherwise any other girl would think she was mad not to go out with a good-looking bloke like Tony.

He grinned and held up both hands. 'Sorry. You can't blame me for trying, now, can you?' His blue eyes twinkled.

Dolly smiled. 'What can I do for you?' She tried to sound businesslike.

'Where's the boss?'

'At the bank.'

'I thought I'd just pop in to see if the wages were ready.'

'I've just started doing the paperwork. Reg said that you might be taking on a big job.'

'Yeh, if he manages to get it and a bank loan, but he'll have to take on more blokes though. Us four can't manage anything that's too big. I tell you something, it's a good job he's got you here. He seems to be spending most of the time doing estimates and sorting out the paperwork. Sometimes, I think he's sorry he ever started on his own.'

'Well, I can't do estimates, but apart from

those, he doesn't have to worry about the paperwork side of the business. Hopefully, I can take
care of that.'

'That's what I told him. I'm glad to see he's
looking after you in here. This place is freezing;
he'll have to get you another stove.'

Dolly smiled to herself. Things were still hard
to get, so Reg must have known the right people,
but even though he had managed to get her a
paraffin stove, she still kept her coat on. She also
had a decent chair, a desk with drawers under-
neath, and there was a typewriter. She wasn't a
very good typist, but she now had a chance to
perfect her skills. She remembered when she and
Penny went to evening classes to learn to type.
They really only went for the dances and to meet
other boys, and you could only go to the dances
if you enrolled in a class. They had a lot of fun
and drove the poor teacher – a Miss James – mad
with all their giggling and mucking about.

Tony broke into her thoughts. 'I made these,' he
said, going to the stack of shelves that stood
against the wall. 'You won't be able to pull 'em
on top of you as they're screwed to the wall.'

'That's reassuring,' said Dolly.

'Right, I'd better be off before the boss comes
in and catches us.'

'We are only talking, and it will stay that way.
Now, be off with you.'

Tony left the office whistling the Frank Sinatra
tune 'Some Enchanted Evening'.

Dolly smiled to herself. Regardless of what
Tony had seen and been through in the army, he
hadn't changed; he was still the happy-go-lucky

26

bloke she had once been engaged to. She sighed. How different things might have been had she not fallen in love with Joe, become a GI bride, and gone to America. Tears threatened to fill her eyes. Despite all that had happened, she still loved her husband, but sadly, he wouldn't be her husband for much longer.

Reg came in and dropped a money bag on Dolly's desk. 'You've got the wages list I gave you?'

'It's all here, and the wage packets.'

'Good, now we can go through them, and the insurance stamps, and the tax.'

'Reg, I'm a bit worried about that. I've never done anything like it before.'

'Don't worry; you'll soon get the hang of it. I had to learn after Penny gave up doing it for me.'

Dolly knew that Penny used to help in the evenings after she finished working as a wages clerk. That was before she had caught polio, and had Gail.

'You know you could always ask Pen to give you a hand if it gets too much. She does help me out now and again.'

'I couldn't do that.'

'Why not? Knowing her, she'd be more than happy to help.'

'She's got enough on her plate.'

'Honestly, I bet she'd be thrilled to bits to give you a hand.'

'I'll see how I get on.'

'If the blokes get the wrong money, believe me, they'll soon be in here complaining.'

After Reg left, Dolly very carefully went over the wages sheets and painstakingly sorted out the money, insurance stamps, and tax. After she had been over it several times, she put the appropriate money, along with a wage slip, in the right envelope, and entered everything in the ledger as Reg had instructed. With a sigh of relief, she got up and put the kettle on. She felt she needed a cuppa after that.

Thank goodness Reg had only three other people, including Tony, working for him at the moment. One was her father, and the other was Penny's youngest brother, Billy. The older brother, Jack, was now doing his National Service. The boys had settled down and grown up since Dolly had gone away, and as Penny had said, since she'd caught polio, and had Gail, they had changed. Dolly also knew that if Reg got this new contract there would be more men working for him so she knew she had a lot to learn, and learn quickly. Perhaps tonight she would ask Penny to show her the ropes.

'All right, love?' Her father asked as Dolly walked into the kitchen.

'Yes, thanks.'

Jim was often home before her; that was if he wasn't in the van driving to the builders' yard to collect some materials. When he was on site, they couldn't work in the dark or in buildings that hadn't any lights, so at this time of the year his working days could be short.

'Pleased to see you got the wages right,' he said.

'Reg helped me. I'm going in to see Penny later, and ask her to show me about this insurance and tax business.'

'It's good to see you're really serious about this job,' said her mother.

Dolly only smiled. She was very grateful to Reg for giving her a chance to do something really useful; not like standing behind a counter in Woolies as she and Penny had done before they went into a factory to help with the war effort.

After dinner, Dolly helped her mother with the dishes, and then went along to see Penny.

'Reg told me you was coming in. I should have given you a hand with the books before this,' her friend said, wheeling her way into the kitchen.

'You've got enough to worry about, without giving me lessons on how to be a wages clerk.'

'Got to make sure you're looking after my old man's business. Don't want to see you go bankrupt, do we, love?' She gave Reg's hand a squeeze. He was sitting at the table, and gave her a broad grin.

'I won't let that happen,' said Dolly as she sat at the table and laid out the notebook and pencil she'd brought along. 'Right ... where do we begin?'

Penny had already made out graphs and lists for Dolly to take away.

After a couple of hours, Dolly could see that her friend was getting tired. 'Right, that's enough,' she said, packing all the papers away, just as Reg's mother came in from the scullery with Gail's bottle.

'I've got to give Gail her supper.' Penny turned her wheelchair round. 'Come and say goodnight before you go, Doll.'

'Course I will,' Dolly said, watching her friend and Reg make their way out of the kitchen.

'D'you know, Dolly,' began Ivy, 'you coming back has made all the difference to Pen. It's like she's been given a new lease of life.'

'I'm pleased about that.'

'You sorry about what happened while you were in America?'

'I'm sorry at what happened to Pen, and that I wasn't here to help her through it.'

'No, I meant about you.'

'I was sad things didn't work out for me and Joe. It might have been different if we'd had another baby, but it wasn't to be.'

Ivy sighed. 'You two girls have had so much happen to you in your short lifetimes.'

'Yes, but in time I shall get over my problems – Penny never will.'

'I know, love.' Ivy gently patted Dolly's hand. 'But we will always be here for her.'

'I know.'

Dolly knew that Reg's mum did so much for Penny and Gail. Penny's own mother, who lived next door to Dolly, did as much as she could, but with one strapping growing lad to feed and clothe, she had to go to work as she was a widow.

Reg came back into the kitchen. 'Pen's feeding Gail and wants a cuppa.'

'I'll take it in if you like,' said Dolly.

'OK,' said Reg, 'and thanks, Dolly.'

'What for?'

'Being here.'

Dolly swallowed hard. She went with Reg into the scullery and when he'd made the tea, she picked up the cup and saucer and made her way to Penny's room.

'She sounds as if she's enjoying her supper,' said Dolly, putting the tea on the small table.

'She's a right little guzzler. Would you like to wind her?'

'I'd love to.' Dolly took Gail and, placing her over her shoulder, gently patted her back. 'Thanks for giving me a hand with the wages sheets.'

'I enjoyed it. It makes me feel useful.'

'Don't you think looking after this little one is useful enough then?'

'Course. But I can only do so much and I still rely on Reg's mum for a lot. I'd still like to be helping Reg. He seems to be working so hard, and rushing here, there and everywhere.'

'Well, he is trying to build up his business. Let's hope I can help to ease his burden a bit.'

'I'm sure you will. Turn round.'

Dolly did as she was told.

'You must have the right touch; she's fast asleep.'

'I think she's just full up. Would you like me to put her in her cot?'

'Yes, please. Then we can go back to the kitchen.'

Dolly carefully placed Gail down, and then followed Penny as she wheeled herself along the passage.

'Is she down, love?' asked Ivy.

'Yes, till the next meal time,' said Dolly.

'I've not had the chance to ask,' said Penny, manoeuvring her wheelchair next to Reg. 'What did the bank say about getting a loan?'

'He said I'd have to wait till I've done all the costing; then he'll look at the figures,' he replied.

'Well, that makes sense.'

'She's always got the right answer.'

31

'I can help you with the costing if you bring home all the figures.'

'You've got enough to do looking after Gail.'

Penny scowled. 'I've only lost the use of me legs, not me brain.'

Dolly hadn't seen that angry look on her friend's face for years.

'Besides, your mum's here all day looking after me and Gail. My mum's just up the road, and she'll be only too glad to have Gail any Saturday afternoon or Sunday.'

'I'll think about it.'

'And I'll be able to tell you if I think some of the suppliers are ripping you off.'

'Things have gone up, Pen.'

'I know. But it still doesn't hurt to let 'em know you're no pushover.'

Dolly was beginning to feel very uncomfortable. 'I think I'd better be going.' She stood up. 'See you tomorrow, Reg.'

'Sure.'

'Dolly, could we go shopping again one day?' asked Penny.

'I'd love that.'

'Good. I'll ask the slave driver here if you can have a Saturday morning off and we can go and paint the town.'

Dolly smiled. 'That sounds great. What about it, boss?'

'She's only been working for me a week and she's already asking for time off.'

'He will,' Penny said, 'and he'll take us up West again like he did before Christmas. Won't you, love?'

'Anything for you, my love.' Reg kissed his wife's cheek.

Dolly felt a lump in her throat. If only she and Joe had been like this. 'Right, I'm off,' she said, making her way out of the room. 'See you tomorrow, boss.'

Once again Dolly walked back home with her head full of thoughts. Sadly, some were regrets. She stood at her front gate, looking up at the sky. It was a clear night and the sky seemed full of twinkling stars. *I wonder how our lives will pan out,* she thought. She shuddered. It was also a cold and frosty night, so she quickly made her way indoors.

Chapter 3

It was almost two weeks later when Reg took Dolly and Penny shopping. It was cold and Penny was well wrapped up, as usual.

Penny's mother had Saturday afternoons off, so she was able to look after Gail. She worked full-time in a factory canteen. The hours were long and the work hard. Although Mrs Watts enjoyed looking after her granddaughter, Saturday afternoons were the only times she felt she was able, even though Penny's younger brother, Billy, loved having the baby around.

Penny didn't often talk about her father, but sometimes said that if only her dad was still alive, then her mum wouldn't have to work and Gail would have a grandfather. Sadly, Reg's father had been killed in the 1918 flu outbreak. Dolly felt very privileged that both of her parents were still alive.

Reg manoeuvred Penny's wheelchair down the ramp that he had made to get her in and out of the van. He kissed Penny and Dolly goodbye and jumped back in the driver's seat. As he started the engine, he called out, 'Don't spend all my hard-earned cash. I'll pick you up here in the café at five. Enjoy yourselves.'

The two friends watched him drive away.

'Right, where shall we start?' asked Dolly, tucking a blanket round Penny's legs.

'Not fussed. I'd like to go to the baby shop and get Gail a pair of those frilly knickers. I read somewhere that they now do them with plastic linings.'

Dolly laughed. 'What about you? Do you want some new knickers?'

Penny grinned. 'Wouldn't mind some nice frilly ones. Remember, it's only me legs what don't work.'

'You are very naughty to have thoughts like that.'

'You must remember what it was like?'

'Please, I don't want to think about that.'

'Why not? You can't live like a nun for the rest of your life. You can always live in hope. Besides, there's nothing stopping you from dreaming.'

'I told you, those days are over.'

'I'll remind you of that in a few years' time.'

'If you don't behave, I shall get on the bus and leave you here.'

'You wouldn't dare. I'll tell your boss; then you'll get the sack.'

'Bully,' said Dolly jokingly.

They spent the afternoon shopping, laughing, and having a great time. Both Dolly and Penny had clothing coupons so Dolly bought some shoes while Penny bought a few blouses. Dolly became a dab hand at manoeuvring the wheelchair in and out of the shops, although not all the shops were wheelchair friendly.

All too soon, they were waiting in the café for Reg to collect them. They sat drinking tea and discussing their purchases.

'What are the clothes like in America?' asked Penny.

'Wonderful. And you can buy everything you can think of, even nylon stockings.'

'That's something I don't have to worry about.'

'Not yet, you don't.'

Penny looked at her watch. 'He's late.'

'Only a couple a minutes,' said Dolly.

'He knows I don't like hanging around having people stare at me.'

'Nobody's staring.'

'Yes, they are. You don't see it like I do.'

'Please, Pen, don't get upset. Reg must have a good reason for being late.'

'I hope so, for his sake.'

Time was moving on, and Dolly was now looking around anxiously as the café owner began clearing the tables and looking at his watch. It was nearing six o'clock and had been dark outside for some time. After drinking more tea, Dolly was wondering how she would get her friend home if something had happened to Reg.

'I'm sorry ladies, but I shut at six,' said the

owner, coming up to them. 'Who are you waiting for?'

'Me husband,' said Penny.

'Can you phone him?'

'No. We don't have a phone at home.'

Dolly took Penny's hand. 'I'm sure he's all right.'

'Suppose something's happened to him. How will we get back?' Penny looked up at the café owner. Tears began to slide down her cheeks. 'I've got a young baby, and I want to get home to her.'

'Please, Pen, don't upset yourself.'

'Look, missus, I can phone the police and they might be able to help you.'

Penny looked alarmed. 'I'm sure something's happened to him. He wouldn't leave us here. He knows I can't get home.'

Dolly felt so helpless.

'Look, I'll phone the police,' said the café owner, 'and you can talk to them and explain everything.'

Penny wiped her eyes. 'Thank you.' She managed to wheel her way through the tables, following the owner right to the back of the café where the phone was.

Dolly sat at a table and waited. Where was Reg?

After a while, a police car drew up outside the café, and an officer walked in.

'Was it you who phoned?' he asked Penny.

Dolly was now holding on to the handles of the wheelchair.

'Yes. I'm sorry to be a nuisance, but my husband should have picked us up at five. It's now nearly half past six and he hasn't arrived.' Tears ran down Penny's cheeks. 'He wouldn't just leave me, not stranded here,' she said, wiping her face.

'And you are?' the policeman asked Dolly.

'Her best friend. Reg, her husband, dropped us off and should have picked us up. You see, we don't know how to get home. We can't get a bus as Penny can't walk.'

'I see. Where do you live?'

'Rotherhithe,' they both said together.

'That's over the water.'

Dolly nodded. She too had tears in her eyes.

'Look, I'll take you in the car. Does that chair fold down?'

'Yes,' said Penny.

'Right. Let's get you, and your chair, in the car.' He began to wheel Penny out of the café.

'Thank you. Thank you so much,' she said to the café owner.

'That's all right, love. I hope everything turns out OK. Come back sometime and tell me what happened.'

'We will,' said Dolly.

As the café owner watched them struggling to get Penny into the car, he thought, *What a bastard, letting the poor girl down like that, unless something has happened to him, then that would be tragic. She has enough to put up with.*

He shut the café door, turned the sign to 'Closed', and put out the lights.

Penny was finally settled in the front seat, while Dolly and the policeman struggled with the wheelchair.

'I've never had to fold it before so I'm not sure how it goes,' said Dolly.

'Don't worry; we'll soon get it sorted. Has your friend been in the chair very long?'

'About six months. She caught polio.'

'That's a damn rotten thing to catch. A mate of mine's young nephew got it; he's in an iron lung.'

'That must be awful.'

'Yes it is.' He closed the boot of the car. 'Right, that's stowed away. Now, let me get you two young ladies home.'

'You won't get into trouble for doing this, will you?' asked Dolly.

'No. We're here to help, as well as arrest villains.'

As Dolly got into the back seat, she felt relaxed for the first time in hours.

'So what's your name?' the policeman asked Penny.

'I'm Penny Smith and this is Dolly...' She waved her hand behind her.

'Taylor,' Dolly quickly interrupted, giving her maiden name.

'What do think happened to your husband then, Mrs Smith?'

'I don't know. I'm really worried about him. He wouldn't let me down if...' she stopped and sniffed back her tears.

Dolly leaned forward and, with a friendly hand, gently patted Penny's shoulder. 'I'm sure he's got a good reason,' she said.

'He bloody well better have. Why couldn't he have got your dad, or Tony, to pick us up? They can both drive the van. Oh my God! You don't think anything's happened to Gail, do you?'

'Who's Gail?' the policeman asked.

'My baby.' Penny broke into tears.

After that remark, Dolly noted that the policeman drove a little faster.

The car turned into Wood Street. 'What number?' asked the policeman.

'Number two,' Penny said softly.

Dolly was full of apprehension and fear. 'This is it,' she said.

'Where's the van?' asked Penny. 'He must be out looking for us.'

Usually, Reg's van would be parked in the street.

'Would you like me to go in first?' asked the policeman.

'No,' Penny said quickly. 'They'll think I've had an accident or something if they see a policeman on the doorstep.'

'I'll go,' said Dolly.

'I'll get the chair out of the boot.'

Dolly walked to the front door and pulled the key through. She turned to see the policeman struggling to get the wheelchair open.

As she went down the passage, she began to worry. What had happened? It was very quiet and she was frightened. 'Mrs Smith, it's me, Dolly,' she called out.

The kitchen door flew open and Ivy rushed into Dolly's arms. 'Dolly, Dolly. Where's Penny? We've been so worried about you. Is she all right?'

'She's fine. She's just being helped out of the car.'

Ivy ran to the front door just as Penny was being pushed inside. 'Oh my God!' she yelled. 'A policeman. What's happened?'

'It's all right, ma'am. Nothing's happened to your daughter-in-law. She's just cold, that's all.'

'Come in.' Ivy quickly closed the front door behind them.

'Mum, is Gail all right? What's happened to Reg? Where is he?' Penny hastily pushed herself down the passage.

'Gail's fine. She's with your mother.'

'Reg. It's Reg. What's happened to him?'

'He's all right, but he's had a spot of bother.' Ivy looked nervously at the policeman. 'His yard was broken into, and someone nicked his van when they were at work. Yer dad came and told us,' she said to Dolly.

Dolly put her hand to her mouth. 'Oh my God! Is he all right?'

'He's fine. They're all at the police station now. Poor Reg, he must be at his wits' end, knowing he couldn't come to meet you. Been there for quite a while now.'

'Do you know if anything else was stolen?' the policeman asked.

'Yer dad said the office had been broken into. The bastards.' Ivy put her hand to her mouth. 'Sorry,' she said, looking very guilty. 'He was just starting to get on his feet an' all. Yer dad and Tony are still with him.'

Dolly just stood, dumfounded.

The policeman looked uncomfortable. 'I'm afraid this sort of thing is happening all the time. I'm sorry, but I do have to go.'

'Would you like to stop for a cuppa?' asked Ivy.

'I would, but I'm afraid I must get on, thank you.'

'That's all right, I understand.'

'Thank you,' said Penny, holding out her hand.

'Good luck,' said the policeman, shaking Penny's hand. 'I hope things turn out all right for you.'

Dolly went with him to the front door. 'Thank you so much. I honestly don't know what I would have done without you.'

'It was my pleasure. I'll come round in a few days to see how things are. I'm sure your local force will have things in hand. We usually know who does this sort of thing.'

'I hope so.'

'As I said, I'm sure it will be sorted soon.'

'Thank you.'

Dolly watched the policeman get in the car and drive away. As she walked back into the kitchen, she felt so sad. Why did people do such things? All Reg wanted out of life was to work, and look after Penny and Gail.

'Mum's making the tea,' said Penny when Dolly walked back in.

Ivy came into the kitchen with the tray of tea things. 'Just waiting for the kettle. That was nice of that policeman to bring you home,' she said, fussing with the cups and saucers.

'I don't think he had much of a choice when the café owner said he was closing,' said Penny sharply.

'Thank God you were there, Dolly,' said Ivy, trying to ease the situation.

'Well, I certainly wouldn't have gone shopping without her,' said Penny hastily.

'No, I know you wouldn't, love. I'll just get the tea.'

Although Dolly was upset about all that had

happened, she felt that Penny was being a bit harsh towards Reg's mother. 'Would you like me to go and fetch Gail?'

'If you don't mind,' said Penny. 'I expect Mum's wondering where we are.'

Ivy came back in with the teapot. 'When yer mum came earlier with Gail, I told her what had happened, so she took Gail back with her and said she'd look after her till you got home. Though, God knows, none of us knew when that would be, or how you'd be able to do that.'

'Well, we're home now, so when you've finished your tea, Dolly, you can go and get Gail,' said Penny, rather abruptly.

Dolly quickly drank her tea, and left. She decided to call in on her own mother who she knew would be very worried and likely to bombard Dolly with questions. She opened her front door and yelled out, 'We're back!'

Grace shot out of the kitchen. 'Where have you been? How did you get home?'

'I'm just getting Gail. I'll tell you everything in a minute.' She left her mother, and went next door to let Mrs Watts know that they were home safely.

After she'd collected Gail, and had explained everything that had happened that afternoon to Penny's mother, Dolly hurried back along the road to number two. She knew Penny was upset and waiting to be reunited with her daughter, but she was a bit worried that her friend was taking it out on her mother-in-law. After all, Mrs Smith was such a kind-hearted person.

Chapter 4

When Grace heard the front door shut, she quickly came out of the kitchen and rushed up to Dolly. 'Thank God you're home. We've been that worried about you. How did you get home?'

'A policeman brought us home in a police car.'

'Oh my God!' said Grace, putting her hand to her mouth. 'Is Penny all right?'

'She's fine now. But we were a bit worried when Reg didn't turn up.'

'He's in a terrible state. Worried sick about you two, as well as the break-in. Your dad's with him now. Bloody rotten buggers, doing this to him.'

Dolly looked at her mother, surprised. She never swore. 'I wonder if Dad and Reg are still at the yard.'

'I don't know.'

'I feel I should go and tell him that Penny's all right.' Reg's yard was only a short bus ride away.

'But you might miss him if they've got the van back.'

'That's true.'

'Would you like a cup of tea?'

'No, thanks. I've just had one at Pen's.'

Dolly sat at the table; she felt so helpless. What could she do? She stood up. 'Mum, I'm sorry, but I can't just sit here waiting about. I've got to go to the yard.'

'But what if...?'

'If they do get home before me and have got the van back, Dad can come and get me.'

'But what if...?' her mother repeated. 'Oh, I don't know. Please yourself.' She knew there was nothing she could say to stop her daughter from trying to help and do something.

Dolly called in at Penny's to tell her she was catching the bus to the yard. Penny was pleased that her friend was concerned about her husband and the business as much as she was.

As Dolly sat on the bus, she wondered if she was doing the right thing. But she knew she had to do something; she couldn't just sit around and wait.

When the bus pulled up at her stop, she hurried along to the yard and was surprised to see a car parked outside, and that the big wooden gates had been run down. There was no sign of her father or Reg.

'Hello,' she said to the man who was standing with his back to her. 'Who are you?'

He turned. Penny could see that he was the police officer who had given her a lift home earlier, but this time he was wearing civvies.

'What are you doing here?' she asked, her voice full of worry. 'How did you know where Reg's place was?'

'I might ask you the same thing,' said the policeman.

'I work here.' Dolly was indignant.

'After I'd dropped you off earlier, I called in at the local nick. They told me where it was, and what had happened. As I was off duty and not doing anything this evening, I thought I'd come and look for myself. Made a mess of the gates, didn't they?'

'Poor Reg,' said Dolly as the two of them walked into the yard. 'He must be very upset about all this.'

She stopped and looked at the mess in front of her. Bags of cement were split open, and lengths of wood had been broken and scattered all over the place. She walked towards her office. The door was banging in the breeze. Inside, by the glow from a street light, she could see papers strewn all over the floor.

She began to pick them up. 'Looks like I shall have my work cut out sorting this lot out.' Tears slid down her face.

'Don't upset yourself. It might not be as bad as it looks.'

She quickly brushed a tear away. 'Sorry.'

'That's all right. Is there a safe here?'

'No. Reg keeps all the money and cheques at home.'

'Well, that's one good thing. They might have been just having a prank. Some people are like that. Think it's fun to try to ruin somebody's business.'

'He served his country, and now he just wants to get on with his life.'

The man smiled at Dolly. 'You must be really fond of your pal and her husband.'

'We all grew up together, and they've been there through all my problems.'

'Now, what sort of problems could a young lady like you have?'

'You'd be surprised.'

Dolly was pleased that the policeman didn't seem to want to pursue that any further. 'Will it be all right if I start clearing this lot up?'

'I should think so.' He began helping her.

Dolly began to gather all the papers and stuff them in her bag. 'I can sort some of these out at home.'

'Look, we can put them in the car and I can take you, and them, home if you like.'

'I can't ask you to do that.'

'You're not asking; I'm volunteering. Besides, it's getting late for a young lady to be out on her own.'

'Thank you.'

When Dolly and the off-duty policeman had finished tidying the office, they made the door as secure as they could, and then once again Dolly was sitting in a car with this young man. 'This is very nice of you. Thank you so much,' she said.

'It's my pleasure.'

'I don't even know your name.'

'It's Harry, Harry Jordan. And yours is Dolly Taylor, if I remember right.'

'Fancy you remembering.'

'Part of my job is to be observant.'

Dolly laughed. 'I see. Is that so you can arrest me if I do something wrong?'

'You never know.'

As Dolly sat back, she realised that this was the first time she'd laughed for a good few hours.

When they turned into Wood Street, Harry asked, 'What number do you live at?'

'Number twenty.'

The car went slowly along the road till Dolly said, 'This is it. Thanks.'

Harry stopped the car and Dolly started to get out. He was round her side almost immediately, and held open the door for her.

'I'll carry this lot,' he said, taking all the rest of the papers they had picked up.

'Thanks,' she said again. As she stood up, she took the papers from him. 'You've been very kind.'

'It's been my pleasure.'

Dolly started to walk away, when Harry said, 'I'm not very good at this sort of thing, but now I'm off duty, could I see you again?'

'I don't know.'

'Perhaps we could go to the pictures or something?'

'I'm sorry, Harry...' she hesitated. To Dolly, it seemed very wrong and unnatural to call a policeman by his first name. 'But I don't think so.'

'I'm sorry. Do you have a boyfriend?'

'No, but...' She stopped, not wanting to reveal anything about herself. She was still too upset about that part of her life.

'I'll call in your office again at the end of the week to see if I can help with anything.'

'You don't have to.'

'It'll be my pleasure. Goodnight then.' With that, Harry got back into his car.

Dolly's father opened the front door and stood looking at the car as Harry drove away. 'Who was that?'

'Hello, Dad. Were you looking out of the window?' Dolly said, slightly annoyed that he hadn't rushed up to her and welcomed her home.

'Sorry. How are you, love? It's been a hard day. Your mum told me how you got home, and all what happened, and that you'd gone to the yard. What did you do that for?' They both walked in and through to the kitchen.

'I wanted to see if you were still there, and what state the place was in.'

'So, who was that?' Jim asked again.

'The policeman that brought me and Penny home. Didn't Mum tell you?'

'What was he doing at the yard?'

'He went to see what damage had been done.'

'Is it his patch then?'

'I don't know. What's with the inquisition?'

'Don't get stroppy with me, young lady.'

'I'm sorry, Dad. I've had a bit of a bad day.'

'You're not the only one.'

'Now sit down the pair of you,' said Grace. 'You've both had a bad day. I'll make us a nice cup of tea.'

Dolly smiled. Her mother always had this wonderful idea that a cup of tea would solve everything.

'Do they know who did it?' asked Dolly.

'No,' said her father. 'But it seems Reg ain't the only one. It must have been a gang of 'em, and they must have a truck, as a lot of the expensive stuff must have been transferred.'

'Harry thought it might have been just vandals.'

Her father looked at her when she said 'Harry', but didn't comment, and continued. 'They knew what they wanted. Trouble is, a lot of those materials are in short supply these days so they thought they'd just come and take it.'

48

'Poor Reg. He must be devastated.'

'He is, poor chap. These people ought to be strung up. He's been serving his country through the war. When he gets back, he tries to make a go of his and Penny's life – and that ain't been easy with the baby an' all – and then this goes and happens. I know what I'd do to 'em if I caught them.' He picked up his newspaper and started to read.

Dolly had never seen her father so angry. 'He has been through such a lot.' She had found it difficult to stop the tears from falling. Thank goodness, she was here in this country to help her friends.

When Dolly had finished her tea, she said, 'I'm just popping along to see Penny.'

'It's a bit late,' said her mother.

'They won't be in bed just yet.'

'What about all these papers?' Grace asked, pointing to the papers that Dolly had thrown on the armchair.

She gathered them up and put them on the table. 'I can ask Reg what I should do with them. The police might want some of them to check on what stock is missing.'

'Don't s'pose they're worried about things like that,' said her father, looking up from his newspaper.

'I won't be long,' said Dolly, adjusting her hat. 'I'll just have a word with Reg.'

Her mother only smiled as she sat down and picked up her knitting.

Dolly was deep in thought as she made her way to Penny's. What would the outcome be? Would they all have a job?

49

'Yoo-hoo! It's only me,' she called, pushing open the kitchen door. 'Hello, Reg,' she said as she walked in.

'Thanks, Dolly, for what you did for Pen today. I was gutted when I couldn't get to pick you both up.'

Dolly thought Reg looked as if he had suddenly aged. 'It was thanks to the café owner and that policeman that it all turned out all right. I was so sorry to find out what happened at the yard, though. It's a right mess.'

'Pen said you'd been there.'

'I've brought a lot of the papers home from the office. I hope I did the right thing. Did the police want to look at them?'

'No. They didn't seem that bothered. It seems the gang's done a few builders' yards round about here.'

'Oh.' Dolly sat at the table. 'Pen putting Gail to bed?' she asked.

'Yes, she is,' said Ivy. 'A cup of tea while you're waiting, love?'

'No, I'm fine, thanks.' After the day they'd had, Dolly knew Penny would want to spend some time alone with her baby.

'Hello, love,' said Tony, walking into the kitchen.

Dolly thought he must have been outside in the lav.

'You did a good job getting Pen home. I can tell you, what with one thing and another, Reg's been tearing his hair out.'

'I'm not surprised,' she replied.

'You should see the bloody mess,' said Tony.

'She has, she's been there,' said Reg.

50

'You have?'

Dolly nodded.

'She's brought a lot of the papers home,' he added.

'We'll get them sorted out tomorrow,' said Dolly.

'You don't have to. We can't do much work at the moment till I can order some more stock.' Reg rubbed his chin. 'Trouble is, I'm not sure if the bank will let me have the stuff on tick. I just hope they find the van in one piece.'

'The police said they usually do,' said Tony. 'It seems that the thieves are not interested in the van. They just need it to get out of the yard so it don't look too suspicious, then they transfer all the stuff into their van that's parked up somewhere.'

'So when they find your van, why can't they find out who's doing it?' asked Dolly.

Reg shrugged.

Penny wheeled herself into the kitchen. 'I know what I'd like to do with the bastards,' she said.

'Wouldn't we all, love?' said Reg.

'You try to make an honest living and this happens,' she said angrily, but there was a catch in her voice.

'Steady on there, love,' said Reg.

'Don't you think we've got enough to put up with?'

'Of course I do, but they don't know that, do they?'

'Well, they bloody well ought to be struck down and finish up in a wheelchair.'

Dolly really felt for her friend. She wanted to

51

hug her and make everything well again.

That night, as Dolly lay in bed, she thought about all that had happened that day. Some people seemed to sail through life with just a few ups and downs, but quite a few people in Wood Street had had more than their share of problems. Through the two wars, some had lost close members of their families. This war had seen most of the houses suffer from bomb blasts, and some were a pile of ruins. Thankfully, everyone tried to rise above it all. She hoped that one day Reg and Penny would be able to do the same, and all that was happening now would just be something to talk about in the future – and to tell their daughter. But, at the moment, only time would help them.

Chapter 5

On Monday morning, as Dolly made her way to work, she wasn't sure what the day would bring. She was worried that Reg might tell her that she would have to leave, as he couldn't afford her wages. She loved being there, even if it wasn't very busy or the best place to work in, and although she didn't get a fortune in wages, she was her own boss in the tiny shed that was her office. Preparing the wages, ordering materials, checking the deliveries, and general office work, kept her busy most of the time, but occasionally, she would have liked other company and more to do.

It was lunchtime when Tony came in. 'So how's my best girl on this cold and frosty morning?'

'Cold and frosty. How's it all going out there?'

'Not good.'

'I can see you, Billy, and Dad are busy clearing up the mess.'

'Reg had to take the casual workers back, as he ain't got the materials now to do that big decorating job that's been on the cards for ages. I can tell you, he's gutted about that.'

'I know. He's spent a lot of money on that stuff. He was telling me that most of it has either gone or been ruined. The trouble is, even the materials that hadn't been paid for will still have to be, and if he don't pay, well, they won't supply him again, and as you know, so much of the stuff is in short supply.'

'I know. It's a bloody shame.'

They sat for a few moments quietly, each with their thoughts.

Dolly broke the silence, and asked, 'Would you like a cuppa?'

'Yes, please. At least they didn't smash the mugs.'

'Or take the teapot and kettle. What we gonna do, Tone?' Dolly asked sadly.

'I dunno. If Reg can't get a loan from the bank, well, that'll be it, I suppose.'

Dolly sat at her desk. 'I hope I don't have to leave. I wouldn't know where to go for a job.'

'I suppose you could try Peek Freans, if the worst comes to the worst. You know Meg Windsor works there and she said it's not too bad.'

'D'you still see Meg?'

'Now and again.'

Dolly didn't want to carry on that line of conversation, as whatever Tony did with his life wasn't really any of her business. 'I wish there was something I could do to help Reg.'

'You just being here for both Pen and Reg is enough, and the fact that you've cleaned this place up. It don't look so bad now the shelves and cupboards are a bit tidier. You do a good job here.'

'I try.'

'I tell you something: it's good that you're back here to give Penny a bit of a boost. She's certainly been a lot happier since you came back home.'

'And I'm glad to be back. If I'd known what had happened, I would have gone mad not being able to get here.'

'So your old man wouldn't have let you come home just to see us, then?'

Dolly shook her head. She really didn't like to say nasty things about Joe, as he wasn't all bad, and they did have some good times during their short marriage.

With their hands wrapped around their warm mugs, they sat quietly for a few moments, before Tony said, 'I'd better get back outside to see what the boys are up to. Thanks for the tea.'

'My pleasure. I'll make some for them.' Dolly smiled at the thought of her dad being called one of the boys. She looked around her. What would she do if she had to look for another job? It wasn't that it was hard to get work, but she liked it here, and she loved being involved with her long-standing friends.

Reg looked very down when he came in later.

'Dolly, I might not be able to pay your wages this week.'

She gave him a big smile. 'I should say, don't worry, I'll work for nothing, but as you know, you provide most of the money that goes into our house as Dad works for you as well.'

Reg looked down, and shuffled his feet. 'I know. I'm hoping to give your dad some work, but all this is going to take a while to build up again, that's if I can get the money to buy the materials.'

He looked so sad that Dolly wanted to throw her arms around him to offer some comfort. 'Look, don't worry about it for now. You're a good honest worker and I'm sure it will all get sorted in the end.'

'It's Pen I worry about. She feels so helpless stuck in that wheelchair all the time.'

'I know.' Dolly had a job to keep the tears from falling. 'I'll go and see her when I get home. Remember she's a tough old bird.'

Reg managed to conjure up a smile. 'She won't be that pleased at you calling her an old bird.'

'I know. Did you want a cuppa?'

'No, thanks all the same, but I'm going to the bank as soon as they open, so keep yer fingers crossed for me.'

'Course I will.'

It was later in the morning when Harry Jordan walked in. This time he was in uniform.

Dolly looked up and said in surprise, 'Harry! What is it? What's wrong?'

He smiled, and Dolly noted that it lit up the whole of his face.

'Nothing. I was round this way so I thought I'd

pop in to see how things were going, and to let you know we've located the van.'

'That's wonderful news. Is it far away?'

'No. Mr Smith's on his way there now to pick it up.'

'Let's hope the bank will loan him the money to get some more stock.'

'It makes me so mad that these sods think they can come in and take what they want,' Harry said angrily.

'You must see this all the time.'

'Yeh.'

Tony pushed open the door. 'Dolly, I saw the copper's car outside. Is everything all right?'

'It's fine. Harry, here, just came to tell me they've found the van.'

'That's great. Does Reg know?'

'He's collecting it now,' said Harry.

Although Tony was pleased at him being there, he couldn't help but scowl when Dolly called Harry by his first name. He began wondering how close they were. 'I was hoping you might have had some good news,' he said, trying to sound as if he didn't care about this bloke coming in and talking to Dolly as if they were good friends or more. 'You've no idea who could have done this, then?'

'No, they were saying at the station that it wasn't just kids out for a lark. It was someone who had a van suitable to take the stuff away after they'd transferred it from Mr Smith's van.'

'Well, that could be any builder or decorator.'

'I know.'

'But why did they have to do so much damage?' asked Tony.

'Thought it would be a bit of a joke, I suppose. Some people are like that.'

Dolly looked from one to the other. To her, this was a pointless conversation. She'd heard it all before.

'Right, I'd better be off,' said Harry. 'See you around, Dolly.'

'Bye, and thanks for dropping in.'

'My pleasure.' He gave her another beaming smile.

Tony was quietly fuming. How dare this bloke think he could muscle in, just because he was a bloody policeman. He decided not to make too much of it. 'He seems a nice enough bloke, for a copper.'

'He is, and he was so concerned about Penny and me.'

'I gathered that.'

Dolly noted there was a hint of sarcasm in that remark.

At the end of the day, Dolly went home, cold and weary.

'You look frozen,' said her mother as she fussed around her daughter.

'I am.'

'Here's a nice cuppa to warm you.'

'Thanks, Mum. What am I gonna do?'

'What d'you mean, love? I thought Reg had got the van back.'

'He has, but he won't be able to pay my wages if he can't get that bank loan.'

'Dad was saying the same thing when he came home.'

'Where is he?'

'Gone to play darts.'

Dolly remembered that her father always played darts on Monday evenings. 'I'll pop in and see Pen after dinner.'

'Yer dad's already had his.'

'Mum. What shall I do if Reg can't afford to keep me on?'

'I don't honestly know, love. Especially if he has to let your dad go as well.'

'It's a bit of a mess all round. I suppose I could go and get a job in a shop, but I did that before, and standing around all day waiting for customers ain't my idea of working. Besides, with all the shortages, and a lot of things still on coupons, there ain't that much to sell. Tony was telling me that Meg now works in Peek Freans. Perhaps I should try there.'

Grace patted her daughter's hand. 'Don't worry about it, love, for now. I'm sure something will turn up and put Reg back on the road again.'

'I hope so, Mum. I really do.'

Grace looked at Dolly. She was proud at having such an independent caring daughter.

'Hello, love,' said Ivy when Dolly walked into her kitchen. 'Pen's in her room.'

Dolly closed the kitchen door. 'Mrs Smith...' Dolly hesitated. 'What will you do if Reg can't get back on his feet?'

'Dunno. His money's been great.' She looked at Dolly, then sat in the armchair and began to cry. 'It looks like everything's going wrong,' she sniffed, fishing around in the pocket of her pinny for a handkerchief.

Dolly rushed to kneel on the floor next to her.

'I'm sorry love,' Ivy said. Giving up searching for a handkerchief, she wiped her tears with the bottom of her pinny instead. 'It seems that everything those two try to do goes wrong.'

'Not everything,' said Dolly. 'Remember, there's Gail.'

That name brought a smile to Ivy's sad face. 'She's a little ray of sunshine, is that one.'

'Is there anything I can do to help them?'

'Just be here for them, love. Now go in and see Pen. And Dolly, don't say anything about me being a bit upset, will you?'

'No, of course not.' Dolly kissed her cheek and stood up. When she stepped into the passage, she thought, *What if I hadn't come home?* These were her best friends, who she had known all her life. She smiled to herself. In some ways, Joe's mother had done her a favour in not liking her. Although she still thought a lot of Joe, she knew her true feelings were this side of the Atlantic.

She quietly pushed open Penny's door. 'How's my favourite god-daughter,' she whispered, with a smile on her face.

'She was guzzling her bottle, but it looks like she's fallen asleep,' said Penny, also trying to raise a smile. 'You can put her back in her cot if you like.'

'It's my pleasure.' Dolly carefully picked up the sleepy baby and held her close. She could see that Penny had been crying. 'And how are you, me old mate?'

'I'll bounce back.'

As Dolly gently kissed Gail's forehead and placed her in her cot, a tear slid down her cheek. When she straightened up, she quickly brushed it away.

'Now what have you got to get tearful about?' asked Penny.

'Lots of things.' Dolly blew her nose.

'Do you still think of the baby you lost?' Penny asked softly.

'What do you think?'

'Sorry. That was a bit insensitive of me. Of course you think about her.'

'But we all know that life has to go on.' Dolly looked away.

'Sorry,' Penny said again, 'but it's just that we've all got such a lot on our plates at the moment. It seems that just as we start to get on top of everything, something comes along and knocks us back again.'

'I know.'

'And I know I'm being a cow to Reg's mum, but I can't help it. I somehow feel I need to take it out on somebody.'

'Well, perhaps it could be me,' her friend suggested.

'You've had enough on your plate.'

'I know, but I'm younger and a lot stronger than I look.'

Penny smiled, just as the door burst open and banged against the wall, waking Gail, who began to cry.

''Ello, love,' said Reg, slurring his words.

His mother was right behind him. 'I'm sorry, love. I tried to stop him coming in, but he just pushed me out of the way.'

Penny looked angry. 'You're drunk.'

'I know. I needed something to cheer me up.' He grinned, and this time he quietly closed the door behind him.

'And alcohol will do that?' said Penny, glaring at him.

'For a little while.' He sat on the bed.

'Who got you in this state?'

'I was with Tony.'

'And is he as bad as you?'

'No, he left me.'

'Shall I pick Gail up?' asked Dolly.

'Yes,' said Penny, abruptly.

Dolly lifted the crying baby from her cot and when Ivy opened the door, they both quickly left the room.

As they walked away, they could hear Penny shouting at Reg.

While Dolly was gently rocking Gail over her shoulder, Ivy sat at the kitchen table. She looked so sad. 'Dolly, love, what we gonna do?'

'I don't know. I really don't. Just be here for them, I suppose. Would you like me to stay?'

'No, love. Thanks all the same. You go on home.'

Dolly put Gail in her pram, then after holding Reg's mum close, she said, 'Are you sure?'

'It'll be all right, you wait and see. He'll be full of apologies when he's sobered up.'

'I'll be off then.'

As Dolly walked past their room, it upset her to hear Penny still shouting at Reg.

Chapter 6

After Dolly left, Ivy took Gail from her pram. She sat back in the chair gently rocking her granddaughter, and let a tear slide down her cheek. 'What we gonna do, my lovely? How will things work out for you and yer mum and dad?' She held the baby close. How she wished things would take a turn for the better for these two, very soon.

When Penny heard the front door shutting, she knew her friend had gone home. As she sat and watched her husband sitting on the bed trying to look sober, she snapped. 'I can't believe you would go out and get drunk!'

'I can only say I'm sorry, love.'

'And you think that's gonna make things better?'

'No. I wish there was something more I could do or say.' He buried his head in his hands.

'I would love the opportunity to go out and get drunk. Instead of that, I have to sit here day after day, week after week, even unable to take meself out to the lav, and you sit there moaning and feeling sorry for yourself. You're a bloody selfish bastard, and I hate you.' Tears were streaming down Penny's cheeks.

'Please don't say that Penny, love. I love you. I'm so sorry,' he said, trying to give her a hug.

She pushed him away.

'Please don't hate me. I love you so much and I wish it was me that was stuck in a wheelchair.' Tears filled Reg's eyes. 'I'm only trying to do me best for you and Gail, but I seem to be stopped every step of the way.' He sat back and wiped his eyes. 'What we gonna do?'

Penny looked at him, and her heart was filled with love. 'Come here.'

Reg swept her into his arms and covered her face with kisses. 'Please don't hate me.'

'I could never hate you, you big lump,' she sobbed. 'I love you. Put me on the bed.'

After they had finished making love, they lay together silently in each other's arms.

'Don't you think you should go and get our daughter?' asked Penny.

Reg kissed Penny's nose. 'I'd better put me trousers on; otherwise I might give me dear old mum a bit of a shock.'

Penny eased herself up on her arm. 'She's seen it all before.'

'I know, but I was a bit younger then.'

'Go on, off with you.'

Reg quietly pushed open the kitchen door. He was filled with love and affection at the sight of his mother, who was asleep, and holding his sleeping baby daughter over her shoulder. He stood in the doorway, watching the lovely scene for a few minutes and then moved into the room before his mum opened her eyes.

'Hello, love,' she blinked. 'Everything all right?'

'Yes, thanks.'

'I must've just closed me eyes. She's been as

63

good as gold.'

'She looks very peaceful. I'd better put her in her cot.' He took Gail from his mother and said, 'You'd better go on up. And Mum, I'm sorry.'

She gently patted his arm, and smiled.

'Thanks.'

'My pleasure, son.'

As Ivy went past Penny's door, she called out. 'Night, Pen, love.'

'Night, Mum,' came back the reply.

Dolly felt very sad as she went home, and she didn't enjoy telling her mother about what had happened earlier.

'Poor Ivy,' said Grace. 'She thinks the world of her little family and she's been there for them all the time. I'll pop in tomorrow and see if she'd like to come in and have a cuppa. She might like a moment or two to have a chat.'

'That would be nice.' Dolly smiled. Her mother always reckoned a cuppa was the answer to every-body's problems. 'I wish I could do something. I feel so helpless.'

'I know you do, love. But remember, even if you weren't here, they would still have to manage.'

'I don't like to hear them shouting. Joe and I never shouted at each other,' Dolly said softly.

Grace glanced at her daughter, and noticed how sad she looked. This was the first time she had mentioned anything like that about her and Joe. Grace knew that Joe's mother hadn't made Dolly welcome, and that he didn't stand up to his mother. Deep down, did Dolly regret coming home? Was she sorry that she hadn't tried to make more of a go with their marriage?

'D'you mind if I go on up?' asked Dolly.

'Course not, love. Yer dad will be in soon. D'you want a drink, or something, before you go?'

'No, thanks.' Dolly kissed her mother's cheek. 'Night. See you in the morning.'

In her bedroom, Dolly opened the drawer in her dressing table and took out a small box. Inside, carefully wrapped in tissue paper, was her delicate silver charm of the Statue of Liberty. Sitting on the bed, she was reminded of the good things that happened during her time in America. The charm was one of many, which had been on the silver bracelet that Joe had given her, the first Christmas she was in America. After that, he had added new charms on every birthday, wedding anniversary, and Christmas. She had loved that bracelet. This charm brought back memories of her friend, Norma, when they both fled to New York. Where was Norma now? Was she still travelling around Europe?

Dolly smiled when remembering all the tourist attractions they visited together, like going up the Statue of Liberty, and the Empire State Building, even going to Macy's. Dolly had admired all the lovely clothes, remembering that clothes were still rationed in Britain. Those had been the real highlights. But she had sold her bracelet to help pay for her journey home from America, just keeping this one charm to remind her of the good times she'd had, and there had been some good times. A tear rolled down her cheek. She was sorry. If only she had known that she could work her way across the Atlantic as a cleaner on a passenger liner, she would never have had to sell her lovely bracelet. That and her engagement ring were the only things she'd had of value back then, and at that time, she needed the money to get home.

Dolly lay on her back staring up at the ceiling; her thoughts still spinning around in her head. What did the future hold for her? Did Joe ever think about her? Why had his mother been so against her? Was the size of her farm so important that she would sacrifice her eldest son's happiness for more land?

'Are you going to marry Sandra to keep your ma happy so that then she'll have both farms? Why didn't you stand up to her, Joe?' she said softly. 'We could have been so happy if we'd moved away. And things might have been so very different if I could have had another baby.'

Dolly wiped away another tear. The thought of her lost baby always made her feel so sad. Like many people, she was angry about the war, but then again, if there hadn't been a war, she would never have met Joe or gone to America. What was the point in raking over the past with all its lost dreams? She slid off the bed, carefully wrapped the charm in the tissue paper, and put it back into its box. As she closed the drawer, she thought about Norma. She had been a good friend who was determined to see Europe. When she told Dolly that she was leaving Deansville, and asked if she would like to go to New York with her, Dolly jumped at the chance. It meant that she might be able to get home and see her family again. It upset her that Joe didn't even try to stop her. Would she ever see Norma again? She had said that one day she would come to London. She had written just the once, and Dolly did wonder that she might have met someone and got married. If that were the case, she would probably never see her friend again. So why, tonight, did she look at the charm and why did she keep it? After all, she would never be able to pass it on to a daughter.

The following morning, Reg came into the office.

'Would you like a cup of tea?' asked Dolly.

'No, thanks... Look, I'm sorry about last night.'

'Reg, you don't have to apologise to me. What you do in your own home is your business.'

'I know, but I've got no excuse to come home drunk. That's not like me.'

'I know.'

'Penny said I should apologise. Not that I didn't want to. I feel such a bastard. She's stuck in a wheelchair, and I go out on a bender.' He sat in the chair and put his head in his hands. 'What we gonna do?'

'I don't know. You've got such a lot on your plate at the moment. I wish I could do more.'

'You just being here for Pen is enough.'

She gave him a weak smile. 'But that don't help the situation here, though, does it?'

'No.'

'Perhaps the bank will help you today?'

'It might take a miracle.' He raised his eyes to the ceiling. 'And him up there seems to be all out of those at the moment.'

'Well, if anyone deserves one, it's you two.'

'Let's hope the bank manager sees it that way.'

'If there's anything I can do...'

'Keep yer fingers crossed for me.'

Dolly gave him a nod as he left the office. 'I'll do that,' she said to herself.

Dolly was busy putting the invoices that she had brought from home into the filing cabinets when Tony walked in.

'How's things?' he asked.

'Not good.'

'Reg's like a bear with a sore head, this morning. It seems he got a bit inebriated last night, and Pen gave him what for.'

'I know. I was there.'

'You was? Poor old Reg. Pen should let him off the hook now and again. He's got a lot to worry about.'

'I know. But don't forget, Penny must be just as frustrated with not being able to help him.'

'That's true.' Tony sat down. 'Dolly, I know I've asked you before and you've turned me down, but couldn't we go out, just once, for old times' sake?'

She looked over at Tony.

'Have a quiet drink somewhere? Just talk over the good times we had once. What have you got to lose?'

'Tony, I know we did have some good times, but we've changed.'

'I promise not to mention anything about us being engaged. I just need some female company. And before you mention Meg, I told you before, she's not for me. So, what d'you say?'

Dolly still had a soft spot for Tony. After all, they were childhood sweethearts, and had got engaged when he went off to war. That was until she met and fell in love with Joe. What should she do? She smiled, giving in. 'Only if you promise not to get morose and nostalgic.'

'My God, you just swallowed a dictionary.' He held his hands up. 'All right, I promise.'

'What time and where shall we go?'

'Seven. And how about a quiet drink somewhere just over the water?'

'That sounds fine. I'll be ready.'

'Good.' He left the office with a grin on his face.

'Mum, I'll be going out tonight,' said Dolly when she got home that evening.

'That's good. Anywhere nice?'

'No, only just for a drink.'

Her mother was tempted to ask 'Who with?', but knew she would be told later. She just hoped it wasn't with that policeman. She didn't trust policemen.

Grace put more coal on the fire. 'Ivy came in this morning. She looked fair done in. She told me Gail's been playing up. It's funny how babies can sense a bad atmosphere.'

'I'll pop in just before I go out.'

'What if...?' she stopped for a moment. 'What if your friend arrives before you get back?'

'Just tell Tony where I am.'

Grace let out a quiet sigh of relief. What if they got back together again? That would be the happiest day of her and Jim's life.

'So, what did Reg's mum have to say?' asked Dolly.

'Not a lot really. Just that she's worried about

Reg, and him not getting the money to get any materials.'

'It must be awful for her,' said Dolly.

'It is. In fact, she had a little weep while she was here, and that's not like Ivy at all. Now I'm working part-time, I asked her if she'd like to go to the pictures, one afternoon. She said she'd think about it.'

'I thought you said you were going to ask for full-time, now that Dad might not be able to get work.'

'I know, but we'll wait and see what happens first.'

Dolly knew that although her mother liked working, she also liked being at home. Working part-time had suited her. Would it all have to change?

At seven o'clock on the dot, Tony knocked.

'Come on in, lad,' said Dolly's father. 'It's good to see you.'

Dolly smiled as she came down the stairs. She was wearing one of the dresses she had bought in America. She knew red suited her, and although it was a plain dress, it was smart. She only hoped she didn't look too overdressed. 'You only saw him at work today, Dad.'

'I know, but this is a social visit... Look at the pair of you. Don't you both look smart?'

Dolly laughed and took her coat off the peg on the wall. 'Come on, move out of the way, and let me get out,' she said to her father, who was standing in the doorway.

'Sorry, love.' He moved away from the door.

'Bye, Mum,' she shouted. She knew her mother was in the kitchen with the door slightly open.

'Sorry about that,' Dolly said to Tony as they walked down the road.

'Not to worry. This is really great, you and me walking down the street together, and I must say you look very nice.'

'Come off it, Tone. You've seen this coat dozens of times.'

'I know, but your frock looks nice. I've just got to pop into the Gregory's for some fags.'

They crossed the road to the newspaper and sweet shop that Ada and May Gregory owned. Ada, the eldest sister, was serving, and when the man left the shop, she looked up as the bell over the door tinkled. 'Dolly, Tony. How lovely to see you both together,' she said with a broad smile, as they walked into the shop.

Dolly quickly closed the door. 'Don't want to let the cold in,' she said. 'How's your sister?'

'She's fine. She's out back doing the tea. She's got a bit of a cold and she doesn't like the cold weather. How's young Reg? We're very concerned about him and his business. Ivy came over and said how much she was worried about him and young Penny. She had the baby with her.' She smiled. 'She's such a lovely little thing. Young Penny and Reg must be very proud of her.'

'We all are,' Dolly said warmly. She loved these two sisters who had always been a part of her life. Dolly had confided in them when she fell in love with Joe and was worried about what to do. Her mother was very angry when she found out that her daughter had been to them for advice. The reason Dolly had asked them for help was that they had both lost their fiancés in the First World War and Dolly had thought that something like that could happen to Joe, so she was unsure about whether or not she should marry him. The sisters had told her to live for the moment, and not worry too much about the future during wartime. They were very upset to see Dolly back home when things didn't work out for her in America.

'Now, what can I get you?' asked Ada.

'Tony wants some cigarettes.'

'Your usual, young man?'

'Please.'

'Off anywhere nice?' asked Ada, placing a packet of twenty Player's on the counter.

'Only for a drink.'

'Well, enjoy yourselves.'

'Thanks. We will,' said Tony, as they left the shop.

'I hope Miss Gregory will be all right,' said Dolly. 'They are lovely ladies, and I'm very fond of them. They were very nice to me when I was undecided whether or not to marry Joe.'

Tony stopped. 'You were undecided?'

'Well, it was a big step.'

'And you asked them for their advice?'

'Well, I couldn't say much to Mum as she was dead set against it.'

Tony turned to face Dolly. 'So if I'd been here, you might not have gone? You might never have met him?'

Dolly didn't say anything.

'Bloody war.' He stopped. 'Just think, we could have been married now and might even have a couple of kids.'

'Tony, please don't start on that again. Besides, the war mucked up a lot of people's lives. Think of those whose loved ones never came back.'

'Sorry. Truce?'

'Truce.'

'But I still think...'

Dolly put her hand up. 'You promised.'

'Sorry. But that was before I found out that you'd had doubts about marrying him.' He grinned and pulling her arm through his, they walked on.

'Don't you start getting any ideas, Tony Marchant.'

Tony was still grinning. 'As if I would.'

Chapter 7

Dolly was enjoying herself just sitting and talking to Tony. She found herself looking at him and smiling as he walked towards her carrying another half of shandy, and a pint for himself. There was still something about him that she liked very much.

'You look happy,' he said, sitting next to her.

'I am.'

'This is like old times.'

'Don't go getting any ideas,' she said jokingly.

He held his hands up. 'As if I would.'

'I wish things were all right for Penny and Reg.'

'So do I. If I had some money, I'd give it to him,

just to tide him over,' said Tony.

'If only the bank would help him out.'

Tony took another sip of his drink and they sat in silence for a while. Dolly began to feel nervous; it wasn't like Tony to be so quiet. He put down his glass.

'It's a good job we've still got a couple of weeks' work,' he said. 'A lot of the stuff was safe in the place we're doing up.'

'But what will happen in a couple of weeks' time?'

'Dunno. D'you know, Doll, I'd be quite willing to go after those blokes who did that to Reg, and give 'em a bloody good pasting.'

'I know how you feel.'

'Why ain't they in the army?'

'Don't know.'

Even though the war was over, there was still conscription, and all young men aged eighteen, unless they were in an exempt occupation, had to serve two years in the army.

'Perhaps they were old blokes, or men who have already done their National Service,' suggested Dolly.

'Could be. Or spivs, or conscription dodgers all looking for ways to make a quick buck.' Tony looked in his empty glass. 'Has your policeman bloke come up with any names?'

She laughed. 'He ain't my policeman. I don't think he's been in the yard. If he has, he didn't come in the office.'

Tony was pleased about that. 'Let's forget about all that for now and remember the good times we once had. D'you remember when we used to sit in the pictures? You would only ever let me put my arm round you. D'you know, Reg used to undo Pen's blouse.'

'I know. She told me.'

'You wouldn't let me do that.'

'No. I know.'

'You used to slap me hand if I tried.'

'Well, I know you, Tony. Give you an inch and you'd take a yard.'

'Can't blame a bloke for trying.'

'Suppose not. I bet you got up to all sorts of things when you was in the army.'

'I wanted to when I got your Dear John letter, but there ain't a lot of girls in the desert. D'you know, I was really upset when I got that.'

Dolly felt embarrassed. 'I'm sorry. I didn't know what else to do. I just had to tell you.'

There was a long silence.

'Have you any regrets about marrying him?' Tony asked quietly.

'Some. But I don't want to talk about it.'

'Sorry. I'll get another drink.'

Tony stood at the bar waiting to be served. He looked at Dolly and smiled. He was longing to hear if Joe had his way before they got married, but he knew Dolly would probably walk out on him if he asked her that, so decided to drop the subject. After getting the drinks, he sat down and said, 'Reg's hoping that Penny might be getting those callipers to help her walk.'

'She did say something about it, but she's not keen. She's not got a lot of patience so I don't know how she'd get on. She gets upset when she remembers the good times we all had together.'

'We certainly had some good times,' said Tony.

They sat for a while, reminiscing. They used to go to Southend for the day and go on all the rides, to the local fleapit to see the latest film, and to the dances at the local club with local lads playing. Dolly remembered that there were always good nights out with Tony.

Tony reminded her of how he and Reg used to fool about as they all walked home together.

'And what about the times we went up West on a special night out?' asked Dolly. 'That was till the war stopped all that and took you away.'

'If there hadn't been a war, would you have still married me?' he asked.

'Probably.'

'I used to love dancing with you.'

'I used to love that as well.'

'We got quite good, didn't we?' said Tony as he sat with his hands round his glass.

'Well, we'd practise enough in your mum's front room.'

Tony smiled at the memory of them laughing and falling onto the settee if they'd got it wrong. 'That and Christmas was the only time that room ever got used,' said Tony.

'Well, you was the only one that had a gramophone.'

'Mum told me that all my records got broken in an air raid. It turned out that she was rushing to get to next door's shelter, and she knocked over that vase that used to sit on top of the records. They all got smashed.'

'I remember the mess that landmine made to your end of the road. Lucky nobody was killed.

What happened to the vase?'

'Strangely, that was all right,' Tony laughed. 'She never did like our taste in music. Mum wrote and told me about what happened to you at Woolies with that flying bomb. That must have been awful.'

'Well, yes it was, but that's all in the past now,' said Dolly, not wanting to be reminded of that terrible day. 'But we did have a lot of laughs back then,' she said, quickly changing the subject. 'Have you got any of the latest records?'

'Nah, didn't see the point, not having anyone to dance with. Would you like to go to a dance again?'

'I don't know. I'd feel guilty about not being with Penny.'

'You'd be with me.'

'I know, but it wouldn't be the same. The four of us always did so many things together.'

'Yeh, but things have changed.'

'They certainly have,' Dolly said softly.

'What about this new music? Have you ever done any jiving?'

'Did a bit in America.'

Tony sat upright. 'Did you? Did you really?'

'I had a go.'

'Was you any good?'

'Not really. You should see some of the youngsters; they really throw themselves about. I expect everybody over here will be doing it soon.'

'In that case, girl, you'll have to teach me, then we can go and show the youngsters a thing or two.'

Dolly laughed. 'You sound like some old man.'

'Well let's face it, we ain't getting any younger.'

Dolly picked up her glass. 'Here's to the good times we had.'

'We could have 'em again.'

'I told you, things have changed.' Dolly smiled at all the happy memories. She looked at her watch. 'I think it's time we went.'

'If you say so.' Tony finished his drink and helped Dolly on with her coat. As he held it, he felt a great longing to hold her and kiss her, but he knew that he had to bide his time if he wanted things to go back to how they once were.

'Thank you, Tony, for a lovely evening.'

'It wasn't much.' He laughed. 'Just a couple of shandies. I might take you out again if that's all it's gonna cost me.'

They walked, arm in arm, and under the street light, Tony saw Dolly smile. 'It should be me thanking you,' he said. 'After all, I think we both deserved a nice night out.'

When they got to Dolly's house, she went to walk up to her door, but stopped and quickly kissed his cheek. 'Goodnight.'

Tony stood and watched her pull the key through the letter box, turn and wave, then go indoors. 'Goodnight, Doll,' he whispered to himself. 'I do still love you, Dolly Day Dream.' Walking away, he ran his hand through his sandy-coloured hair. 'If only you could love me again,' he said.

Dolly closed the door, and stood for a while before she went into the kitchen where she knew her mum and dad would still be up and waiting for her to come home. She had enjoyed this evening, but worried that it was happening too soon. She didn't want to get involved with anyone else, even if it was Tony, who she had known all her life. The memories she had with Joe were still with her.

'Hello, love,' said her mother, as Dolly pushed open the kitchen door. 'Did you have a nice time?'

'We only went for a drink. And yes, it was nice just sitting and talking about old times.'

'Would you like some cocoa?'

'No, thanks.'

Her father turned the radio down, and sat up. 'Young Tony's a nice bloke.'

'I know, Dad, but please don't read anything into it. We're just good friends.'

'I know, love, but it's nice to see you going out again.'

Grace was smiling, fit to burst.

'So,' said Reg when he walked into the office the following morning, 'I hear you went out with Tony last night.'

'My God, he didn't waste any time in telling you, did he?'

'Well, he is a bit like a cat with two tails this morning.'

'We only went for a drink.' Dolly turned to her filing cabinet. 'You're as bad as me mum and dad.'

'Well, we would all like to see you two together again.'

'Sorry. It's not to be.'

'Anyway, I just popped in to tell you I might be out all morning.'

'Anywhere exciting?'

'I've got to see a bloke – a Mr Edwards – about

some work. Yesterday, he came round the place we're working in and said if he buys the materials, could I provide the labour at the right price.'

'That's great.'

He went to the door. 'Wish me luck.'

'Of course I do.'

Dolly was really pleased at the news, and was humming to herself when Tony walked in.

'You seem happy,' he said. 'Was it my stimulating company last night that brings a smile to your face?'

'No, it was the thought that Reg might be finding some work.'

'Yeh, that'll be great. It seems this bloke's got a big house, and it's got quite a bit of bomb damage. He wants Reg to do the work. When Reg told him what had happened and couldn't provide the materials he said he'd get them, so that'll be great.'

'Do you know how much has to be done?'

'No. But hopefully it's enough to keep the four of us going for a few weeks.'

'D'you fancy a cuppa?' asked Dolly.

'No, thanks. I'd better get outside. If he comes in and sees me sitting here drinking tea, he might sack me.'

'I don't think he'll do that.'

'See yer, Doll. And thanks for last night.'

It was late afternoon when Reg came back into the office. Dolly could see by the look on his face that he'd got the job.

'So when do you start?'

'Week after next. We should finish the job we're on by then.'

'Where is it?'

'It's over Poplar way. They've had it pretty bad over there.'

'I'm so pleased for you, Reg. Let's hope this leads to more work.'

'So do I.' He left the office, whistling.

Dolly called out to her mother when she opened the front door. 'Just popping into Penny. Won't be long.'

'Hello, Mrs Smith,' she said when she walked into the kitchen of number two. 'Penny in her room?'

'Yes, love,' Ivy replied, with a beaming smile.

'Everything all right?' Dolly asked softly.

Ivy nodded. 'Go on in.'

Carefully, Dolly opened the door to Penny's room. Gail was in her cot, and Penny was softly cooing to her daughter, gently stroking her head. She looked up. 'I'm glad you popped in. I owe you an apology. I'm sorry about the other night.'

'Forget it.'

'I can't. I couldn't help meself. Everything just got on top of me.'

'I'm not surprised. Give me a cuddle.'

'I hear you went out with Tony last night.'

'How d'you know?'

'Your mum popped in.'

'I might have guessed.'

'She was dead pleased.'

'I know.'

'Well?'

'Well, what?'

'Are you seeing him again?'

81

'I see him nearly every day.'

'D'you know, Dolly Taylor, sometimes you can be so dammed annoying.'

Dolly was pleased that her friend had called her by her maiden name. 'I know. Now, what was all that about with you and Reg?'

'Oh, that. It was me getting all stroppy cos I'm stuck in this bloody chair and can't get out and about.'

Dolly knew things were hard for her fun-loving friend. 'Look, things might be getting better, and as soon as the weather gets a bit warmer perhaps me and you could go out again.'

'I'd like that. Especially if I've got me new legs by then.'

'Not heard anything yet?'

'No. Now everything's free, I expect I'll have to wait me turn.'

Dolly was pleased she'd managed to turn the conversation around, but why didn't she want to tell Penny about last night, when there wasn't anything to tell? 'It's good Reg has got some work. At least, he can keep everybody in a job.'

'It's good. Mind you, I think he should give up trying to run his own business and just go out and get a job. That way, we'll have a proper wage coming in every week and not have to rely on taking anything that comes along.'

'I thought you liked him having his own business.'

'I did.' Penny turned to her baby. 'But, at least, then I'll know she won't go short of anything.'

'I'm sure that would never happen.'

The door opened and Ivy popped her head

round the door. 'Would you girls like a cup of tea?'

'That'll be nice, Ma,' said Penny. 'We'll come in the kitchen and have it.'

'Do you want me to bring Gail?' asked Dolly.

'No, she'll be all right.'

Dolly could see that Penny was still really down, despite the good news that Reg had got some more work.

'I hear you and Tony went out last night,' said Ivy.

Dolly laughed. 'It was only for a drink.'

'I know, but it's nice to see you two getting along together. Didn't like that other girl. What was her name?'

'Meg,' said Penny.

'Well, me and Tony are old friends,' said Dolly.

'I know,' said Ivy as she poured the tea into three cups.

'It's good Reg has got another job,' said Dolly, hoping to change the subject.

'Yes, bless him. He does try so hard.'

'I know. Let's hope it brings in more for him.' Dolly looked at Penny but she didn't appear to be at all interested in this conversation. 'I know it's cold out, but have you been out today?' she asked Penny.

'Where the bloody hell can I go?'

Dolly knew that sometimes Mrs Smith would leave the baby with her mother, or Penny's, then wrap Penny up and push her around the market. Although, it was hard work for her. 'Sorry I asked.'

'Can't even go over to the bloody sweet shop or the grocers. Can't get through the bloody door

83

with this thing, can I?'

'The Gregory sisters always bring stuff out for you.'

'I know. But it ain't the same as going in a shop and choosing things yourself. Won't ever be able to take me daughter to the shops or school.' She quickly turned her wheelchair round and left the room.

'Sorry, Pen,' Dolly called out. 'Sometimes I forget and say the wrong things.'

'Don't upset yourself, love,' said Ivy. 'We all do, at times. Things are really getting her down lately. I wish there was something I could do.'

'I wish there was something we could all do for her. It must be frustrating not being able to do the normal things you have to do for your daughter.'

'You two have certainly had a rough deal in your lives.'

Dolly gave her a weak smile. 'I don't think we're the only ones.'

'I know, but you're both so young.'

Dolly wanted to get away from this conversation. 'Pen was saying that she's not heard anything from the hospital about giving her crutches.'

Ivy shook her head. 'Mind you, I don't know how she'll get on with 'em. She's not got a lot of patience as it is.'

Penny pushed open the kitchen door. 'I hope you're not talking about me.'

'Course we are,' said Dolly. 'I was just asking if you'd heard any more about the crutches.'

'No. Anyway, I don't want crutches; I want new legs.'

'What about these callipers? Will you get them?' asked Dolly.

'Don't know. I expect the blokes in the forces will come first. I expect if we could afford it, we could get them ourselves, but that idea is well and truly out of the window now.'

'You never know,' said Dolly. 'I best be going back. Mum will have the dinner on the table. See you tomorrow.'

'Sorry for being a bit of a cow,' said Penny.

'That's all right.' Dolly kissed her friend's cheek before leaving. She hated to see Penny so unhappy. *She might feel better when the weather changes,* she thought.

Later, Dolly told her mother about the conversation she'd had with Ivy Smith. 'I'm really worried about Penny. She seems to be far away at the moment and not all that happy.'

'Well, let's face it, the poor girl hasn't a lot going for her right now. She's probably had a bad day. We all have them at times.'

'I know.'

'Things will look better when the weather turns. Has she heard any more about getting those things for her legs?'

'No, not yet. I wish they would hurry up and get it all started.'

'Well, we all know how long these things take, especially if they're free... Are they free?'

'Don't know. I would think so, seeing as everything else is free now.'

'This National Health Service is a godsend. Fancy not having to worry about whether to go and see a doctor – or not, if you really couldn't afford it.'

'A bit different to America. I can remember when I went to a doctor over there; Joe's mother nearly went mad at the cost. They only went to see a doctor if the local drug store couldn't help them.'

'Well, thank goodness that's not going to be a problem here now.'

Dolly smiled. Her mother always seemed to have an answer for any situation.

Chapter 8

It was a few weeks into February, and Reg was busy finishing up the old job and getting the boys started on the new one.

'Everything all right, Dolly?' he asked at the end of one Friday when he walked into the office.

'Yes, thanks. I've worked out this week's wages. Do you want to check them?'

'They should be all right. In fact, you're getting to be quite a dab hand with everything now.'

She smiled. 'Has Mr Edwards come up with any money this week?' She had never met this man, but Penny had told her that she was a bit concerned that he wasn't all Reg had said he was, and he might not even pay them every week as he'd promised.

'Yes,' he said, putting a small leather case on her desk. 'He's so pleased with us and what we're doing that he told some of his business associates. He reckons he can get us some more work.'

'Oh Reg, that's wonderful news.'

He grinned. 'Yeh, it certainly is. He said there should be enough here to cover the wages, and what's left over to share out with everybody. It's a bit of a bonus as he's more than pleased with what we've done.'

Dolly smiled. 'Now that is good news.' Despite Penny's fears, she felt she had to say, 'He seems a nice bloke.'

'He is, and he seems to know a lot of people, so that could be good for us if we carry on doing a good job for him.' He left the office, whistling.

Dolly smiled. Perhaps things were on the up at last for Penny and Reg.

'Hello, Dad,' said Dolly when she arrived home that evening. Her father was sitting in his armchair reading the paper. 'That was a nice surprise in your wages this week, wasn't it?'

'It certainly was.'

'So what's this Mr Edwards like, then? Reg certainly thinks a lot of him. And he reckons he could get him a lot more work.'

'We'll just have to wait and see.' Jim returned to his newspaper.

Dolly was a little surprised that her father didn't show a bit more enthusiasm about Mr Edwards. As he'd never been to the office, Dolly had no opinion about him. All she was concerned about was that he was paying everyone's wages.

'Thought Dad might have been a little bit more enthusiastic about this Mr Edwards,' said Dolly to her mother, later, as they were finishing washing up the dinner things. 'Has he said anything to you?' she asked, putting the plates in the cupboard.

'Only that he reckons he's a bit of a wide boy. Got a posh car, by all accounts.'

Dolly laughed. 'Is that all?'

'Well, you know what yer father's like. Thinks anybody who's got a posh car and smart clothes is a wide boy, especially if he don't appear to be working for a living.'

'I can't wait to see him.'

Later, when Dolly popped in to number two, Penny shouted, 'I'm in the kitchen.'

'You on your own?' Dolly asked her friend.

'Reg took his mum for a drink. It's her birthday. They've only gone to the Earl of Beaconsfield and they knew you'd be in to look after me ... not that I need looking after.'

Dolly knew the pub well; it was only at the bottom of the road, but she was still worried that they hadn't called on her to come in right away. 'I wish I'd known it was Mrs Smith's birthday, I would have bought her a card.'

'You know what she's like; she didn't want any fuss. Besides, she does so much for me that she deserves a couple of drinks with her son.'

Dolly was pleased that Penny seemed to be feeling better about things in general.

'Put the kettle on and we'll have a cuppa,' said Penny. 'And you can make Gail's bottle while you're out there.'

'Course,' said Dolly as she went into the scullery.

After a while, when she was nursing Gail, Dolly asked Penny if she knew anything about this mysterious Mr Edwards.

'I was a bit worried when Reg first told me about him, but now I don't care, just as long as he pays Reg to work for him.'

'Dad reckons he's a bit of a wide boy.'

Penny laughed. 'I know what he means, but you know what people are like. Just cos he's got a flash car and nice clothes, that don't mean a thing.'

'How do you know all that?'

'Reg told me.'

'Is he worried about him?'

'No. He thinks someone must've died and left him a business.'

'Oh,' said Dolly, a little disappointed there wasn't something more sinister about this Mr Edwards.

'Your trouble is, you've seen too many films where there has to be a baddie.'

Dolly laughed. 'Well, it gives us something to talk about.'

They spent the rest of the evening talking, and cooing over baby Gail. Mr Edwards' name wasn't mentioned again. It wasn't long before Reg and his mother walked in.

'Sorry we've been so long, but everybody kept wishing me a happy birthday and if I'd drunk all the drinks bought for me, I'd be on me knees be now.' Her cheeks were slightly flushed and her eyes were sparkling.

Reg kissed Penny, then Gail and Dolly. 'So, how's my best three girls?'

'You stink of beer,' said Penny.

'I know and it ain't even me birthday.'

Dolly kissed Ivy and wished her a happy birthday. 'Sit down. I'll make you a cuppa, for a change.'

Smiling broadly, Ivy did as she was told.

Reg was full of Mr Edwards and what a great guy he was. 'And that was real good of him to give us a bonus today.'

'Just as long as the work keeps coming, that's all I worry about,' said Penny. She smiled and pointed at her mother-in-law who was sitting in the armchair, asleep.

'Come on, Mum, time for bed,' said Reg, gently taking her arm.

'Oh, I must have just closed me eyes. Sorry about that, girls.'

'That's all right, Mum. You go on up. See you in the morning,' said Penny, as Ivy bent over and kissed her.

'Night, girls.' She waved, and left the room.

'She's not a bad old stick,' said Reg.

'She's been good to us,' said Penny.

Dolly was pleased her friend was back to her old self.

At the office, the following week, Dolly looked up and was surprised to see Harry Jordan walk into the office, in his police uniform.

'Hello,' she said. 'What are you doing this side of the water?' He had told her that his patch was the other side of the Thames.

He took off his cap. 'Had to come over this way so I thought I'd just pop in to see you.'

Dolly noted, not for first time, that he had a

lovely ready smile. 'Don't suppose you've heard any more about the break-in?'

'No,' he said as he looked out of the window. 'Everybody busy, then?'

'Yes. They're all out working.'

'That's good. Pleased to hear that Mr Smith's getting back on his feet again.'

'We all are. Would you like a cup of tea?'

'Sorry. I am on duty.'

'Of course.'

He looked at his watch, and then said hurriedly, 'I've really come to ask you if you'd go out with me one evening?'

Dolly was surprised. 'I don't know.'

'Just to the pictures or something.'

'I don't know. I don't think so,' said Dolly.

Once again he looked at his watch. 'I'd better be going. I'll call in again when I'm round this way. That'll give you time to think about it.' He smiled and putting on his cap, opened the door.

'Thanks for dropping by.'

'My pleasure.'

After Harry had left, Dolly was pleased he'd called in, but she was also surprised that he'd asked her out again. She would have liked him to stay a little longer. It was nice to have someone to talk to and, after all, he was nice for a copper, but was there an ulterior motive for asking her out? Did he want to know more about who Reg worked with, and where?

That evening, when Tony and Reg came back to the office, she told them that Harry Jordan had been there, just in case someone had seen him, and told Reg. She never mentioned about him

91

asking her out, not that she had anything to hide, but it might just upset them, even if she was only thinking of dating a policeman.

'What did he want to come sniffing around here for?' asked Tony.

'He just wanted to know how things were, that's all.'

'He didn't say if they've found out any more about the break-in, then?' asked Reg.

'No.' She could see that Tony wasn't very happy that Harry had been there.

'Did you tell him where we were?' asked Reg.

'I just said you were all out working. Why? Is there something wrong?'

'No. It's just that I don't like the cops asking questions about what we're doing, that's all. They should spend more time looking for the blokes that nearly put us out of business. If you're ready to go, I'll go and get the van started.'

Sometimes, if they were around at Dolly's leaving time, Reg would give her a lift home. After all, they did live in the same street.

'He seems a bit touchy. Is everything all right?' she asked Tony as she put on her hat and coat.

'He's fine. It's just that he don't like the idea of the old bill sniffing round here. Can't say I like it either. Was it you he wanted to see?'

'What if it was?'

'Nothing, I s'pose. Come on, Reg's waiting.' Tony was definitely a bit miffed.

Dolly grinned to herself as she climbed into the van.

Once March arrived, the evenings became lighter,

and at last, it seemed that spring was on its way. Reg only came into the office on Friday afternoons to sort out the wages and take them to the site he was working at.

'Reg, do you go to the bank before you come here?' asked Dolly.

'No. Why?'

'Does Mr Edwards always give you the money in cash?'

'Yes. Why?'

'How does he know how many hours you all work?' she asked as she counted out the money, recorded it in the wages book, and filled the envelopes.

'I suppose he works it out, just like you do. What's with the questions?'

'Nothing.'

'Has that copper been sniffing around again?'

'No, why should he?'

'It's just that I don't like everybody knowing me business.'

Dolly got on with her job, and nothing more was said. When the wages were sorted out, Reg got ready to leave. Dolly knew she had asked too many questions and should apologise. 'I'm sorry, Reg, if I've offended you. It's just that I worry about things being all above board.'

He smiled. 'Don't be daft. Of course it's all above board. Just cos we don't see any paperwork, or order any materials, as long as Mr Edwards pays us in cash, that's all we've got to worry about. I'll just go out and check that gate.'

Dolly knew Reg was still worried about another break-in, even though there was hardly any stock in the yard.

When he returned, he asked. 'All done?'

Dolly nodded.

Reg picked up the envelopes. 'Right, I'm off. See you tonight.'

Tony only popped in the office now and again, as they seemed to be going from one job to another. Reg was thinking about getting another van. After ten years of rationing, there was talk of petrol soon not requiring coupons.

'I'm thinking of getting a car,' said Tony, on one rare occasion he was in the office. 'Mr E seems to have a lot of connections. He said he'd look out for a good second-hand one for me, and maybe a van for Reg.'

'Can you drive?' asked Dolly.

'Course. Learnt when I was in the army, didn't I. And I passed me test. So would you come out with me then?'

'Might.'

'Good. That's something to look forward to. Right, see you tomorrow.'

Dolly smiled as he left. He was such a charmer.

An hour later, Harry Jordan walked into the office.

'Hello,' said Dolly. 'This is a surprise, twice in one month. Is everything all right?'

'Yes, thanks.' He took off his cap. 'Did you give any thought to what I asked you before?'

She smiled. 'Thanks for the invite, but at the moment I don't feel like going on a date. Sorry.'

'Well, you can't blame a bloke for trying. I expect it's the uniform that puts you off. I'd promise to wear civvies.'

Dolly laughed. 'I should hope you would.'

'Now that gives me some hope.'

'Harry,' she still felt awkward at using his first name, 'the last thing I want to do is give you some hope.' Dolly was getting a little embarrassed. 'Was there anything else?'

'You don't happen to know the address where Mr Smith is currently working, do you?'

The sudden turn in the conversation had surprised Dolly. 'Over the water, Poplar way. Why? Have you heard any more about the break-in?'

'No. Do you happen to know who he's working for?'

To Dolly, this time, Harry had quickly become very businesslike. 'No. Just as long as he pays the wages, that's all I care about.'

'You must have an address.'

'Why?' she asked again. 'Is there something wrong?'

'No. What about if you want to contact him?' He sat down.

'Is there something wrong?' she asked again.

'No. It's just that we're making a few enquiries about some dodgy dealings with a gang on our side of the water. There's a lot of wheeling and dealing going on at the moment, and we think it's not quite kosher.'

'Oh.' She didn't want to mention Mr Edwards just in case he was the one Harry was enquiring about. Dolly was getting cross with this man. Was he only interested in her to find out about Reg and where he was working? 'Should you be telling me this?'

'Not really, but I know you are a nice bunch of people and I wouldn't like it if Mr Smith was involved with anything that's not quite above board. D'you happen to know where they get their supplies from?'

'No. Should I?'

'Well, it's just that I should have thought so, given you're in charge of invoices and all that.'

'The customer always seems to provide all the supplies.' Dolly was beginning to get a little nervous. 'Would you like a cup of tea?' was all she could think of saying.

Harry smiled. 'No, thanks. Perhaps next time. There was a lot of looting during the war, both sides of the water, and now we think that as materials are hard to get hold of, the gangs may have started up again. After all, Mr Smith had stuff stolen, didn't he?'

'Oh,' was all Dolly could say.

Harry stood up and put his cap back on. 'Maybe I can call in again?'

'Yes. That'll be nice.'

With that, he left, and Dolly began to panic. Was it a date he really wanted, or was that an excuse for something else? What if Harry had been talking about Mr Edwards? What if there was something about him that wasn't quite right? Harry's attitude had made her feel very uneasy. She wouldn't mention it to Reg as she had already upset him by asking him too many questions about his boss. Perhaps she could ask Tony out tonight, tell him about Harry's visit, and try to find out if this Mr Edwards was all that Reg thought he was.

Chapter 9

After Harry left the office, Dolly was very nervous. What if this Mr Edwards was part of a gang? What sort of gang was he in? Where did he get his materials from? Dolly had heard Reg talk about big black market deals going on. Was Mr Edwards involved with anything like that? What if Reg, Tony, and her dad were involved with some kind of a dodgy practice? Where would that leave them? Surely, Reg wouldn't let himself get involved if he thought everything wasn't above board.

She knew she was letting her imagination run away with her. After all, Reg had Penny and baby Gail to think about. As for her dad, Dolly knew that he'd seen enough of the world to know that getting involved with anything that was wrong didn't get you anywhere except in prison. She had to stop thinking this way, but she couldn't concentrate on anything, and her thoughts were going around in circles.

Harry's visit to the office had planted these seeds in her mind. She should have told him who they were working for, although, Reg had never given her the full site address. He'd always casually said that it was over the water, Poplar way. Could they really be working for gangsters?

Now that Dolly only had the wages to deal with, and sometimes a few letters for Mr Edwards to type up, she didn't have to deal with orders, so she had a lot of time on her hands. That gave her time to let her imagination run away with her. But, it struck her that if something happened to Penny or the baby, and Reg was needed, she would not know how to get in touch with him. She knew that she now had to find out who they were working for, and where they were working.

Dolly sat down and looked at the phone. She felt as if she wanted to run away and hide. She didn't want any of the people she loved to be involved with gangsters, but were they gangsters? Maybe Penny was right: Dolly had been watching too many films. But why had Harry been asking so many questions, and putting all these ideas in her head? She would ask Tony tonight, and, hopefully, get some answers.

It was then that the phone rang, making her jump. What if it was Mr Edwards? What would she say to him? She cautiously picked up the receiver. 'Hello, Smith's Builders and Decorators,' she said nervously.

'Dolly. This is Tony. Could you pop in to Penny's and tell her that Reg will be late tonight. He's going to look at another job with Mr Edwards.'

She breathed a sigh of relief. 'Yes of course. D'you know where they're going?'

'No. But it sounds as if it could be a very big job.'

'Tony...' Dolly was very worried. Why hadn't Reg told Tony where he was going? Did Reg know? 'Tony, could I see you tonight?'

There were a few moments of silence, then Tony said, 'Did I hear right? You want to go out with me?'

98

'Yes, please.'

'Wow. Course. What time?'

'Will you be ready by seven?'

'I should say so. See you then.'

'Bye,' said Dolly.

'Bye,' said Tony.

She put the receiver down and looked at her watch. She had another three hours till she was with Tony. Only then, would she have some answers to the thousand and one questions that were buzzing around inside her head.

Dolly popped in to see Penny before she went home, to tell her that Reg would be late that evening, and the reason why.

'He didn't say where, then?'

'No. I wasn't given an address; I was just told that he was going with this Mr Edwards to look at a job.'

'I hope it's a big one that will keep the boys busy for weeks,' said Penny when she heard all that Dolly had to say.

'I'd best be going. I'm out tonight.'

Penny looked up from giving Gail her bottle. 'Anywhere nice?'

'No. Just for a drink.'

'And may I ask who with?'

'You can, because if I don't tell you, I'm sure someone else will. I'm going out with Tony.'

'Wonderful.'

'Don't get too excited. It's only for a drink.' There was no way that she was going to tell her best friend about the visit from Harry Jordan, or the real reason behind why she was going out with Tony.

'Now, let me see,' teased Penny, 'that's the second time, so far this year, that you've been out together, alone.'

'You'll have us walking down the aisle next, you old busybody.'

'That would be fantastic. And by the way, a busybody, yes, but I'm not old! When you're stuck here day and night, there's not a lot to do but fantasise. Now, be off with you. You can tell me all about it tomorrow.'

As Dolly walked back to her own house, she told herself that she would keep whatever Tony told her to herself, for now.

It was dead on seven o'clock when Dolly opened the front door to Tony, who was grinning like a Cheshire cat.

'Hi, Doll. Ready?'

She could see that he was looking really smart. In the hall light, his blue eyes were sparkling and his sandy-coloured hair had been carefully combed into place.

'I'll just grab me handbag,' she said, and left him standing on the doorstep as she rushed into the kitchen to pick it up.

'Have a good time,' shouted Grace, as Dolly rushed out.

'We will.'

Dolly was pleased it was Monday and her father had gone to play darts, otherwise she might have been tempted to say something to him about Harry's visit and his enquiries about the mysterious Mr Edwards.

Outside, Dolly took Tony's arm. 'So, where shall we go?'

'I don't care. I just like the idea that you want to go out with me.'

Dolly had to choose her words carefully. Although she liked Tony, she didn't want him to think that she was only interested in questioning him about Mr Edwards. 'Perhaps we could go to that pub we went to before.'

'That's fine with me.'

On the bus, Tony was telling Dolly about the lovely house they were doing up. 'You should see it. The rooms are very lofty, and the fireplace in the front room is marble. And it's got a bathroom. I'd like to live in a place like that.'

'Is anybody living there at the moment?'

'Nah, from what we can gather, it belonged to Mr Edwards' old mum. They must've had a few bob at one time.'

'So where does he live now?'

'Dunno. We don't see a lot of him. He just pops in to tell us what to do, and then sometimes him and Reg go off.'

When they were settled in the pub with their drinks, Dolly asked, 'How does this man manage to get hold of the materials when everybody else is struggling?'

'Apparently, he's got a lot of connections. But don't let's talk about him; let's talk about us.'

'There's not really an "us", is there?'

'I don't know. I was hoping this is what you asked me out for.'

'Sorry, Tony.'

'So why did you ask me out, then?'

As much as she wanted to tell him about what Harry had told her this afternoon, she knew she couldn't, as he seemed to think that Mr Edwards was all above board. 'I was lonely and wanted some nice company.'

'I suppose you do get a bit lonely being on your own all day.'

'It wasn't so bad when I had to phone suppliers and sort out invoices, but I don't do that now, so I do get a bit fed up.'

Tony reached across and touched her hand. 'You're not thinking of leaving, are you?'

'I don't know. Nobody just pops in like before. Some of the reps used to come in, just for a warm and a chat, at times.' She was beginning to feel very sorry for herself.

'So even yer policeman ain't been sniffing around, then?'

Dolly picked up her drink. With her other hand under the table, she crossed her fingers. She didn't like telling lies. 'I've not seen him for a while.'

They fell silent. Dolly was finding it hard not to talk about Mr Edwards, and she could see that Tony was getting restless. 'Do you want to go?' she asked, after they'd had a second drink.

'Only if you want to,' he answered casually.

'I'll just finish me drink. Then we can be off, if you like.'

'OK.' He didn't argue or make any comments.

As they walked home from the bus stop, Dolly felt very guilty. She had only asked Tony out to find out more about Mr Edwards, but he didn't seem to have a bad word to say against him. If her father was still up when she got home, she would

102

ask him what he thought about the man. But was she taking too much notice of what Harry had told her?

'I'm sorry we didn't seem to hit it off tonight,' said Tony. 'You seem as if you've got something on your mind. Are you all right? Is the job getting you down?'

'No, I'm fine.' Dolly smiled. 'I'm sorry I've not been more stimulating company.'

'Perhaps we can go out another time, when you feel more like it, that is.'

'I'm sure I will. Goodnight Tony, and thanks.'

'Thanks for what?'

'Being there for me when I needed you.' Dolly went to her front door and pulled the key through the letter box.

Tony walked away. He knew there was definitely something worrying Dolly. What was it? Was she trying to tell him she was going to leave? Reg and Penny would be very sad to see her go. If that was the case, why couldn't she tell him? He would try to get into the office tomorrow and find out what the problem was.

Dolly was pleased when she opened the kitchen door and saw that her dad was alone. 'Mum in bed?' she asked.

'Yes. So you've been out with Tony, then?'

'Only for a drink,' she said, sitting in the armchair that was the other side of the fireplace.

'That's nice. You know me and your mum would like it if you two got together again.'

'I know, but it's not to be.'

'That's a pity. He's a nice lad.' Jim smiled.

'Well, I'm going on up now. Don't forget to put the guard in front of the fire when you come up.'

She sat forward. 'No ... Dad ... Dad, can I talk to you?'

He looked worried. 'Course you can.' He sat down again. 'What's wrong? You in any kind of trouble?'

'No.'

'So what's bothering you?'

'I'm worried about Reg.'

'Why? What about?'

'Harry – that's the policeman who brought us home that time – came into the office today.'

'What did he want?'

'I'm just coming to that. He asked if I knew who you were all working for. I didn't mention any names, as he was talking about some kind of gang, but he didn't say who or what they were involved in.'

'And you think he was talking about Mr Edwards?'

'Well, what do we know of him?'

'Not a lot, I'll grant you, but he seems a nice enough bloke, and he seems to be putting quite a bit of work our way.'

'Where does he get the materials from? I don't get any invoices.'

'I don't suppose you do. Reg don't have anything to do with that side of things now. He just tells him what's wanted and it arrives. Don't ask me how he manages to get hold of the stuff, but that's not our problem. Just as long as he comes up every week with our wages, and yours, we've got nothing to worry about.'

'He don't even send a banker's draft or cheque; he always pays the wages in cash.'

'So that should make your life a bit easier, not having to go to the bank.'

'I don't even know the address where you're working.'

'Do you have to?'

'What if Penny wanted to get in touch with Reg?'

'I'm sure Penny's got his address. I think this copper's started to put some silly ideas in your head.'

'But are they?'

'Did you mention any of this to Tony?'

'No.'

'Well, don't let Reg hear you say anything. And Dolly, next time that copper comes in, tell him to mind his own business. Anyway, I'm off now. Looks as if we could have a busy time in front of us. Night, love. And don't worry about too much.' He kissed her cheek.

'Night, Dad.' She picked up the poker and gently stirred the coals. Was she reading too much in to what Harry had told her?

Chapter 10

The following morning, Dolly was surprised, and full of panic, when Reg knocked on their front door. 'What's wrong?' she asked. 'Is Penny all right?'

'She's fine. I got home quite late last night and

after taking the boys to the job, I thought I'd come and take you to work. I've got a bit of paperwork we need to go over.'

'Hang on. I'll just put me hat on and get me bag.'

'Bring a scarf, as it's a bit nippy this morning and you might need it in the office.'

When Dolly was settled in the van, Reg said, 'This van's freezing. I'll be glad when I get one with decent windows and a floor that stops the draft from coming right up me trouser leg.' He laughed.

'Tony said that Mr Edwards is looking out for one for you.'

'Yeh. He reckons one should come along soon.'

'You sound in a good mood.'

'I am, and I can tell yer, Dolly, the day I met Bert Edwards was the best thing that ever happened to me and the firm.'

'Why's that?'

'He's got some good connections, and he's putting plenty of work our way. I might even have to take on some more blokes.'

'That's good,' she said flatly.

'I thought you might be a bit more enthusiastic about it.'

'Well, I don't know anything about the man.'

'I can tell yer, he's a bit of all right.'

Dolly began to wonder if Harry had got things all wrong, so she kept her thoughts to herself.

'I'll light the Primus, and then you can put the kettle on,' said Reg when they went into the office. He placed a folder on the desk. 'This is a list of the work we're going to do. We're doing up a block of flats that have been badly damaged. There's six in all.'

'Does Mr Edwards own them?'

'Dunno. I didn't ask. I've got a list of the materials I think we might need. I want you to help me try to sort out the days it'll take and work out roughly what the wages bill will be. We can do one flat at a time, OK? Bert just wants to have some idea of what the overall cost might be.'

So, it's Bert now, is it? Dolly thought. 'That sounds reasonable to me,' she said, trying to sound businesslike. 'But it will only be a rough guide.'

'That's all Bert wants, for now.'

They spent quite a few hours going over the figures.

'Well, that seems to have got things a bit straight,' said Reg. 'You can get all this lot typed up, this afternoon, and then I can present it to him. It'll look a bit more professional then, rather than me writing it on scraps of paper. Right, now I'll take you to the café for a coffee and a bite to eat.'

'If you say so, boss.' Dolly certainly didn't want to upset Reg by telling him about Harry now. She would bide her time.

When they'd settled down, and with her fingers wrapped round the mug of hot coffee, Dolly asked, 'What about the invoices for pricing all the materials?'

'That's the good thing – I don't have to worry about that.'

'He manages to get everything, then?'

'I should say so. He must have some really good

connections, as anything we ask for, he manages to get. I tell yer, Doll, it's wonderful not having to scrimp and try to make something out of nothing.'

'Don't you worry about where he gets the stuff from?'

'Nah, that's his problem.'

'Reg, what if it's not all above board?'

'As I said, that's his problem, not ours. We just do as we're told.'

Dolly sat back. Was she reading too much into this? Reg seemed happy with the situation. After all, it was his business, and he was nobody's fool. 'Penny's not heard any more about these callipers then?' she said, to change the subject.

'Not yet. I told her we'd try to get to the hospital soon, to see if we can get her sorted out. I'm afraid I've let things slip a bit, what with worrying about getting work, then the break-in, and then having to try to find materials. So, what with one thing and another, I'm afraid I've let some things go, but for Christ's sake, don't tell Pen that. She'll have a right go at me.'

'Are her legs any thinner?' Dolly had been shocked when she first saw her friend's legs, and how thin they looked, but she knew that Reg would massage them every night to try to make them stronger.

'Nah, it's the muscle wasting away. I just hope she'll have the patience to be able to manage when the time comes.'

'It will be hard work for her.'

'I know. Right, if you've finished, we'll get back, and you can start to type up all those notes I've made.'

'I'm glad I learnt to type properly when I was in America.'

'I didn't know that's where you learnt. I thought it was night school, when you and Penny used to go.'

'We did go to night school, but it was more to muck about and meet the boys.'

Reg laughed. 'You two were always out for a good time. But you still came back to me and Tone.'

'It was while I was on the farm I did a bit of typing.' Dolly had told them all about the farm. 'I also used to help a friend who worked in the school. She was the one I went to New York with.' Dolly let her thoughts drift to Norma.

'Right,' said Reg. 'It's time to get back, so you can get down to some work.'

'It'll be good to be busy again,' she said as they left the café.

That evening, Dolly went into Penny's again. 'Reg not home yet?' she said. Everyone knew when Reg was home, as his old van was parked in the street.

'No. Why?'

'Nothing. He was in the office all this morning and we were going over a lot of figures, and trying to sort out times for the jobs and the wages.'

'I'm glad to hear he's keeping you busy.'

'By the sounds of it, this new job is certainly going to keep all of them very busy.'

'And I'm glad to say that my young brother seems to have really taken to this building and decorating lark.'

'He's a good lad. Who'd have thought that he

would have grown up to be such a good worker, when you think of all the things he used to get up to? I reckon he'll have all the girls after him soon. He's so good-looking, now all his spots have gone.'

'Well, he does come from good stock. It's a good job he's Reg's apprentice. I wouldn't want him away as well as Jack.'

Like everybody else, Dolly knew that conscription was still in place. 'At least now, there's no fear of 'em being sent off to fight,' she said. She was pleased to see that her friend was in a happy mood. 'Reg was talking about taking you to the hospital before long, to try to sort out these callipers.'

'I know. I've tried not to worry him too much as I know he's busy and wants to make sure all these jobs go smoothly. Besides, I'd rather wait till he's got this van he's been on about. Just as long as it don't freeze me to death.'

Dolly laughed. 'I must admit, this one's a bit of a rust bucket. It's even colder in there now than when we went to the West End that time.'

'Well, the blokes that did the yard knocked a few more holes in it.'

'Tony said that if the money they're earning keeps up, and he can afford the payments, he'd like to get himself a car.'

'You will be posh then when you go out.'

Dolly didn't comment on that remark.

'So when you going out with Tony again?'

'I don't know. When he asks me, I suppose.'

Penny smiled. 'So you want to go out with him again?'

'Well, it's better than sitting with me mum and dad.'

'You know you're always welcome in here.'

'I know. But sometimes I feel that you and Reg need a bit of time on your own.' Dolly didn't mention that Tony might not ask her again as it wasn't a very successful evening, thanks to her asking too many questions.

Reg came in, whistling. He poked his head round the door. 'Hi girls.'

'You sound in a good mood,' said Penny.

'I certainly am.' He walked in, carrying an armful of flowers. 'This bunch is for you, Dolly. This one is for me mum, and this one, my darling, is for you.' He kissed Penny as he handed her a lovely bunch of roses.

'Thank you, Reg,' said Dolly. 'What are these for?'

'Does there have to be a reason?'

'You ain't knocked them off, have you?' asked Penny.

'I knew my dear wife would say something like that. No, my love, I ain't knocked 'em off. It's just that Bert Edwards has agreed all the figures that me and Dolly worked out, and he reckons that we've got more than enough work to keep us going for at least another four months, and there could be a lot more after that. So thank you, Dolly, for helping me, and doing such a good job. When you've finished typing them up properly, I'll take them to Bert.' He kissed Dolly's cheek.

Penny laughed. 'It's not every boss that gives his staff flowers and a kiss.'

'I know,' said Dolly, 'and I shall always be

111

grateful to you, Reg, for giving me a start.'

'Think nothing of it. Right, I'll take these out to Mum and make us all a nice cup of tea.'

'It does me good to see him so happy,' said Penny. 'I wish I could meet this Bert Edwards and thank him personally.'

'So do I,' said Dolly. But she knew her reasons were very different to Penny's. She wanted to see what sort of man he was.

Dolly's wish was granted, when at the end of the week, a man in a lovely, thick, tan-coloured coat with a dark brown fur collar walked into the office. He looked all around.

'So this is where he keeps you.'

'I beg your pardon, Mr...?'

'Edwards. I'm the one who pays your wages.' He took off his brown trilby hat, and smoothed down his slick, straight black hair.

'Oh.' Dolly took a quick intake of breath, and felt herself blushing. He wasn't as old as she thought he might have been, and he was very good-looking in a swarthy sort of way. 'What can I do for you?'

'Not a lot. I just thought that as I was this side of the river, I'd pop in and see who it is that looks after the boys. This is a bloody cold office.'

'I'll survive.' Dolly knew she had to be polite to this handsome man. 'Can I get you anything? A cup of tea perhaps?'

'No, thanks. You made a neat job of that typing.' All the time he was talking, his dark eyes were looking around the poky room.

'Thank you.'

'Reg said you've known each other all your lives.'

'Yes, we all live in the same street.'

'That's nice.' He walked to the door. 'I'll see that you get some more heat in here.'

'You don't have to.'

'Nobody can work like this.' He put his hat back on. 'See you around. Bye.' With that, he left.

Dolly went over to the window. 'Well, that was certainly short and sweet,' she said to herself, watching him drive away in a very nice dark-blue car. She thought he looked a bit like Tyrone Power. He had a small, thin black moustache, which did make him look a bit like a gangster. She smiled ... and his coat wasn't bad, either. But what did he really want? It would be rather nice if he did get her some more heat, but maybe he said that just for something to talk about. After all, she didn't work for him.

She sat back down and looked around. What could she do now? Everything was in its place and she knew she was getting restless. What if she started to look for another job? She knew that Penny could get back to doing the wages now that there weren't any invoices to worry about, so she wouldn't be leaving Reg completely in the lurch. She felt like a spare part most of the time, now that she didn't have suppliers to chase, or invoices to sort out and make sure they were paid on time. She sighed. This was something she would have to give a lot of thought to.

It was the last week in March when Penny received a letter from the hospital. Her scream sent Ivy rushing to her room. 'Whatever's the matter?' she asked, full of panic.

Penny was laughing. 'Sorry, Ma, I didn't mean to frighten you, but I've just had the most wonderful news. Look.' She passed the letter to her mother-in-law.

Ivy bent over, and kissed Penny loudly on the cheek. 'Wait till Reg hears about this. He'll be beside himself. I'll just go and make us both a cuppa.' As she left the room, a tear slid slowly down her cheek. Of course, she was as pleased as Punch. This was something everybody had been waiting a long time for. It was about time the two of them had a bit of luck. What with Reg getting all this work, and now this. She felt like running up the street shouting about it, but how would Penny cope? She wasn't the most patient of young women. Would she want her own home, after she learns to walk again? What would this mean to the family now? As Ivy filled the kettle, she got cross with herself for thinking such thoughts.

'Let's just take one step at a time,' she said to herself, 'and see what the outcome will be.'

Everybody was very pleased to hear that at long last Penny was going to the hospital to get splints for her legs. She knew that learning to walk again would be a long process, but she didn't care.

'So when do you go?' asked Dolly, that evening, when she'd first heard the good news.

'Tuesday, April the eleventh.' The date was etched in Penny's brain.

As the date had got nearer, so Penny had been filled with fear and dread. 'What if I can't cope?', 'What if they hurt?', 'What if they're not for me?'

she had asked, many times.

Everybody had tried to reassure her. They told her to remember Douglas Bader, the Second World War pilot who was captured by the Germans. He had lost his legs and had been fitted with tin ones. Then there was President Roosevelt: he'd been the president of the United States, and had been diagnosed with polio. None of this seemed to help quell Penny's fears.

When the big day arrived, everybody was filled with anticipation. Dolly couldn't concentrate on the little that she had to do.

At the hospital, the doctor that Penny saw was a young man who she thought didn't look old enough to be qualified. He began by asking questions. She told him about when she first caught polio and then about having Gail. He seemed very surprised at how well she appeared to be managing.

'I've got a very good family around me,' she said, clutching Reg's hand.

After a long talk with the doctor, during which time he took lots of notes, he finally said that he was going to look at Penny's legs.

'Can you stand at all?'

She shook her head. 'I can't feel anything.'

'Don't worry about that. Now, I'm going to lift you onto the bed.' He swept her up in his arms as if she was as light as a feather. 'Have you been massaging her legs?' he asked Reg.

'Most nights.'

'Good. Now the muscle is wasting away, we will have to try to get you sorted. How often can you get here?'

115

'Not that often,' said Penny, her face full of fear. 'My husband has to work.'

'What about parents?'

'Reg's mum looks after our baby, and my mother has to work. She was widowed in the war.'

'I'm sure we'll find some way,' said Reg. 'We've got to,' he added softly.

'I see.' The doctor went back to his desk and wrote some more. 'I would like to give you some exercises. Do you think you could help her with those?'

'I'll do anything.' Reg swallowed hard. He was almost in tears.

'Good. Later, I'm going to send you to get fitted for your boots. They have to be made to measure and have sockets put in the heels so the splints can fit into them. Now I'm going to measure you for your callipers. You'll have to come back here for the fitting. When I'm satisfied that everything is in place, and you feel a little confident, I'll transfer you to your local cottage hospital. Do you have one near you?'

'Yes, it's not too far away.'

'Will you be able to get to it?'

'We'll find a way,' said Reg.

'Good. They will sort out your exercises. They have bars to help you to walk. You must be very patient. You are not going to be able to walk right away, as your muscles are very weak. They need to be stronger for you to stand, and it's going to take time. You'll have some bad days when you insist that you can't do it. But with a lot of patience and love from the family to help you every step of the way, you will.' He looked at Reg before getting up to measure Penny's legs.

Penny couldn't believe that after all this time she was going to walk again. Tears slowly ran down her cheeks.

Reg squeezed her hand. 'You'll soon get the hang of it, love, and you'll be running down the street 'fore you know it.'

'And I'll be able to take Gail to school.' Penny brushed her tears away.

The doctor looked at them, but didn't say a word. He'd heard all this before. This young lady had a lot of anger, tears, and heartache in front of her, but, he thought, if she was determined enough, one day she would get there.

Chapter 11

Ivy had been looking out of the window on and off all morning, so when at last Reg's van pulled up, she heaved a sigh of relief and said in a whisper to Gail, who was sleeping peacefully, 'Your mummy and daddy are back home, darling,' then she hurried to open the front door.

She helped her son to get the wheelchair from the back of the van, and then steady it while he lifted Penny from the front seat.

Usually, she would be sitting in her wheelchair in the back of the van, but today she was excited and wanted talk to Reg, even if it was freezing cold as the wind came up through the floor.

'I can't wait to hear about it all,' said Ivy, excitedly, as she opened the front door wide enough for Penny to manoeuvre herself through.

'How's Gail been?' asked Penny.

'As good as gold.' Her mother-in-law smiled. 'She's fast asleep at the moment.'

'She'll be waking for her bottle soon,' said Penny.

'I'll see to it, Ma,' said Reg. 'And while I'm out there, I'll make us all a cuppa. We're both gasping.'

'Kettle's simmering on the gas ready. How did it go?' Ivy asked as Penny wheeled herself into her room.

'It's going to be a long process,' she said, removing her hat, scarf, and gloves.

As Ivy helped Penny with her coat, she said, 'I expect it will be.' She was finding it hard to contain herself, but she knew from experience that she had to wait for Penny to be forthcoming with the information.

Gail stirred, and Penny leant over the cot and gently picked her up. 'I'll take Gail into the kitchen for her bottle.'

Ivy was relieved when Reg called from the kitchen to say that tea was ready, and took Gail from Penny as she wheeled herself along the passage.

'I've got to get fitted for boots,' said Penny. 'Can't say I fancy wearing boots, especially in the summer.'

'What will the boots do?'

'They need holes put in the heels for the callipers.'

'Oh,' was all Ivy could say.

Penny, and Ivy, who was carrying Gail, went into the kitchen just as Reg came from the scullery carrying the tea tray.

'Has she told you all that happened?' he asked his mother.

'Just that she's got to have boots.'

'Yeh. They have metal sockets in the heels for the callipers to fit in to. She was measured for those today. When they're ready and we've seen the doc to make sure everything's OK, she's then got to try to walk for a bit, holding on to some bars. When Pen's got a bit of confidence, she's got to go to the cottage hospital for exercises and learn how to walk.'

All the while, Penny, who was now holding Gail, sat quietly looking from one to the other. After all this time, she was used to people talking over her head as if she wasn't there.

'Oh, love,' said Ivy. 'I'm so pleased for you.'

'It's going to be a long process,' Penny said, with a weak smile.

'I expect it will be. But you've got plenty of time.'

'She needs her nappy changed. I'll take her into my room. Have you made her bottle, Reg?'

'It's in the scullery. I'll go and get it.'

'Bring it in.'

Ivy felt very hurt when they left her. She knew that they wanted to be alone, but she dearly wanted to know how often they would have to go to the cottage hospital. How would they be able to cope? It wasn't that far away, but Reg had to work. Would Penny be able to manoeuvre her wheelchair all that way?

I won't be able to push her, thought Ivy, not if I'm pushing the pram. Perhaps I can leave the baby with someone, but how long for?

All these thoughts were racing around in her head as she gently stirred her tea.

That evening, Dolly couldn't wait to go and find out how Penny had got on at the hospital. She wasn't surprised to see Mrs Watts in the kitchen talking to Ivy.

'This is good news,' said Penny's mum, smiling. 'I can't wait to see her walking.'

'I should say so,' said Dolly.

'It's gonna take time,' said Ivy. 'Go on in, love,' she said to Dolly, 'Pen's waiting for you.'

'So how was it?' Dolly asked, as soon as she pushed open the door to Penny's room.

'All right, I suppose.'

'That don't sound very encouraging.'

'Probably because I thought I'd be fitted for those callipers right away.'

'So what happened?'

'I answered a lot of questions, and now I've got to wait for the boots and callipers to be made and fitted, then I've got to go to the cottage hospital to learn to walk.' She looked away.

'You knew it would be a long process.'

'I know. That's what everybody keeps telling me.'

Dolly could see that her friend was understandably feeling down.

'It seems to be taking for ever.'

'But just think, you've got the better weather coming. When you feel confident, we can go for a little walk round the block and I can push Gail in her pram. She'll soon be sitting up and taking

120

notice. Oh Pen, you've got so much to look forward to.' Dolly could only see a bright future ahead for her friend.

Penny smiled. 'You've always got an answer; I'll say that for you.'

'Well, I always try to look on the bright side of things. Now, come on, tell me all about this doctor? Was he dishy?'

It was a sunny Saturday afternoon in April. Dolly was standing at the bus stop when Meg Windsor came up to her.

'Hello, Dolly. Long time no see. How are you?'

'I'm fine, how about you?'

'I'm great. Off anywhere nice?'

'No, just going to do a bit of shopping.'

'So am I,' said Meg. 'We could go together.'

'It depends where you're going,' said Dolly, not really wanting to go with Meg.

'Just up West. I'm looking to get meself one of these new-look coats that are all the rage. One of the girls at work got herself one from C&A last week and it's really smashing.'

'They are nice.'

'I love the way they fit in the waist; the new length looks really good with high heels.'

Standing next to Meg, who was slim and looking very smart, Dolly suddenly felt very plain and dowdy. She hadn't really bothered with too many clothes since she had come back from America, partly because she didn't have anywhere to go and partly because working for Reg meant that she wasn't earning a great deal of money.

'So, how's Reg treating you? I was hoping for

that job.'

Dolly knew that, but didn't make any comments about it. 'It's fine. Don't see a lot of him; they're all out working.'

'Here's our bus. Come on, let's go upstairs, then we can have a fag.'

'I don't smoke,' said Dolly.

'You always was a goody-goody.'

When they were settled down, Meg asked, 'How's Tony keeping, these days?'

'He seems fine.'

'Are you two going out together?'

'Just now and again. Don't see a lot of any of them now they're busy working over the water.' Dolly didn't want Meg to know it had been weeks since they had gone out.

'I hear he's gonna get a car. That'll be one up for your street, seeing a car parked there.'

'Who told you that?'

'Me mum. She knows all the gossip that's going round. Seems she met Tony's mum out shopping the other day.'

'Oh,' was all Dolly could say.

When the conductor came up for their fares, Meg asked him. 'You gonna drop me off later?' She gave him a real come-hither look.

'I might, if yer play yer cards right,' he said with a wink.

Dolly looked away. She was embarrassed at the way Meg was behaving.

When the conductor had moved on, Meg said, 'I can see by that look, you don't approve of me having a bit of a laugh with blokes.'

'Do what you like, Meg.'

'You never used to be so straight-laced. I would have thought that after living in America all that time you would have been a lot more... I dunno ... easy, I guess.'

'Well I'm not easy, as you put it. I'll get off the next stop and catch another bus.'

Meg put her arm out. 'No, please don't go. I'm sorry. I ain't got that many friends to go out shopping with. Besides, it's always more fun to go with someone. Could it be just us for today?'

'What about the girls from work?'

'No, they've got their own mates, and well, sometimes I get a bit fed up going out on me own. And let's face it, blokes don't wanna go shopping, do they? They only want one thing.'

Dolly suddenly felt sorry for Meg. She knew what it was like to be on your own when going anywhere, be it shopping, pictures, or even just for a walk. She remembered the laughs she and Penny used to have. Hopefully, those days would come back again when Penny learnt to walk.

They wandered around looking in all the shops. Meg loved trying on clothes, and they laughed at some of the hats and outfits they wore. When they went into C&A, Meg made straight for the coats department.

'What d'you think of this?' she asked Dolly, holding one up.

'It's really nice. I love that colour. It's a sort of tweedy blue. Try it on.'

Meg gave her handbag to Dolly, and then tried the coat on.

'It fits you a treat,' said Dolly. 'And it does look very nice.'

Meg did a twirl in front of the mirror. 'It feels really smashing.' She ran her hand over the lovely material. 'Why don't you try one on?'

Dolly had looked at the label. She knew she couldn't afford the price, not on her wages. 'I'd better not,' she laughed. 'Just in case I like it. I'm a bit short this week.'

'I can always lend you a few bob. I know you'll always pay me back. So, go on.'

'No. I'd better not. Anyway, you getting that coat?'

'I should say so.'

After shopping, they had visited the Lyons Corner House for a cup of tea, and now they were standing at the bus stop, discussing their afternoon.

Meg tucked her arm through Dolly's and said, 'D'you know? I've really enjoyed meself this afternoon. Thank you.'

'So have I,' said Dolly, 'so thank you.'

'Have you? Have you really?'

'Yes, I have.'

'Here's our bus,' said Meg.

When they were settled, and making their way back home, Meg said. 'We'll have to do this again, sometime.'

Dolly then realised what a good time she'd had with Meg. All these years, she hadn't been too fond of her, and now she'd enjoyed her company. Was it because she was always worried that she would take Tony from her when they were engaged? But that was a few years ago; that worry was all over. 'I dunno about that,' she said. 'As soon as Penny can walk with her callipers, then we'll be off. She's really missed shopping and all that.'

Meg removed her arm, and sat back. 'Yes, it must've been really hard for her with a baby an' all.'

'She's been very brave.'

'How's she getting on? Mum said that when she's been fitted with those leg iron things, she'll be going to the cottage hospital to learn to walk again.'

There didn't seem to be a lot that Meg's mum didn't know about everything and everyone. 'Yes she is. But I think it's gonna be a long job.'

'It must be hard. I've seen some of those kids strutting about all stiff legged. Mind you, some of 'em can even run. Can't see Penny ever doing that.'

Dolly's thoughts quickly turned to when Gail would be running about. How would Penny manage to chase after her daughter?

Meg went very quiet, and looked out of the window. Dolly wondered what her thoughts were.

That evening, when Dolly went into her friend's house, and called out to say that it was only her, Ivy asked her to take the baby's bottle into Penny.

As Dolly pushed open the door, Penny said, 'Me mum reckons she's been a bit fretful this afternoon.'

'Must be the weather,' said Dolly. 'Do you want me to feed her?'

'You can if you like.'

Dolly took the baby out of her cot. 'She's very wet.'

'You can change her.'

Dolly knew where everything was and set about changing the baby's nappy. When she'd finished, and had settled down to give Gail her bottle, she told Penny about her afternoon.

'You went shopping with Meg Windsor?' Penny's tone was one of surprise.

'Met her at the bus stop. As we were both going up West, we decided to go together. She bought herself one of these new-look coats, and it looked really smashing on.'

'So, you thinking of getting one?'

'Dunno.'

'Don't she work at Peek Freans?'

'Yes. Why?'

'Just interested, that's all. I heard they get good money, so she can afford a nice coat.'

'I expect she can.'

'Dolly. Are you happy working for Reg?'

'What made you ask that?'

'Dunno really. Don't suppose you have much to do now there's no ordering.'

'There's not a lot to do at the moment.' Dolly sat back and put Gail over her shoulder. She noted that Penny didn't seem to be very interested in her baby at the moment. Did she have something on her mind? Was she trying to tell her that Reg didn't need her anymore? 'Is there something you're trying to tell me?'

'No. Course not.'

'So, what's wrong?'

'I'm worried about going to the hospital. My legs are all soft and weak. Will I be able to stand?'

'I thought Reg massaged your legs very night.'

'He does. But you ain't seen them for a while. I

126

don't like showing people. They're all white and thin, like a couple of sticks.'

'Don't get upset about it now. Wait and see what the doctor advises. They must get those sorts of problems all the time.'

'I suppose so, Dolly, but I'm really frightened.'

'What about?'

'What if I can't get on with them? I'll be stuck in this chair for the rest of me life.'

'Don't talk daft.'

'Is it being daft?'

'Look, you've always been a stubborn old whatsit. If you can have a lovely baby like Gail, here, and manage as well as you have done, I'm sure you'll get over anything that life puts in your way. Now stop being so down.'

Penny smiled at her friend. 'Not so much of the old,' she said, but deep down, she wasn't sure if she had the strength to carry on.

Chapter 12

It was the first week of May, and as Dolly was walking home, early one evening, she heard someone calling out her name. She turned round, and was very surprised to see Meg Windsor hurrying along to catch up with her.

'Hello,' said Dolly. 'Don't often see you round this way.'

'No, I'm going to see me Aunt Rene, who lives in Princes Street. The poor old dear fell over and me Mum asked me to pop in on me way home.'

'Oh, I'm sorry. Is she all right?'

'Not too bad. She's a bit shook up, that's all, and at her age that ain't good.'

'How old is she?'

'Dunno. Must be in her seventies. Been out shopping lately?'

'No. What about you?'

'I went and got that nice blouse I tried on a few weeks back, remember?'

Dolly knew the one she meant, and it was very nice. 'What colour did you get?'

'The blue one.'

'Well, it certainly suited you.'

'So you ain't been out buying at all, then?'

'No.' Dolly didn't want to say she couldn't afford it.

'Has Penny got those legs iron things yet?'

'No, she's waiting for them to be made. But it shouldn't be long now.'

'So there'll be no stopping her then.'

'I hope not.'

'Will she be wanting her old job back?'

Dolly was taken aback. 'I don't know.' Although Dolly had given it just a passing thought, to hear Meg talk about it, she realised it could become a reality.

'Well, don't forget, if you ever want a job, I can always put in a word for you at Peek Freans. The girls are all right and the money's not bad. It can get a bit boring at times putting packets of biscuits in boxes all day, but at the end of the week, it's worth it.'

'Thanks, Meg.'

'Anyway. See you around,' said Meg as she turned into her aunt's road.

Dolly carried on. Meg had certainly given her food for thought. Would Penny want to come back to work when she was able to walk unaided? This was something Dolly would have to think about in the future, so perhaps going to Peek Freans wouldn't be all that bad.

When Dolly arrived home, she was still concerned about her job. Although she didn't have a lot to do now, and the thought of leaving had been going around in her head for a while. She didn't really know what she wanted. After all, she was still her own boss, up to a point. Would she like being told what to do?

'Hello, Mum. All right?'

'Yes thanks, love. What about you? You look a bit worried.'

'It's nothing really. I met Meg Windsor on me way home and she was telling me about her job at Peek Freans.'

Her mother stopped laying the table and looked up. 'You ain't thinking of leaving Reg, are you?'

'I don't know. There's not a lot to do now. What about when Penny learns to walk again? Will she want to go back to work?'

'I shouldn't think so. Don't forget she's got a baby to think about.'

'I know. It's really only the wages to do, now Reg is more or less working for Mr Edwards, plus a few invoices he asks me to type up for him. Let's face it, Penny could do that at home.'

Grace continued to put the knives and forks on

the table. 'What about when Reg gets on his feet again and starts working for himself? He'll need you then.'

'There is that, I suppose.'

'Well, don't start worrying about that now. Just wait and see what happens.'

'I'll make a few discreet enquiries when I go in there later.'

'Yes. But be careful. You know how sensitive Penny can be.'

Dolly smiled. Everybody knew about Penny's moods since being in a wheelchair.

Penny was all smiles when Dolly walked in. 'You look pleased with yourself, what's happened?'

'Had a letter today. We go to the hospital next week, Doll. I'm going to be fitted with me callipers. Although I'm happy, I'm also very worried. What if I can't get on with them?'

'Course you will. I've told you before, you're a stubborn old whatsit, and you won't let anything beat you.'

'I'm worried that when I go to the cottage hospital they might make me do things I can't. I don't want to let Reg and Gail down.'

'Of course you won't.'

'Reg was saying that perhaps after I've been a couple of times, you'll be able to take me. It's not too far away, and you'd still be paid. That way, he won't have to stay away from work.'

Any thoughts of Dolly getting a better job had now gone. She smiled. 'That'll be great. Taking you for a walk and getting paid for it; that can't be bad.'

'And when I get the hang of it, we can go shopping.'

Dolly put her arms round her friend. 'We'll do anything you want.'

They spent the evening talking about the times they used to have. Before long, Dolly could see that Penny was getting tired. 'I'll be off now, then,' she said.

As Dolly walked along the road to number twenty, she thought about what Penny had said, about taking her to the hospital. She dearly wanted to help Penny, but in some ways, she felt trapped. She needed a new job and more money. Now that clothes were getting more fashionable, she felt very dowdy. Was she being selfish? Was she destined to become a frumpy old maid?

The next morning, when Dolly was sitting reading a book, Tony came into the office.

'What are you doing here? Why ain't you at work?' she asked.

'I had to collect some stuff for Bert Edwards.'

'Where did you have to go to?'

'Somewhere round Woolwich way. I thought that as I was on the ferry, and coming over this way, I'd pop in and see you. Why?'

'Just nosey, I s'pose. So what you doing here, then?'

'No reason. It's just that I don't see a lot of you now. That all right?'

Dolly smiled. 'Of course. So, was it a big warehouse?'

'Nah, just some bloke's yard. I tell you what though, Doll, this bloke ain't half got some stuff in there.'

'What sort of stuff?'

'Building material. I ain't seen nothing like it. No wonder we don't have any trouble when we ask for stuff. It was a like an Aladdin's cave. If Reg got to know this bloke and could get the stuff himself, I reckon he could really get back on his feet and be on his own again.'

'Could you just walk in?'

'Nah, you should see the security. I tell yer, if we'd had that we wouldn't have got broken into.'

'I'm surprised Mr Edwards let you into his secret.'

'Well, it seems he had a pressing engagement.' Tony grinned. 'He obviously puts pleasure before business.'

'D'you want a cup of tea while you're here?' Dolly wanted to find out more.

'I'd better not. See you sometime.' With that, he blew her a kiss and was gone.

Once again Dolly was left wondering about this Mr Edwards. What sort of people did he know?

That evening, Dolly was still full of questions.

'Tony popped in today,' she casually said to her father when they were sitting down to dinner.

'I gathered that. He was gone a long while. Reg gave him a bit of a rollicking when he got back.'

'Why?'

'The time he took to get the gear. He should remember that time costs money.'

'Oh. He was telling me about the place he went to. It seems it was full of building materials.'

'So I believe.'

'Just as long as it's all above board,' said Dolly quietly.

'You're not still on about Mr Edwards, are you? I thought you'd dropped all that nonsense. It's a pity you ain't got more to do in that office, then you wouldn't have the time to go off on one of your fantasies.'

Dolly was taken back. It wasn't like her dad to talk to her like this.

'I'll go and get the pudding,' said her mother, and she quickly went into the scullery, returning almost immediately with a bowl full of stewed apples. 'I'll bring the custard over; it's only on the dresser.'

Dolly could feel an unusually strained atmosphere in the room. Did her dad know more than he was letting on?

Grace began to dish the fruit into bowls. 'I got these apples at the Blue Anchor market, today, and I'll tell you, those blokes ought to be ashamed of themselves. All the apples at the front are really lovely and polished, but they take the stuff from the back of the stall, shove 'em in a bag, and it's not till you get home that you find you've got a lot of rotten ones. Still, I suppose we should be grateful that fruit ain't on ration.'

Dolly wanted to laugh. Her mother was trying so hard to ease the situation. But why was her father being like this?

The following evening, just as Dolly had got home, there was a knock at the front door. The family all looked at each other. Nobody ever knocked at this time.

'I'll go and see who it is,' said Dolly.

She was very surprised to see Tony. 'What you doing here?' she asked.

He quickly looked about him. 'Doll, can we go for a drink tonight?'

'If you want to. What is it?'

'I'll tell you tonight.'

'You're making it all sound very mysterious.'

'Who is it, love?' called out her mother.

'It's only Tony.'

'Well, ask him in.'

'D'you want to come in?' Dolly asked Tony.

'No, thanks all the same. I'll see you at seven. Is that all right?'

'That's fine.' She watched him walk away and then closed the door. What was it that he wanted to see her about? It was making her feel very uncomfortable.

At seven o'clock, Dolly was waiting in the front room looking out for Tony. As soon as she saw him coming along the road, she rushed out to meet him.

'Be back later,' she yelled out to her parents as she opened the front door. They were in the kitchen listening to the wireless. She took hold of Tony's arm and said, 'Now, what's this great mystery?'

He laughed. 'It ain't no big mystery, as you call it. I just want to show you something.'

'Where we going?'

'You're so impatient. When I saw you yesterday, I thought you needed cheering up. Besides, I wanted to see you again. So when I finished tonight I went to see a bloke up near South Bermondsey station who sells second-hand cars, and told him I was bringing me girl along tonight to get her approval about the car I've had me eye on.'

'Oh, you.' Dolly gently smacked his arm. 'And here's me thinking you was going to tell me something juicy about Mr Edwards.'

'Oh, Doll, you're not still on about that, are you?'

'I'm sorry, but I can't help thinking there's something not right about him.'

'Well, if there is, we can forget about it tonight, cos I'm gonna take you for a little drive.'

'Will the owner let you?'

'He will if he wants to sell it.'

'I'm so pleased for you, Tony.'

'Are you? Are you really?'

'I said so, didn't I? Now, come on, let's get the bus.'

'D'you know. This could be the last time we catch a bus.'

'That'll be lovely.'

'We can go anywhere you want.'

'Tony, I hope you're not doing all this just to get me to go out with you, are you?'

'Not really. I've always wanted me own car, and now we're earning a few extra bob, the chance has come, and petrol is coming off ration very soon. Alf, that's the bloke who's selling it, reckons that there'll be a big demand for second-hand cars, so I'm gonna take the opportunity with both hands.'

Dolly knew that they were all earning more than when it was just Reg's business. She would dearly have liked to ask for a rise, but now she had less to do, she didn't think she had a good enough reason.

When they got to the bomb site that had been turned into a forecourt for cars, Tony rushed up to a little blue car. 'Well, what d'you think?'

'It looks very nice.'

'It's a Morris Eight. I've had me eye on it for a while, but didn't dare put down a deposit on it, not when Reg's business was a bit rocky.'

Dolly could see that Tony was really excited.

'It was up on blocks all through the war. The bloke who owned it was injured. He can't drive anymore and wants to sell it. Wait here while I get the key from Alf.'

As Dolly walked round the car, she was reminded of the big cars they had in America. Joe, like most people over there, had a large comfortable car, but it was a big country and they drove a lot of miles.

'Well, what d'you think?' asked Tony, as Dolly settled herself into the passenger seat. He switched on the engine.

'I think it's very nice.'

'Good. Right, we'll go for a little spin, and then I'll come back and do the paperwork. Then, my dear lady, we can go for a drink to celebrate. What d'you say to that?'

'I think that sounds a great idea.'

'Good.'

They drove around for a little while, and when they were back in the forecourt, Alf was standing there to meet them. 'Well?' he said. 'Do you like it?'

'It's not bad,' said Tony. 'The brakes stick a bit,

136

and I think the price is too high.'

'Come into the office and we'll talk.'

Dolly wanted to laugh. Tony had already told her that he was going to buy it, but he was now trying to reduce the price.

They wandered over to the wooden hut that wasn't unlike the one she worked in. 'I'll wait outside,' she said, not wanting to get involved in anything that Tony was going to say. After all, it was his money.

It wasn't long before Tony came out, smiling. Alf was right behind him, and they shook hands before Tony walked away.

'Did you get it?' asked Dolly.

When they were out of sight of Alf, Tony took Dolly in his arms, and kissed her full on the mouth.

Dolly reeled back in surprise. 'What was that for?' she asked.

'You brought me luck. I got it for less than I thought I would.'

'I'm so pleased for you, but when can you drive it?'

'When all the paperwork's done, and I've got it insured and registered for petrol coupons, then, my dear Dolly Day Dream, we can go off to the country or the seaside. The choice is all yours. We can go wherever you fancy.'

Dolly smiled. Nobody had called her that for years. They always said she was a dreamer; always looking for something out of reach.

This was like the good old days when they had a lot of laughs together. Could those days come back when Penny was walking again? Dolly had always liked Tony's company, and she did miss going out. But she knew she mustn't let him get his hopes up and think that things would go back to how they once were.

Chapter 13

All day, Dolly had been thinking about Penny. This was the day that she had her callipers fitted. How would she manage? Would she have the patience to persevere? That evening, as soon as she got home from work, she rushed into number two.

'So? How did it go? When are we going to see you running up the road?' she asked, pushing open the door to her friend's room.

Penny looked up at Dolly. Tears were streaming down her face.

Dolly dropped to her knees and held her friend close. 'What is it? What went wrong?'

'Nothing. It's just that it's so difficult.' She wiped her tears away. 'I never thought it would be so hard just to stand up.'

'Come on, tell me all about it; it can't be that bad.'

'It was.'

'Penny, what happened?'

Penny looked at her friend. 'After the doctor strapped those things on me legs, he and Reg helped me to stand between the bars. They felt so heavy and cumbersome, it was like wearing leg irons, and the boots looked so big. I stood there for a little while, and then the doctor put one foot in front of the other, but I just couldn't move. I lost my grip and slid to the floor. If the doctor and Reg hadn't been there, I don't know what would have happened. How could I have got up?'

'Don't be daft. They would never have left you on your own.'

'I know. That's what me mum said when she came in to find out how I got on. But I don't want to have to rely on people for the rest of me life. Oh Dolly, what can I do?'

Dolly, still holding her friend close, said, 'You will make it, I know you will, but you must be patient.'

'I don't feel like that at the moment.'

'Pen, you mustn't give up.'

Penny wiped her cheeks. 'I know you're right, but I don't know if I can do it.'

'Of course you can.' Dolly didn't know what else to say, so she picked up one of Penny's boots and turned it over. 'With these soles and heels, they're gonna last you a little while.'

'Forever, if I never wear them.'

'Don't talk daft. Now come on, show me these contraptions.' Dolly looked around the room. 'What have you done with them?'

'I made Reg throw them out.'

'What? You can't do that.'

'Why not? They're mine.'

'I know, but really they belong to the hospital.'

'You sound just like Reg.'

'Penny, try to see a bit of sense. You can't expect things to be perfect right away. You have to persevere and learn to walk again.'

'I don't have to do anything.'

Dolly wanted to shake some sense into her friend. 'Think of Reg, for a change. And Gail. You want to be walking by the time she starts toddling about, don't you?'

'Of course I do.'

'Well, then.'

'I knew you'd have a go at me, but I just can't do it.'

'Course you can. I never had you down as a quitter at the first hurdle. Did you see any little kids while you was there?'

'Some.'

'And were they walking with calipers?'

Penny nodded.

'I bet some of them shed a few tears at the beginning.'

'I must admit some were really good, and running, but there was a little girl who was crying.'

'Well, you're not a little girl. You're a mum and a wife, and I don't want to hear that you've given up.' Tears were now rolling down Dolly's cheeks.

'What you crying for?'

'I don't want to nag, but you make me. Oh, please, Penny, have another go.'

'I think we'd better go into the kitchen. Come on, wipe away those tears, and let's see a smile. After all, it's me that's got the problems.'

Dolly smiled and did as she was told.

When they went into the kitchen, Ivy was sitting in an armchair, nursing Gail.

'Hello, Dolly,' she said, 'I guessed it was you who came in.' She looked a little sad as she put Gail over her shoulder. 'She's been as good as gold today.'

'I've been hearing all about today,' said Dolly, sitting in the chair opposite Ivy. 'It wasn't a good one, by all accounts.'

Ivy looked at Penny.

'Don't start,' said Penny. 'I am here, you know.'

'We do know,' said Dolly. 'Now, where's these callipers?'

'Reg put 'em in the lav,' said Ivy, gently patting Gail's back.

Dolly stood up.

'Don't bring 'em in here,' said Penny, her voice full of alarm.

'I won't.'

When Dolly opened the lavatory door, she looked at the callipers standing up against the wall. They were dreadful looking things, with a thick leather strap to go around Penny's waist. There were also straps that would go around her legs. She picked one of them up – it seemed quite heavy – and sat down on the toilet seat.

Poor Penny. Dolly's heart went out to her friend. She wondered how anyone could be happy having these things strapped to their legs. They looked like torture instruments, and probably did feel like leg irons.

'But she's got to be positive,' she said out loud. 'And I'm going to be with her, every step of the way.'

Dolly wandered back into the kitchen. 'Well, you certainly ain't gonna win any beauty contests wearing those,' she said, 'but at least you'll be able to give Gail a run when you've mastered them.'

Penny only gave her friend a weak smile.

A couple of days later, Reg came into the office.

'How's Penny today?' asked Dolly.

'Still very down. I tried to get her to put the callipers on again last night, but she refused.'

'When do you have to go back to the hospital?'

'Monday, next week. I've got to try to get her to wear them indoors, but she won't hear anything about it.'

'She'll see sense, soon. Give her time.'

'God, I hope so. When she can manage to wear them a bit longer and gets used to walking a bit between the rails, then she'll be going to the cottage hospital. They would like to keep her in and try to get her walking every day, but you know Penny, she'd scream blue murder if they kept her away from Gail.'

'Do you think she'll master them?'

'I hope so. I really do. The doc said that one day, when her muscles get stronger and she can stand, she may only need crutches, then a stick, so you see it could all be positive, if we can get Penny to see it that way.'

'I'm sure she will as time goes on.'

'I hope so. Anyway, here's the time sheets ready for you to work out the wages for tomorrow. I could have dropped them in to you tonight at home, but I don't want to bring work home right now.'

'Is everything all right, Reg? I mean, other than Penny.'

'Yeh, it's fine.' He gave her a beaming smile, but Dolly thought he looked a bit worried. Was there more bothering him than just Penny?

That evening, Dolly was surprised when she turned into her road to see Reg's van parked outside his house. She was always home before him. As they had light in the flats they were doing up, they often stayed to finish a room.

They must have finished that job, Dolly thought. *Strange, he didn't mention it when he was in the office.*

'Hello, Dad,' she said, when she went into her own house. 'Don't often see you home before me. Everything all right?'

'Course.'

'Reg didn't mention you'd finished that flat when he came in the office this morning.'

'He don't have to tell you everything, does he?'

'No.' Dolly was taken aback. Normally, her father would say, 'Yeh, we've just finished a room, and we're all ready to start a new one tomorrow.' Sometimes, he would tell them all about the colours they'd used, and what posh fittings they'd installed. As he wasn't forthcoming with anything more, she thought she'd better leave it.

On Friday afternoon, Dolly was getting a little concerned. Reg always brought the money to the office first thing in the morning so she could make up the wages, but today he was late. All day, she had been looking out of the window waiting for him to arrive. She had got a bit cross, and hoped she would be able to do everything before it was time to go home. She looked at her watch again. It was almost five o'clock. She usually left at half past. Once again she looked out at the yard, but there wasn't any sign of Reg. She didn't know what to do.

She was still standing at the window when, to her surprise, Tony drove into the yard in the car that he was buying. She quickly opened the office door. 'You've got your new baby, I see.' She noticed that Tony wasn't his usual smiling self. 'Tony, what's wrong? Where's Reg?'

'Don't worry.'

'Now you have got me worried. Is it Penny or the baby?'

'Neither. Reg has been called away. He told me to tell you to take the wages sheets and envelopes home and he'll sort it all out when he gets back. I'll give you a lift. It's a good job I was able to pick up me car this afternoon.'

'Haven't you been to work?'

'Not this afternoon.'

'Why?'

'I'll tell you later. Come on, get yer coat.'

'I'm getting very worried. What's happened?'

Tony didn't answer, and as Dolly sat in the car, a horrible feeling came over her. Had something awful happened to Reg?

'Dolly, don't ask me too much at the moment, as I don't really know a lot. Just that Bert came in and took Reg away with him.'

'What? Kidnapped him?'

'D'you know, you've got such a vivid imagination. At times you can be such a daft cow.'

'Thanks.' Dolly sat back. She was annoyed with Tony. How dare he call her that!

'I can assure you that Bert didn't kidnap Reg. They just left together, that's all. Reg said to let you know about the wages. Satisfied?'

'If you say so.' What was it that made Reg leave a job? 'Have you finished the flat you were doing?'

'Nearly. We ran out of plasterboard. I think that's where Reg went.'

'Oh you...You let me believe all sorts of things might have happened to him.'

Tony laughed. 'I knew you'd think like that. You thought that the big bad man had taken him away.'

Dolly was cross. 'All right, clever clogs, so I worry about the people I like.'

'Do you worry about me?'

'No.'

'Well, that's told me.'

They continued the journey in silence.

When Dolly took the wage slips into Penny, she said, 'I don't know where Reg is. Tony told me to bring these in here, so Reg could sort it out when he gets home.'

'My brother's been in; he's worried about his wages,' said Penny. 'He said that Reg went off with this Mr Edwards.'

'That's what Tony said. By the way, Tony's got his car.'

'That's good, so where's he gonna whisk you off to?'

'I haven't a clue.'

'But you are going to go out with him?'

'I told him, only if he behaves himself.'

'Poor bloke, he's been hanging on for years.'

'I have told him not to.'

'Ain't you got any feelings for him at all?'

'I like him, I always have done, but it can never

be the same as it was.'

'Dolly, don't you think it's about time you forgot about Joe and started to live again?'

'I can't blot out that part of my life.'

'I don't suppose you ever will, but I reckon you should try, otherwise you'll end up being an old maid and stuck on the shelf forever.'

'Thanks. Anyway, I'd better go home; Mum will have the dinner on the table. See you later.'

'Bye, Doll,' said Penny, as her friend left. She thought it would be lovely if Dolly got back together with Tony. He really loved her, and he would look after her.

Penny pushed herself into the kitchen.

'Was that Dolly I heard?' asked her mother-in-law.'

'Yes, she brought in the wages sheets. It seems that Reg has gone off with Mr Edwards, and the money. I'll kill him if he's gone out drinking, and with the wages as well.'

Ivy smiled to herself. She remembered the last time Reg came home after having a little too much to drink. He would have to be a brave man to face Penny's wrath again – that was, of course, if he really was out drinking.

'Hello, Dad,' said Dolly as she walked into the kitchen. Her father looked up from his newspaper. She was determined not to mention Mr Edwards. She took off her hat and fluffed up the back of her hair. 'I've just taken the wage slips into Reg, but he's not there just yet. He'll be doing them at home when he gets back, so you might have to wait a bit for your money.'

146

Jim folded his newspaper. 'It's a good thing neither your mother, nor the rent man, is waiting for their money, then.'

Dolly didn't know what to say to that, so she added, 'Tony's got his new car. He brought me home in it.'

'Is it nice?' asked her mother.

'Yes, it is.' She had already told them that she'd been with Tony to look at it.

'He's a nice lad,' Grace said. 'Will you be going out with him sometimes?'

Dolly smiled. 'I expect so.' She knew her parents. Like everybody else, they would love it if she and Tony got together again.

It was about eight o'clock when Dolly went to see Penny. She could see that Reg's van still wasn't in the road.

'Cooee! It's only me,' she called out as she went into the house.

'We're in the kitchen,' Penny called.

Her friend was sitting at the table looking at the wage sheets. The envelopes were still empty.

'Reg not been in then?' asked Dolly.

'No. He ain't come home yet.'

Dolly could see that Penny was furious.

'I do hope he ain't gone drinking with all the money. You know what a silly sod he can be when he's had a skinful.'

'God, I hope not,' said Dolly. She knew that Reg could be more than generous when he'd had a few drinks, and as most people lived from week to week, they didn't have enough savings to carry them over. 'Everybody's relying on their money.'

'I know that, don't I?' Penny said angrily.

147

Dolly felt a bit sorry for Reg, but he should have come home with the money first before going out with Mr Edwards.

Dolly stayed for a while, but could see that Penny was becoming more irate. She didn't want to be around when Reg finally got home. 'I'll be off now,' she said. 'See you tomorrow.' She kissed Penny's cheek, and then whispered, 'Don't be too angry with him.'

Chapter 14

Dolly woke with a start. Someone was banging on the front door. She looked at the clock; it was three in the morning. Who the hell was it at this time? She jumped quickly out of bed.

Her father was shouting. 'All right, all right. I'm coming. Keep yer bloody hair on.'

She opened her bedroom door to see her mother standing at the top of the stairs. 'Who is it, Mum?'

'I don't know.'

Dolly put her hand to her mouth. 'Oh my God! You don't think anything's happened to Penny, do you?'

'I don't know.'

Dolly stood watching, as her father, in his bare feet, and wearing only his pyjama bottoms, opened the front door. To her horror, a policeman was standing there.

'Sorry to disturb you at this time of night, sir,

148

but Mrs Ivy Smith at number two asked me to call. Is there someone called Dolly living here?'

'Yes. My daughter. I'll call her.'

Dolly raced down the stairs. 'No need, Dad. I'm here. What is it? What's wrong?'

'Could you come with me, please?'

'OK.'

She pushed past her father and the policeman, and ran bare-footed along the road to Penny's house. Tears were streaming down her face. What had happened? Was it Penny or the baby? The front door was wide open, so Dolly ran straight in. First, she pushed open Penny's door, but she wasn't in her room, then she ran into the kitchen where Penny and Ivy were both crying. Penny was in her wheelchair, and her mother-in-law was sitting next to her, holding her hand.

Dolly dropped to her knees. 'What is it? What's wrong?'

'It's Reg,' sobbed Ivy.

'Oh my God! Has he had an accident in that old van?'

Ivy shook her head. 'He's in hospital – St Olave's. The policeman thinks he's been in some sort of fight.'

'What?' cried Dolly. 'So why the policeman?' She sat down on the floor just as the policeman and her parents arrived in the kitchen. She quickly put her hand to her mouth. 'Oh my God! He's not...?'

'Dolly, I've brought yer slippers and dressing gown,' said her mother, placing the blue candlewick gown over her daughter's shoulders. 'You're gonna catch yer death a cold rushing out like that. Jim, I've got your coat, too.'

'What's wrong, officer?' asked Jim, first looking at his daughter's ashen face, and then quickly at Penny and her mother-in-law.

'Mr Smith is in hospital.'

'Why?' asked Jim.

'We don't know,' said Ivy. 'We think he's been in a fight.'

'So why come here at this time of night?' Jim asked the policeman.

'I was told to take Mrs Smith to the hospital.' He looked at Penny sitting in her wheelchair. 'But...'

'He must be very bad for the police to come here to get Pen,' Ivy said, giving a little sob. 'Please God, don't let him...'

At that moment, Gail decided to make herself heard.

'Dolly, can you go and get Gail?' asked Penny.

'I'll go and get her,' said Grace.

'Is he badly hurt?' Dolly asked the policeman, terrified at what the answer might be.

'I'm afraid I don't know.'

Grace returned after a short while, with baby Gail wrapped in a blanket.

'Thanks. Give her to me,' said Penny.

'Is this your baby?' asked the policeman.

'Yes, and Reg is her dad.'

The policeman looked uncomfortable. 'I'm sorry. I'd help if I could, but I need to get back to the station.'

Jim Taylor accompanied the policeman to the front door. When he returned, he said, 'I feel quite sorry for the lad. He's only young, and to be confronted with us lot must have been quite daunting. He said he'll take me to St Olave's.'

'You can't go with him, not in yer pyjamas,' said Grace.

'I ain't got time to get dressed as he's just going off. I've got me coat.'

'I've got to get to the hospital somehow,' said Penny.

'You can't do that now,' said Jim. 'Wait till I get back; maybe the policeman can sort something out.'

'How will you get back?' Dolly asked her father anxiously.

'I'm hoping the policeman can bring me back. If not, I'll grab a cab.'

'Have you got any cash on you?' asked Grace.

'No. I don't normally take money to bed with me.'

'I'll get me purse,' said Ivy.

'No, don't worry, Ivy,' Jim said. 'I'll pay the cab when I get back.' With that, he left.

'Shall I make us all a cuppa?' asked Ivy.

'I'll give you a hand,' offered Grace.

'It's all right. I can manage.'

'I'd rather. It'll give me something to do.'

Ivy gave Grace a weak smile as they both went into the scullery.

'D'you think we ought to tell Tony?' asked Dolly, who was now standing at the doorway.

'Why? What good would that do?' asked her mother.

'He might be able to shed some light on all this.'

'Dunno,' said Ivy.

'What d'you think, Pen?' Dolly asked her friend. Penny looked at Dolly. 'I don't know. Don't bother Mum, though. She has to get up very early, and I don't want to worry her. She's got enough on her plate as it is. Would Tony mind being woken up at this time?'

'He might know something,' said Dolly.

'I don't reckon he'll mind, when he realises what it's all about,' said Ivy.

'What if I never see Reg alive again?' sobbed Penny.

'You mustn't think like that. Reg's a fighter,' said Dolly.

'But he must be bad if the police have to come here for me.' Tears streamed down her face.

Dolly wanted to cry with her. 'I'll go and get Tony,' she said, leaving the kitchen.

She hurried along the road in her dressing gown and slippers, feeling pleased that she had something to do, but also needing Tony there.

At Tony's house, she had to knock twice before a light came on. After a short while, he opened the door.

'Dolly! What on earth are you doing here at this time in the morning?' He was only wearing his pants. He ran his fingers through his hair.

'It's Reg,' she said. 'Can you come to the house?'

'Who the bloody hell is banging on the door this time of night?' shouted Mrs Marchant, from upstairs.

'It's Dolly. Go back to bed, Ma.'

'What does Dolly want?' she asked, coming down the stairs. 'Hello, love. What's wrong?'

Dolly burst into tears.

'Come on in, love. It's bloody cold standing out there.'

'No, I must get back to Penny,' she sobbed. 'Can you come with me, Tony?'

'Course I can. I'll just put some clothes on. Ma, I'll let you know what it's all about when I get back.'

'OK, love.'

As they hurried back along the road, Dolly's tears subsided. She felt relieved that Mrs Marchant didn't want an explanation, and that Tony had put on his trousers.

Tony was surprised to see Dolly's mother in Reg's house. 'So what's this all about? Dolly gave me a quick rundown on the way here, but to be truthful, it don't make any sense.'

'Would you like a cup of tea, Tony?' asked Grace.

'Yes, please, Mrs Taylor.'

'I'll go and get another cup.'

'Do you know what this could be about?' asked Penny.

'No. I only know that Reg went out with Bert Edwards to get some stock. As you know, we were waiting for those plasterboards. I told you that, Dolly, didn't I?'

She nodded.

'Didn't the copper tell you anything?' he asked Penny.

'No. He wanted to take me to the hospital – that was till he saw I was in this...' She banged the arm of her wheelchair, making Gail jump. 'Sorry darling,' she said, kissing her daughter's head.

'So what did he say? Is he coming back?'

'We don't know.' Penny wiped away her tears.

Tony looked at Dolly. 'You all right? You look frozen.'

'Can somebody go and get some more coal?' asked Ivy. 'We might just manage to get the cinders going again.'

'I'll go,' said Dolly.

'No. I'll go,' said Tony. He was glad he'd had the sense to grab his coat on the way out of his house. He went outside to the coal bin.

Dolly was sitting at the kitchen table with a 'little girl lost' expression on her face. 'What we gonna do?' she asked Penny as Tony was coming back in.

'I don't know,' Penny said softly. 'I wish I could walk.'

Dolly leant over. For a while, they both held each other close.

Tony sat at the table and just looked. He didn't know any words of comfort.

Grace and Ivy walked out into the scullery, looking at each other, both with the same thoughts. When would things go right for these two girls?

Penny went to her room. Dolly carried Gail, and placed her gently in her cot.

'Why don't you try to get some sleep?' said Dolly. 'I'll help you get into bed.'

'No, I'm all right.'

'You can't sit there all night. We don't know how long Dad will be, or whether he'll have any news. As soon as he gets back, we'll wake you. Come on, Pen, try to get some sleep.'

'All right. Go and get Ivy to give you a hand.' She looked across the room at the callipers standing against the wall. 'This really will make me do my best to try and walk again.'

'You can worry about that later. Let's get Reg

home first.'

Between them, Dolly and Ivy got Penny settled, then they went back into the kitchen.

'Look, why don't you and your mum go back home,' Tony said to Dolly. 'And you, Mrs Smith, go to bed. I'll stay here and wait for Mr Taylor.'

'What if he don't get back till later?' said Dolly.

'I can sleep on a clothes line. Besides, it ain't the first time I've slept in a chair. Now go on, be off with you.'

Dolly and her mother went back home. Neither of them felt like going to bed, so they both sat in the armchairs and waited for daylight to come.

'Are you family?' asked the nurse at the reception desk when Jim and the policeman had walked into St Olave's Hospital.

The policeman explained the situation.

'As you know, it's relatives only at this time of night,' the nurse replied, looking at Jim standing in a coat and slippers, 'but, under the circumstances, I'll see what I can do.' She picked up the phone and made a call, repeating all that she had been told.

After a while, a young woman, who Jim could see by her manner was probably a senior nurse, came up to him.

'I'm the night sister, Nurse Moore. Follow me, please,' was all she said.

The policeman turned to leave. 'I'd best be getting back to the station now.' He held out his hand.

'Thanks, mate,' Jim said, shaking the policeman's hand. He then followed the night sister along the corridor.

She finally stopped outside a set of double doors and said, 'He's in here, but you can only stay a short while.'

Quietly, they went into the darkened ward and along to Reg's bed.

Jim looked at him lying peacefully. He didn't have to ask how he was. Even in the half-light, he could see that Reg had a bandage round the top of his head, and his face had been stitched and cleaned. It looked as if there were black bruises beginning to appear round his eyes, and his cheeks were swollen.

'What you been up to, mate?' whispered Jim, but he knew he wouldn't get a reply.

'You say his wife's in a wheelchair?' asked Nurse Moore.

'Yes, and she's got a young baby. Is he gonna be all right?'

'It will take time. Come with me to my office.'

As Jim followed, he was dreading what she might tell him.

'Please sit down,' Nurse Moore said, sitting behind her desk. 'Mr Smith has been badly injured in a fight. The police think it's something to do with gang warfare, and they want to question him as soon as he recovers consciousness. That's all I know.'

Jim tried not to shout. 'Gang warfare? What the bloody hell was he doing with a gang?'

The night sister wrote everything down as they talked. 'You can see that he has been hit around the head and face. Why is Mrs Smith in a wheelchair?'

'Sadly, she caught polio, so can't get here easily. That's why I'm here. I'm a neighbour. Mrs Smith and my daughter are best friends.'

'I see...' Nurse Moore looked at some notes in front of her. 'We think, at the moment, that most of his injuries are superficial and will heal in time. There will also be some scarring, but that will fade.'

'So have you any idea when he'll be able to come home?'

'Unfortunately, no. He may have to have some X-rays, but only a doctor will be able to tell you that.'

'I was hoping you could tell me more.'

'Sorry.'

Jim's thoughts turned to Penny. 'How's his wife going to get here to come and see him?'

'Do you have a car?'

'No. Could the hospital help?'

'I'll make some enquiries.'

'OK, thank you, Sister. I'll be getting back now to give the family the news.'

'How are you going to get home?'

'I can get a cab.'

Nurse Moore watched him walk away. It was at times like this when she found her job very difficult.

It was starting to get light when Jim pulled the key through the letter box at Penny's house. He carefully crept along the hall to the kitchen and could see Ivy and Tony asleep in chairs. They looked so peaceful. He didn't want to disturb them, so he left quietly and went along to his own house. As soon as he'd opened the front door, Dolly and Grace were there to greet him.

'Jim, you're back. Have you been into Penny's?'

'Yes, they're all asleep.'

'Come on,' said Dolly, 'we'll go back in. They'll want to know what's happened.'

Just at that moment, Tony appeared behind them.

'I thought you was asleep,' said Jim.

'I heard you come and go,' said Tony. 'Penny called me just as you left. Reg's mum is making some tea, so I said I'd come and find out how you got on.'

'I'll go in and tell Penny,' said Jim.

When they all walked into number two, Penny asked, 'How bad is Reg, Mr Taylor?'

'I'll make you all a fresh pot of tea,' said Ivy.

Jim sat in the armchair and told them everything.

'So, what you're saying is, they don't really know how badly he's been injured,' said Tony.

Jim shook his head. 'Not at the moment. The night sister said he may need some X-rays, but only a doctor would be able to say for certain.'

'They wouldn't tell a neighbour, anyway, would they?' said Penny. 'I've got to get there.'

'What hospital did they take him to, Mr Taylor?' asked Tony.

'St Olave's.'

'So he was this side of the river, then?'

'Seems like it.'

'How did they get this address?'

'I don't know. Perhaps he had something in his pocket.'

'Don't forget he had the wages on him,' said Dolly.'

'That's a good point,' said her father. 'D'you think someone beat him up for them?'

'Could be, if he was flashing the cash in a pub,' said Tony.

'If that is the case, I'll kill him!' said Penny.

'What about the van? I wonder where that is?' Tony was desperately trying to make sense of it all.

'Could be anywhere,' said Jim.

'Tell you what, Pen; I'll take you to the hospital a bit later on. With a bit of luck, Reg might be conscious by then and able to tell us what happened – and where the van is. Mr Taylor, and Dolly, can you come too? It will probably need all of us to help get Pen in and out of the car.'

'What about her wheelchair?' asked Dolly.

'I can't take that; me boot's not big enough, but I should think the hospital can lend us one.'

'Thank you,' said Dolly. 'I knew you'd come up with a solution.' She kissed Tony's cheek, even though everyone was looking.

Tony grinned. 'Right, let's all try to get some sleep. We've got a busy day ahead of us.'

'Thank you, Tony,' said Penny.

'That's what friends are for.'

Dolly sat wiping her eyes. Why did Tony have to be such a nice person? She knew she should love him, but something held her back.

'Night all,' he said as everyone began to move away. 'See you later.'

Tony walked along the road wondering about Reg lying in hospital. What had he got himself

involved in? Had Dolly been right to be suspicious of Bert Edwards? Was he involved with
something dodgy? And what about the wages?

*If this is the end of Reg's business, I'll have to look
for a job, as I've got me car to pay for,* he thought.

But he knew that the first thing to do was get
Penny to the hospital. When he had made sure
that Reg was OK, they would sort something out
between them.

Chapter 15

At ten o'clock that Saturday morning, everybody
was in the Smiths' house ready and waiting for
Tony. When he arrived in his car, they were all
relieved that he hadn't overslept.

'Right,' he said. 'Let's get Penny in first.'

'I'll try to be as helpful as I can,' said Penny.

'Don't worry about it. We'll try not to hurt you,'
said Tony. Then looking at Dolly and her father,
added, 'When we've got Pen sorted, you two can
get in the back.'

'You should have got a four door, son,' said Jim,
grinning, and giving Tony a pat on the shoulder.

'Be grateful for small mercies,' he said with a
smile, even though for the rest of the night he'd
been wondering how badly injured Reg was, and
how long they might all be out of work. If it was
going to be long term, then he had better find
himself another job real quick, if he wanted to
keep up the payments on his pride and joy.

After a bit of a struggle – with Tony on the inside, pulling, and Jim on the outside, pushing – they finally managed to get Penny out of her wheelchair and into the car. Finally, they were all inside and settled.

'Don't worry about Gail,' said Ivy, bending down and peering through the window. 'Me and Grace will look after her. Good luck, and give my son my love.'

'Course I will,' said Penny, who up till now hadn't said a word. She quickly wiped the tears from her eyes. She didn't want anyone to see how she felt about her wonderful friends and how helpful they were being. She was also worried about Reg. What state would she find him in?

Dolly glanced over the road and saw both of the Gregory sisters standing at the doorway to their sweet shop. They looked concerned, and as the car went past, they waved. Dolly thought that they were very caring ladies. She would have to pop in there later and let them know what had happened.

'Penny, if you get the chance, d'you think you could ask Reg where the van might be?' asked Tony. 'Cos if we've got that, it would make it a lot easier for you.'

'I'll try, that's if they'll let me see him.'

'They should do,' said Jim. 'After all, you are his next of kin.'

After that, everybody was quiet and tense with apprehension. Normally, they would all be chatting away, but today, they were full of their own thoughts as they made their way to the hospital. How badly was Reg injured? How would they all manage?

When they arrived, Tony got out of the car, quickly followed by Jim and Dolly.

'I'll go and find a wheelchair,' said Dolly as she disappeared inside. She went to the reception desk, and explained the situation to the young nurse there.

'Wait here; I'll go and get a porter.'

'Thank you,' said Dolly.

In a short while, the nurse returned with a young man pushing a wheelchair.

'Right, where's the patient?' he asked, in a jokey manner.

'Outside,' said Dolly, and she led the way.

Tony and Jim were standing by the car when the young man came up to them. 'Now what have you been up to?' he asked Penny as he looked into the car.

'I've come to see me husband,' she said.

'Right, let's get you sorted out. Have you got any movement at all?'

Penny shook her head. 'Not in me legs.'

'D'you want any help, mate?' asked Tony.

'You just keep the door wide open. And you, sir,' he said to Jim, 'can you hold the chair steady? I should be able to manage.' He turned to Penny. 'Now, you, young lady, lock your arms around my neck. When I say "ready", keep your head down and be prepared to be whisked away.'

Dolly smiled. They needed someone to lighten the atmosphere. She stood back and watched her friend doing as she was told.

'Ready?' asked the porter.

Dolly was worried that Penny would bang her head, but this young man was a professional.

Penny was lifted clear of the car and seated in the wheelchair.

'Thanks, mate,' said Jim. 'That was a jolly sight easier than us getting her in.'

'It comes with practice. Now where d'you want to go?'

'Don't know,' said Penny.

'Well, we'll start at Reception. They can tell you what ward your husband is in.'

They all followed the porter as he made his way to the desk. 'They won't let you all in to see the patient,' he said.

'We know that,' said Dolly. 'It's just that we want to be with Penny, in case she needs us.'

He gave Dolly a lovely smile. 'If he's permitted visitors, you know you can always come back at visiting hours, but only two at a time are allowed round the bed.'

'Thank you,' she said.

After looking through a ledger and making a phone call, the nurse at the reception desk told them what ward Reg was in, adding that they had to see the ward sister first.

After wandering through a maze of corridors, the porter said, 'This is Sister's office.' He knocked on the door.

'Come,' called a voice.

'You wait out here,' the porter said to Dolly, Tony, and Jim, and pushed Penny inside, closing the door behind him.

'Sister,' he said to the stern-faced woman who sat behind a desk. 'This is Mrs Smith. She's come here to find out about her husband who was admitted in the early hours.'

163

'Yes. Night Sister Moore left me some very detailed notes.' She turned to Penny. 'I understand that a neighbour – Mr Jim Taylor – came here.'

'Yes. I was very worried after the policeman called, and as you can see, there was no way I could get here, so Mr Taylor came here for me. Is Reg very badly injured?'

'He has regained consciousness and the police have been to see him. At the moment, he is having X-rays to see what damage has been done.'

'Will I be able to see him?'

'I should think so. How did you get here?'

'A friend brought me in his car.'

'There's three of them outside,' said the porter. 'I told them that only Mrs Smith will be allowed to see her husband.'

'Yes, that's right.'

'They had to come with me to get me in and out of the car,' explained Penny.

'I understand,' said the sister. She picked up the phone and dialled a number. 'Is Mr Smith back in the ward?' she asked the person on the other end of the line.

The answer must have been 'yes' as she then said, 'Right, porter, can you take Mrs Smith along to ward B6 where Nurse Pearce will be waiting for you.'

Penny began to feel sick. What was she going to see? 'Thank you,' she said to the sister, as the porter wheeled her round and they left the office.

Outside, in the corridor, Dolly rushed up to Penny. 'Is everything all right?' she asked.

'I don't know. He's just come back from having

164

X-rays. I'll let you know.'

With that, the porter pushed her away along the corridor.

The door was opened into a long ward, and a young nurse came up to them. 'Mrs Smith?' she asked.

Penny only nodded.

'Your husband is down there, on the left-hand side.' She pointed.

'Thank you.'

Slowly, the porter wheeled Penny along the ward.

'Hello, Bob,' shouted out one man. 'We gonna have nice young ladies in our ward now?'

'You should be so lucky,' said the porter. 'Besides, you'll have Sister after you for shouting out and waking all the others.'

'We've been awake for hours. You should know what it's like being in hospital. There's no rest for the wicked.'

When they stopped at the bottom of Reg's bed, Penny gasped when she saw the state of her husband's face.

'I'll leave you for a little while, and then I'll come and take you back to your friends,' said the porter, pushing Penny right up beside Reg.

'Thank you,' said Penny.

He closed the curtains around the bed before he left.

Penny reached out and touched Reg's hand. 'Reg, it's me.'

He opened his eyes as best he could, as they were bruised and badly swollen. 'Penny. How did you get here?' He was having difficulty speaking.

'Tony brought me in his car. What's happened to you?'

'I got into a bit of a fight, and I think I've come off worse,' he said softly.

'Well, you certainly look as if you have.' She stopped to wipe the tears from her eyes.

'Who told you where I was?'

'The police came to the house last night.'

'I'm so sorry. Is Mum all right?' He closed his eyes again.

'A bit shook up. Dolly's dad came earlier this morning to find out what was wrong.'

'He did?'

'Well, I was desperate to know where you was and how bad you were.'

'I didn't know Jim had been here.'

'How did you get yourself in this state?' Penny sobbed.

Reg squeezed her hand. 'Don't cry, love. I'm so sorry. It probably looks a lot worse than it is.' He tried to sit up, but fell back against the pillow.

'They told me that you've been to have an X-ray.'

'I think they were looking for a brain.' Reg winced as he tried to laugh.

'Where do you hurt?'

'All over. I think I've had a good kicking.'

'Do you know who done it?'

He slowly shook his head.

'Was you with Bert Edwards?'

'Yes.' He winced and turned his head away.

To Penny, it seemed as if she had only just begun talking to Reg, when, suddenly, the curtains were pulled back.

'Sorry, Mrs Smith,' said the porter. 'I'm afraid you've got to go now. You can come back tonight during visiting hour.'

'And how the bloody hell am I going to be able to do that?'

'I'm sorry, Mrs Smith. I only take orders.'

The porter slowly pulled Penny away from Reg's bed and carefully pushed her back along the ward.

With Penny still crying, there were murmurs from the other patients who were saying that it was more like a prison than a hospital.

Dolly, Tony, and Jim all jumped up when they saw Penny being pushed towards them so soon.

'How is he?' asked Tony.

'Is he all right?' asked Dolly.

Penny wiped away her tears. 'He looks a bit of a mess.'

Jim looked at the others. He had been hoping that Reg might look a bit better than when he saw him earlier.

Penny sobbed and reached out for Dolly's hand. 'What we gonna do?'

'I don't know.'

'Penny, did you ask him where the van was?' asked Tony.

'No, I was only with him for a short time, and then I couldn't ask him much as he seemed to be in a lot of pain.'

'Look, if you like, me and Dolly can come back tonight and ask him. If we can get the van, then we'll be able to bring you here. Would that be all right?'

Penny nodded.

'I'll go and find out what time visiting hour is,' said Dolly.

'Good idea,' said Tony.

Dolly came back in a short while. 'Seven till eight, and only two at a time round the bed.'

'Right, that's it. Me and Dolly will be back here tonight.'

'Perhaps you'll be able to find out how bad he is,' said Penny as she was being pushed along the corridor towards the exit.

With the porter's help, they got Penny into the car. When they were all seated, they were off. Once again they were all very quiet.

Tony broke the silence. 'He didn't say who did it, did he?'

Penny shook her head. 'The police have been to see him. He did manage to say that Bert Edwards was with him, but he didn't say if he'd been hurt as well.'

'He might not know,' said Dolly.

'I don't suppose you managed to look around while you was with Reg?' asked Jim. 'Just in case he was there as well.'

'No, sorry. The curtains were pulled round us,' Penny replied.

Dolly gently placed a hand on Penny's shoulder. 'Don't worry about it; we'll have a good look around when we're there.'

Penny touched her friend's hand. She knew that these people would do anything for her and Reg. What had he got himself into?

They finished the journey in silence, each lost in their own thoughts.

When they all arrived home, and after updating

Ivy, Dolly went across the road to see the Misses Gregory.

'Hello, Dolly,' said May Gregory. 'You were all off early this morning.'

'Yes, we were. We went to see Reg who's in hospital.'

'Oh my dear. Whatever's happened? We saw Mrs Watts going in first thing to see Mrs Smith. She looked very agitated when she came out.'

'We don't know a lot at the moment. All we know is that he's been in some sort of fight. A policeman came last night to tell Penny, but as you know, she couldn't get there, so me dad went with the policeman to the hospital. He's in St Olave's.'

'Just a minute.' May went to the back door. 'Ada,' she called out. 'Come out here.'

With that, Ada Gregory came into the shop. 'Now what is it?' she asked, irritably. 'Hello, Dolly. Is everything all right?'

'Young Reg is in hospital,' said May.

'No...What's wrong with him?'

'It seems he's been in a fight,' said Dolly. 'We don't know that much about it at the moment. We took Penny to see him earlier, but she was only allowed to stay for a few minutes. Me and Tony are going back this evening to see if we can find out how it happened. I'd thought I'd pop in and tell you, so if anybody asks, you can tell them that's all we know, so far.'

'How did you manage to get Penny to the hospital?' asked May.

'Somehow, between us, we managed to get her into Tony's car.'

'The poor girl,' said Ada. 'How's she going to

169

get to see Reg?'

'Hopefully, when we get the van, it will be a lot easier. We don't know where it is at the moment.'

'Thank goodness young Tony's got a car,' said May.

'Mrs Smith told us that Penny has to go to the hospital to try to learn to walk again on those calliper things. How's she going to do that?' asked Ada.

'I don't know. We haven't even thought that far ahead yet.'

'Well, it's a good job that you're back over there to help her out,' said May.

Dolly swallowed hard. 'Yes it is. Could I have a packet of cigarettes for Reg?' she said, putting her money on the counter.

May handed over a packet of ten Ardath, and then pulled out a small box of chocolates from under the counter. 'And take these for Penny.'

'Thank you. But what about the coupons?' asked Dolly. Sweets were still on ration.

May waved her hand. 'I don't think we need worry about that. They're not much, but it's just to let her know that we are thinking of her.'

Dolly smiled. 'I'll let you know how things are when we find out more.'

'Thank you. We'd appreciate that,' said Ada.

As she crossed over the road, Dolly thought about all the times she had felt sorry for herself since coming back from America. Yes, her marriage had gone wrong; she had lost her baby and could not have any more, but Penny had had far more bad luck. She might have had a baby, but then caught polio and couldn't walk. What with

Reg now in hospital, they could all be out of work. What did she have to complain about? At least she could get another job.

Dolly pushed open the front door and called out, 'It's only me, Mum.' Going straight up to her bedroom, she threw herself on the bed, and cried.

It wasn't long before her mother pushed open the door. 'You all right, love?' She sat next to her daughter, gently stroking her hair. 'I'm sure everything will sort itself out.'

Dolly sat up, threw her arms round her mother, and between deep heartbreaking sobs, gasped, 'Mum, what's Penny gonna do?'

'I don't know, love. We'll just have to wait and see. Yer dad said you didn't manage to see Reg, then?'

Dolly shook her head. 'No, me and Tony are going tonight.'

'Don't get yourself so upset. You might know a bit more after you've seen him.'

'I hope so.'

'Now, come on downstairs and have a bite to eat. It's been a while since you've had something.'

Despite being so upset, Dolly gave a little smile. Her mother always thought that food and a cup of tea would solve all their problems.

Chapter 16

'So, what you gonna do then, love?' asked Mrs Marchant.

'I dunno, Mum.' Tony was finishing off the last of his sandwich.

'Well, you've got that car to pay for, and if Reg ain't got any work, how you gonna manage for money?'

'As I said, I don't know. Hopefully, I might know a bit more tonight, after me and Dolly go to the hospital and talk to him.'

'Well, don't forget I rely on your money now to pay the rent.'

'I know that, Mum.' Tony gave his mother a smile. 'Don't worry; I'm sure everything will work out fine for us.'

'I hope so.'

'I know I can get another job.'

Mrs Marchant smiled and patted her son's hand. She knew he was a good lad.

Tony was confident he would find work, but like the rest of his friends, he was concerned about Reg. He was also worried about what would become of his mother if he were ever to marry Dolly. With his sister, Rose, now married to a doctor and living in Scotland, there'd be no regular income. He picked up the cup of tea his mother had just placed in front of him. With his elbows on the table, and both hands wrapped round the cup, he

172

stared into space. *That's if, one day, I'm lucky enough to get Dolly to marry me,* he thought.

That afternoon, Jim Taylor was sleeping in the chair, and Dolly was quietly reading, when there was a knock on the door.

Grace came in from the scullery just as Dolly stood up. Jim made a few snuffling noises and went back to sleep.

'Go and see who it is, love,' Grace said softly.

When Dolly opened the front door, she was surprised to see Tony standing there. 'I thought you'd be like me dad – having forty winks.'

'No. Dolly, can you come with me for a walk?'

'I'd love to. I'll just get me coat, and tell Mum.'

'Wrap yourself up, love,' said Grace. 'It might be May, but it's a bit chilly out there.'

When they were outside and walking slowly along the road, Tony said, 'This is all a bit of a mess, ain't it?'

Dolly only nodded.

'So what we all gonna do?'

Dolly stopped. 'How d'you mean? I thought we were going to see Reg tonight?'

'We are. But what if he won't tell us much?'

'Course he will. We're his friends.'

'But what if he's involved with something really dodgy?'

'How d'you mean?'

Tony shrugged.

'Why? D'you think he is?' asked Dolly.

'I don't know. I never really trusted Bert Edwards.'

'What? And you thought I was being paranoid

173

about him.'

'Well, I didn't like to let on, but after you told me about your copper friend telling you about the gangs–'

'He ain't my copper friend,' Dolly quickly interrupted.

'Whatever...Well, I started to take more notice of Reg's comings and goings, to try to find out if anything was going on.'

'And did you?'

'Nah, but Reg did start to get very secretive.'

'In what way?'

'He never said where he was going, or who with, and sometimes, when we wanted to know what to do next, he'd be missing nearly all day. That's not like him. He was always with us on the job.'

'Oh, Tony. Let's hope Reg can tell us something, and that we're both wrong about Mr Edwards.'

'I hope so. Dolly, what if Reg can't get any more work?'

'How d'you mean?'

'Well, if Bert Edwards is a wrong'un, he could make things very hard for Reg if he wanted to start on his own again.'

'He can't do that, can he?'

'I don't know. I'm just putting me thoughts into words.' He took Dolly's hand and gave it a squeeze. 'And I just needed you to talk to.'

'So, what you're saying is that we could all be out of work.'

'Could be. What would you do if push comes to shove?'

'I can always go to Peek Freans, I guess. What

about you?'

'I suppose I can always get work. After all, there's a lot of rebuilding and refurbishing work going on, and I'm quite skilled at most things.'

'Well, let's hope it don't come to that. Look, it's a bit cold out here; let's have a sit down in that café.'

'Good idea.'

Hand in hand, they crossed the road. They both knew that everything could change for them in the next few days.

That evening, as Tony drove to the hospital with Dolly, they were both quiet. It was with some relief when Tony finally pulled up outside the hospital.

They stopped at the reception desk and asked the nurse if Reg was still in the same ward. She informed them that he was, so they made their way to room B6. They stood outside with the other visitors, waiting for the doors to be opened.

When the Sister finally came to open the door, and before anyone could move, she said, 'Please remember, only two people around the bed at a time, and you must leave when I ring the bell.'

The regulars hurried in, straight to the bed of their loved ones.

Dolly remembered Penny telling her that Reg was on the left-hand side, so they made their way along the ward, looking at every person in their bed, till they came to him.

'My God, mate, you look as if you've been in a fight,' said Tony.

'Ha ha, very funny,' said Reg slowly. With his

swollen lips, he was having difficulty speaking.

Dolly was shocked to see how bad his face looked. It was badly bruised, and there were some stitches round his left eye.

'Hello, Dolly,' said Reg, holding out his hand.

'Oh, Reg, what have you been up to?'

'It wasn't me, it was the other blokes.'

Dolly noted he said 'blokes', so there must have been more than one.

'I can see you look a bit of a mess,' said Tony, 'but how are you feeling, mate?'

'Not good. How's Pen?'

'Worried,' said Dolly. 'D'you think you'll be in here long?'

'Dunno.'

Reg hadn't tried to sit up, and Dolly could see that as well as having difficulty speaking, he was squinting because of the stitches.

'Where's the van, Reg?' said Tony, not wasting a moment to get to the things he wanted to know. 'If you've got the keys, we can go and get it, then we can bring Penny here.'

'I don't know where it is. After giving me a good kicking, they took the van and drove it away.'

Tony looked at Dolly.

'Don't worry about that now,' said Dolly. 'We'll try to get something sorted out.'

Reg gave her a weak lopsided smile. 'Thanks.' He closed his eyes.

Dolly could see that Reg was exhausted. After a while of him not saying much, she looked at Tony. 'Perhaps we'd better go,' she said softly.

Tony nodded.

Dolly stood up. 'Reg, we're gonna be off now.

I'll just leave these ciggies that the Gregorys gave me to pass on to you.'

There was no response as she placed the cigarettes on the bedside table.

'Take care,' said Dolly, trying hard to keep her feelings hidden.

'Bye, mate,' said Tony. 'See you again.'

Reg just raised his hand.

As they walked back along the ward, Dolly couldn't help but shed a few tears.

Once they were outside, Tony said, 'Who the bloody hell did that to him? I tell you something, Doll, when we find out who did it, I'll go after them.'

'Don't talk such rubbish. Try to see a bit of sense for once in your life. If they did that to Reg, what do you think they would do to you?'

'I'm sorry, love, but it makes me so bloody angry.'

'I know how you feel, but that's not doing Reg or Penny any good.'

'You're right. If only we knew where the van was.'

'Look, why don't we go to the police station and find out if they know anything.'

Tony gave Dolly a quick kiss on the cheek. 'I knew you would talk a lot of common sense. I do love you, Dolly Taylor.'

She smiled. He'd called her by her maiden name.

The local police station was just around the corner, and as Tony parked the car, he said, 'What if they won't help us?'

'I don't know. We'll cross that bridge if and when it happens.'

Tony gave her the grin that she remembered with such affection.

As they explained all that had happened to the policeman at the desk, he wrote everything down in a notebook. When they had finished, he asked, 'So you want to know where Mr Smith's van is?'

'Yes, please. It would make it easier for us to get his wife to the hospital. She's in a wheelchair,' said Dolly.

'I see. Wait here while I try to get some information.' He disappeared through a door at the back of the counter.

Dolly and Tony sat down on a bench that ran along the wall. While they waited, Tony took hold of her hand. 'When we do find the van, we'll be over our first hurdle.'

'I hope so,' was Dolly's reply.

They both jumped up when the policeman returned. 'Well, it seems we don't have any paperwork here about a van. We only know that one of our officers found Mr Smith in the road in a sorry state and took him to St Olave's.'

Dolly could feel the tears start to trickle down her cheek. 'Is there anywhere else we can go?' she asked.

'Not really. D'you know where Mr Smith was before he was beaten up?'

Dolly shook her head. 'He did say that the gang that hit him drove off in the van.'

'So really then, it could be anywhere.'

She nodded.

'Well, thanks anyway,' said Tony. 'When we go

and see him again, he might be able to tell us a bit more.'

'I hope so,' said the policeman, and closed the book he'd been writing in.

'Thank you,' said Dolly, and they both turned and walked away.

'Good luck,' the policeman called after them as they left.

Once they were outside, Tony became angry again. 'What the bloody hell was Reg thinking of, letting himself get into this mess?'

'I don't know,' said Dolly. 'I only wish I did.'

As soon as they arrived in Wood Street, they went straight into see Penny.

'How was he? Did you see him? Is he all right?' she asked.

'Hang on a bit, love,' said Tony. 'One question at a time.'

'Sorry.'

'Yes, we did see him, but he wasn't very talkative. And I must say, he does look a bit of a mess. We didn't stay very long. He don't know where the van is, as it seems they – whoever it was – drove off with it, so it could be anywhere.'

Dolly stood, holding Penny's hand.

'Would you two like a cup of tea?' Ivy asked Dolly and Tony.

'Yes, please,' said Tony. 'We was going for a drink, but Dolly here wanted to see you first.'

Penny looked up at Dolly. 'Thank you,' she said, but her friend didn't answer.

'He didn't say if he was going out somewhere after work, did he, Pen?' asked Tony.

179

'No. I've no idea why he would even be over this side of the water. He wasn't looking at another job, was he?'

Tony shook his head. 'If he was, he kept it very quiet.'

Ivy put the tea on the table. 'Help yourselves to sugar.'

'Thank you,' said Dolly, putting sugar in her tea and stirring it gently.

'He hasn't said anything to you, Dolly, has he?' asked Penny. 'Do you know where he might be working next?'

'No. I don't see a lot of him, now Mr Edwards sees to most things. Reg just gives me the money for the wages, and that's about it.'

'Did he have the wages on him?' asked Penny.

'Don't know,' said Dolly.

'He was out most of the day,' said Tony. 'In fact, we ain't seen a lot of him at work just lately. We thought he was off with Bert Edwards pricing up other jobs... This is all a big mystery.'

'I'm sure it'll all sort itself out,' said Ivy.

'I hope so,' said Penny. 'If they find the van, things will be lot better. That's if you don't mind driving it, Tony.'

'Course I don't mind. We did go to the police station to see if they might know where it is, but they don't. Monday, we're going to one over the water, near to the job we're doing, to see if it finished up over there. If not, they still might be able to help us.'

'I do hope so,' said Penny, adding softly, 'and thank you.'

Chapter 17

To Tony, Sunday always seemed to be a long day, but today he had a quest. It was early afternoon, and he'd gone along to see Penny to ask her for some of Reg's petrol coupons.

Dolly's head shot up. 'You can't have those,' she said. She was busy painting Penny's toenails at the time.

'Why not?' asked Tony.

'Because they're for pink industrial petrol. That's one of my jobs: sending receipts to the ministry. And if you get caught, you could be looking at a prison sentence.'

'Who will know?'

'I think the police are on the ball,' said Dolly.

'I just want to take Penny to the hospital this afternoon, as visiting is allowed, and I ain't got a lot of petrol. I've just about got enough to get to work in the morning, and then hopefully, they'll find the van and Reg's coupons.'

'I can't let you do that, Tony, it's not worth the risk,' said Penny.

He dropped himself into the armchair. 'So what am I gonna do now, then?'

'What do you normally do on a Sunday?' asked Dolly.

'First thing, I helped me mum with the washing. It's hard work getting it out the copper and through that old mangle.'

'I never thought you were the domestic kind,' said Dolly.

'I am where me old mum's concerned. Now, I don't know... I could probably take a baby for a walk.'

'Now that I'd like to see,' said Penny.

'So where is our god-daughter, then? I suppose we should take her out. You wanna come with me, Doll? We can go over the park.'

'She's a bit young to go on the swings, Tony,' said Dolly.

'Anyway, she's spending the day with her other gran,' said Penny, 'but thanks for the offer.'

'Well, how about me and you going to the park, Doll?'

'Great. We can take this big baby in her push-chair.'

'I'd like that,' said Penny. Although she was very disappointed at not being able to see Reg today, she didn't want Tony to get into trouble for using pink petrol. At the moment, they had enough problems to contend with.

'Right,' said Dolly. 'When your varnish has dried, we'll get you wrapped up, and then we'll take you for a walk.'

It was now the middle of May, and nice just being out in the welcoming early sunshine. The friends spent the afternoon walking round the park, and generally having a nice time.

The following morning, Tony called for Dolly to take her to work in his car.

'This is nice, I like having me own chauffeur,' she said, settling herself down.

'You'll be wanting me to wear a peaked cap next.'

She grinned. 'Now that is a good idea. Thank you for yesterday. I really enjoyed being out, and I know Penny did.'

'It don't take much to please you, does it?'

'No. Not really.'

'We'll have to do that more often. Fancy me taking out a couple of good-looking birds. It didn't even cost me much, just a cup of tea.'

Dolly laughed. It had been good to relax for a few hours. After all, who knew what was in store for them.

Before they had left Penny, the previous evening, Tony had told her that he and Dolly would go along to the yard in the morning to see if they could do anything.

'As we said last night, I can't go to the job till we get the materials. As we'll be going to the police station, later, to see if they know anything about the van, I thought we'd both start the day together.'

'We don't even know if we've got a job to go to,' Dolly said sadly. 'It's such a great big mess.'

'Don't upset yourself. We might know more today.'

Dolly smiled at him, but she really couldn't see a way out of all this. 'Dad said he might go along to the site a bit later on, to see if anything's happening there.'

As they were driving along, content with each other's company, Dolly said, 'I'm going to learn to drive.'

Tony laughed. 'Whatever for?'

'Well, I've been thinking; petrol will be off ration soon, and if and when we get the van back–'

'What?' interrupted Tony. 'You can't drive that old rust bucket – that's if Reg would let you.'

'Well, would you let me drive your car?'

'Dunno.'

'I did a bit of driving when I was in America.'

'You never said.'

'Didn't have any need to. I didn't have a licence, as it was only round the farm.'

'Well, you'll find driving on the roads over here a bit different to America. Besides, you'll have to get a licence and pass a test.'

'I know that.'

'If Reg did let you drive his old van, you'll have to do things like double-declutch.'

'What's that?'

'I'll show you, if and when the time comes.'

'If I was able to drive the van, then I could take Penny to the hospital and perhaps help her to use her crutches, then she might be able to walk again.'

'In that case, I'll help you.'

Dolly smiled. 'Thank you. I knew I could rely on you.'

Tony touched her hand. 'Looks like I'm seeing a whole new Dolly Taylor.' He was secretly hoping that this might be the turning point of their friendship.

When they arrived at the yard, they were surprised to see Harry Jordan sitting outside in a police car. As soon as they stopped, he got out.

'Hello,' said Dolly, as Harry came up to them. 'Are you here on official business?'

'Sort of.'

'You'd better come into the office,' said Tony.

The three of them made their way across the yard, and as they went inside the office, Harry took off his cap.

Dolly set about lighting the stove. 'What can we do for you?' she asked.

'It seems that my station didn't have a lot to do yesterday, so they were phoning around as someone had been enquiring about a van.'

'That was us,' said Dolly. 'Reg was involved in a fight, and he's in hospital.'

'Sorry to hear that. Is he badly hurt?'

'He's been beaten up a bit,' said Tony.

'Oh. Well, we might have found the van.'

'That's wonderful news,' said Dolly. 'Where?'

Harry took out his notebook and read through it. 'A van was parked outside a pub and causing an obstruction. At first, we thought it might have been involved in a robbery we're investigating, and when I saw it, I recognised it as Mr Smith's.'

'Could it have been used in a robbery?' asked Tony.

'I don't think so. The robbers were reported to have had a red van, and Mr Smith's is a dirty, white, rust bucket.'

Dolly wanted to smile. Reg would be most upset to hear his old van described in that way, and by Tony, as well.

Harry closed his notebook and put it in his pocket. 'Did Mr Smith say if Bert Edwards was involved?'

'Reg told his wife that he was with Bert Edwards, but we don't think he's in the hospital,' said Tony.

'When can we collect the van?' Dolly asked.

'Get some form of ID, and his insurance from his wife. Come to my station to do the paperwork, then you can take it away.'

'Were the keys in it?' asked Tony.

'Yes, so somebody must have left it in a hurry.' Harry stood to leave. 'I expect I'll see you later. Bye for now.'

'Bye,' said Dolly.

'Well, that was a turn-up for the books,' said Tony. 'Fancy that copper phoning round for us.'

'As Harry said, they probably had nothing else to do.'

Tony noted that she'd said 'Harry'. 'Or it could be that he felt sorry for us when you told him about Penny and the baby.'

'Well, I was pretty upset. Anyway, what we gonna do now?' asked Dolly.

'First, I should go to the site and see if anything's happening there. Then I'll go and see Penny and collect all the papers I'll need to pick up the van, now we know where it is.'

'As I said, Dad might go to the site a bit later on. Would you like me to come with you?'

'No. I think it's best you stay here in case someone comes round.'

'Who would come here?'

'I don't know.'

'All right.' Dolly was a bit peeved that Tony didn't want her with him. 'If you should see Bert Edwards, you won't do anything silly, will you?'

'Ah, you do care about me, after all.'

'No, it's just that I don't want to have to visit

someone else in hospital.'

'You're all heart, Dolly Taylor.'

Dolly smiled.

'What will you do with yourself while I'm gone?'

'I'm going to sort out anything from the cupboard that I can, bundle it all up, and take it home so that Penny can go through it. Then she might know a bit more about what's been going on.'

'Miss Efficiency. I can see now why Reg wanted you to work for him.'

'Go on, be off with you.'

Tony left, grinning. He knew he was going to have to work hard for Dolly's affections, and wait until the right time to tell her that he still loved her and wanted to marry her.

After he had gone, Dolly realised that things with Tony were starting to be like they were all those years ago. He was so easy to talk to. But, she knew that she had to be very careful; she didn't want to give him any ideas that they could get together again. Marriage was still a definite no-no as far as she was concerned.

It was almost lunchtime when the office door opened again. Dolly looked up, and was surprised to see Bert Edwards standing there. She was hoping it was Tony, back with the van.

'Hello,' she said.

'Hello, Dolly. May I call you Dolly?' he asked, taking off his trilby and smoothing down his straight black hair.

She nodded. 'What can I do for you?' She was

trying to remain calm, but she was very angry with this man, and a bit scared of him. She knew that if she started to accuse him of anything, it might turn out very bad for her. She secretly prayed for Tony to return.

'I've just been to the site and heard from Tony that Reg is in hospital.'

'Yes, and he's in a pretty bad state.'

'Have you been to see him?' Bert asked.

'Yes. He told his wife that you were there with him. Is that right?'

'Yes I was, but it wasn't me they wanted; it was Reg.'

'Why?'

Bert sat down. 'It seems he owed them a lot of money – some bookmakers and card sharps don't like that. They were fed up with waiting for their cash.'

'What?' Dolly quickly sat down.

'It seems he's been doing a lot of gambling, and got in with the wrong sort.'

'But you just said you was with him.'

'I was.'

'So why didn't you stop them hitting Reg?'

'I know these blokes, and they told me to scarper while I still had legs I could walk on, so I did.'

'But you never called the police?'

'As I said, you don't mess with that sort.'

'Reg never used to gamble.' Dolly suddenly felt very angry. 'Did you get him to meet your mates?'

'I must admit that at first we did both go to a game or two, but then it started to get out of hand. I tried to warn him time and time again, but as the stakes got higher, he went to bigger games, and just wouldn't listen.'

'I'm sorry, but I don't believe you. Why did you start taking him with you?'

'He's not a child. He has got a mind of his own and said he liked a flutter.'

'I know, and if he thought he could get some easy money for Penny and the baby, that's all he would think of.'

Bert shrugged. 'What could I do?'

'Are these blokes who beat him up mates of yours?'

'Good God, no!'

'So why didn't they beat you up?'

'I don't owe 'em any money.'

'Do you know who they are?'

'Not really. I know of 'em, but Reg got into different high-stake games, and all I know is that you don't mess with those sorts of gangs.'

Dolly was hoping that Tony or Harry would walk in. She didn't feel safe with this man. Did he have dealings with gangs?

'Do you know where they took the van?' she asked, even though she knew that it was at the police station. She was hoping that Bert Edwards might accidently let on that he knew more than he was saying.

'I remember one of 'em drove it away, so it could be anywhere.'

'Till we get it back, we can't take Penny to the hospital to see him.'

'I am so very sorry.'

'So is Penny. What about the work? Tony's gone to the site to see if they've all still got a job.'

'Course they have. Those plasterboards have arrived now, and I've been over and talked to 'em, so they're getting on with it. I know the owner wants the job finished as soon as possible.'

Bert Edwards put on his trilby, and after carefully pulling it down over his right eye, he stood up and walked towards the door. As he went out, he turned to Dolly. 'Tell Reg not to worry. I'm sure things will work out... Bye.'

Dolly went to the door and watched him drive away. Was everything he had just told her true? Did Reg really get in with a bad crowd? She couldn't tell Penny any of that – she would go mad, and poor Reg could finish up back in hospital.

She went back to her chair and looked out of the window. If only Tony would come back.

A bit later, Dolly went to the local shop for a magazine. She needed something to do, to take her mind off all that had happened these last few days. As she slowly made her way back to the yard, she was surprised to see Harry Jordan waiting outside again.

'Hello,' she said. 'So, twice in one day. What have I done to deserve this? Have you seen Tony? Has he got the van?'

'I don't know; I've been out on duty all the morning. Can we talk?'

Dolly was filled with alarm. What was he going to tell her? 'Course, come on in.' She unlocked the door to the office.

'Dolly, I was concerned about you.'

'Me. Why?'

'You looked very worried.'

'I am worried, about Reg and Penny, and me job.' She wasn't going to tell him that Bert Edwards had visited, not till she'd had a word with Tony.

Harry took off his cap, and sat on a stool. 'In a way, this is a social call.'

'But you're on duty.' Dolly was full of worry. What was he going to say?

'I know, but I do have a reason. Perhaps I could take you out somewhere nice, just to take your mind off things.' He held up his hands. 'I know I asked you out once before and you turned me down. Now, I would like us to be just friends.'

'Why?'

'You're such a nice understanding person, and always seem to be concerned about everybody else.' He smiled. 'And besides, I've been given two tickets for a show up West. So how about you coming with me next Saturday.'

Dolly was taken aback. 'Why me?'

'Would you like to go?'

'Well, yes. I haven't been to a show for years.'

'So what do you say?'

'I'd love to.'

'Good. I'll pick you up at your house about five. Perhaps we could have a bite to eat first.'

'I don't know...' Dolly sounded hesitant.

Harry held up his hands. 'I promise it will be just as friends.'

'All right,' Dolly smiled. 'Thank you very much.'

'I'd better go. See you on Saturday.'

'Yes, thank you. Oh, will you be at the station

tonight when we pick up the van?'

'No. I'll be off duty by then. Bye.'

'Bye,' she said as she watched him go.

Dolly did not see Harry's big smile as he left. He really did like this young lady, and hoped that this might be the first of many dates.

Dolly sat and thought about what had just happened. She had agreed to go out with Harry Jordan. What would her mum and dad say? Or Penny and Tony. It was only to go and see a show. Why was Harry given the tickets? What if she'd refused? She would ask him on Saturday.

Chapter 18

When it was time to leave the office, Tony drove into the yard in his car. Dolly was disappointed that he didn't have the van. She could see her father and Billy in the car, and decided she would wait till her and Tony were alone before she told him of her plans for Saturday.

'Everything all right?' Tony asked as he breezed into the office.

'Fine. What about you? Have you been working?'

'Yeh, Bert Edwards came in and told us what to do. He said he wanted the job we're on finished as soon as possible, so I thought I'd better leave getting the van till tonight.'

'He came in here and asked about Reg.'

'He did tell me he was coming here. So, what

did he have to say?'

'Not a lot, really. What did he tell you?'

'I'll tell you when we get home. I don't want yer dad or Billy to hear too much just yet, till we know more.'

'OK.'

'Yer dad was already at work this morning when I got there, so was Billy. He's a good lad, and he's very worried about Reg.'

'He thinks the world of Gail.'

'It was good to be working, and Bert told us not to worry about being paid as he will see to it. Right, let's go and get all the stuff we need to pick up the van, then we can take Penny to the hospital tonight.'

'What about your car? Who will drive that?'

'I'll leave it at the police station. In the morning, I can go to work on the bus and bring it home then. Ready, Doll?'

She nodded, and plonking her hat on her head, she picked up her handbag, and the papers she'd been through, and made her way outside with Tony.

'Hello, Dad; Billy. Everything all right, then?' said Dolly, climbing in the back of the car and sitting next to Penny's brother.

They both nodded.

'Not bad,' said her father who, after Dolly had got in the car, settled back in the front seat. 'How about you?'

'Been doing a bit of sorting out of stuff to show Penny.'

'That poor girl,' said her father. 'I tell yer, she's a real brick.'

'Comes from good stock,' said Billy.

Dolly smiled at him and patted his hand.

When they arrived at Wood Street, Tony parked his car outside Penny's house.

'Tell Mum I'll be in a bit later,' said Dolly to her father.

'OK, but don't forget it's darts night; she'll have me dinner all ready.'

'I won't be long.'

Before they went in, Tony said to Dolly, 'When we see Reg tonight, don't mention that Bert came in the office today.'

'Why not?'

'Let's wait and see what he has to say first.'

'All right.' She wasn't going to question Tony's reason.

Tony quickly told Penny about the van, and what paperwork they needed to collect it. She showed them the cupboard that held that sort of information.

'If Tony gets the van, and is back in time, we can take you to see Reg tonight,' said Dolly.

Penny's face broke into a smile. Dolly thought that she looked as if a great weight had been lifted from her tired, sad, face with that bit of news.

'That will be wonderful, thank you,' said Penny. She held out both her hands. Dolly and Tony held them for a moment. 'Thank you, both.'

'Right,' said Tony, 'I must go and tell me mum what I'm up to. Dolly, I'll see you a bit later.'

'D'you want me to come with you to collect the van?' she asked.

'No, it's fine. I shouldn't be long.' He kissed

them both on the cheek before leaving.

'I'd better go and have me dinner,' said Dolly, 'and then I'll be back. See you in a little while.'

'Thank you, Dolly,' said Penny.

As Dolly left, she noticed a few tears trickle down Penny's cheek. She felt guilty about not telling her friend everything she knew about Reg being in hospital, but was it all true? All being well, they would have some answers tonight.

All evening, Dolly was in with Penny, and they were both hoping that Tony would arrive soon with the van.

'It's too late to go to the hospital now,' said Penny, after looking at the clock once again.

'I wonder what's happened,' said Dolly. She was starting to worry.

'Perhaps he can't get the van started,' said Ivy.

'I'm sure if that was the case, he would have got some help from a garage or something,' said Dolly, trying to be optimistic, even though she was worried that the thieves might have done a lot of damage to the van.

'Did he take his car?' asked Penny.

'Yes,' said Dolly.

'So, really, he should be back be now,' said Penny.

Dolly agreed. She was very worried now. Had something happened to Tony?

For what seemed like forever, Tony had been trying hard to keep his composure as he went through endless questions regarding Reg's van. He had tried to convince the police that he had permission from Reg's wife to collect it. Even the letter from Penny that he'd brought along was met with suspicion.

'Come on, fellas,' said Tony, trying to sound full of ease, even though he was worried that it wasn't going to help him. 'Let's face it, who would want to take that old rust bucket?'

That must have convinced the policemen, as finally, they handed over the keys.

Tony got into the van, worried that there might be some damage, but when the engine burst into life, he almost said a prayer of thanks. He looked at his watch and, realising that he didn't have any spare time to go back and collect Penny, decided to go on to the hospital alone.

He parked the van quickly and hurried into the hospital, straight to the ward where he hoped Reg would still be. Sister raised her eyebrows as he hurried past her and along to Reg's bed. He had only just sat down when the bell went for everybody to leave.

'Well,' he said, 'I've got the van, so I can bring Penny in tomorrow.'

There was no response from Reg, who had his eyes closed.

'Do you know the blokes what did this to you?'

Reg slowly shook his head.

Tony was getting frustrated at the lack of response. 'Look, mate, you'd better wake up your ideas cos tomorrow when Penny gets here, she'll want to know what this was all about.'

The ward sister shook the bell again, only louder and more urgently this time.

Reg opened his eyes.

'Sorry, mate, but I've got to go,' said Tony as he walked away, but he knew that Reg was watching him.

As Tony walked towards the door, Sister gave him a withering look. 'Goodnight,' she said sharply.

'Goodnight, Sister,' said Tony with a broad grin.

'Well, that was a complete waste of time,' he said out loud, as he sat back in the van. 'I should have gone straight home.' He put the van into gear and made his way back to Wood Street.

Dolly was still in with Penny when she heard the key being pulled through the letter box. She was quickly on her feet and in the passage to meet Tony.

'Where have you been?' she asked abruptly, as he walked through the front door.

'To the hospital.'

'You should have come here first for Penny,' she said as they walked towards the kitchen.

'Sorry, Pen,' said Tony, pushing open the kitchen door. 'But there wasn't time. I was ages at the police station filling in forms and going through a lot of old rigmarole. I wasn't even sure they'd let me have the van.' He turned to Dolly. 'I was hoping to see your copper mate, but he wasn't on duty.'

Dolly felt herself blushing. 'I told you before, he ain't my copper mate.' What would they all say when they knew she was going out with Harry on Saturday night?

'Anyway,' continued Tony, 'I knew that if I

came here first, it would be too late to take you to see Reg. You know what a stickler that ward sister is as far as time is concerned. As it was, I was only with him for a couple of minutes.'

'Did he have anything to say?' asked Penny.

'No. He just lay there with his eyes shut. Mind you, he looks a lot better; most of the swelling's gone down.'

'Thank you, anyway, Tony,' said Penny. 'I really do appreciate all you two are doing for me.'

'That's what friends are for,' said Tony. 'Right, I'll just run along to Mum; she'll want to know what happened.'

'Dolly, would you pop along to mum and let her know what's happening?' asked Penny.

'Course.' Dolly walked with Tony to the door. 'Did Reg say anything?'

'No. I wasn't there long enough. We can take Penny with us tomorrow. See you in the morning.' He quickly kissed her cheek, and then he was gone.

Dolly watched him walk away. She thought he looked tired and unhappy. Had Reg said anything to him? Did he know it was all about Reg's gambling? Had Bert Edwards told him? There were so many questions that she needed to ask Tony, but they would have to wait till they were alone again. And what about Penny? Would she believe that Reg had been gambling heavily?

Back in the kitchen, Dolly smiled and stood quietly as she watched Penny talking to her daughter.

'Daddy will be back again soon, darling, then everything will be fine again.' She looked up.

'Dolly, I didn't hear you come back in. Tony looked a bit down. Do you think Reg is all right?'

'I would think so. He did say he looked a bit better. Anyway, you'll be seeing him tomorrow and then you can ask him yourself.'

'Do you mind if I go to bed? I feel a bit drained,' said Penny.

'I'm not surprised. Would you like me to massage your legs?'

'No, that's all right. You must be tired as well.'

'Well, it has been rather a funny old weekend. Would you like me to put Gail to bed?'

Ivy, who was sitting quietly concentrating on her knitting, said, 'It's all right, Dolly, I'll see to her.'

'Don't forget to tell Mum,' said Penny.

'Course not. Goodnight,' said Dolly as she kissed her friend. 'See you tomorrow.'

Dolly walked to Mrs Watts' house, wondering what tomorrow would bring.

That night, as Dolly lay in bed, she was finding it hard to get to sleep. She had so much on her mind. First, there was Reg and his gambling debt; then there was her going out with Harry on Saturday. Was she doing the right thing? She turned over. She was still young and free, so really she could do as she pleased, but then again, after making one mistake, she didn't want to upset her family. Still, it was only to see a show.

Chapter 19

After being in the office for all of Tuesday morning with nothing to do, Dolly decided to leave early.

'Dolly, what you doing home so soon?' her mother asked. 'Is everything all right?'

'Everything's fine. It's just that I was so bored in there on me own, so I decided to come home.'

'That's all right then.'

'Is there anything I can do for you?'

'No, thanks. Everything's taken care of. Are you going to the hospital tonight?'

'Yes, we're taking Penny with us.'

'That's good. You going in there now?'

'No. I'll wait till tonight to see Pen.'

Grace looked at Dolly suspiciously. This wasn't like her daughter. Ever since she had come back from America, she had spent every spare moment in with her friend.

Dolly went up to her bedroom. She sat on her bed, and began to wonder what she was doing with her life. She was restless. One of the reasons was that her job didn't give her enough to do, but she couldn't leave, not while Reg was in hospital and the men were all working. Who would do the wages and everything that went with it? Would Penny be willing to start to do all that again? One thing was certain: Penny would need to try to make the effort to walk again. She just needed someone to encourage her.

She jumped off the bed and ran downstairs. 'Just going to see Penny,' she called out to her mother.

Grace didn't say a word.

'Hello, Mrs Smith.'

'Dolly, you must call me Ivy. Everyone else does. You're home early. Penny's in her room having a lay down.'

'I'm just going to the lav,' said Dolly, going straight outside.

Ivy looked at her suspiciously.

Dolly picked up the callipers and marched back into the kitchen.

'What are you going to do with those?' asked Ivy, in alarm. 'You know she won't have them in the house.' She was very worried at what Penny would say.

'I know that, but things have got to change. She's got to walk again. Sitting around here all day and feeling sorry for herself ain't helping her or Gail.'

The door was suddenly pushed open as Penny wheeled herself into the kitchen. 'I thought I heard your voice. What the bloody hell are those leg irons doing in here?' she yelled, pointing at the callipers, and looking angrily at her mother-in-law. 'I thought I told you I never wanted to see those things again.'

'It wasn't Ivy who brought them in here; it was me,' said Dolly.

'You? Why?'

'Because you are going to start using them, and I'm gonna help you. Now, where's those boots?'

'I'll get them,' said Ivy, and quickly left the room.

Penny glared at Dolly. 'Who the bloody hell do you think you are, coming in here and demanding I do what you tell me?'

'Somebody has to.'

'Besides, you should be at work; not coming in here and having a go at me.'

'Have you finished?'

Penny sat sulking.

'We've all been fussing around you for far too long. Somebody has to make you buck up your ideas.'

'You can't make me.'

'We'll see about that.'

Ivy returned with the boots.

'Right, now I'm going to put these on you, and then hopefully, me and Ivy will be able to put the callipers on,' said a determined Dolly.

Penny looked terrified. 'I can't do it, Dolly.'

'I've never known you to be a quitter,' said Dolly, lifting up Penny's foot and carefully pushing it into the boot.

Ivy stood, just looking on.

Tears were rolling down Penny's face, as Dolly pushed her other foot into the boot.

'There, that's the first hurdle over.'

'What if I fall over? You two can't get me up again.'

'She's right, Dolly,' said a very worried Ivy.

'Then I'll go and get me mum to give us a hand.'

'That's right, get the whole street in to see what an idiot I am, who can't even stand up.'

Dolly knew this wasn't going to be easy. 'We

might be better going into your bedroom and getting you on the bed, first.'

'I can't believe this,' said Penny. 'And we all thought that Hitler was a dictator.'

Dolly ignored that remark, turned the wheelchair round, and pushed it into the bedroom.

Normally, Penny could help herself getting in and out of the chair and onto the bed. She could use her arms to lever herself up and use the pulley that Reg had constructed, but now she just sat in her chair.

'Come on, help us,' said Dolly.

'I don't want to.'

'You are acting like a spoilt brat.'

'And you are acting like some sort of Gestapo.'

'Oh Penny, can't you see I only want to help you.'

Penny looked away.

'Wouldn't it be wonderful if you could be at least standing when Reg comes home?'

'He might be home tomorrow, so you gonna work a miracle?'

'I'm going to try. Now help us.'

Ivy stood by, watching and waiting. What would happen when Dolly left? Would Penny take this out on her, and have her running around? She would do anything for her daughter-in-law, but she knew that Penny could sometimes have a very short fuse.

Dolly was struggling to get Penny on the bed. 'Come on, Pen, help me.'

'I don't want to.'

Dolly sat on the bed. 'I never thought you were a quitter. D'you know, when I left the States, I had to work my way back. I can tell you, it was bloody hard work, cleaning toilets and people's sick, but I wouldn't give up, as I knew that I wanted to come back home.'

'Quite the little martyr, ain't you.'

Ivy stood quietly and watched the scene. She wasn't going to say anything, even if she did agree with Dolly.

'Ivy, give me a hand to get this lump on the bed.'

Ivy looked very worried.

'Come on. She won't bite.'

'I might,' said Penny.

Ivy went round to the other side of the bed. Between them, they managed to get Penny onto it.

'What now, clever clogs?'

'Sit up.'

'Why?'

'So that I can put this strap round your waist.'

The callipers had a thick strap with a buckle to keep them held up.

'Don't want to.'

Dolly sat next to Penny and took hold of her hand. 'You've got to try. Do you want your daughter to be walking before you?'

Reluctantly, Penny sat up.

'Good girl,' said Dolly. 'Now, when I've done that and attached these leg straps, and fixed them into your boot, I'm gonna slide you to the bottom of the bed and let you put your feet on the floor.'

Dolly fastened the leather straps round Penny's thighs.

Ivy looked at Dolly in amazement. 'Will you be able to do that?'

'We won't know till we try. Don't worry, Pen, we will hold you.'

'What if I fall over?' asked Penny, suddenly taking an interest, amazed at all that was going on.

'Well, you'll only fall back on the bed and I promise you that you won't hurt yourself.'

Dolly was silently praying that everything would go as she hoped.

When the callipers were strapped to Penny's useless legs and fixed into the boots, Dolly carefully pulled her friend to the edge of the bed.

'Now, sit up. When your legs stick out, me and Ivy will hold you as we help you to lower your legs to the floor.'

'I can't, Dolly. I'm frightened.'

'Well, just give it a go.' Dolly held on to her friend's hands.

Penny sat up and inched her way to the bottom of the bed till her legs were sticking out over the edge. 'Now what?'

'Right, Ivy, you put your arms round Pen's waist, your side, and I'll do the same this side.'

Dolly quickly glanced over at Gail who was lying on her back kicking her little legs in the air. A tear ran down Dolly's face. She just prayed that this would work, and then suddenly, she burst out laughing.

'I'm glad you think this is bloody funny,' said Penny as she sat on the bed with her legs out in front of her, and with her mother-in-law and best friend holding her round the waist.

'I was just thinking: what if someone looked

through the window? They might think this is some sort of funny game.'

Ivy gave a little snigger. Penny, who up until now had a miserable look on her face, started grinning, then she too burst out laughing. Soon, the three of them were laughing, not just with joy, but also with relief that they had got this far.

Gradually, they inched Penny into an upright position and then slowly lowered her legs to the floor.

'Don't let go of me!' she cried out, grabbing Dolly and Ivy's arms as she tried hard to get her balance.

'Course we won't,' said Dolly, wondering what to do next. 'Now, I'm gonna move round and stand in front of you, to stop you from falling forward. Don't worry; I won't let you go till I think you've got your balance. If I think you might fall, I shall push you back. All right?'

Penny nodded.

'Right, here goes.'

Penny was full of fear as Dolly, who was still holding on, slowly made her way round to stand in front of her friend.

'Right, Pen, I'm going to let go very slowly...'

Gradually, she let one arm drop, but held it close to Penny. Then she did the same with her other arm.

Ivy had her arms round Penny, almost crushing her. She wasn't going to let her go.

'Do you think you've got your balance?' asked Dolly, who had her arms out ready to push Penny back on the bed.

'I don't know.'

'Shall I let go?' asked Ivy.

'No. Give me a moment or two to find out.'

'Good girl,' said Dolly. 'See that bit wasn't so bad, was it?'

Penny grinned at Dolly. 'I forgot how we are both the same height.'

'I think you've shrunk a bit.'

'Could I sit down again?'

'Course, if that's what you want.'

Dolly helped her friend to sit back on the bed.

Ivy let Penny go, and breathed a sigh of relief. 'I never thought you'd be able to do that, Dolly.'

'If the truth be known, neither did I.'

'I did it though,' said Penny, proudly. 'Well, nearly.' She looked over at her baby. 'Soon, my darling, your mummy will be standing by herself.'

'Will you be willing to have another go?'

'Give me a little while to get me breath back,' she said, smiling.

'I'll go and make a cuppa,' said Ivy, and she quickly left the room. Outside, she wiped her eyes on the bottom of her pinny. She didn't want them to see her tears.

When Ivy returned with the tea, it was to see Penny and Dolly laughing.

'Are you going to have another go, love?' asked Ivy.

'I think I might.'

Dolly threw her arms round her friend and hugged her tight. 'I knew you could make it.'

'We'll have to see about that, but I'll say this for you: you should be a police officer. No criminal would be safe if you were in charge.'

'Think of what you've got to tell Reg tonight.'

'I don't think he'll believe me, after all the fuss I made at the hospital when I tried them on there.'

'Yes, but that was because it was the first time you'd seen them, and knowing you, you probably tried to do too much – like run before you could walk.'

'Very funny.'

'You willing to have another go?' asked Dolly.

'Just be careful with me.'

Dolly felt elated when she went back home.

'Hi, Mum,' she said, walking into the kitchen with a huge grin on her face.

'You look happy,' said her mother.

'I am. You'll never guess what I've done.'

'Something good by the expression on your face.'

Dolly pulled out a chair from under the table and sat down. 'I've managed to get Penny to put her callipers on, and stand up.'

'What? How?' Grace also pulled out a chair and sat herself down on it. 'How on earth did you do that? Everybody knows she won't even look at 'em.'

'I know, but after a bit of nagging, me and Ivy managed to put them on, then we gradually got her to stand on her own. It was only for a minute, but at least it's a start.'

'She didn't even do that at the hospital.'

Everybody knew about Penny's first encounter with her callipers, which according to her, was a complete disaster.

'I know,' said Dolly, bursting with pride. 'I think being in her own home with people she knows is better than in a room with strangers. She's terrified of making a fool of herself.'

'You must be very pleased with yourself.'

'I am, but all she needed was a bit of a push ... well, more of a pull, really.' Dolly added, smiling.

'Wait till Reg hears about this. It might help him to get better.'

'I hope so.'

Jim was also pleased to hear what had been happening that afternoon. 'At least it's a start. Wait till Reg hears about this,' he said, repeating what his wife had said earlier. Everybody was concerned about the family.

When Dolly finished her dinner, she went along to Penny's, and waited for Tony to bring the van round to take Penny to the hospital.

'Hello, girls,' he said as he walked into the kitchen. 'Ready?'

Penny nodded. 'See you later,' she said to her mother-in-law who was standing at the door ready to wave them off.

Like everybody else, Ivy was also smiling at the news Penny would pass on to her son.

'I've got the ramp in place,' said Tony.

He took hold of Penny in her wheelchair and pushed it into the road. Then, he carefully manoeuvred the wheelchair into the back of the van, putting blocks under the wheels. When it was in place, he chained it to the side.

'There,' he said to Penny, 'that should stop you from falling about. And I promise to drive slowly.'

Penny just sat there, smiling. She was so happy. She was going to see her husband and she couldn't wait to tell him her wonderful news. Just being able to stand, even if it was only for a minute or so, had been such an achievement for her. Could this be the start of her walking again? Thank goodness Dolly was there to nag and bully her.

Dolly had promised Penny that she could tell Tony the good news.

'Had a good day?' asked Dolly.

'Not bad. We're really getting stuck into this flat we're doing up, and it looks great. What about you?'

'I came home early today, as there wasn't much I could do. I spent a bit of time in with Penny. We had an interesting afternoon, didn't we, Pen?'

Penny was sitting behind them. 'Yes, we did.'

'So what did you do that was so interesting?'

'Dolly got me to stand up wearing me leg irons.'

'What?'

'Careful,' said Dolly. 'Keep your eye on the road.'

'Did I hear right?'

'You certainly did,' said Penny.

'How did she manage to get you to do that?'

'With a lot of nagging and bullying.'

'Well I'll be...'

'I was only on me feet for a moment, but at least it's a start.'

Dolly sat looking out of the window, feeling like the cat that had got the cream. She knew that, from now on, things could only get better as far as her friend was concerned.

Chapter 20

They arrived at the hospital in plenty of time before the doors to the wards were opened. Tony pushed Penny into the reception area, but, to their amazement, Reg was sitting there fully dressed.

'Reg!' Penny called out as she pushed her way towards him.

'Hello, love,' he said, kissing his wife. He then turned on Dolly. 'Where was you this afternoon? Why wasn't you in the bloody office when I phoned?'

She just stood there, dumfounded.

'I don't pay you to spend the afternoon at the pictures.'

'Hello, Reg,' said Penny. 'So good to see you. Are you coming home?' There was more than a hint of sarcasm in her voice.

'I could have been home hours ago, if someone was doing what she's paid for.'

'Dolly was with me.'

'I still don't pay her to come home and sit and talk about make-up and things.' He was clearly very angry.

'You could have caught a cab,' said Penny, beginning to get upset.

'What would I have paid him with? Shirt buttons.'

'Didn't you have any money on you?' asked Penny.

'No, I was robbed, remember?'

'You look a lot better,' said Tony, trying to defuse the tension.

'I feel a lot better. Now, can we get going? I want to see me baby.'

They all went quietly to the van.

'Do you want to drive?' asked Tony.

'No, you can do it. I'll sit in the back with Pen.'

'I'm so pleased you're coming home,' said Penny, who was clearly upset at her husband's outburst.

'So am I. How's Gail?'

'She's fine. Reg, I've got a lot to tell you.'

'And I've got a lot to tell you, but let's wait till we're home and on our own, shall we?' He emphasised the 'we'.

'You look tons better than the last time I saw you,' said Penny. 'When do the stitches come out?'

'I've got to go to the cottage hospital sometime. What about you and mum? Are you both OK?'

'We're both fine.'

Dolly sat quietly taking in all what Reg had said. Did he honestly think that she was never in the office? She was very upset at Reg's outburst. Tony had gently patted her hand and smiled as she climbed into the van. She wanted to cry. She guessed Penny was dying to tell him her news, but she must have decided to wait till he had calmed down.

When they arrived home, Dolly quickly said her goodbyes and hurried to her own house.

'Thanks, Dolly,' said Penny. 'See you a bit later on?'

Dolly only nodded.

Tony quickly went up to her. 'I'll be round in about half an hour. Let's go for a walk or something.'

She just nodded again. She was so near to tears.

'Dolly is that you?' Grace called out as her daughter quickly made her way upstairs.

When there wasn't any answer, she followed Dolly to her room. Pushing open the door, she was shocked to see her daughter sitting on the bed, crying. 'What is it? Is it Reg? Whatever's the matter?'

'Reg is home, and I think I've lost my job ... and Reg hates me.'

'Why?'

'When we got to the hospital, he was already waiting to go home. He had expected us to go and pick him up. It seems he was discharged this afternoon, and he phoned the office when I wasn't there.'

'Did he know what you was doing?'

She shook her head.

'Well, when he does, he'll be round here with his tail between his legs.'

Dolly didn't answer.

'Is he better now?'

'Not really. He's still got to have the stitches out.' She gave a sob. 'But the bruises have gone down a lot.'

'Come on downstairs, love.'

It was just after Dolly had got downstairs that Tony knocked at the front door.

'Come in,' said Dolly. 'I must look a sight. I'll just nip upstairs and put on a bit of make-up.'

Tony went through to the kitchen. 'Hello, Mrs

213

Taylor. Did you hear the news about Reg? That was a right turn-up for the books, wasn't it?'

Grace nodded. 'Dolly's really upset.'

'I know, but I'm sure Penny will give him what for. He'll come round here full of apologies when he knows what Dolly achieved this afternoon. Penny's really over the moon.'

'She told you then?'

Tony nodded.

'Dolly's worried she's gonna lose her job.'

'I don't think she's got any worries on that score.'

'Sorry about that,' said Dolly as she came back into the kitchen. 'I'm ready.'

'See you later, Mrs Taylor.'

'Bye, love, and try not to worry too much.'

As they walked along, Dolly put her arm through Tony's. He didn't comment, as he knew she wanted some form of comfort.

'Do you know why Reg finished up in hospital?' asked Dolly.

'Not really. Why, do you?'

She nodded. 'Bert Edwards came into the office, this morning, and told me that Reg had been gambling. The blokes he was with beat him up because he owed them a lot of money.'

Tony stopped and turned towards Dolly. 'Bert Edwards told you all that?'

'Yes. I asked him if the blokes were mates of his. He said no, they played for far too much money for his liking. Tony, what has Reg got himself into?'

'Christ knows. But why did Bert Edwards tell you?'

'Cos I asked him.'

'Let's go in the pub; then we can sit and talk quietly.'

When Tony returned with Dolly's shandy, she sat playing with the glass. 'What we gonna do?'

'I honestly don't know. Bert did come on site and told me not to worry about wages or materials. It seems he's got all that covered. But what's all this about Reg?'

Dolly told Tony everything else that Bert Edwards had told her.

'So why didn't you tell me all this before?'

'When have I had the chance? I didn't want to say anything in front of Penny. I thought we could ask Reg ourselves and see what he has to say about it.'

'You should have told me.'

Dolly had tears running down her face. 'Don't you start on me.'

'Dolly, I'm so sorry, please don't cry.' Tony put his arm round her shoulders and pulled her close.

She wiped her eyes.

'Do you want to go?'

She shook her head. 'It seems I can't do anything right.'

'How can you say that? Look what you've got Penny to do.'

'I expect I've lost my job.'

'I shouldn't think so. In fact, after that piece of information, we could all be out of a job.'

'What makes you say that?'

'Bert might not give Reg any more work if he really is into this gambling thing.'

'Why should that affect his work?'

'Think about it. Bert gives him the money for materials and wages, and then he goes off and, well, you know what happened. So what will stop him from doing it again?'

'Surely Reg has got more sense than that?'

'Has he? They say if you're an addict, it's hard to break.'

'Reg can't be an addict, can he?'

'I'm not sure. I do remember when we was in the army, he was always looking for a card game, so I can't honestly say I don't think he is. He's been acting very strange just lately, going off when we were waiting for materials, or to be told what to do next.'

'Do you think he'll tell Penny what it was all about?'

Tony shrugged. 'Wouldn't like to say. But I bet she has a real go at him about the way he went for you.'

Dolly didn't answer.

'I've been thinking about that outburst, and I don't know what he thought you could do even if you had been in the office. You couldn't have got him home, and you couldn't have come to the site looking for me, as you don't know where it is. So what the bloody hell was he shouting about?'

'I don't know. It could be his guilty conscience.'

'You could be right.'

Dolly sat back. 'Why does life have to be full of problems?'

'Let's face it, love. Most of them are man-made.'

Dolly thought about her own life...Yes, they were.

'Are you going to work tomorrow?' asked Tony.

'I don't know.'

'By the time we get home, Reg might have calmed down.'

'To be truthful, I'm not sure what I want to do.'

'Surely you don't want to go to Peek Freans?'

'I don't know,' Dolly said again. 'It's got to be better than standing around in Woolworth's.'

At this moment, her mind was in turmoil.

It was a couple of hours later when Dolly was standing with Tony at her front door.

'Do want to come in?' she asked.

'Thanks all the same, but I'd better go home.'

'Thank you for being here for me,' she said.

He kissed her cheek. 'I'll always be here for you, Dolly Day Dream.'

As she turned away, she felt full of guilt. She hadn't told Tony that she was going out with Harry Jordan on Saturday to see a show. But why did she feel guilty? After all, Harry was just a friend.

'Hello, love,' said Grace when Dolly pushed open the kitchen door. 'Reg has been round here for you. He said he was very sorry and would you go in and see him when you came home.'

'I don't think so,' she said, putting her handbag on the table.

'Why not? He said he was so very sorry at what he said.'

'I don't care.'

'He also said that he thought you were a marvel at getting Penny to stand. He is genuinely sorry, Dolly, and I think you should go and see him.'

'I'm sorry, Mum, but I can't face him at the moment.'

'Well, please yourself. But I've never known you to hold a grudge.'

'And I've never been shouted at in a public place before. No, he'll have to wait. I'm going to bed.' She kissed her mother's cheek. 'See you in the morning.'

'Goodnight, love.'

'Goodnight, Mum.'

Dolly climbed the stairs with a little grin on her face. She was glad that Reg was sorry, but maybe Penny had sent him. What would he say if he knew she knew all about his gambling? Well, they would both have to wait till tomorrow for some answers. After she'd had her say, she might not even have a job. She was sure that everything would sort itself out, but she was too tired to worry about anything tonight, so went to bed.

Despite all that was said during the previous day, Dolly decided to go to work. It was her way of showing Reg that she wasn't a shirker. She knew Tony had taken her dad and Penny's brother, Billy, to the site that morning, and she had been thinking about what to do.

'Are you going to work?' asked her mother when Dolly walked into the kitchen.

'Might as well. Got nothing else to do, although there's not a lot to do there.'

'You could go in and see Penny.'

'No. I don't think so. Not till I'm ready.'

'Please yourself. But you can't let this get to you.'

'No, I know.'

'What do you want for breakfast? You could have a bit of that dried egg on toast.'

Dolly wrinkled her nose. 'Thanks, but I'll just have a bit of toast, then I'll be off.'

When Dolly closed the front door behind her, she was very surprised to see Reg pull up outside her house in his van.

'Dolly,' he said, coming up to her. Placing his hands on her shoulders, he tried to kiss her cheek.

Dolly quickly stepped back. 'Hello, Reg,' she said coldly.

'Are you going to work?' he asked.

'Course.'

'Get in the van. I'll take you.'

'That's all right. I'll get the bus. You stay here with Penny.'

'No. I need to talk to you.'

'Reg, you've just come out of hospital. I'll call in on me way home tonight.'

'No. I need to talk to you,' he repeated, but more forcefully this time.

Dolly could see there wasn't any point in arguing, so hitching up her straight skirt, she climbed up into the van and sat next to him.

'I'm sorry about yesterday,' said Reg.

Dolly didn't answer.

'When Penny told me what you'd got her to do, I was over the moon. If I collect you after lunchtime, this afternoon, could you come in and do it again?'

'I don't know.'

'Please. I'm begging you. And I'll pay you a bonus.'

Dolly smiled to herself. She'd never had a bloke

begging her for anything. 'I don't know,' she said again. 'Anyway, I don't need money to help my friend,' she said tartly.

'I know, so can you forgive me for yesterday?'

'I was very upset about that,' she said quietly.

'I know,' Reg repeated. 'And believe me, I'm really sorry.'

'I was hurt and very angry. It was the first time I'd ever left the office early.'

'I know that,' he said again. 'But I just wanted to get home. Anyway, once we get to the office and I can sort out some paperwork, we can come back home.'

Although she knew the answer, she asked, 'Have you got last week's wages? I've done the wages list and the envelopes are ready.'

'I'll have to go to the bank first. They're all waiting for their money and those blokes pinched it.'

'Do you know who did it?'

'No.'

'So you couldn't help the police then?'

'I wouldn't tell 'em even if I did know.'

'Why ever not?'

'As I told Penny, I don't want two broken legs. So, can we drop this subject? I'll be in later with the wages money.'

Dolly remembered that the last time Reg asked the bank for money, they had refused. She knew it would be pointless him asking again, but she wasn't going to say anything just yet.

When they arrived at the yard, Dolly unlocked the office door. 'You coming in?' she asked as Reg stood back.

'No. I think I'd better go along to the site first

and make sure everything's all right there. When the bank opens, I'll go along and get the money for the wages.'

'Let's hope the bank has some money for you then,' Dolly said to herself as she turned away.

'See you later, then,' Reg called out, and then left.

Inside the office, Dolly stood at the window and watched him drive away. How was Reg going to get any money? The bank wouldn't help him. She only hoped that he wasn't going to look for the men who beat him up.

The telephone rang, making her jump.

'Hello, Smith's Builders and Decorators,' she answered. 'Can I help you?'

'Dolly, it's me, Harry.'

'Harry, what can I do for you?'

'I'm just ringing to ask how you are.'

'I'm fine, thank you.'

'Mr Marchant managed to pick up the van, then?'

'Yes. We went to the hospital last night, and they let Reg come home.'

'That's great news. Is he OK?'

'Still very bruised.'

'Well, at least he's home. Everything still on for Saturday?'

'Yes. I'm really looking forward to it.'

'So am I. I'll see you then. Take care, bye.'

'Bye.'

Dolly replaced the receiver and sat back. Harry seemed to be a nice considerate man for a policeman, and she really was looking forward to Saturday.

Chapter 21

It was well into the afternoon when Reg turned up at the office.

'Right,' he said, 'gather up the wages envelopes; we'll do the wages at home. Then when the lads finish tonight, I can give them their last week's money.'

Dolly was surprised he had the money. She put everything into a bag. 'I'm ready,' she said, picking up the keys.

'Good. Let's go.'

They drove along in silence for a while, and then Reg asked, 'Have you seen anything of Bert Edwards?'

'He did come into the office on Monday.'

'What did he have to say?'

'Not a lot. He was more interested in getting to the site and making sure they had the right materials.'

'So, he didn't say anything about being with me that night?'

Dolly crossed her fingers. 'No, not really. He just said he was with you, but didn't know the blokes that beat you up.'

'He did know them. He did a runner as soon as he saw them, so they came after me.'

'Why? What had you done to them?'

'It seems Bert had a few gambling debts, and they came for their money.'

'So why did they attack you?'

'Gawd only knows! Might have thought I owed them money.'

Dolly was confused. Who should she believe? 'So you managed to get the money for the wages then?'

He lightly patted her knee. 'Course I did. Now, when we get home, I want to see Penny standing. I tell you something, Doll, if we can get her walking again then that will be the best thing that's happened in a long while.'

He sat back, and Dolly could see that he was smiling, but her mind was in turmoil. Who was telling the truth? And how did the bank manage to let Reg have the money for the wages when he had said before that they wouldn't? She had to see Tony tonight, to see if he could throw some light on this situation.

When they arrived at home, Dolly got out of the van and went to make her way to her own house.

'I thought you'd come in here,' said Reg.

'Later.'

'We're supposed to be doing the wages.'

Dolly realised that she was still employed by Reg. 'OK,' she said, following him inside and through to the kitchen.

'Dolly,' Penny called out when they both walked in. 'I hope this stupid lump of mine has apologised.'

Dolly kissed Penny's cheek. 'Yes, he has.'

'Have you forgiven him?'

Dolly shrugged. 'Not sure.'

'Hospital or not, I can tell you I had a right go

223

at him. Fancy leading off like that.'

Dolly only gave her a weak smile. 'I've done all the wages sheets, and the envelopes are already.'

'Good,' said Reg, settling himself at the table.

As soon as they finished, Dolly was on her feet. 'I'm just popping home to let Mum know I'm back. I'll be back in a jiff.'

'OK,' said Reg. 'Now, I want to see this miracle.'

'Ha ha, very funny,' said Penny.

Dolly could see there was a lot of tension between the two of them.

'I'll get things started here,' said Reg.

Penny looked at him. 'I'll wait for Dolly to get here first.'

'Please yourself.'

Dolly could see that Reg wasn't pleased at being pushed aside.

'It's only me, Mum,' Dolly said, pushing open the kitchen door. She was surprised to see her mother sitting at the table with some papers scattered over it.

Grace quickly scooped them up. 'You're home early. Is everything all right?'

'Not bad. What you doing?' asked Dolly.

'Nothing.'

'What's all this?'

'Nothing,' repeated her mother.

'Come on, Mum, what are you trying to hide?'

Grace sat back. 'If you must know, I'm trying to make ends meet.'

'What? But I thought things weren't too bad, now me and Dad are working, and with you only doing a few afternoons a week.'

'The only reason me hours have been cut down is because we've stopped making parachutes. Cloth is still hard to get. Till things get better, they're only keeping some of us on.'

'Why didn't you say you was finding it hard?'

'I didn't want to worry you, more so now things ain't that great with Reg.'

'So, what's the problem?'

'I've got a bit of stuff on the never-never, and I had a letter today to say they'll take the stuff back if I don't pay for some of it.'

'What did you get?' Before her mother could reply, Dolly said, 'No, not that three-piece in the front room.'

Grace nodded. 'Well, the other one was so scruffy, and the settee had got torn when the window was shattered, so I put me name down for a new one. When the dockets arrived, your dad wasn't here, so when the shop said they'd got some in, I went and bought it. I needed something to help cheer me up.'

Dolly had been surprised when she'd got back from America to see the new furniture. Her mother had told her that as the other suite had been damaged with glass from the bombing, she was entitled to the dockets that were needed to buy furniture. Dolly was amazed. Her mother was always so sensible. She never did anything without a great deal of thought.

Dolly put her arms round her mother. 'Don't worry; we'll get this sorted out.'

Grace began to weep. 'I've never done anything silly in me life, and now it looks as if I'm in trouble.'

'We're all guilty of doing silly things. Look at me.'

'I did miss you and your dad so much,' she said, wiping her eyes.

'Don't worry about it now. When Dad gets home, we'll all sit down and try to sort this out.' Dolly kissed her mum's cheek.

'Your father will go mad when he knows what I've done.'

'Course he won't.'

'He's never bought anything on hire purchase.'

'It's very different now with all the shortages. You have to buy things when the shops have got them.'

'That's why I did it.'

Despite the war being over for several years, Dolly knew that many items were still rationed. There was such a lack of goods, and everybody was complaining.

'How much do you owe?' she asked.

Her mother picked up a piece of paper and handed it to her daughter.

'Ten pounds? That's a month's wages for me.'

'I know.'

Dolly looked at her mother with concern.

'I was paying off the tally man five shillings a week. And now with me on shorter hours, and all the worry about you and your dad's job, I got a bit behind.'

'Please, Mum, don't worry about it.'

Grace wiped her eyes. 'I knew I should have said something before.'

'I'm sure we can get it sorted out. Mum, will you be all right if I go back to Penny's?'

'Course, love. Her needs are greater than mine.'

'I don't like leaving you like this, but Reg wants to see Penny standing again.'

'I understand.'

Dolly kissed her mother's cheek. 'I won't be too long. By the way, I'll be picking up our wages.'

Reluctantly, Dolly left her mother, and walked back to Penny's house.

'Right. What's happening?' she asked as she pushed open the kitchen door.

'Not a lot,' said Ivy who was sitting, holding Gail. 'She won't let Reg help her. She's waiting for you.'

'I'll just get her calipers.'

'Reg took 'em in the bedroom.'

Dolly grinned at Ivy. 'She can be a bit stubborn.'

'You're telling me.'

'You coming in the bedroom?'

'No. I'll stay here and wait.'

'OK.'

Dolly pushed open the door. 'It's only me.'

'I know,' said Penny, 'I heard you come in.'

'So what's happening?'

'Nothing,' said Reg. 'She won't let me do anything.'

Dolly grinned. 'Perhaps she just needs a gentle touch.'

'Well, you know what an impatient bugger he is. I'm terrified he'll let me go.'

'Right. I'm here now. Let's do what we did before. Reg, sit Pen on the bed. I'll put her calipers on.'

Dolly did what she did before, encouraging

Penny to move to the edge of the bed. When she was standing, and Dolly was sure that her friend had her balance, they very carefully let her go. Penny stood for a little longer this time, and when she fell back on the bed, Reg smothered her face with kisses.

'You are such a clever girl,' he said, sitting on the bed next to his wife.

'I'm determined to walk again,' Penny said, with tears slipping down her cheeks.

'Of course you are, and we are all going to help you. Do you want to do it again?' he asked.

'OK.'

When it was time for Dolly to leave, Reg went to the front door with her.

'I can't tell you how happy I am. I will give you that bonus, then I'll take you two up West on Saturday and you can both have a spend-up.'

'Thanks, Reg, but as I said before, I don't need paying to help my friend.' Dolly knew she had to tell her friend about Saturday, and soon.

'Come on, Dolly, don't get uppity. I must show you what this means to me and Pen.'

'I do know what it means to both of you, to all of us.'

'Right. That's settled.'

As Dolly went home, she had already decided that any extra money she got, she would give to her mother. She also knew that she couldn't go shopping, as Harry would be picking her up at five o'clock. She wanted to see Tony to find out about the money that Reg had suddenly acquired. For Dolly, once again, her life was beginning to get complicated.

As her dad was home, Dolly decided not to say anything about the money her mum owed. After she had helped with the washing-up, she said, 'Mum, I'm just popping along to see Tony. I won't be long.'

Her mother, who was drying her hands on the roller towel that hung behind the door, quietly pushed the door shut.

'Oh? I thought you was going to help me try to sort out my problems,' she said softly.

'I will, Mum, but I must go and see Tony first.'

'Please yourself.'

Dolly could see that her mother was put out as she followed her out of the scullery and into the kitchen.

'Take as long as you like, love. You're seeing quite a bit of him lately.'

'Who's that?' asked Jim, who was sitting in the armchair reading the newspaper.

'Tony,' said Grace.

'He's a nice bloke. You could do a lot worse.'

'I've told you before,' said Dolly, 'Tony is just a friend, nothing more.'

'Yer dad was only saying.'

'I know, Mum.'

Grace continued, 'Not all mothers-in-law are like the one you had.'

Jim folded his newspaper.

'What?' said Dolly. 'What's brought this on?'

'We're just saying, that's all,' said her mother.

'I have got other men friends, you know. In fact, I'm going out with one on Saturday.' She was angry with herself for telling them in this way.

'Who?' asked her father.

'Harry Jordan. He's taking me to see a show up West, if you must know.' Dolly was getting angry.

Her father sat up. 'Is he that copper?'

'Yes.'

'Well, I certainly don't approve of that. Does Tony know?'

'Not yet, and Dad, I am over twenty-one, you know, and can do what I like.'

'We know that, love,' said her mother. 'But we don't want you messing up your life again.'

Dolly picked up her bag and left. She hated this feeling. She was sorry at getting cross with her parents. What was it that was making her so bad-tempered?

'Hello, Dolly,' said Tony when he opened his front door. 'D'you wanna come in?'

'No, thanks. I just want to talk to you.'

'I'll just get me coat.'

As they walked along, Tony said, 'What's the problem?'

'How do you know I've got a problem?'

'By the look on your face. I thought Reg said he was sorry for his outburst.'

'He has, and we got Penny standing again, this afternoon.'

'You did? That's great. So, what is it?'

'Tony, how did Reg manage to get the money for the wages?'

'Christ knows.'

'You don't think he was daft enough to go gambling again, do you?'

'I hope not.'

'Reg told me those blokes were after Bert Edwards, but because he did a runner, they had a go at Reg instead.'

Tony stopped and faced Dolly. 'What?'

'Who do we believe?'

'I don't know.'

'If that was the case, surely Reg would have told the police,' said Dolly.

'I would have thought so. I can't see any bloke taking a beating like that and not grassing the real villains up.'

'Perhaps he was frightened they'd come after him again.'

'Well, I can understand that,' said Tony, 'but why would Bert Edwards come to the site, this morning, when he knew Reg was out of hospital?'

'I don't know, not after the way Reg got beaten up. What if Reg knows about more than one gambling place?'

'I can't answer that. I know he's a bit of a daft bugger, but to get involved again, he must be off his head.'

'What I can't understand is how he got the money for our wages. Before, the bank wouldn't let him have money for materials,' said Dolly.

'He must have got it from somewhere.'

'D'you think Bert Edwards gave it to him?'

'Wouldn't like to say. He might if he wanted the job finished.'

'I suppose that could be it, but Penny will kill him if she ever finds out.'

'Well, she mustn't hear it from us. It's up to him what he tells her,' said Tony.

They walked to the park and sat down on a bench.

'What a week this has been,' said Dolly. 'I'll be glad when Saturday comes.'

'Why, what's happening Saturday?'

Dolly knew she had to tell him. 'I'm going to the theatre.'

'That's nice. Who with? Anyone I know?'

'Harry Jordan.'

'What? That copper?'

'Shh! Keep your voice down!' She noticed a couple who were walking their dog look over at them.

'I thought you had more bloody sense than that.'

'Don't you start. What's wrong with that? I'm free, and I can go out with who I like.'

'I know that, but a copper... Doll, he's probably only taking you out to find out about Bert Edwards.'

She laughed. 'Now, what do I know about him?'

'Believe me, he'll find a way.'

'You're as bad as me mum and dad. I'm fed up with people trying to run my life for me.'

'I think it's because we're worried about you.'

'I made one mistake, but I'm a big girl now, Tony.'

'I know.'

'Besides, I really want to go to the show on Saturday, and Harry has got the tickets.'

'You should have said; I would have taken you.'

'It's a bit late now,' said Dolly.

Chapter 22

As they approached her house, Dolly knew Tony wasn't very pleased with her. Just lately, she seemed to make everybody cross with her. But why did she have to do what they wanted? She knew deep down that they all worried about her. After all, she had been independent before, and that had turned out to be a big mistake. Was this how the rest of her life would be: people trying to tell her what was best for her?

'Tony, I'm sorry if I've annoyed you.'

'It's your life, and let's face it, you've always done what you wanted to.'

'Please, don't let us fall out.'

When they reached Dolly's front gate, Tony looked at her. He did love her, and he didn't want anybody else moving in. He had lost her once before, but now he had been given a second chance. If only she would let him show her how much he loved her.

'Tony, I'm only going up West to see a show with Harry. It's no big deal, so please don't let this upset what we have.'

'What do we have, Dolly?'

'Hopefully, a very good friendship. I know I can always talk to you.'

'You know I will always want more.'

'Yes, and I feel guilty about you not going out with other girls.'

'How can I? When I see you, I want to take you out.'

'You know you can always take me out.'

'But what if I want, you know, for us to be a proper couple? Get engaged? Talk about our future together?'

'Can't you see I don't want that?'

'Why?'

'I made one big mistake.'

'But you've got your lifetime in front of you.'

'So have you. That's the reason why I don't want you waiting for me to change my mind.'

Tony smiled to himself. Perhaps there was some hope for him. 'I can wait.'

'Tony, I've told you how I feel.'

'Just because one marriage went wrong, that don't mean to say that we couldn't make it work.'

'Perhaps we should stop going for a drink. Make a clean break.'

'If that's what you want.'

She nodded.

'Right.'

With that, Tony turned and walked down the road.

Dolly stood watching him. She knew she had hurt him and, in her heart of hearts, she hadn't wanted him to walk away. She also knew she was being silly, but it was too soon after being married to Joe. She was frightened at having another relationship. More so now that she had seen Tony with Gail, knowing that she couldn't have any more babies. That wouldn't be fair to him.

There was a very strange atmosphere when Dolly

walked into the kitchen. She could see that her mother had been crying. 'You all right, Mum?' she asked.

Grace shook her head. 'Yer dad's gone to the pub.'

'Well, that's nothing new.'

'He's very annoyed with me over this money thing.'

'Why didn't you wait till I got home? We said we would talk it over together.'

'And he ain't very pleased with you either.'

'Why? What have I done?'

'You going out with this copper.'

'My God, we're only going to see a show. I'm not going to jump into bed with him.' Dolly was beginning to get fed up with everybody telling her what to do.

'You don't have to be so crude.'

'I'm sorry, Mum. It's just that I've just had Tony telling me I shouldn't be going out with Harry.'

'It's only cos we love you. We don't want you to make another fool of yourself.'

'Thanks.' Dolly was so angry with everyone. 'What did Dad have to say about the money you owe?' she asked abruptly.

'Not a lot really. Just that I was stupid, and old enough to know better.'

'That wasn't very nice.'

'I don't think he feels very nice at the moment.'

'Well, at least he got paid.'

'I know.'

'Did he offer you any money towards what you owe?'

'He said he would.'

'Good for him. With the extra I'm going to get from Reg, that should keep the bailiffs from the door.'

'It's not a laughing matter.'

'I know. Sorry, Mum. Do you want me to stay here till Dad gets in?'

'No, thanks all the same. You going to see Penny?'

'No. I'm going up to bed.'

'It's a bit early for you.'

'I know. I just want to be on me own for a bit.'

'Does Penny know you're going out with this copper?'

'No. I'll tell her in me own good time.'

'All right, love. See you in the morning.'

'Night, Mum.' Dolly kissed her mother's cheek.

'Night, love.'

As Dolly climbed the stairs, she thought of all the trauma that had happened these past few days. She shouldn't have said anything about going out with Harry, but then again, she didn't have anything to hide. Besides, she didn't think it was anybody else's business. She also knew that she had to tell Penny that she couldn't go shopping on Saturday. That was going to cause another problem when her friend discovered the reason why.

The following morning, when Reg came into the office, Dolly noticed that he didn't look all that pleased. 'Everything all right?' she asked casually.

'No. Not really.'

'Oh dear.' She wasn't going ask what was wrong. She knew that he would tell her in his own time.

'Would you like a cuppa?'

'Yeh, why not.'

Dolly picked up the kettle and gave it a shake. 'There's enough water in here.' She put the kettle back on the Primus stove. 'I might be needing some more paraffin soon.'

'You can go along to the shop and get it.'

'OK.' Nothing was said about money for the paraffin.

'Are you still going to take Penny shopping on Saturday?'

Dolly looked up from the mugs she was washing up. 'Why?'

'Only Tony said you're going out with that copper.'

Why did Tony have to tell him? 'Yes, we're going up West to see a show. I was going to pop in tonight to tell Penny. Perhaps we could make it the following week?'

'She's gonna be very disappointed.'

'I'm really very sorry, but this was planned a while ago.'

'You don't think he's only taking you out so he can find out about me business, do you?'

'Why would he do that?' She gave a false laugh. 'Have you got something to hide?'

Reg looked away. 'No. It's just that I don't like coppers.'

The kettle began to boil. Dolly picked it up and went to the bench. She put the tea leaves in the pot and poured the water over them.

'I'm sure Harry's not looking to interrogate me about your business,' she said, trying to keep the conversation light-hearted.

'We shall see.'

After Dolly had added milk and sugar to the mug, and poured out the tea, she handed it to Reg.

'Thanks.'

'Is there anything special you want me to do today?'

'No. Not really. I think Bert might have some invoices for you to type up. He said he'll be over later.'

'It's good that he's putting plenty of work your way.'

'Yes it is.' Reg stood up. 'I'd better be off.'

'I'll pop in tonight and tell Penny about Saturday.'

'OK.'

Dolly watched Reg drive away. She picked up his mug and saw that he'd hardly touched his tea. Now she had to sit and wait for Bert Edwards to turn up, meaning that it could be another boring day.

The thought of Meg and the Peek Freans' factory came into her mind. Perhaps it wouldn't be such a bad idea to go and see her. In some ways, it might be good to get away from Reg and Tony. After all, living in the same street and all working together might be the reason she was feeling low. Perhaps she needed new people to work with, to talk to, and to have a laugh with. All these thoughts were still going round in her head when she saw Bert Edwards drive into the yard.

He walked into the office looking very smart and dapper, as usual. He politely removed his trilby and smoothed down his dark hair.

'Hello, Dolly. Everything all right?' he asked, placing his hat on a chair.

'Yes, thanks.'

'Reg don't look too bad after his little run-in with those blokes, does he?'

'He does look a lot better now. He said you might have some invoices for me to type up.'

'Yes I've got them here.' He opened his briefcase, and took out a handful of papers. 'What I would like you to do is to type these up, and then enter them in this book.' He handed her a black hardcover book. 'They're handwritten, but hopefully you'll be able to understand them. If not, leave them out, and we can go through them together. Any chance of this being done today?'

Dolly quickly looked through them. 'I would think so.'

'Good. I'll give you a ring later and tell you what time I can get over to pick them up.' He gave her a big smile. 'I wish you was over the other side of the water.'

'I think the price of premises would put Reg off.'

'Probably.' He picked up his trilby and put it back on. 'Bye for now.'

Dolly watched him drive away. Thank goodness she had something to do. She took the cover off the typewriter and settled down to do something useful.

It was well into the afternoon, and Dolly had been typing almost non-stop. She sat back and stretched. She had been intrigued at some of the documents. Most of them were just receipts, but there were some invoices for materials, and she was surprised at what Bert Edwards was paying for some of them. It was a lot cheaper than Reg had paid. She made a note in the ledger, and wondered if she should tell Reg of the supplier, but it was just a name and no address. There were also a lot of invoices for a Mr Jack Greenbank. Did he own the property they were working on?

The phone rang, making her jump. She picked up the receiver. 'Hello...'

'Dolly, it's Bert Edwards. How are things going? Have you finished?'

'Yes. Everything's ready for you.'

'That's great. I'll be over in half an hour. Is that all right?'

'That'll be fine.'

'Thanks. Bye.'

She replaced the receiver and began clearing away. She had enjoyed being busy.

After Bert Edwards had left the office, Dolly decided to make her way home. She knew she had to call in to Penny and tell her about Saturday.

She was dreamingly looking out of the bus window, when she saw Meg Windsor walking along. Dolly banged on the window and beckoned to her. Getting off the bus at the next stop, she waited for Meg to catch up with her.

'Hello, Dolly. Long time no see. How's things?'

'Not too bad. How's your aunt?'

'She's bearing up, poor old dear. I hear that you've got Penny walking again.'

Dolly laughed. 'I don't know who told you that. I only managed to get her standing.'

'And I also heard that Reg was beaten up. What has he been up to?'

'You certainly seem to have a good source of information.'

'Well, you know what me mum's like. Been shopping lately?'

'No. What about you?'

'Not done a lot. Say, how about you and me going shopping on Saturday?'

'Sorry, I can't.'

'Going anywhere exciting?'

'I'm going to the theatre.'

'That sounds exciting. Is that with Tony?'

Dolly didn't know whether to lie to her or not. 'No.'

'This sounds interesting. Is it anyone I know?'

'I don't think so.'

'So, how is the romance going with Tony?'

Dolly was pleased that Meg didn't push for a name and said casually, 'There is no romance.'

Meg smiled. 'So does that mean there's still hope for me?'

Dolly didn't answer that. 'Are they still looking for girls at Peek Freans?' she asked.

'Why?'

'Well, I don't get a lot to do all day, and I feel I need something else to keep me out of mischief.'

'Why don't you come one day and talk to the foreman. If there's anything going, he'll be able to help you.'

'Thanks, I will. What's his name?'

'Len Yates. He's not a bad bloke, as long as you keep your head down.'

'Are you going to see your aunt?'

241

'Yes, just got to take her a few bits in. Me mum does a lot of her shopping as she can't get out now.'

'Oh, I'm sorry to hear that.'

'Thanks.'

When they got to Meg's aunt's road, she said, 'Don't forget, come and see Len.'

'I will,' said Dolly as they parted. Suddenly, she had a spring in her step. She had something to look forward to. Meg wasn't a bad sort; in fact, she wished Tony could see that. But Dolly knew she had to keep all this to herself, just in case nothing came of it.

Dolly pushed open the front door to Penny's. 'Yoo-hoo! It's only me,' she called out.

'Hello, Dolly,' said Ivy, opening the kitchen door. 'Everything all right?'

'Yes, thanks.'

'Penny's not here.'

'What? Where's she gone?'

'Reg took her to the hospital.'

'Why? What's wrong?'

Ivy was grinning. 'Nothing. She wanted to show the doctor that she was standing, and wanted some advice.'

Dolly plonked herself into the armchair. 'I was really worried there, for a minute.'

'Sorry about that, but I'm so pleased for her. She really is trying to make some progress.'

'I know.'

'And it's all down to you.'

Dolly smiled. At least she had done something right for once. 'Tell Reg to let me know what happened and how she got on.'

'Course I will. They should be back soon; they've been there most of the afternoon.'

Dolly was pleased that her friend was trying to get on with her life. Now Dolly knew that she too had to start thinking about her future, regardless of what other people thought.

Chapter 23

Dolly had only been home a short while when she opened the front door to Reg.

'Hello, Reg. How did Penny get on today?'

'Can you come in to see Penny?' he replied.

Dolly was a little apprehensive; he didn't sound very happy. 'I'm just popping along to see Penny, Mum,' she shouted to her mother who was in the scullery preparing dinner.

'Don't be too long, dinner's nearly ready,' came back the reply.

When Dolly arrived in Penny's kitchen, she could see by the look on her friend's face that she was very pleased with herself.

'Dolly, come here.' Penny held out her arms, and when Dolly bent down, she was hugged. 'What would I do without you?'

'What did the doctor say?' asked Dolly when she was finally released from Penny and able to stand up.

'He was very pleased with me, and guess what? I managed to walk a few steps between the parallel bars, just holding on. It felt so funny being upright again and walking, even if it was only a few steps.' Tears were trickling down her face.

Dolly, too, had tears. 'I'm so pleased for you,' she managed to say. 'So all my nagging paid off?'

'The doctor said I should be very proud of you, and meself. I told him you were a bit of a nag.' Penny wiped her eyes.

Dolly also brushed away her tears. 'So, what's next?'

'I've just got to keep on doing what we did, and as my confidence grows, perhaps take a step or two and walk just holding on to your hand. Reg said you can come home early, any day, and as I get better at it, you can spend the whole day with me. I've got to go to the hospital, but Reg can take me there.' She clasped Dolly's hand. 'I am so grateful to you for being here and helping me, and making me see sense. Who knows, by the time Gail starts school, I might even be able to take her.'

'That would be wonderful,' was the only answer Dolly could give her friend.

Penny was bubbling, talking fit to burst. She was making plans and said, 'On Saturday, Reg will take us up West. We'll go to that café again, and we can tell the owner what happened the last time we were there. Hopefully, Reg will pick us up on time.' She looked up at her husband. Her eyes were full of love and affection.

Dolly knew she had to say something about Saturday, but was reluctant to burst Penny's bubble. Should she cancel going out with Harry? Her mind was going over and over.

'I don't think Dolly can make it,' said Reg,

glaring at her.

'Why's that? Have you got a date or something?' asked Penny. 'I'm sure Tony won't mind. You can always go out with him any time.'

'I'm not going out with Tony,' Dolly said softly.

'You look very guilty. So who *are* you going out with?'

'I'm going to see a show with Harry.'

'Who the bloody hell is Harry?' Penny was clearly very cross.

'He's that copper that's been sniffing around,' said Reg. 'You know, the one who drove you both home that time.'

'What?' said Penny. 'You're going out with a copper? So cancel it.'

'I can't. He's booked the seats.'

'He's more important than me then?'

'No, course he isn't. We can go shopping next week.'

'I want to go this Saturday.'

Dolly was getting annoyed with her friend, but knew she mustn't say too much. Penny was being very difficult. 'I'm really sorry, Pen.'

'So when was you going to tell me about this little arrangement?'

Dolly didn't answer.

'Take me into the bedroom, Reg, before I say something I shouldn't.'

Reg turned the wheelchair round.

'I never thought you'd go out with a copper,' Penny said as she and Reg left the room.

Dolly slumped into the armchair.

Ivy, who was sitting opposite, hadn't said a word until now. She went over to Dolly and put

245

an arm around her. 'Don't take on so, love. She'll calm down. You know how het up she gets when things don't go her way.'

Dolly began crying. 'I didn't mean to upset her,' she sobbed. 'All I'm doing is going to see a show. Is it that bad for me to want go out?'

'Of course it's not,' said Ivy. 'You're young, and you should be going out and enjoying yourself.'

'I wish everybody thought like that.'

'The trouble is, they all think they know what's best for you.'

'I made a big mistake once and now they won't let me forget it.'

'Give 'em time, love. Give 'em time.'

'I'd better go home. If Penny wants me, she knows where I am.'

'Go on, love. And don't worry too much about it.'

Reluctantly, Dolly went home. The last thing she wanted to do was upset her friend. Couldn't they all see that she only wanted to go out with someone different for a change?

'So how did Penny get on at the hospital?' asked Grace when her daughter walked in.

'Very well, it seems.'

'You don't look very happy about it,' said her mother, putting her knitting to one side.

'She's very angry with me for not being able to go shopping with her on Saturday.'

'Oh dear.'

Dolly sat in the armchair. 'I can't believe all the fuss that me going out is causing.'

'It's because we've all got your happiness at heart, love.'

'I think that a lot of this is because we all live and work too close together. Perhaps I should think of changing my job, and mix with different people.'

'Where do you think you might go?'

'I've been thinking about going to Peek Freans. I saw Meg the other day and she said they're looking for girls.'

Surprised, Grace looked at Dolly. 'Would you be happy stuck in a factory all day?'

'I don't know till I try.'

'You're more or less your own boss at the moment. It won't be the same.'

'I know. But at least I'll be with other girls. It can get very lonely being on your own all day with no one to talk to.'

Grace was inclined to agree, but chose not to say anything.

As Dolly stared into the fire, watching the coals gently settle, she made up her mind. She would go to Peek Freans and see if there was a job going, and she wouldn't say anything to anyone till she found out.

After a restless night, Dolly made up her mind to go along to Peek Freans on her way to work.

'You're up early,' said her mother when Dolly walked into the kitchen.

'Yes I'm going along to see Meg, and to find out a bit more about a job. If I leave it till later, Reg might come into the office and offer to bring me home. I can't tell him I'm going to see about another job, can I?'

'No, I suppose not,' said Grace.

247

Dolly made her way to Drummond Road, hoping to find Meg amongst the many workers as they went into the factory. She noted that they all seemed to be happy and chatting. Could she be one of them soon?

'Dolly! Dolly Taylor!' Meg called out, coming up to her. 'What you doing here this time of the morning?'

'Hello, Meg,' said Dolly. 'I've come to see if there's any jobs on offer.'

'Let's go and see, shall we?'

'What? Now?'

'Why not?' Meg grabbed Dolly's arm. 'I know the boss is in. He always arrives first to make sure the machines are up and running before the rest of us get in. He's not a bad bloke as long as you keep the work going.'

Dolly was amazed at the vast amount of huge machines that spanned the endless walkways. She followed Meg as they went up the stairs to the office.

Meg knocked on a glass door. 'Mr Yates,' she said, pushing open the door. 'Is it all right if we come in?'

Mr Yates looked up. Dolly was surprised to see that he wasn't as old as she thought he might be. Meg had said that he'd been with the firm for years. He must have started when he was very young.

'Come in, Meg. What can I do for you?'

'My mate, Dolly, here, is looking for a job.'

'Hello, Dolly.'

She smiled at him.

'So where are you working now?'

248

'In an office, for a building firm.'

'And why do you want to leave them?'

Dolly thought that to say she was lonely sounded a bit feeble, so she said, 'It's a one-man band, and I think his wife might be coming back to work for him soon.'

Meg quickly looked at Dolly, but said nothing.

'I see. I can give you an application form. You will need to have a medical. Do you think your boss will give you a reference?'

'I would think so.'

'If we take you on, you will be working on the machines. Do you think you would like that?'

'Expect I could get used to it.'

Mr Yates opened a drawer in his desk, and handed Dolly some papers. 'Fill these in and bring them back to me.'

'Thank you,' she said, taking them from him.

'Bye for now.' Mr Yates stood up and shook her hand.

'Bye,' she said.

When they were back outside the factory, Dolly said, 'Well, that didn't seem so bad.'

'So what d'you think?' asked Meg. 'Would you like it here?'

'I don't know.'

'It's very noisy when all these machines get going.'

'It'll certainly make a change from being quiet all day.'

Meg put her arm though Dolly's. 'A word of warning: you'll have to watch Len Yates; he's a bit of a ladies' man.'

Dolly laughed. 'A bloke is the last thing I want

in my life.'

'I know. But I think you're daft, cos if I could get Tony Marchant into my life, well I'd be a very happy bunny.'

Dolly said goodbye and went to work.

It had been another long boring day in the office, and Dolly was waiting for Reg to arrive with the wages sheets and money. She would then be able to fill the envelopes. She had started to fill in the application form for what she hoped would be her new job, but she was worrying about getting a reference from Reg. She decided she would wait till she had actually got the promise of a new job before she said anything. The papers were in her bag, and she would finish them that evening. Maybe this was the change she needed. *Who knows*, she thought, *hopefully, it will be for the better.*

She was standing at the window when she saw Reg's van pull into the yard.

'Hello, Reg. Is everything all right?' she asked him when he walked into the office.

'Everything's fine. I just thought I'd take you home.'

'What about the wages?'

'Bring the wages sheets and the envelopes. We can do those at home.'

'They're all done.'

'Good. Ready?'

When they were both in the van, Reg said, 'Penny's really sorry about the way she went off yesterday.'

'That's all right. I know she's under a lot of pressure.'

'That's still no excuse. You should be able to do what you want.'

Dolly didn't answer.

'Anyway, can you come in tonight and let her be nice to you?'

'I suppose so.'

'I've asked Tony to come as well. We can play cards for a bit. D'you remember? We used to like doing that some evenings before we both got called up.'

Dolly nodded.

'I'll get a couple of bottles of beer in, and some lemonade, so you girls can have a shandy. What d'you say?'

'That'll be nice.' Dolly wondered why Reg was suddenly being nice, and harping back to how things were before they went off with the army.

'Come in about seven.'

'What about the wages?'

'We can do them first.'

'OK.' Dolly was very suspicious about this. She was pleased when Reg pulled into Wood Street. When she got out of the van, she called out, 'See you at seven.'

'Look forward to it,' he said.

When she went indoors, she said, 'Hello, Mum. I'm going to Penny's tonight.'

'Is everything all right, then?'

'Reg gave me a lift home. He said he wants me and Tony to go in for a game of cards.'

Her mother smiled. 'That's how it used to be. A lot of water has flowed under the bridge since those days.'

'It certainly has,' Dolly said nonchalantly. She

251

was also wondering if Reg would let slip about his gambling habit.

'Did you manage to get along to the factory?'

'Yes, and I've got an application form to fill in and take back to a Mr Yates.'

'When are you going to do that?'

'I'll get around to it sometime.'

Dolly had changed her clothes and was now watching the clock. There was no way she was going to Penny's before the agreed time. She waited till the clock struck seven.

'See you later, Mum,' she called out as she left the house.

She still felt very uneasy about seeing Penny, and was unsure whether to knock and wait to be invited in or just to walk in as she had always done. The decision was taken out of her hands when Tony followed her through the front gate.

'Hello, Doll. You waiting for me?'

'Of course.'

She pushed the front door; it was open.

'Hello, Dolly, love...Tony,' welcomed Ivy, coming into the passage. She was holding Gail. 'I thought I heard voices. They're in the kitchen. I'll be along; I'm just putting her down.'

'Thanks,' said Dolly and Tony together.

Dolly looked at the sleeping baby. 'She's gorgeous. Makes you feel as if you want to eat her.'

'I don't think Penny would approve of that,' said Tony, noticing the way Dolly was looking at Gail.

'Come on in,' said Reg, opening the kitchen door. 'Drink, Tone?'

'Please.'

'What about you, Dolly?'

'Yes, please.' Dolly looked at Penny, who was sitting in her chair. Should she kiss her as she always did when she walked in?

The problem was taken away from her when Penny held out her arms. 'Come here and give us a kiss, you big lump.'

Dolly went and held her friend tight. 'Not so much of the big lump.'

'I'm sorry I gave you a bad time,' whispered Penny. 'Me and my big mouth.'

Dolly didn't reply. She thought it best not to mention it. She didn't want to spoil the evening.

'That's it, I'm off,' said Tony, throwing his cards on the table.

'Spoilsport,' said Penny, grinning.

'It's all right for you; you've been winning.'

Penny counted the money that was sitting in front of her. 'Four pence,' she said. 'What can I buy with that?'

Dolly laughed.

'It's all right for you, too,' said Tony, grinning at Dolly. 'You've also taken some of my hard-earned cash.'

'Right, all together,' said Reg. 'Ah...'

Everybody joined in, and then fell about laughing.

'I must go as well,' said Dolly. 'Just look at the time. It's all right for you,' she said, looking at Penny. 'You don't have to get up for work in the morning.' As soon as she said it, she knew it was the wrong thing. All evening, she had been on her guard and had been careful of what she said, in case it might shatter the fragile atmosphere.

'I only wish I did,' said Penny.

'I'm sorry, Pen. I didn't mean anything.' She knew she had to keep this light-hearted. 'Besides, it might not be too long now before you're itching to get back to work again.'

Dolly noted that Penny quickly looked at Reg. Was it a knowing look? Was she thinking of going back to the office? It was then that she remembered they hadn't done the wages, and Reg hadn't said anything about them. Perhaps he'd do them tomorrow – that's if he had the money.

'D'you know, I've really enjoyed meself tonight,' said Penny. 'It was just like old times. We must do it again soon.'

'I dunno if I could afford it,' said Tony, laughing. He kissed her cheek. 'And I've enjoyed it as well, but I must be off. Besides, you girls need your beauty sleep.'

'Cheeky bugger,' said Penny.

'You coming, Dolly?'

'Yes.' She gathered up her handbag. After the goodbye kisses, they left.

When they were outside, Dolly said. 'We didn't get our wages, did we?'

'No. Have you done them?'

'I've done the envelopes, but Reg didn't give me the money for them. He said we would do it tonight.'

'He must have forgotten.'

'That's if he had the money.'

'Don't worry your pretty little head about it. He'll probably bring it round in the morning.'

'I hope so.'

'I'll walk you to your door,' said Tony.

'You daft apeth. I only live down the road.'

'I know. It's just that I want to do this.' He took Dolly in his arms and gave her a long and loving kiss.

Dolly clearly enjoyed it and didn't push him away.

'Thank you,' Tony said. 'D'you know, I had a great time tonight. It was just like the old days.'

'Yes, it was, but please, Tony, don't get any ideas. I'm very fond of you, but nothing more.'

'We shall see.' He gave her a peck on the cheek, and walked away whistling 'Some Enchanted Evening'.

Dolly pulled the key through the letter box and let herself in. There was just the light on in the passage, and the kitchen door was closed, so she knew her parents were in bed. She, too, went to her bedroom.

As she snuggled down, she thought about that evening. Why hadn't they done the wages? Was Penny going to do them? After all, it was only putting the money in the envelopes. Was Penny thinking about going back to work? If so, it would be all the better for Dolly to get a good reference.

She gently touched her lips. She had enjoyed Tony's kiss. It wasn't wild and passionate, just gentle and loving. It had been a long while since she had been kissed like that. Now, she had tomorrow evening to look forward to, and it could be something very different.

Chapter 24

In the office, the following morning, Dolly was patiently waiting for the hands on the clock to move to twelve. She would then be able to leave the office and take the questionnaire to Mr Yates. If she was offered the job, she knew she would have to tell Reg, and ask for a reference. That was something she wasn't looking forward to. Last night had been just like old times, with plenty of laughter and joking about. Nobody had mentioned about her going out with Harry tonight, and things seemed to be getting back to how they used to be. Did she want all that to end? This could be the start of a new beginning for her, but was that really what she wanted? Her mind was in turmoil; she really didn't know what she wanted to do. She was surprised that Reg hadn't been in to see her. She still hadn't been paid. What had happened to the wages? Had Penny done them?

At last, it was twelve o'clock. She put on her hat, and left the office. She was just locking the door when Reg's van turned quickly into the yard. He jumped out and jogged up to Dolly.

'I'm so glad I caught you.'

'What's wrong? Anything happened to Penny?' Her friend was always the first person Dolly thought of when something out of the ordinary happened.

'No. Penny's fine. It's just that I forgot to give out

the wages last night, so I thought I'd better do it this morning while everybody was still at work, just in case someone was going out before I had the chance to hand over the money. I've just come from the site, so do you want a lift home, or are you off somewhere?' He handed Dolly her wages.

'Thanks,' she said, putting them straight into her handbag. 'If you're going home, I'll come with you.' She smiled to herself. Once again she wasn't going to do what she wanted. Why didn't she have the nerve to refuse a lift and go to see Mr Yates?

'There's that bit extra I promised you.'

'Thank you, but I told you, I didn't need to be paid for helping my friend.'

'I know.'

Dolly was still wondering where Reg had got the money from. Had Penny filled the envelopes?

'That was a good night, last night,' said Reg. 'We must do it again this Friday.' He turned his head slightly towards her. 'That's if you're not doing something else.'

'That would be nice.'

Dolly wondered what would happen if she got the job at Peek Freans. Would they still want her around?

She felt very awkward as she sat next to Reg in the van. So many things seemed to be happening. After tonight, she didn't think she would be seeing Harry again, so that could be one hurdle over with. Then, next week, all she had to do was visit Mr Yates and wait and see what that would bring.

There was little conversation during the journey

home, and Dolly was relieved when they turned into Wood Street. 'Thanks for the lift, Reg.'

'See you later,' he called after her as she opened her front door.

Dolly decided not to reply.

When she was in the kitchen, she opened her wage packet. She gasped when she saw that Reg had given her an extra ten shillings. It wasn't on her wages slip. Why did he give her so much? She thought she might get five shillings, but ten? She was still staring at it when her mother walked in from the yard.

'Just been putting the sheets through the mangle and hanging 'em on the line. I hope they dry. I hate wet washing draped everywhere. You all right, love?'

'Yes, thanks. Just a bit shocked, that's all.'

'Why? What's happened?'

'Reg has given me ten bob for helping Penny.'

'Ten bob? That's a lot of money just for helping someone.'

'I know. It's not on me wages slip.' She handed the ten-shilling note to her mother.

'I can't take all of this.'

'I said I'd give it to you to help you with your money problem.'

'I know, but ten shillings.'

Dolly grinned. 'Go on, take it, before I change me mind.'

'But...'

'What's really worrying me is what he will say if I get this job.'

Grace pulled out a chair from under the table and sat down. 'I don't know, love. Are you still going for it?'

Dolly nodded. 'I've got to get this back to Mr Yates.' She held out the application form. 'But it'll have to wait till Monday now.'

'I'm sure everything will work out all right. Thanks for this, love,' said her mother, putting the ten-shilling note in her overall pocket.

Dolly spent the afternoon getting ready for her big night out. After she had washed her hair, she sorted out what she was going to wear. She decided on a black straight skirt and pale pink long-sleeved blouse. She needed to look smart, but not over the top. She was still a bit apprehensive about going out with Harry. She wasn't sure if they had enough to talk about. Could Reg be right? Had Harry asked her out because he wanted to talk about the business? Well, she would know by the end of the evening, but for now, she was just going to enjoy herself.

She wasn't sure what women wore for a night at the theatre. She still had a pair of nylons that she'd brought back with her from America. Taking them out of the drawer, she sat and admired them. They were so fine and delicate-looking. She only hoped they wouldn't get a ladder in them, as this was her last pair. Clothes were still rationed and nylons were hard to get, as well as expensive. She thought it a pity that it wasn't a fine day. She still had to wear her only coat, but she would be able to take it off in the restaurant and the theatre. She was now beginning to get excited. Harry would be here for her in two hours.

'You look very nice,' said Grace when Dolly went into the kitchen.

'Thank you.'

'Is Harry picking you up here?'

'Yes.' Dolly looked at the clock. 'He said he'd be here about five. I'll go in the front room and look out for his car.'

'OK, love.'

Dolly put on her small black hat and, picking up her handbag, went into the front room to look out of the window. She was very nervous. It wasn't five o'clock yet and all sorts of fears were going thought her mind. What if he couldn't make it? What sort of fool would she look, then?

It wasn't long before Harry's car slowly drew to a stop outside the house.

'Bye, Mum,' Dolly shouted as she went out the front door.

'Bye, love. Have a good time.'

Harry was out of his car and opening the passenger door. 'Your carriage awaits, madam.'

Dolly smiled. 'Thank you.'

'You look very nice,' said Harry, settling down behind the wheel.

'Thank you.'

'Where would you like to eat?'

'I don't mind. Did you have anywhere in particular?'

'No, not really.'

As Harry pulled away, he asked, 'How does Lyons Corner House suit you? I don't think any of the better restaurants are open till later, and I'm not keen on eating after nine. So, is that all right with you?'

'That's fine by me. I don't like eating too late, either.'

He turned his head towards her and smiled.

Dolly thought that Harry looked very different out of uniform, and when he smiled, he had a lovely warm look about him. 'I'm really looking forward to tonight,' she said.

'Good. So am I. How's your friend, Penny, these days?'

'She's fine, thank you.' Was this the moment he was going to ask about Reg?

'I expect she's very pleased that her husband's home.'

'Yes, she is.' Dolly stiffened slightly.

'Are you all right?'

'Yes, thanks.' She waited for Harry to pursue with this line of conversation.

'Do you miss America?' he asked instead.

'I miss all the lovely things the stores had. They didn't suffer from any shortages at all through the war. I couldn't believe some of the things I saw in the New York stores.'

'That must have been very exciting.'

'It was.'

'I hope to travel when all the restrictions are lifted.'

'Where would you like to go?'

'America. When you see how those cops work, it must be very thrilling.'

'It's not how the films show it.'

'I don't suppose it is, but I would still like to travel, and America would be my first choice.'

'It's such a vast country. They think nothing of driving miles just for something small.'

'It's also a very beautiful country.'

'I would have liked to have seen a lot more of it, but it wasn't to be.'

'It must have been a great disappointment to you when your marriage went wrong.'

'Yes, it was,' Dolly said softly.

'I'm sorry. I didn't mean to upset you.'

'That's all right.'

They continued the journey in silence, till Harry said, 'I'll just park along here.'

'I didn't think there would be so much traffic at this time of the evening.'

'I expect everybody's been shopping. You wait till petrol comes off ration, then we'll see a lot more cars on the road.'

'I want to learn to drive.'

'Do you? Well, it might be a good idea to apply for your licence before everyone else decides to.' Harry pulled the car into the kerb. 'Right, this'll do. Lyons is just over there.' He got out of the car and was round Dolly's side before she had a chance to get out.

Harry held her elbow as they crossed the road. When they reached the other side, he changed over and took her other arm, so that he walked next to the kerb.

Dolly was impressed. It was the sort of thing that Joe would do. Years ago, the men always walked on the outside of the pavement to stop the ladies getting splashed by the horse-drawn carriages as they passed. It was old-fashioned; not many English men did it these days, but Dolly was secretly thrilled by the gesture.

When they were seated in the café, they studied

the menu.

'What do you fancy?' asked Harry.

'I don't know. It all looks very nice. What are you going to have?'

'I like the pies.'

'I'll have the same as you then.'

The waitress took their order, and Dolly sat back. 'This is very nice of you, Harry. Thank you.'

'It's my pleasure to take out a nice young lady. Now, about this driving, who's going to teach you?'

'I don't know. I was hoping Tony would, but he's worried about his car, and the petrol, of course.'

'I could teach you.'

'Oh, no. Thanks, all the same, but I can't expect you to be bothered with me. Besides, I might ruin your car. I was going to ask Reg if I could have a go in his van, but Tony said I'd have to learn to double-declutch, whatever that is.'

Harry gave a little laugh. 'He's quite right. But if you get a more up-to-date car, you won't have to do that.'

Dolly was relieved when their meal arrived as it put an end to that conversation.

When they had finished their meal, Harry ordered two coffees. 'Sugar?' he asked. When Dolly nodded, he passed her the bowl. 'I forgot to tell you, we're going to the Victoria Palace to see The Crazy Gang. Do you like them?'

'I've never seen them, but I've heard them on the wireless. They're very funny.'

'I've been told the show is very entertaining.'

Dolly was thrilled when they finally stood in front of the theatre. It looked so very grand.

'Have you been here before?' asked Harry as they joined the queue of people waiting to go in.

She shook her head. 'Dad took me to the Palladium, once, before the war. I don't remember what we saw as I was terrified of falling off me seat. I was only little. We were up in the gods and my legs dangled. It's so high; I really did think I would fall over the edge.'

Harry laughed. 'Well, you don't have to worry about that today as our seats are downstairs.'

'In the stalls?'

'Yes.'

'They must have cost quite a bit.'

'I told you, they came with the job.'

'That must have been a very happy customer.'

'I don't know about that. He'd bought them before he went to court.'

Dolly laughed. 'He should have waited till after he'd been sentenced.'

'That would have done us out of a great night out.'

The queue began slowly moving. Dolly could feel the excitement mounting. Harry had bought a programme, and Dolly was surprised when he produced some sweet coupons for a small box of chocolates. When they settled into their seats, he took her hand and asked, 'Happy?'

'I should say so. Thank you so much.'

At last, the orchestra started up, and Dolly was the happiest she had felt for a long while.

At the end of the show, Dolly was sad that all too

soon it was over.

'Would you like to go for a drink?' asked Harry as they slowly walked along the street.

Dolly felt as if she was in a dream. London was really lit up now. It was so different from the dark days of the war. The lights; the people; everybody looked happy and seemed to be enjoying themselves as they walked along laughing and talking.

'Yes, please,' she said at last. She didn't want this evening to end. She was surprised at how easy it was to talk to Harry. He made her laugh at his stories of what went on in a police station with some of the drunks and people who weren't quite right.

When they settled in the pub, he was smiling as he walked towards her with her shandy and his beer. 'Are you sure you wouldn't like anything stronger?'

'No, thank you. This is fine. Do you live near the police station?' Dolly asked, for something to say.

'Not too far. I live with my sister and her husband. He's also in the police, so she knows all about shifts and things. Mum and Dad live in Wales. We went there at the beginning of the war, but I had to get away. It was like living in the back of beyond. I'm much more of a London boy. Anyway, have you enjoyed yourself, this evening?'

'Yes, very much. I thought the show was lovely, and very funny.'

'If you like, we could do this again.'

'I'm not sure about that.'

'Give it a while, but promise me you'll think about it.'

'I will,' said Dolly. Although she had enjoyed Harry's company, she was very unsure of her future, and did not want to commit herself to another relationship just yet.

She thought she must be smiling all the way home, and when they drew up at her front door, Harry was quickly out of the car and letting her out.

'Thank you for a really lovely evening,' said Dolly.

'It was my pleasure.'

Was Harry going to kiss her goodnight? Did she want him to? When she pulled the key through the letter box, he was standing right behind her. 'I'm afraid I can't ask you in for a drink. Mum and Dad are in bed.'

'That's all right. I just want to make sure you get in OK.'

Dolly pushed open the front door and with her back to Harry, said, 'Goodnight, and thank you once again for a lovely evening.'

'Goodnight, Dolly. I do hope we can do this again.' With that, he turned and walked back to his car.

As he drove away, Dolly felt disappointed that he hadn't made a move to kiss her. She did miss being kissed, and being loved.

Harry, too, was thinking about their evening. He liked Dolly very much, but knew he had to take his time with her. How he had wanted to kiss her and hold her tight. Hopefully, that time would soon come.

Chapter 25

'Did you have a nice time?' asked her mother, as Dolly pushed open the kitchen door.

'Yes, thanks. You're still up?' Dolly was surprised to see her parents sitting in front of the fire.

'Been listening to a play,' said Grace, leaning over to the dresser and turning the wireless off.

Dolly looked at her suspiciously. Had there been a play, or were they just waiting up for her?

'So how was it?' asked Grace.

'Lovely. The show was wonderful.'

As usual, Jim was sitting in his armchair, looking through his newspaper. 'So, what was it like going out with a copper?' he asked, putting his paper to one side.

'Harry bought me dinner, chocolates, and a programme.' Dolly opened her handbag. 'Here, have a look at what we saw.' She handed her father the programme. 'We were in the stalls.'

'Very posh,' Jim said, quickly glancing through it. 'I must say, it does look very nice.' He leaned forward and handed the programme to Grace.

She also had a quick look through and handed the programme back to Dolly. Then, rolling up the ball of wool that was on her lap, she pushed the needles through it and put it in her knitting bag.

'It was,' said Dolly, disappointed that her parents hadn't shown more interest. 'I'm going to bed now.'

'Do you want a cup of cocoa?' asked her mother.

'No, thanks.'

As she lay in bed, Dolly thought about the evening. She really had enjoyed Harry's company. He was nice to talk to, and she was pleased that he hadn't asked about Reg's business or pushed for any more dates. He had seemed very interested in her time in America, and it seemed he was keen to go there too.

The following morning, Dolly didn't know whether to go and see Penny or not. Would her friend be angry with her for not going shopping yesterday? Would she be interested in hearing what a wonderful evening Dolly had had? Why, after all these years of friendship, was she worrying about what Penny might think? Why couldn't she lead her own life?

Dolly knew why. She still felt guilty at going away and not being there when Penny was struck down with polio.

Later, when Reg called and asked her to go and see Penny, the decision to visit was made for her.

'Did you have a nice time last night?' Penny asked, as soon as Dolly walked in.

'Yes, thanks.' Dolly was very careful not to elaborate.

'So what was the copper like?' asked Reg.

'Very nice.'

'You seeing him again?' asked Penny.

'We didn't make any more arrangements.'

'If you're not busy today, I thought you might help me have a go at trying to walk again. So will you help?'

'Of course I will. You know that. You don't have to ask.' *So that's the end of the conversation about my night out,* thought Dolly. 'Do you want to have a go now?'

Penny nodded.

Dolly was trying hard to keep her thoughts under control. Why hadn't Penny asked about the show? She knew Penny loved anything like that. It was obvious she was still very angry. 'Shall I get your boots and callipers?'

'They're in the bedroom, ready.'

'OK. Let's go.' Dolly opened the kitchen door and Penny wheeled her way through.

Dolly put Penny's boots on, while Reg just stood and watched. She then tried to sit Penny up and strap the callipers round her waist.

'Give me a hand,' said Dolly to Reg. She was getting angry with both of them, as they didn't seem to want to help. Dolly stood up. 'Are you going to help me, Reg, or not?'

He moved forward and, between them, they got Penny up on to her feet. She stood for a moment or two on her own, and then tried to throw her leg forward as if walking, but she lost her balance. Dolly and Reg quickly caught her.

'Penny, that was wonderful!' said Dolly. 'You're certainly getting there. When do you go back to the hospital?' She lowered a smiling Penny onto the bed.

'We can go tomorrow. Reg has got to have the last of his stitches out, anyway.'

'Do you want to have another go now?'

'In a minute. Reg, can you get us a cup of tea?

Then we can do it again.' She looked at Dolly. 'That's if you haven't got a date or something.'

Dolly noticed the sting in her friend's voice. 'No. I am at your command.' She knew her reply was facetious, but she didn't care. She was hurt by Penny's attitude.

After they had finished drinking their tea, Penny said, 'Right, let's have another go.'

Dolly and Reg pulled Penny up and she leant on their shoulders. She tried to swing her right leg forward, but it wouldn't move. She threw herself back on the bed, where she just lay and cried. 'I feel so bloody useless,' she sobbed.

Reg put his arms round her neck. 'Don't worry, love, it'll come,' he soothed. 'Remember how thin your legs are. The doctor said you've got to build up your muscles.'

'That's all very well for him to say. He ain't the one who's trying.'

'I know, love, I know.'

Dolly stood and watched as Reg held Penny tightly. Feeling like a spare part, she silently left the room and headed back to her own house. As she made her way along the road, she noticed Tony walking towards her.

'Hello, Doll. Just thought I'd come and ask if you had a good time last night?'

'Yes, thank you. Why is everyone so interested in me having a night out with someone?'

'It's cos he's a copper. What is it? You look upset.'

Dolly could feel the tears welling up. 'I am,' she said.

'What about?'

'I can't say.'

Tony put his arm around her. 'Now come on, you can tell me anything.'

Dolly felt the tears silently run down her cheeks.

'Tell you what; we'll go for a drive.' He very gently steered her along the road to his house. 'Come in, while I get me keys.'

Dolly stood in the passage, and Tony was back almost immediately. They were silent as he drove them to the park. When they arrived, he said, 'Do you want to walk, or just sit and talk?'

'Can we just sit in the car for a bit?'

'Course we can. Now come on, what's the trouble?'

With that, Dolly put her hands to her face and burst into tears.

Tony put his arm around her and gave her a piece of rag that he kept in the car to clean the windows when they steamed up. 'Sorry, but it ain't very clean.'

She managed to give him a watery smile. 'Thanks.'

'Feel better now?'

She nodded. 'Thank you.'

'So, what's this all about?'

'I've just been in with Reg and Penny, as she wanted to try to walk again.'

'And what's wrong with that?'

'It was their attitude towards me. They didn't want to know anything about me going out last night.'

'You are daft. What was wrong with that? They were probably worried that you might get too interested in this copper.'

'I ain't a child, you know.'

Tony laughed. 'We all know what a sucker you are for a bloke in uniform.'

'What? Joe was a very nice person, even if he was weak where his mother was concerned. I made one mistake and that's going to be with me for the rest of my life.'

She went to open the car door, but Tony stopped her.

'I think you're being very silly,' he said.

'Thanks!'

'Anyway, how did Penny get on?'

'She's really trying.'

'So how about you stop feeling sorry for yourself and concentrate on helping Penny?'

'Do you think I'm feeling sorry for meself?'

'Not everyone can get excited about you going out one night. It's not the be-all and end-all, is it?'

'S'pose not.' Dolly now felt foolish, but said, 'That's not the only thing that's worrying me, though.'

'What other little problem have you got? Come on, you can tell Doctor Tony.'

'I'm thinking about getting a job at Peek Freans.'

'Yes, you've been thinking about that on and off for quite a while now.'

'I went to see the manager and I got an application form to fill in, but I'll need a reference from Reg.'

'Right, I can see your problem. Do you think he'll give you one?'

'I don't know. What if Penny says no?'

'She wouldn't be like that. You two have been

friends all your lives.'

'I know, but at the moment I'm really out of favour.'

'I can't see her stopping you from getting another job.'

'I hope not. Oh Tony, what am I gonna do?'

With that, Dolly began to cry again.

Tony leant across the seat and took her in his arms. 'Please don't cry, Doll. Things ain't that bad.'

'But what if I don't get the job? What will happen then? I'll never get another one without a reference.' Dolly gave a big sob.

'Get the job first, before you start worrying about Reg. Come here, you daft apeth.' He lifted her tear-stained face and gently kissed her lips, softly at first, and then, as Dolly didn't resist, he became more ardent.

When their lips parted, Tony said, 'Dolly, I do love you, and I hate to see you so upset. Please let me help.'

Dolly wiped her tears away with the back of her hand. 'I'm sorry, Tony; I shouldn't burden you with my troubles.'

'I keep telling you, it's no burden being with you. Let me take you out tonight and try to sort something out.'

'How can you do that?'

'We'll think of something.'

'All right, but can we go home now?'

'Of course.' Tony was pleased that Dolly didn't get cross over the kiss. Perhaps she did have feelings for him again. He knew he mustn't hurry her, but he was certain that they would marry one day.

Only time would tell.

Although she was comforted by Tony's kiss, Dolly knew she had to tell him that things could never be the same as they were before. She was very fond of Tony, but knew she would never marry him.

That evening, after dinner, Dolly helped her mother with the washing-up. 'Mum, I'm going out with Tony tonight for a little while.'

'That's all right, love. You don't have to tell me.'

'I know. But I thought I'd let you know, just in case Reg comes and asks where I've gone.'

'He won't do that, will he?'

'I don't know. Penny was a bit upset when I left them this morning.'

Dolly began putting the clean dishes away. She hadn't told her mother what had happened; just that Penny had tried to walk. She had been very upset by her friend's attitude, but now she'd had some time to think about it, and talk it over with Tony, she realised she had sounded childish and pathetic.

'You've got to give that girl a medal for trying,' said Grace, interrupting Dolly's thoughts.

Dolly smiled. 'She's determined to walk before Gail starts school.'

'Well, at least she's got a few years, then.'

When Tony came round to collect Dolly, he asked, 'Where would you like to go?'

'I don't really know.'

'As it's a nice evening, we could go for a drive to Greenwich. We'll have time to walk for a bit, before it gets dark.'

'Sounds nice. All right.'

When they got out of the car, they walked along hand in hand for a while.

'Mum had a letter from my cousin, Vera. D'you remember her? She became a nurse.'

'Course I do.'

'Well, she's coming down from Norfolk in a couple of weeks' time to see us for a few days. She said she's got a new fella. He's something in the bank. She said they've been seeing each other for a little while now.'

'That's smashing, Tony. Is she bringing him?'

'I don't know. I don't think so.'

'I bet your mum will be pleased to see her.'

'I should say so.' He laughed. 'You know me mum. Everything that can't be washed will be polished.'

'That's what mums do.'

'I know, but she's just me cousin, not flaming royalty.'

'Do you think she might marry this new fella?'

'Mum hopes so. If he's Mr Right for Vera, she'll be over the moon. That bloody war. It was so tragic when her first bloke got killed. Mum didn't think she'd get over it.'

'It ruined so many lives,' said Dolly, 'but life does have to go on.'

'Well, it certainly ruined ours,' said Tony.

Dolly gave a little shiver.

'You cold?' asked Tony.

'No.'

'Come on, let's go and get a cuppa.' Tony put his arm around Dolly and pulled her to him.

'Tony, what are you doing?'

'Trying to warm you up.'

'I'm fine, thanks.'

Dolly was worried that he was going to kiss her again as he'd done earlier that afternoon. She had enjoyed it, but she was frightened about getting too attached. She did like Tony, but she was terrified of falling in love with him again. She knew that mustn't happen.

Chapter 26

Back in the office on Monday morning, Dolly was busy typing up some invoices that Bert Edwards had put though the letter box over the weekend, when the phone rang.

'Hello, Dolly,' said Bert Edwards. 'Did you find the invoices I dropped off last night when I was round that way?'

'Yes, I did. I'm typing them up now.'

'Good. I'll try and pick them up later today as I'm looking at another big job that I hope Reg can take on.'

'That's no problem. Any idea what time you'll be here?'

'What time do you leave?'

'About five.'

'I should be able to get over before then.'

'OK.'

'Thanks, bye.' With that, he hung up.

Dolly put the receiver down. 'It had better be

before five, as I want to take my form back to Mr Yates,' she said to the phone.

At half past four, Dolly noticed Reg drive into the yard. She was surprised when he went to the back of the van, pulled down the ramp, and pushed Penny down it. She rushed outside. 'What are you two doing here?'

'We've just come from the hospital,' said Penny. 'We thought we'd take you home.'

'That would be lovely,' said Dolly, 'but I'm waiting for Mr Edwards to collect some invoices he asked me to type up.'

'I can take them,' said Reg. 'We went to the site before we came here. By the way, what do you think of my good looks, now?'

Reg turned his face to one side and Dolly could see that all the stitches had been removed.

'That's better,' she said. 'You look your handsome self once again.'

'Don't encourage him,' said Penny. 'And guess what I did today?'

'Let me see...' said Dolly, grinning.

'I walked halfway along the bars. It wasn't very far, but I did it.'

Dolly bent down and hugged her friend. 'Penny, I'm so proud of you,' she said, wiping away a few tears.

'Not as proud as I was. We've been there all day. It was very hard work and it took a bit of time, but I did it in the end, and that's all down to you. What would I do without you?' As she held Dolly close, she quietly said, 'I'm sorry if I was off with you yesterday, but truth is, I was a bit jealous. I would love to go to the theatre.'

Dolly stood up. Tears were trickling down her cheeks. *This is how things should be between us,* she thought. 'Would you like me to bring the programme in, or will it upset you?'

'I'd love to see it, and then you can tell me what the show was like.'

'Right,' said Reg, 'if you're ready, we can make our way home.'

Dolly was starting to think that taking the application form back to Mr Yates wasn't meant to be. Every time she thought she was free to go, something would come up and stop her from getting there. As she sat next to Reg in the van, she knew she could have said that she was going somewhere else. Was her guilty conscience still stopping her?

When Dolly arrived home from work, she rushed indoors to tell her parents how Penny had got on at the hospital.

'I bet she's as pleased as Punch,' said Jim.

'There'll be no stopping her now. She's such a brave girl,' said Grace, wiping away a stray tear with her hand.

'And Reg has had all his stitches out.'

'That's good,' said Grace.

When they had finished dinner and had washed up, Dolly walked into the kitchen and said, 'Penny wants to see my programme. She's hoping that when she can walk with just sticks, Reg will take her to the theatre.'

'It's a shame that people like her aren't allowed to do these things,' said Grace.

'It could be because it's a fire risk,' said Jim.

'Probably,' said Dolly. 'Anyway, I'll be off to see Penny in a minute. I want to find out more about the walking she did.'

'Course you do,' said Grace, smiling. 'It seems that all sorts of good things are coming to Wood Street.'

'Why? What else is new?' asked Jim as he took his jacket from the nail behind the kitchen door. He was off for his usual game of darts.

'I saw Tony's mum today,' said Grace. 'She's as pleased as Punch that Vera is visiting soon.'

'I know; Tony told me,' said Dolly. 'Did she tell you that Vera's going out with a man who works in a bank?'

'Yes,' said Grace. 'Sounds as if she's done all right for herself.'

'Cooee! It's only me,' Dolly said softly as she pushed open Ivy Smith's kitchen door.

'Hello, Dolly,' said Ivy. 'Sit yourself down. They're in their room seeing to Gail.'

'Is Gail all right?'

'She's fine. It's just that sometimes they want a bit of time on their own.'

'What do you think of what Penny did today?'

'That was wonderful. She's over the moon. And it's all down to you.'

'And you. You helped her to get started.'

Ivy smiled. 'Sometimes, I think they get a bit fed up with me being around all the time.'

'Now, what would they do without you? You've been marvellous.'

'I've only done what I think is helpful.'

Dolly could see that Ivy was feeling down. 'I know it's none of my business, but you look a bit sad. Is everything all right?'

279

'I'm fine.' She got up and went into the scullery.

Dolly followed her. 'Has something been said?'

Ivy filled the kettle. 'Reg was saying earlier that the government is going to be building new towns. If that happens, they might stand a chance of getting a house of their own.'

'Dad was talking about that; he'd seen it in the paper. It would be wonderful if Reg could get a house, but how far away would it be? What about his business?'

'Dunno.'

Dolly could see that Ivy was upset. 'Do you know where they're going to build these new towns?'

'No, but I daresay it'll be miles away in the country somewhere.'

'I reckon it'll be years before that happens. You know how these things are.'

'There's a lot of people who need houses, what with all the bombing and the so-called slum clearance. It was bound to happen.' Ivy gave Dolly a weak smile. 'I expect by then Gail will be walking and going to school... I can't imagine that little 'un going to school.'

Dolly reached out and gently patted Ivy's hand. 'Come and sit down.' Clearly, Ivy was worried that her son would move away from her. 'I expect you felt like this when Reg first started school.'

She gave Dolly a sad smile. 'And a right little bugger he was as well I can tell you. D'you know, he'd be crying all the way to school, saying he didn't want to go, then as soon as he saw his mates, he'd run off without so much as a kiss or a goodbye wave.'

'I suppose that's boys. They're not clingy like girls can be.'

The kitchen door opened and Penny came in, with Reg right behind.

'So what are you two nattering about?' asked Reg.

'You!' said his mother.

'Oh dear, now what have I done?'

Dolly laughed. 'I've been hearing all about you going to school.'

'I suppose I was a bit of a handful.'

'And as the only one, a bit spoilt, I expect,' said Penny. 'With two other brothers, me mum didn't have time or the patience to spoil any of us.'

'Please; you'll have me in tears soon,' said Reg, bending down and kissing Penny's cheek.

'I suppose you didn't turn out too bad,' Penny said lovingly.

'Thank you.'

'Now, Dolly,' said Penny, 'let's have a look at your programme. Reg has promised that he will take me to the theatre when I can walk with just me sticks.'

'First, I want to hear all about this trip to the hospital and you dashing about,' said Dolly.

'It'll be a while before I start dashing about, but give it time.'

For a long while, they sat and discussed Penny's day at the hospital, and then, Dolly's night out.

As Dolly walked home, her thoughts were still muddled. She wondered if she should stay working for Reg or make a move. 'I'll think about that tomorrow,' she said to herself, closing the front door behind her. Seeing her parents had gone to bed, she made her way upstairs.

On Tuesday, Dolly's day in the office had been very quiet, giving her the opportunity to mull things over. When it was almost five o'clock, she decided that it was time to make her move and take the application form back to Mr Yates.

She left work and made her way to the Peek Freans' factory. As she got near, she spotted Meg, who was busy talking to some of the other girls. Dolly didn't want to interrupt, but Meg caught sight of her.

'Dolly!' she called out, waving goodbye to the group and going to greet her. She took hold of Dolly's arm. 'Have you got the job?'

'I don't know. I'm just bringing the form back.'

'Well, you certainly took your time. I don't think that will go down very well.'

'What with one thing and another, I've just not been able to get here.'

'You should have brought it round to me. I could have taken it in for you. Still, no matter. Right, let's go and see the man.'

'Is he still here?' Suddenly, Dolly felt very nervous. Was she doing the right thing?

'D'you want me to come in with you?'

'No, thanks. I'll be all right on me own,' and off she went.

Meg waited for her, and when Dolly came out of the office, she asked, 'Well?'

'I've got to get a reference.'

'Will Reg give you one?'

'I hope so.'

As they walked home together, talking about many things, Meg said, 'Mum told me that Vera is coming to visit for the weekend soon. I bet Mrs M's pleased about that.'

'Yes, she is.'

'And she's bringing a man friend with her – lucky her.'

'They don't know for sure if she's bringing him.' Dolly thought that Meg's mother was better than the bush telegraph. She must have spent her day going around and winking out any information she could get from all and sundry.

'Mum reckons she'll be sorry when this rationing and queuing lark ends,' Meg continued, 'as she loves standing around and talking. How sad is that?'

'I expect a lot of women will feel that way.'

'Wasn't it a terrible shame about Vera's first bloke?'

'Yes, it was.'

'Well, if she has found someone else, then good luck to her. I need to find meself a bloke.'

'I'm surprised you haven't already got a fella,' said Dolly.

'It ain't for the want of trying. I'll tell you what; why don't you and me go to a dance one Saturday night? Some of the girls go to the Hammersmith Palais. There's quite a few tasty blokes, and the band's great. I've been with 'em a couple of times, but they was a bit too cliquey for me.'

'I'm surprised at that. You seem to fit in with most people.'

'I try, but I think sometimes I try a bit too hard and it puts 'em off.'

Dolly thought that was probably right.

'So how about it?'

Dolly thought about the fuss that going out with Harry had caused. Would going dancing have the same effect? 'I don't think so – not at the moment.'

'Well, perhaps we can make plans when you start here.'

Dolly thought that might be a bit of a problem. Did she really want to go out and about with Meg?

Chapter 27

Motorists were overjoyed when on Friday 26 May, and after ten years of rationing, petrol was finally off ration.

Tony had collected Dolly from work, and as he drove her home, he said, 'As it's Whitsun bank holiday on Monday and the weather looks fine, what say we go to the coast for the day on Sunday?'

'That'll be nice.'

'Bring yer cossie and we can go for a swim.'

'No, thank you. It'll be too cold.'

'Coward.'

'It would be nice if we asked Reg to bring Penny along as well.'

'Yeh, why not? He can follow with the van.'

As they drove home, they were surprised at the cars waiting at the petrol stations.

'Everybody's going mad. Look at that queue,' said Tony as they went past the line of cars.

'Have you got enough petrol for Sunday?' asked Dolly.

'Yeh, I used the last of me coupons in the week.'

Dolly settled back. This was going to be a lovely weekend.

That evening, Tony told Reg of their plans for Sunday.

'I'm all for it,' Reg said. 'How about you, Pen? Look, Tone, save taking your car, we can all go in the van. That way, we can even take Gail with us.'

Even though it was wearing out, Reg was very attached to his van.

'So, you'll have two to push along the front,' said Penny, her eyes sparkling with excitement.

'I'll see about doing us a few sandwiches,' said Dolly, 'although they might only be Spam.'

'Whatever it is, it'll taste great,' said Penny. 'It's been a long while since I've seen the sea.'

Dolly swallowed hard. Her friend had so much to look forward to.

On Sunday, they all made their way to Brighton.

Penny, in her wheelchair, and Gail, in her pram, were both strapped into the back of the van.

Dolly sat in the back with them and surveyed the happy scene. Penny looked blooming, and Gail was very good as she was being gently rocked. *This is how friends should be,* she thought.

'Bloody hell! Look at all this traffic,' said Reg.

'I thought it might be busy, but this is daft,' said Tony. 'I reckon every car what's roadworthy must be on the road today.'

'And by the looks of those on the side with steam coming out of 'em, some ain't very road-worthy at all.'

'I expect a lot of 'em have been on blocks while their owners have been away,' said Tony as they slowly made their way along the crowded roads.

At long last, they arrived at Brighton.

'Right, I'll park here,' said Reg, 'and then we can get Pen and Gail out. It's a bit of a way from the pier, but it's not too bad. Is this OK with you, Pen?'

'It's fine. Just the smell of the sea is wonderful.'

When they were out of the van, with all of the bags and paraphernalia that goes with a baby and a day out, they set off along the promenade.

'It's such a lovely day,' said Dolly as she pushed Gail along. Reg took charge of Penny.

'Wait till we can bring Gail to play on the beach,' said Penny, over her shoulder.

'She won't be able to make too many sand-castles here,' said Tony.

'No, we'll have to go to Ramsgate or some-where where it's nice and sandy,' said Penny.

They settled themselves on the beach with deckchairs, and relaxed. After they'd eaten their sandwiches, Tony asked Dolly if she fancied a walk.

'Why not?'

'We'll come back for you, Pen, and then we can walk along the pier and get a cup of tea. Will that be all right with you, Reg?' asked Tony.

'That'll be fine. I'll just sit here and close me eyes for a minute or two.'

'You sure you'll be all right on your own?' Dolly asked Penny.

Reg coughed.

'I ain't on me own. I've got me family round me,' said Penny.

'Course you have – sorry, Reg. Just as long as the tide don't come in and sweep you all into the sea... Bye,' said Dolly.

'See you later,' said Penny, as Tony and Dolly walked off.

Soon, Tony and Dolly were walking along hand in hand. Dolly hadn't objected when his hand took hold of hers.

'That was a funny thing to say about leaving Penny on her own,' said Tony.

'It's just that I was wondering; if they have to move, Reg will have a lot to shift. A pram and a wheelchair, it's not easy over those stones.'

'Stop worrying. They ain't kids.'

'I know. I'm sorry.'

'Just enjoy yourself. Take a deep breath and enjoy the sea air.'

'This is wonderful,' Dolly said. 'Thank you so much for suggesting this day out.'

'I ain't done nothing. I just sat next to Reg.'

'I know, and it's nice not to have anything to think about.'

As they walked back, they could see that Reg was busy changing Gail's nappy.

'He's certainly turned out to be a good dad,' said Tony.

'I think it's a case of having to be. Do you think he's given up gambling?'

'Don't know, but at least he spends more time

at work now.'

'You're back,' said Reg, putting Gail in her pram.

'Right. Who's ready for a cuppa?' said Tony.

'I am,' said Penny, 'and I fancy some fish and chips.'

'Now that sounds like a good idea,' said Tony.

'I'll put this lot in the van,' said Reg. 'We don't wanna walk about with smelly nappies.'

'OK,' said Tony, 'we'll slowly make our way to the pier.'

They walked along laughing at some of the fashions. Dolly was reminded of how she and Penny used to do that. Reg caught up with them and they made their way to a tea shop.

Later, when they were all settled in the van, they began the journey home.

'D'you know,' said Penny, 'I really feel I've caught the sun today. Do I look like it?' she asked Dolly.

Dolly laughed. 'You have got a bit of a red nose. I'll put some cream on it when we get home.'

'I'm just gonna make a bit of a detour,' said Reg.

'Why?' asked Tony. 'Not sure this old van will make it up Reigate Hill.'

'No, it's not that. I wanna go and look at this Crawley New Town.'

'Why?' asked Tony. 'You ain't thinking of moving, are you?'

'No, course not. I'm just nosey, that's all.'

Dolly looked at Penny, who didn't say a word.

They continued the journey in silence till Reg turned off the main road. They passed lots of houses in various stages of being built. He stopped the van and got out.

Tony was right behind him. 'You sure you're not thinking of moving?' he asked.

'No, I told you, I just want to have a look and see what they're like. Let's get Pen out; she'd like to have a nose around.'

Dolly stood by the van while Reg and Tony took out the pram and the wheelchair. She looked at Tony, who just shrugged.

They wandered around looking into half-built houses and some that were almost finished.

'These are wonderful,' said Penny as she pushed herself thought the open doorways. 'What's the bathroom like, Dolly?'

Dolly went upstairs. She stood and looked in wonder. These houses were lovely. 'Great,' she called. 'It's a pity you didn't bring your callipers, as you might have been able to get upstairs.'

'I tried that at home and very nearly fell on me face. Besides, I knew I wouldn't be able to get on the beach with 'em on.'

After a while, Reg said, 'Right, let's be off.'

Once they were all back in the van and going again, Reg asked, 'What do you think of them houses?'

'They're wonderful,' said Dolly. 'You ain't thinking of moving out this way, are you?'

'Nah, you have to have a job here.'

'So you've been enquiring about it then?' asked Tony.

'Nah, I read about it in the paper.'

All this time, Penny hadn't said anything.

'What did you think of 'em, Pen?' asked Dolly.

'They looked lovely, but I couldn't get up the stairs to go to the lav, could I?'

'I think they're building bungalows, so you wouldn't have any trouble then,' said Reg.

'You've certainly gone into it,' said Tony.

'Course I ain't. Just interested in the buildings, that's all.'

Dolly looked at Penny. Were they thinking of moving?

'I don't think your mum would be very happy if you moved away,' she said.

'Who said anything about moving?' Penny quickly said.

Suddenly for Dolly, the whole day's happiness had melted away.

When they finally arrived home, Penny said, 'I know I've not done a lot, but I feel worn out.'

'It's all that fresh air,' said Reg, opening the front door and pushing Penny into the passage.

'I'll bring Gail,' said Dolly.

'And I'll bring all the stuff in from the van,' said Tony.

'Did you have a nice time?' asked Ivy when they went into the kitchen.

'We've had a wonderful day,' said Penny. 'Mind you, I'm dead tired now.'

'Well, I'll be off,' said Dolly. 'See you all tomorrow.'

'I'll be off as well,' said Tony.

When they were outside, Tony said, 'Well, that little outing was something, wasn't it?'

'Keep walking,' said Dolly, 'just in case Penny is looking out of the window.'

'She must know we're gonna talk about it.'

'I know. What do you think? Would Reg be able to move?'

'I can see his point; they're smashing houses.'

'But what about his business, now he seems to be back on his feet?'

'I don't honestly know, Doll. I think we'd better just wait and see before we jump to any conclusions.'

Dolly knew Tony was right, but that didn't stop her from worrying. She didn't want her friend to move away. What about the people who worked for Reg? As Tony said, she mustn't jump to conclusions.

'Did you have a nice day?' asked her mother, as Dolly walked in.

'We had a wonderful day, and the weather was perfect.'

'That's good. Did you want something to eat?'

'No, thanks. We had the sandwiches I made, and later we had fish and chips. It's funny how it tastes better when sitting on the seafront and eating it out of paper.'

'How was Gail?'

'She's so good. She can sit up now and she loved looking at the sea. On the way back, we stopped off at this new town they're building at Crawley.'

Up until then, her father had been busy reading his newspaper. He peered over the top of it. 'What's it like?'

'There's some really nice houses.'

'Could you go in any and have a look round?' asked Grace.

'Only the empty ones, but they're smashing.

The bathrooms and kitchens are lovely.'

'Was Tony interested in them?'

'He thought they were very nice, but it was Reg who seemed more interested.'

'It's been in the papers, all about it,' said Jim, suddenly taking an interest in the conversation and putting down his newspaper. 'I think you need a job to go to before you can put your name down for a house.'

'So Reg said. You should have seen the traffic, though, and the breakdowns. I can tell you, it's really put me off driving.'

'Well, it is a bank holiday weekend, and with petrol just coming off ration, it's bound to be busy,' said Jim. 'I expect it'll settle down.' He picked up his newspaper and carried on reading.

'Do you think Reg might be thinking of moving, then?' asked Grace.

Once again Jim put down his newspaper. 'How can he do that, Grace? I can't see Ivy wanting to move to the middle of nowhere. Besides, what about his job? Nah, you ain't got any worries on that score. It's taken Reg too long to build up his business.'

'Would you like to move away from here, Jim?'

'Dunno. It ain't something I'd ever thought about. What about you?'

'It would be nice to have a lovely new bathroom and a modern kitchen.'

'You wouldn't want to move away from here, would you, Mum?' Dolly asked.

'I might, but it would be hard leaving all the neighbours, and everything we grew up with.'

Dolly was surprised at her mother's answer.

On Monday morning, as it was a bank holiday, Dolly went in to see Penny.

'Look at me face,' said Penny as soon as Dolly opened the door.

Dolly grinned.

'It ain't no laughing matter.'

'I dunno. Red suits you. Come on, I'll put some cold cream on that lovely red nose. Is Gail all right?'

'Thank goodness we had the sense to put that umbrella over her. Mind you, her little legs look a bit pink, but I have creamed them.'

'Is Reg taking you out today?'

'No. I know it's a bank holiday, but he's gone to the site to check up on supplies.'

That remark put Dolly on edge. Did he need to go to the site today, or was that an excuse? She still worried about Reg.

'Hello, Dolly,' said Ivy, walking in with Gail's bottle. 'I hear you had a lovely day yesterday.'

'Yes, we did.'

'Pen said that Gail slept all night through. Must have been all that lovely fresh air. It's gotta be better than all the dirt and dust that's around here.'

Dolly immediately wondered if Ivy had been told about the visit to Crawley. 'Did Penny tell you about all those new houses we saw?'

'Yes, I did,' said Penny, and then quickly to her mother-in-law, 'I told you how we had to make a detour because of the traffic.'

On her way back home, Dolly saw Tony drive

293

past and park outside his house. She wondered where he'd been and if it had anything to do with Reg. As he got out of his car, he waved to Dolly before running to catch up with her.

She told Tony about that morning's conversation with Penny, then asked, 'So why has Reg gone to the site?'

'He went to find out if the stuff was still OK. He's still a bit paranoid since the break-in.'

'You don't think he's...?'

Tony put up his hand. 'Stop! He's not gone off gambling, if that's what you think.'

'I can't help worrying about him. Perhaps there's something more going on.'

'What d'you mean?'

'Well, Ivy was talking about the dirt and dust around here, and Penny said we had to take a detour because of all the traffic. Was that right?'

'I'll grant you there was a lot of traffic.'

'Well, what if it's to do with looking at those houses?'

Tony shook his head. 'D'you know, Dolly, I've never known anyone to add two and two and make ten out of 'em.'

'What d'you mean?'

'Well, you always jump to the wrong conclusions. Look at how you thought Bert Edwards was a gangster. He turned out to just be a clever businessman.'

'We all make mistakes.'

'I know. But you see things before they make any sense.'

'Thanks. Well, I'll see you later,' Dolly said, and went indoors.

Chapter 28

On Wednesday evening, Penny and Reg asked Dolly and Tony in for another game of cards. They had a lovely evening, full of laughter.

'Do you know when Vera will be here?' Penny asked Tony.

'Saturday morning, sometime.'

'Will it be all right if I go along to see her?'

'Course it will, but if you like, I can ask her to come along and see you.'

'No, thanks all the same. Now the weather's warmer, I'm going to try to go out on my own a bit more,' said Penny. 'Will I be able to reach the door knocker from me chair?'

'Is that wise?' asked Reg. 'Going out on your own?'

'It is only up the road. I'm all right all the time I'm on the straight bits, but it's just that I'm not very good with kerbs at the moment. When I'm on me own, I'm frightened I'll tip meself out.'

Dolly wanted to hug Penny. It was at times such as this, when she realised how restricted her friend was.

On Friday evening, when Dolly went in to see Penny, she was surprised to see Vera sitting there.

Vera immediately stood up and hugged Dolly. 'Hello, Dolly. It's great to see you after all these years. How are you?'

'I'm fine and how are you?'

'Very happy.'

'It's been a long while.'

'I know, and so much has happened in all our lives. What about this gorgeous baby?' Vera looked in the cot at Gail who was kicking her legs in the air. She turned to Dolly and said, 'I'm so sorry your marriage didn't work out. Aunty wrote and told me.'

Dolly wasn't happy about Mrs Marchant passing that news on to her niece, but it was all in the past now. 'It was just one of those things,' she said.

Penny said to Dolly, 'I was just telling Vera here how I got on at hospital and that it was all down to you really.' Looking at Vera, she added, 'She's such a nag.'

'Good job someone is,' said Dolly.

They sat for a while talking about so many things, but Dolly could see that Vera was most interested in Penny and her attempts at walking.

'Would you like me to come along in the morning and tell you about some exercises you can do?' asked Vera.

'Thanks, all the same, but won't you want to be with your aunt?'

'We can only talk about so much. OK, I'll pop along sometime. Are you going anywhere?'

'No.'

'Good. Right, I'll be off then. See you later.'

Just as Vera left, Tony walked in. 'Hello, all my lovely girls. Where's that old man of yours?' he asked Penny.

'He's just gone over to the shop for some fags.'

'Vera looks good,' said Dolly.

'Yeh, she seems very happy with her new friend. Has she told you that he'll be here on Sunday? Mum's running about like a thing possessed, worrying about what to give him for dinner.'

'Surely he knows we only get a shilling's worth of meat,' said Ivy, who had been sitting quietly and taking in all that was said. 'Your mum can't do much with that.'

'I know, but you know me mum. Vera told her not to worry. He's only going to be here in the afternoon.'

'Well, she seems very happy,' said Dolly.

'Yeh, I think she is, but I'll still give him the once over. After all, if he's gonna be one of the family, I've got to know all about him.'

'Is Vera gonna marry him?' asked Penny.

'Dunno.'

'Oh you ... you were getting us all eager.'

Tony laughed, and Dolly looked at him. Had Vera said something to him? After all, they had always been close cousins. She really hoped that Vera had found someone. She deserved some happiness.

It was a sunny Saturday afternoon in June, and Dolly was deep in thought as she crossed the road to go into the Gregorys' shop. That morning, she had received a letter from Mr Yates to say that there wasn't a vacancy on the shop floor, but there could be an opening available shortly in the typing room. As she could type, would she be interested? She would have to go along and take a test. As she couldn't type very fast, Dolly wasn't sure about taking up the offer. She pushed open

297

the door to the shop and put all her thoughts behind her.

'Hello, Dolly,' said Vera, who was inside.

'It's so nice to see all you young people around here again,' said May Gregory.

'And it's nice to be back,' said Vera. 'Living just round the corner seems ages ago.'

After a chat about how things used to be, Dolly and Vera made their way out of the shop.

'How did you get on with Penny this morning?' asked Dolly.

'Fine. I do admire her. She's so determined to walk again.'

'I know, but she wasn't when I first came home from America.'

'You've done a grand job, Dolly. I only wish you and Tony could get together again. He does love you, you know.'

Dolly shifted from one foot to the other and looked down. 'Did you know I can't give him any children?'

Vera nodded. 'Do you think that's so important?'

'Have you seen him with Gail?'

'Have you been to see a doctor?'

'Yes. When I lost the baby, the doctor here told me that something had gone wrong with me tubes, and the doctor in America said I couldn't have any more ... that's one of the reasons why Joe and I split up. And then there was his domineering mother. So you can see how it is.'

'Do you still love Tony? After all, you were engaged once.'

'We were very young then.'

'You know he still loves you.'

Dolly looked up the road. 'I'd better be going. Me mum might wonder where I've been.'

'I hope to see you tonight. I think Tony wants to take me and his mum out for a drink. He'd like you to come as well.'

'Are you sure?'

'That's what he said. I'll send him along to tell you what time. Is that all right?'

Dolly nodded, and crossed back over the road to walk home. Did Tony really want her to be there? Was Vera also trying to get them back together?

A short while later, Tony came along to tell her that he would pick her up at seven o'clock.

Once again Dolly looked in the mirror to make sure her hair and make-up were in order. When Tony knocked on the door, she called out to her parents, 'See you later.'

'Have a nice time,' came her mother's reply.

Dolly laughed. 'We're only going for a drink.' With that, she picked up her handbag and left the house.

'You carriage awaits, madam,' said Tony, opening the car door for her.

'Thank you, kind sir.'

'Hello, Dolly,' said Vera and Mrs Marchant from the back seat.

'Hello,' said Dolly as she got in.

'I feel like royalty,' said Mrs Marchant. 'Fancy my boy having a car.'

Dolly laughed. 'So where are we off to?'

'You'll know when we get there,' said Tony.

After a short drive, Tony parked outside a pub

in Blackheath, and they all got out of the car.

'It's years since I came here,' said Vera as she stood looking around. 'I was a student nurse in those days.'

'I know,' said Tony. 'I thought I'd bring you to the pub you used to frequent in your mad youth.'

'We worked too bloody hard to have a mad youth. What with dodging the bombs, taking patients to the shelter and patching up those we could...' Vera stood silent for a while, reminiscing. 'Those were good and bad days, but thank God they're all over now.'

'And now you're going to start a new life,' said Mrs Marchant.

Vera took her aunt's hand and kissed her cheek.

'Come on,' said Tony, 'let's go and have this drink.' He took his mum's and Vera's arm, and led them into the pub.

Dolly could see how happy they all were.

When they were seated and had their drinks, Tony raised his glass. 'Here's to me cousin. I wish her every happiness in her future life with John. And I'm really looking forward to meeting him tomorrow.'

'Thanks, Tony,' said Vera.

They all raised their glasses.

'You're going to get married?' asked Dolly, surprised.

Vera had a beaming smile. 'Yes, I'm getting married on the first of July.'

As Dolly was sitting next to Vera, she gave her a hug. 'I'm so thrilled for you.'

'Dolly, you must come to tea tomorrow and meet John,' said Mrs Marchant, who was positively glowing.

'Are you getting married in the church?' asked Dolly.

'Yes, we hope to, but it will be a very quiet affair. A couple of nurses are coming, and a friend of John's who will be best man. Tony here is giving me away, but Dolly ... would you like to be my bridesmaid?'

Dolly was taken aback. 'What? Me? What about one of the girls you work with?'

'No. I want to keep it in the family.'

'But I ain't family.'

'No, but you are a very good friend of the family, and I have known you all your life. It won't be a white wedding, just a nice dress and hat.'

Dolly was stunned. 'What can I say?'

'Please say yes.'

'Vera, I would be very honoured.'

'Thank you,' Vera said, giving Dolly a hug.

The rest of the evening was filled with laughter and much talk about the forthcoming wedding.

When Dolly got home that night, she was pleased that her parents were still up, and told them all that had happened that evening.

'That's wonderful,' said Grace. 'We ain't had a wedding in this street for years. And Vera wants you to be a bridesmaid. That's nice of her. Pity it's not a white wedding.'

'I think they want to keep it quite a low-key affair.'

'Will she still be able to stay at work when she's married?' asked Jim.

'It seems so,' said Dolly. 'Vera said that as there's such a shortage of nurses since the National

Health started, and now that the government's bringing in nurses from abroad, they are gradually lifting a lot of the restrictions.'

'I should think so too,' said Jim. 'After all those years of training, it always seemed daft to me that nurses had to give it all up just cos they got married.'

'Well, those days are over now, Dad.'

'And a good job too,' said Grace.

'By the way, I won't be here for tea tomorrow, as Mrs Marchant has invited me over there.'

'That's nice,' said Grace. 'Will Vera's new man be there?'

'Yes, and after tea, he's taking Vera back to the hospital as she's on duty tomorrow night.'

Chapter 29

On Sunday afternoon, when Dolly left her house to have tea with the Marchants, she couldn't help but notice the nice car parked behind Tony's second-hand Morris. Dolly thought that it had to belong to John. Working in a bank, he must have earned a lot more than Tony did.

When she knocked on the front door, it was opened almost immediately by Tony. 'Come on in,' he said, kissing Dolly on the cheek.

Dolly thought she would have to follow Tony along the passage to go into the kitchen, but instead, he stopped and said, 'In here,' and pushed open the door to the front room.

On the settee, next to Vera, sat a good-looking young man with neatly trimmed dark hair. 'Hello again, Dolly,' said Vera, jumping to her feet. 'Come on in and meet John.'

John stood up and held out his hand. 'Pleased to meet you, Dolly. I've been hearing a lot about you.'

He was head and shoulders taller than Dolly. As she took his hand, she noticed that he had long slender fingers. 'And I'm pleased to meet you,' she said, 'not that I've really heard that much about you.'

'Vera has rather sprung me on the family. Never mind, we've got a few hours to get to know one another.'

'Tea, Dolly?' asked Mrs Marchant.

'Yes, please.' Dolly could see that she was in a bit of a flutter. 'Do you want me to help?'

'No, thanks. You're a guest.'

Dolly wanted to laugh at that. She dared not look at Tony as she knew he must be grinning.

'Vera told me that you've been to America,' said John.

'Yes, that's right. I was a GI bride, but unfortunately it didn't work out.'

'That must have been such a disappointment.'

'Yes, it was.'

'America is such an up-and-coming country.'

'Don't you get any wild ideas,' said Vera. 'I'm British through and through.' She gave Dolly a sly look.

'I hear you are going to be Vera's bridesmaid,' John said to Dolly.

'Yes, that was a complete surprise.'

'Your tea, Dolly,' said Mrs Marchant, walking into the room and handing Dolly a posh cup and saucer.

'Thank you.' Dolly looked at Tony. He looked over to the corner of the room and raised his eyebrows. Seeing the almost empty cabinet, she realised that Mrs Marchant had used her best china. Usually, it was locked away.

When they began to talk about the wedding, Dolly relaxed.

Vera said, 'We've been to church, and the date's to be Saturday, July the first, at three o'clock.'

'I'm pleased that you're getting married in our local church. You, Tony, and Rose were christened there,' said Mrs Marchant.

'And Tony's going to give me away,' said Vera.

'I can do that all right.' He grinned.

'Will Rose be coming to the wedding?' asked Dolly. She thought about Tony's sister, who'd not liked Dolly when she broke off her engagement to Tony to marry Joe.

'No, she won't be able to make it,' Mrs Marchant said sadly. 'They are both very busy and Scotland is such a long way away.'

'That's a shame,' said Dolly, and looking at Vera, said, 'Was there any particular colour you would like me to wear?'

'No. I don't think so. I hope to get a nice blue suit, but I'll let you know nearer the date.'

Dolly managed to suppress a gasp. She had been married in blue. 'Blue suits you,' she said.

'I was hoping she'd have a white wedding,' said Mrs Marchant.

'We've been all through that,' said Vera. 'And I

told you, I'm not one for dressing up.'

'Well, at least you're getting married in a church.' Vera was flushed with excitement as she spoke. 'We've been to see the priest. We were concerned about having to go to the church services for the three Sundays beforehand to hear the banns being read. That would have been difficult as we both work away, but the priest said that as long as someone can attend, just to make sure everything is all right, then that should be fine...' she looked at Mrs Marchant, who nodded, 'and Aunty has kindly offered to go.' She then turned to her cousin. 'Tony, you can join her, if you like.'

'Thanks all the same, but I think I wait till the wedding,' he said.

'And John has to go to his local church and get a certificate,' Vera continued.

'That shouldn't be a problem,' John said, 'as my parents are both regular churchgoers.' He squeezed Vera's hand.

After a little while of general chit-chat, Mrs Marchant stood up. 'I'll just go and see to the food.'

'I'll give you a hand,' said Dolly, and quickly followed her out of the front room.

When they were in the kitchen, Dolly was surprised at the lovely spread. 'This looks wonderful. How did you manage to do so much in such a short time?'

'Vera did most of it. They brought most of the fillings for the sandwiches and the cakes. What do you think of John, Dolly?'

'He seems all right. What do you think?'

'He seems a nice enough bloke. As long as he

305

looks after Vera, that's all I worry about. Now, let's get these sandwiches uncovered.'

Dolly lifted off the clean tea towels that covered the plates. She smiled. This was surely a feast for a king.

After they finished eating their tea, John went to his car and brought in a bottle of wine.

When everybody's glass was full, he stood up and looked at Vera. 'Here's to you, my darling. I hope we have a long and happy marriage.'

Tony gave a toast to the happy couple. 'To John and Vera. Cheers!'

Dolly could see the love in Vera's eyes, and was happy for her.

For a while, they sat and chatted. Dolly was pleased to see how well they were all getting on. John was a very agreeable man. She guessed he must be slightly older than Vera, who was now in her late twenties. He seemed very much at home with the family.

From the way he talked, Dolly could tell that he'd had a good education. He must have come from a very solid family. 'Will your family be coming to the wedding?' she asked.

'I should say so. They're pleased to think that someone like Vera is brave enough to take me on.'

Vera smiled at him. 'They are very nice people.'

So, Vera has already met them, thought Dolly.

When it was time for Vera and John to leave, everyone went to the front door with them. There were lots of hugs and kisses, and finally, they were off.

Tony put his arm round Dolly's waist, and they all waved till the car turned the corner.

Mrs Marchant gave a big sigh. 'Thank Gawd, that's all over!'

Tony laughed. 'It wasn't so bad. John seems like a nice bloke. What do you think of him, Doll?'

'Don't know, really. Didn't have a lot to say to him, but Vera thinks the world of him. Did you notice how she looked at him? That's got to be a sign of true love.'

'And she's been to see his parents,' added Mrs Marchant. 'She told me they've got a big house, Cambridge way, so I was very worried about him coming here.'

'You've got nothing to be ashamed of, Ma.' Tony kissed his mother's cheek.

'Where will they be living?' asked Dolly.

'He's buying a small house near where he works,' said Mrs Marchant.

Tony put his arm around his mother's shoulders. 'Let's go and have what's left in the bottle that John brought with him.'

'So what was he like?' asked her mother, as soon as Dolly walked into the kitchen.

'Very nice. He works in a bank.'

'That's a good job,' said her father.

'Do you know what date the wedding's going to be?' asked Grace.

'July the first. They're getting married at St Mary's, but Vera was worried about having to attend the church three Sundays beforehand, as they work in Norfolk.'

'Surely, there must be a way round that?' said Grace. 'Look at all the hurried weddings that took place during the war.'

'They were nearly all with a special licence,' said Dolly, remembering her own wedding.

'I suppose that could be a way round it,' said Jim.

'Tony's mum said she'd go to the church for Vera.'

'Will Mrs M want any help with food? With most stuff still on ration or in short supply, it must be very hard to serve up a good wedding breakfast and a nice cake.'

'We're going to a hotel after the wedding. They're arranging it all themselves, so that'll be a lot of worry off Mrs Marchant's mind. And, Vera wants me to be her bridesmaid, but it won't be a white wedding.'

'Oh, that's a shame. What is it about you young girls that you don't want all the nice things?'

'I think it's cos we've been brought up on austerity, so think that sort of thing is a big waste, or in short supply, or on ration.'

'Well, I still think a white wedding would have been nice. What does Mrs M have to say about it?'

'I think she feels the same as you, but remember it's Vera's choice.'

'Of course... Right, I'm off to bed. You coming up, Jim?'

'Might as well.' He stood up and kissed Dolly on the cheek. 'Night, love. See you in the morning.'

'Put the guard in front of the fire before you go up, love,' said Grace. 'See you in the morning.'

With that, they both left Dolly sitting quietly and staring at the burning coals. She was so pleased for

Vera. Things had worked out well for her. *If they would only do the same for me,* she thought.

Back at the office on Monday, Dolly had been kept very busy with a lot of invoices that Bert Edwards had put through the door. He wanted them typed and entered into the ledger.

When he called in to collect them at five o'clock, he said, 'I'm very pleased with all that you do for me, Dolly. Do you mind doing all this extra work?'

'Not at all. In fact, I'm pleased for something to do. Since Reg went into business with you, I've not had that much to keep me busy.'

'That's good, cos a bloke I know wants someone who can type, so will it be all right if I tell him you'll do it?'

'Of course, but you'd better make sure that Reg knows and he says it's OK.'

'Fine. I'll get all that sorted out,' said Bert Edwards. He gathered up all the papers, put them in his briefcase, and left.

Dolly sat back in her chair. 'Well, that's that. I'm obviously not meant to leave here,' she said to herself. Standing up, she put on her hat, gathered up her handbag, and after locking the office, made her way home.

That evening, when Dolly went in to see Penny there was definitely an atmosphere in the kitchen. 'Is everything all right?' she asked.

'I don't know,' said Penny. 'You tell me.'

'I'm sorry, but I don't know what you're talking about... Oh, is this about Mr Edwards asking me to do some typing for his friend? I did say he'd better clear it with Reg first.'

'No. It's not that, Dolly,' said Ivy. 'You see, I met that girl's mother, today.' She turned to Penny. 'What's her name?'

'Meg.'

Dolly froze. She knew what this was about. 'And?' she asked, trying to make light of it.

'It seems that you are going to leave Reg and work at Peek Freans,' said Penny. 'So when were you going to tell us this news?'

'I had been thinking about it a while back, but now Bert Edwards has given me more work.'

'Oh, so you're gonna stay? Thank you,' said Penny sarcastically. 'I thought you would be more grateful to Reg for giving you a job without references.'

Dolly looked at her, surprised.

'That's without, of course, him letting you take time off whenever you felt like it.'

Dolly stood and looked at her friend. 'I can't believe this,' she said. 'The only time I left early was to come home and help you try to walk.'

'That's without your boyfriend coming in. God only knows what you got up to then.'

'What? Are you talking about Tony?'

'No. Your copper friend.'

'Harry Jordan? You must be joking. I'm really surprised at you Penny, and yes, I was planning on going to Peek Freans, but I changed me mind. Now I'm not so sure I did the right thing.' She picked up her coat, and on her way out she turned to Ivy. 'I'm more than surprised at you, listening to Meg's mum gossip.' She walked out and slammed the front door after her.

'Hello, love. Everything all right?' asked her mother when Dolly arrived back at home.

'No, it's not.'

'What is it? What's wrong?'

Dolly slumped into the armchair.

'Dolly, love, what is it?' Grace looked at her sad face, and put an arm around her daughter's shoulders.

Dolly told her what had happened.

'Trust that Meg's mother to stir things up. I reckon she goes out of her way to cause trouble. I'm surprised at Ivy. I would have thought that she would have had a word with you before telling Penny about it.'

'Well, what's done is done.' Dolly sniffed and wiped her nose. 'So it looks as if I shall finish up working with Meg. It's a pity really as Mr Edwards was going to give me some more work.'

'I don't know what your dad will say when he gets home.'

'Don't tell him tonight. Let him enjoy his darts.'

'Will you go into the office tomorrow morning?'

'I don't know. I'll have to give 'em the keys back.'

'Was Reg there?'

'No.'

'He might have a different view on all this.'

'I don't know. Penny was pretty upset, and she does have a lot to say as far as the business is concerned.'

311

Chapter 30

As Dolly was getting ready for work the following morning, she was very unsure about going. Reg hadn't turned up last night. When she asked her dad for his advice, he just shrugged and told her it was up to her. He didn't want to get involved. Her mother wasn't very happy about that.

Dolly picked up her handbag and, after kissing her mother goodbye, said, 'I might be home soon.'

'Good luck, love.' Grace knew that after she'd washed up the breakfast things she'd go and have a word with Ivy Smith. She knew Dolly would be cross about that, but, after all, she was still her daughter.

Dolly was surprised to see Bert Edwards waiting for her when she arrived at the yard. 'Hello,' she said as he got out of his car.

'I thought I'd come over first thing.' He went to the boot and took out a large box. Dolly opened the office door, and he followed her in and placed the box on her desk. 'If you can get these done by the end of the week, Jack will be very grateful.'

'Mr Edwards, I might not have a job here after today.'

'What?' He sat in the chair. 'I thought you was happy here.'

'I am ... was.'

'So what happened?'

Dolly thought there was no point in hiding it, so she told him.

'And this is because Reg's mother listened to a lot of tittle-tattle?'

'Well, it was true.'

'Don't you worry about it. I reckon if it comes to it, you could still work for me and Jack. Would you mind working at home?'

'I don't know.'

'You'd be a lot cheaper than getting an agency to do the work. Besides, I like the way you set the time sheets out – you are very neat. Reg will be bloody sorry. He'd be daft to get rid of you.'

'Thank you.'

'Well, if you can get on with this lot, I'll have a word with Reg and try to sort something out. But don't worry about it.'

Dolly felt quite elated after Bert Edwards had left. At least she would still get work, and be able to work at home if Reg gave her the sack. But what about a typewriter? She couldn't afford to buy one. Well, she'd worry about that if and when the situation arrived.

She set about sorting all the papers and started singing to herself. She felt a lot better now she had some kind of future, and it would probably be better than working in a factory.

As Dolly was going through the contents of the box that Bert Edwards had left for her, she anxiously waited for Reg to burst in and give her the sack.

In the afternoon, when she was busy sorting out the invoices, the phone rang and made her jump.

'Hello?' she said nervously.

'Hello, Dolly. How are you?'

'Oh, hello, Harry. I'm fine, thank you.'

'I've got some more tickets for Saturday, for a show you might be interested in. Are you free?'

Dolly quickly decided that although she might not have a job very soon, she would decline, just in case things did work out for the best. 'I'm sorry, Harry, but I'm afraid I have to say no.'

'Oh, that's a shame. Is there someone more important than me?'

'Well, not really. It's just that...' Dolly put a hand behind her back and crossed her fingers, 'I've promised Penny we'd go shopping as I let her down before.'

'I see, but it's such a shame as I know how much you enjoyed our other little outing.'

'Yes, I did.' Dolly was pleased that he didn't say 'date'.

'Never mind. Perhaps next time I'll be lucky. By the way, have you done anything more about learning to drive?'

'I've applied for my licence.'

'That's good. As soon as it arrives, I suggest you start to get things rolling. With petrol off ration there will be a lot of people who want to learn to drive.'

'All right, I'll see about getting started.'

'Good. And don't forget, I'm here to offer my services as your instructor.'

Dolly laughed. 'Thanks for the offer, I'll let you know.'

They carried on talking about things in general and when she replaced the phone, she knew she had done the right thing. Somehow, she felt a lot better about her future. She would learn to drive and get a car. She knew that if she asked him, Harry would help with both of those.

It was almost five o'clock when Reg drove into the yard. Dolly had been dreading this moment all day. Although she was now tidying up and getting ready to leave, she was pleased that she hadn't covered the typewriter or put her coat on.

'Hello, Reg,' she said when he opened the door.

'You're still here, then,' he said flatly.

'It's not five yet,' she replied sarcastically as she stacked up Bert Edwards' papers.

'I understand that Bert's going to give you a lot more work,' said Reg, pointing to the pile.

'That's right, but I told him to first make sure that it would be fine with you.'

'Yeh, as long as he pays me enough. After all, I'm the one that pays your wages, and the light bill.'

'So is it all right with you?'

'You've decided to stay, then?'

'I would have told you if I was going to leave. It's just that I...'

'Don't bother to try to explain things. Look Dolly, we've known each other for many years and as I told Penny, she don't own you. She should be grateful that you're here and helping her as much as you can. Look at all the evenings you've come in and helped her to walk.'

Dolly plopped herself back down on her chair. 'Thank you, Reg. I would hate it if me and Penny fell out.' She smiled. 'She is getting on with this walking lark. Soon, she'll be rushing about all

315

over the place.'

'I think it'll be a while before that happens.' He looked uncomfortable. 'You know I blame me mum, listening to all that rubbish about you. And you know what Pen's like. She mulls things over and ends up making six out of nothing. Right, are you ready? I'll take you home.'

Dolly wanted to throw her arms round Reg; she felt so relieved.

That evening, as soon as Dolly had finished helping her mother with the washing-up, she went back in to see Penny.

Ivy was standing at the kitchen table doing some ironing. 'Hello, Dolly,' she said, putting the flat iron on the stand by the fire. 'Reg said you'd be in. I'm so sorry about yesterday. I should have kept me mouth shut, but it just came out, and you know Pen, she just jumped on it. I wish I could have cut me tongue out.'

'I was very upset about it.'

'I know. Yer mum came in and had a bit of a go at me.'

'I'm sorry about that.'

'That's all right. I can understand her concern. Anyway, Reg gave Penny and me a good talking to and we're both so sorry we upset you.'

'I'd better go in and make me peace with Pen,' Dolly said.

She knocked gently on Penny's door. Pushing it open, she said softly, 'It's only me,' and went in.

'Hello.' Penny still sounded a bit off. She nodded towards the door. 'I suppose she's said she's sorry?'

316

'Penny, what can I say?'

'I think it's all been said.'

'So you're still angry with me then?'

'It was just the way you kept it to yourself – getting another job.'

'Well, I'd decided not to say anything till I'd made up me mind. Anyway, it's all over now, but if you'd rather I don't stay, I'll go back home.'

'Please yourself,' Penny said, in an offhand way.

Dolly knew she shouldn't retaliate; she had to bide her time, so with that, she turned and left.

Ivy heard the front door shut, and went into Penny's room. 'Where's Dolly gone?'

'Home. And don't you start. I've had enough of Reg having a go at me. I can't help that I feel betrayed.'

Ivy wanted to laugh. 'Betrayed,' she said. 'After all you two have been to each other, all these years.'

'Yes, well, yes.'

'So what did you say to her?'

'Just what I thought.'

'Penny it was my fault. I shouldn't listen to gossip.'

'It's just as well you did. Now I really know what my supposedly true friend was thinking.'

'I'm sure she would have told you if she was going to leave Reg.'

'Well, she'd have to if she wanted a reference.'

'And would you have stopped her?'

Penny looked at her mother-in-law, surprised by her comments. Usually, Ivy was meek and just agreed with whatever Penny said.

Is she getting fed up with all my moaning? Am I

317

being unreasonable? These were the thoughts that were running through Penny's mind.

'You're home early,' said Grace when Dolly walked back indoors.

'It seems as if I'm still in somebody's bad books.'

'But Reg said...'

'I know, but Penny has other ideas.'

'You know, Dolly, this is so silly. Remember, she can't have a lot to do all day except mull over every little thing that's said. I reckon you should ask her out shopping again. I think that would do you both good.'

Dolly looked at her mother. It wasn't like her to say things like that. She laughed.

'What's so funny?' asked Grace.

'Me and Penny. We're acting as if we're a couple of spoilt kids, not like a couple of old married women, well one married and one divorced. Thanks, Mum, I'll ask her tomorrow.'

The following evening, when Dolly went in to see Penny, she was pleased to see that Reg was still around. Some evenings, when he was out, Dolly wondered if he had really given up gambling. Penny had never been told why Reg had been beaten up. She still thought it was because he'd had the wages on him. Tony had told Dolly that he'd had a word with him, and Reg made Tony promise that he would never tell Penny, as he was worried she would leave him. He also promised to stop gambling. Unfortunately, there was always an element of doubt that he might not have kept his word.

318

Ivy had made a pot of tea and offered one to Dolly.

She shook her head. 'No, thanks. I've just had one.'

Penny was sitting in her chair, quietly nursing her daughter.

'Reg, are you doing anything on Saturday afternoon?' Dolly asked.

'Nothing I can think of at the moment. Why?'

Penny looked up. She was very tempted to ask if Dolly was going for an interview for her new job, but quickly changed her mind.

'I was wondering if you could take me and Pen out shopping again?'

Penny was speechless.

'What d'you say, Pen?' asked Dolly. 'Do you fancy going up West? We could even tell that café owner what happened the last time.'

'I'd love to.'

'Right, that's settled. I can be ready by two.'

'I shall be waiting.'

Suddenly, the air had been cleared, and very soon, they were all laughing and joking as before.

When Dolly left, Reg went to the front door with her. 'You didn't have to do that,' he said.

'Yes, I did. I hate any bad feeling between me and Pen, and I knew she'd jump at the chance of going out again.'

'Thank you.' Reg kissed her cheek. 'We have to go to the hospital next week. Who knows, she might be walking for a bit longer then.'

'I hope so. She's done so well just lately.' Over the past few weeks, every time they could, they put Penny in her calipers and set about trying to help her walk.

As Dolly went home, she thought of Harry. Now she was doing something positive on Saturday, she didn't feel so bad at letting him down.

'So, you and Pen are going shopping tomorrow,' said Tony as he drove her home from work on Friday. 'I would have taken you if that's what you wanted.'

'You know you can't get Penny and her wheelchair in your car.'

'I will when she walks with her callipers.'

'I hope by then I've got me own car.'

'You do have to have a licence to drive, and pass a test, you know.'

'I'm waiting for my licence to arrive. It should be here any day.'

'What?'

'I've already applied for one, a few weeks ago. It was just as well, as Harry said now petrol is off ration, a lot of people will want to learn.'

'And I suppose he offered to help?'

'Yes. Are you jealous?'

'Of course I am. You know I'd teach you.'

'I might take you up on that.'

'You'll need L-plates.'

'I know.'

To Dolly, it was just like old times as she and Penny wandered around the shops, at least those that Penny could get through in her wheelchair.

It was a warm June afternoon, and after a wonderful morning shopping, they were sitting in the café waiting for Reg.

320

The café owner had been pleased to see the girls again. 'Teas and cake are on me,' he said when they told him what had happened since the last time they were there. 'When I told me missus all about it, she gave me a right old rollicking, I can tell you. She reckons I should have got me van out and taken you home. To be honest, love, I didn't even give that a thought.'

Penny took his hand. 'Please don't worry about it. It all worked out fine in the end. And I'm pleased to say my husband is now going to get a better van.'

'Did they ever catch the blokes what did that to your old man's business?'

Penny shook her head.

'There's some right bastards about – sorry ladies...' The café owner looked embarrassed. 'I'd better get back behind me counter.'

Reg turned up right on time. Dolly and Penny thanked the café owner, said their goodbyes, and then they all made their way back home.

'Have you two had a good afternoon?' Reg asked.

'It's been wonderful,' said Penny. 'I think I might even have spent a bit more than the tanner you gave me.'

He laughed. 'I knew I shouldn't have let you two out on your own. You'll end up bankrupting me.'

Dolly turned round and looked at Penny sitting in the back of the van. She was pleased that things were now better between them.

She had just been home a short while when someone was at the front door.

'Hello, Tony.'

'Hello, Doll. Did you and Penny have a good day?'

'We certainly did. And I had a look at some suits for the wedding. I'll have to ask Vera if she's any idea what colour she'd like me to wear.'

'She hopes to be back here next weekend, so you can ask her then. Saw yer mum this morning; she said your driving licence had arrived.'

'Yes, I only had time to quickly glance at it before I went out with Penny.'

'Well, I've got you a little present.'

'You have?'

Tony took a brown paper bag from behind his back and handed it to Dolly.

When she opened it, she laughed and gave him a hug. 'Thank you.' She took the shiny L-plates from the bag.

'Right. How about you have your first lesson tomorrow morning?'

'Are you sure you want me driving your car?'

'Well, you've got to learn in something.'

'I'd love to. Thank you so much.'

'Well, that's settled then. We shall start at ten in the morning. Now I suggest you go and study *The Highway Code*.'

'I will, sir, and thank you.' She leaned forward and quickly kissed Tony's cheek.

As he walked away, he began to whistle 'Some Enchanted Evening'.

Dolly closed the door and grinned. She did like him, but...

Chapter 31

It was Sunday morning when Dolly nervously walked to Tony's house clutching her shiny new L-plates.

'Hello,' he said, coming to the front door and putting on his coat. 'See yer later, Mum,' he called out. 'Right. Shall I put them on?' he asked, pointing to the package Dolly was holding.

'No. I'd rather wait till we are out of sight. I don't want the whole street looking at me.'

'Please yourself. Get in and we'll be off somewhere quiet.'

Tony drove to a road and stopped the car. 'Is this quiet enough for you?'

Dolly looked about her. There were large empty spaces now where houses had once stood. The rubble had all been cleared away and the street was very quiet.

They both got out and swapped seats.

'I'm very nervous,' said Dolly. 'I'm frightened I'm gonna damage your car.'

'I shall be right beside you.'

Dolly got into the driver's seat. With Tony sitting beside her, they went through the procedure on how to start to drive.

After an hour, Dolly was hot and bothered. She was terrified of damaging Tony's pride and joy, especially when she grated the gears. When she looked at him, he was still trying hard to smile.

'Right that's enough,' she said. 'Is it always this hard?'

'It'll come. Don't worry.'

'I do worry. I wish there was some other way I could learn.'

'You've got to be patient.'

'That's not one of my good points.'

'I know that, don't I? Perhaps we can try in the evenings as it's so light.'

'Only if you're sure.'

'I'm sure, but I'm worried that when you do pass your test and get your own car, you won't want me to take you out anymore – will you?'

'No. I shall be taking you out. But I think that will be a while yet.'

'So how did you get on?' asked her father when Dolly walked into the kitchen.

'OK, I think. I grated the gears a few times; I'm terrified that I'll damage Tony's car.'

'Well, I reckon he's a bloke in a hundred,' Jim said. 'I certainly wouldn't let you loose in my car if I had one.'

'Is he taking you out again?' asked Grace.

'Yes,' said Dolly.

Grace smiled. 'Well, you couldn't have been that bad.'

'Mum, did you go along to see Mrs M?'

'Yes, I did. She showed me the frock she's got for the wedding. It's really nice, and I like the way the hat picks out the navy colour. It's a lovely little hat, and it suits her.'

'I know.'

'She's a bit worried about Vera, though.'

324

'Did she say why?'

'She just hopes she's made the right choice.'

'I don't think she's got any worries about John. He seems a nice enough bloke.'

'Yes, but she's worried he might look down on her, and her house.'

'I don't think so. After all, he's Vera's choice. And she's been to his house and met his family.'

'I know. But as I told her, we've all got our family's happiness at heart. We can only hope for the best for 'em.'

Dolly knew she had to get off this subject before her mother brought up her big mistake.

At lunchtime, on the following Saturday, Tony picked Dolly up from the office to take her home to see Vera.

'She's only here for the day,' he said as Dolly got into the car. 'I'll be taking her back to catch her train later; you can come with me if you like.'

'I'd like that,' said Dolly.

When they arrived at Tony's house, Dolly gave Vera a hug and a kiss, and they quickly began to talk about the wedding.

'I've made up my mind,' said Vera. 'I shall be in a blue suit, with probably a black hat, so, Dolly you can wear any colour you fancy. Is that all right?'

'That'll be lovely.'

'I've got a couple of days off before the wedding, and the week after. We shall be going away for a few days, not sure where yet. John says it's going to be a surprise.'

Vera looked so happy, and Dolly was pleased

for her.

They carried on chatting for a while, and then Mrs Marchant prepared a small tea.

After they had finished, Vera said, 'It's time I was off. I'm working the night shift this week and don't want to get into Matron's bad books.'

'But you ain't had any sleep today.'

'Don't worry, Aunty. From Monday, I shall be on days, so I'll have Sunday to recover.'

'I do worry about you,' said Mrs Marchant.

'Well, you don't have to. Ready then, Tony?'

'Ready when you are, Vera.'

They said their goodbyes, and Tony drove Vera to the train station. Dolly went with them.

'Have you got your L-plates with you?' Tony asked Dolly as they drove back after dropping off Vera.

'No, course not.'

'That's a pity. You could have driven home.'

Dolly looked at the other vehicles around them. 'I don't think I'm ready to go on busy roads just yet.'

'You'll have to get used to other traffic if you want to drive.'

'I know, but I'll wait till I've had a few more lessons.'

On Sunday morning, Dolly was just about to go into Penny's when she saw Tony coming out of the Gregorys' shop.

'Hello,' she said, 'I'm just popping in to see Penny.'

'Do you fancy going for a drive this afternoon?' he asked.

'Yes, I'd love to, if it's all right with you.'

'Bring your L-plates.'

'Thanks. See you later.'

Although, as she went in to see Penny, she still wasn't sure if she wanted to drive.

Dolly told Penny all about the visit to Mrs Marchant's to see Vera.

'As it's less than two weeks to the wedding, I shall have to take meself up West again to buy a frock. I saw a nice one in C&A when we went shopping last week.'

'Why didn't you buy it then, you daft apeth?'

'I didn't have enough money at the time, and I didn't know what colour to buy.'

She wasn't going to tell Penny that the reason she'd suggested going shopping was because she still felt guilty about going out with Harry. She changed the subject. 'Anyway, I'm going out driving again with Tony, this afternoon. Can't say I'm really looking forward to it.'

'You won't say that when you pass your test and get your own car.'

'If I can afford one, that is.'

'You'll get one. You've always got what you wanted.'

Dolly wasn't sure if there was a little bit of jealousy in that remark.

'Right, are you going to take over or not?' Tony asked, tapping the steering wheel.

'Can't say I really feel like it now.'

'Oh, come on. Don't be daft. When you've got your own car, you can go out whenever you want.' He gently patted Dolly's hand.

327

'I know, but I'm concerned about all the traffic. It puts me off, and last time I grated your gears.'

'It won't always be like that.'

'I know, but I don't feel that happy about it.'

'So what do you want to do?'

'Don't know.'

'We'll go for a little drive, and then see how you feel. Is that all right?'

'OK,' agreed Dolly, but she knew she didn't want to drive today.

On Monday evening when Dolly left work, she went straight in to see Penny. She knew that her friend had been to the hospital that afternoon and just had to find out how she had got on.

'Dolly, I did it!' said Penny, her face full of joy. 'I walked on my own between the bars, and with just my sticks. It was only a few steps, but I didn't hold on.'

She had tears running down her face. Reg, who was standing next to her, was smiling.

Dolly knelt down and held her friend tight. 'I'm so pleased for you.'

'And it's all down to you, Dolly,' said Reg, proudly. 'You was the one that got her onto her feet in the first place.'

'When I feel more confident, I want to cross the road and go into the Gregorys' shop. Will you come with me?'

'Do you have to ask?' said Dolly, who by now was also in tears.

Penny went on to describe how she had walked. 'At first, Reg and the doctor held on to me, but then they gradually let go. I was terrified, I can tell you. I only took a few steps, but it's a start.'

Over these past weeks, Reg had been taking Penny to the hospital to help strengthen her muscles and help her to walk along the bars. Dolly was really pleased at her progress, and it seemed that her friend was now more determined to walk again.

'So that's our good news,' said Reg. 'How are you getting on with your driving? Tone said you're not doing too badly.'

Dolly wiped her eyes. 'I'm not doing that good. I've grated the gears a couple of times, and that makes me nervous. I'm terrified I'll do some damage to his car.'

'You just need to relax,' said Reg. 'It's all about confidence, as Penny says.'

'I suppose so,' said Dolly. 'Well, I have to go in for me dinner, now, as it's Dad's darts night. But I'll be in a bit later.' She kissed Penny's cheek, then left.

Over dinner, Dolly told her parents what had happened with Penny.

'Well, I think that's wonderful news,' said Grace.

'It'll be nice for her to get out and about again,' said Jim.

Dolly felt great. Suddenly, her life was wonderful. She was happy with her job, and she was determined to learn to drive and get herself a small car. When that happened, she would take Penny out, along with Gail, and they would be able to go anywhere they wanted. She felt as if a great weight had been lifted from her shoulders, all because her friend was happy. *After all,* she thought, *I was the one to get it all started.*

This was the third Sunday that the banns for Vera's wedding were being read. Tony had arranged to take Dolly for another driving lesson later that afternoon. As the Taylor family were eating their breakfast, they were disturbed by someone knocking on the front door.

'Who can that be at this time?' said Grace, placing the cosy over the teapot.

'I'll go,' said Dolly, putting the toast she was eating back on the plate. She opened the front door to find Tony standing there. 'Tony, what is it? What's wrong?'

'Sorry it's so early, but it's Mum. She's not well.'

'Oh, I'm so sorry. Is she that bad? Is there anything I can do?'

'Who is it, Dolly?' called her mother from the kitchen.

'It's Tony.'

'Well, ask him in.'

'You'd better come in,' said Dolly, standing to one side to let him pass.

'Hello, Mrs Taylor … Jim…' he said, giving them both a nod. 'I was just telling Dolly here that Mum's not too well.'

'Oh dear,' said Grace. 'What's wrong?'

'She got a rotten headache. I think it's all the worry about this wedding that's getting to her. She's worried about not being able to hear the banns being read this morning. She's not that happy about going to church, anyway, so I said I'd go to stop her getting in a state. Will you come with me, Doll?'

Dolly looked at him with surprise. 'Course I will. What time?'

'The service starts at nine.'

'Right, it's now half past eight. I can be ready in a bit. Tell your mum not to worry. We can make it in time.'

The service was just beginning when Tony and Dolly slipped into the last pew. It was very peaceful. The last time they were here was at Gail's christening. Today, Tony was clutching Dolly's hand as they sat, then stood, and followed what everybody else did. Then, at last, the banns were read. There were going to be quite a few July weddings. When Vera and John's names were read out, Tony smiled at Dolly and squeezed her hand.

'It would be nice if it was our wedding,' he whispered.

Dolly gave him a withering look. After the service, as they made their way home, she said, 'Did you have to say that?'

'Sorry. I was only thinking out loud.'

She really couldn't be cross with Tony. Being in church had given her a warm feeling, too.

'Well, anyway,' she said, 'you know I can't get married in a church.'

Chapter 32

For Dolly, the rest of the week flew by. Then, at last, it was Saturday 1 July, and Vera's wedding day.

When Dolly woke up, she was pleased to see that the sun was shining. At breakfast, while she was eating a piece of toast, her mother was telling her how much she was looking forward to the day ahead.

'We don't get many weddings in this street,' she said.

Dolly didn't rise to that. 'Vera said she was pleased you were both going to the church, but sorry she couldn't invite you to the do after.'

'We didn't expect to be invited to that, but your father took a bit of persuading to go to the church. But as I told him, he's seen Vera grow up. It will be nice for her to see some familiar faces as she walks down the aisle. I expect there'll be more family on her husband's side, so I told your father that we will need to help make up the numbers on Vera's side. From what Mrs M said, they've all got cars.'

The wedding was at three o'clock, so Dolly had plenty of time to do her hair, take her clothes along to Tony's, and help Vera get ready. She was looking forward to it, and had managed to take herself back to C&A to buy the dress she had seen while shopping with Penny. It was a soft pink colour with small cap sleeves, and a sweetheart neckline. Her mother said that it looked very nice.

All morning, she seemed to be running backwards and forwards between her and Tony's house. She was so happy for Vera as she helped with her hair and painting her nails.

Vera had arranged for a taxi to take her, Tony, Mrs Marchant, and Dolly to the church, but the rest of the guests, including Dolly's parents, had to walk. The church was within easy walking distance, so a few other neighbours would be there, including Penny. Reg was to take Penny in her wheelchair, with Ivy pushing Gail in her pram.

'Now, are you sure you've got everything packed for tonight?' Mrs Marchant asked Vera as they waited in the kitchen.

'Yes, Aunty. My case is in Tony's car, waiting. He can bring it along after the ceremony. Is that all right?'

'It's fine by me,' said Tony, just as the flowers arrived. He had already taken his car to the church early that morning so he could take his mother and Dolly on to the reception.

Vera had a bouquet of red roses, and Dolly had a small bouquet of carnations. The smell was lovely. There was a carnation buttonhole for Tony and a lovely rose corsage for Mrs Marchant.

'Vera, this is so lovely,' said Mrs Marchant as she admired her flowers. 'But you know something ordinary would have done for me.'

'Aunty, this is my wedding day and I want to see you looking lovely, which, by the way you do. This is just the finishing touch.' She kissed her aunt's cheek, and then pinned the flowers on to her dress.

Mrs Marchant thought about her late sister and choked back a sob. How she would have loved to be here, to see her lovely daughter getting married. Her thoughts were interrupted by a shout from the passage.

'Sounds as if the taxi's here,' said Tony. He looked at everyone. 'I must say, I'm proud to be escorting such a bevy of beauties. You all look really smashing.'

'Thank you,' said Vera. 'Right, let's be off.'

Tony sat in the front of the taxi, and Vera, Mrs Marchant, and Dolly sat in the back. As they made their way slowly along Wood Street, they saw the Gregory sisters waving outside their shop and they all waved back.

It only took a few minutes to get to the church and Dolly was surprised at the number of people waiting there. 'You two are very popular,' she said to Vera.

'Some of the nurses have come down, and of course, there's John's family,' said Vera, who was positively blooming.

'Well, you can't go in yet,' said Mrs Marchant. 'You've got to be late; it's tradition.'

'I'll drive you round the block again,' said the taxi driver.

By the time they had returned, everybody had gone inside the church.

Dolly felt proud and very honoured to be walking up the aisle behind Vera and Tony. She smiled at the people sitting in the pews, and was surprised to see about the same amount of people on each side. She did wonder who would be there. She could see Penny, Ivy, and Reg who was holding Gail. Gail was busy trying to eat the ribbon that was on her bonnet. Then, there were Dolly's parents. Her father hadn't wanted to come, but her mother had made him. Then to her surprise, she saw Meg and her mother. Meg gave Dolly a discreet wave. There were also one or two of the other neighbours.

Dolly thought that John looked very handsome. He turned slightly to take Vera's hand, and gave her a wonderful smile.

After the service and the signing of the register, the wedding party made their way back down the aisle. This time, Dolly was holding Tony's arm, and he was grinning like a Cheshire cat.

'I like this,' he whispered, patting her hand.

Dolly just carried on smiling at the congregation.

After the wedding photographs had been taken, and the confetti tossed over the happy couple, the two of them went off in John's car to the hotel where they were holding the reception.

Mrs Marchant and Dolly waited for Tony to go round the back of the church to collect his car. In no time at all, he was back, and then they too made their way to the hotel.

The hotel was set in lovely grounds in Surrey, just outside of London. Inside, John and Vera were standing in the doorway to welcome their guests. There were hugs and kisses for everyone. The meal was wonderful and the speeches sincere.

Dolly felt very honoured to be sitting at the top table along with Vera, John, the best man who was a fellow doctor, Tony, Mrs Marchant, and John's parents. There was a lovely two-tiered cake, and the wine was flowing.

After the food, everybody moved into the ballroom where there was a small band playing.

When they had settled quietly in the corner of the room, Mrs Marchant said to Dolly, 'He must have a few bob to pay for this lot.' They were watching Vera and John having the first dance.

'Vera said that John is an only child.'

John's mother came over to them. 'Mrs Marchant...' She held out her hand. 'We haven't had a chance to talk. I'm John's mother, Isabel, and this is my husband, Claude.'

Claude gave them both a nod. Dolly thought that Mrs Marchant might jump up and curtsy.

'I'm Ruby,' she said softly.

'We are both so pleased to meet you,' said Isabel. She turned to look at Vera and John. 'Don't they make a happy looking couple?'

'Yes, they do,' said Mrs Marchant.

Tony came over with a drink in his hand.

'And you must be Vera's cousin,' said Isabel. 'I've heard a lot about you.'

'All good, I hope.'

'I must say, you looked after Vera very well in the church.'

'Well, let's hope John looks after her from now on. After all, it is his job.'

'I'm sure he will. Come along Claude,' said Isabel, 'we must go and circulate. Ruby, I hope we can talk later.' They moved away.

Dolly wanted to laugh.

'You all right, Mum?' asked Tony.

'I'm fine now I've met those two, but I'm a bit worried about Vera. That Isabel seems a right old stuck-up cow.'

Tony laughed. 'I don't think she is. It's just her way. I was talking to her through the meal and she seems very nice. Don't forget, she's just as worried about John as you are about Vera. They might both come from different backgrounds, but that don't matter, just as long as they're happy.'

Dolly almost gave Tony a round of applause.

'Right, do you both want another drink?' asked Tony. 'Remember, it's all free.'

'Don't you go drinking too much,' said Mrs Marchant.

Tony bent and kissed his mother's cheek. 'I do love you, but I'm not a little boy any longer.'

'I know that, but I can still box your ears if you get out of line.'

'I'll go and get those drinks.'

'I'll come with you and give you a hand,' said Dolly.

'Thanks, Doll.'

As the evening wore on, the younger ones began wandering about in the lovely gardens. Although, as with most green spaces, most of it had been turned over to grow food, but all the mature trees, and some rose bushes, were still there.

Vera and John were staying at the hotel for the night. Tomorrow, they were off to Scotland for a few days, and were planning to pay a visit to see Tony's sister, Rose, and her husband, as they were not able to get to the wedding.

Mrs Marchant found an aunt of John's and

337

they were busy discussing what they did during the war and the effects of rationing.

'Fancy a stroll outside?' Tony asked Dolly as they smooched around the dance floor to a slow, dreamy tune.

'Yes, please. It's so hot in here.'

All day the temperature had been rising, and the hotel staff had thrown open all the doors and windows to try to let in some air.

'That's a bit better,' said Tony, once they were outside. As most of the other men had done, he had already taken off his tie and jacket.

'Look, there's a seat under that tree. Let's go and sit down,' said Dolly. 'This has been such a wonderful day; I don't want it to end.'

The evening breeze very gently rustled the leaves on the tree.

'I only hope things will work out well for Vera,' said Tony.

Dolly smiled. She was pleased he was concerned about his cousin. 'I'm sure they will. John seems a nice bloke.'

'You looked really smashing today, Doll.'

'Thank you, kind sir. You didn't look too bad yourself.'

Tony put his arm round Dolly's shoulders and she snuggled into him. Slowly, she turned her face towards his and he gently kissed her lips. When she didn't pull away, he kissed her with more passion and she responded. Then, he gently pulled away, stood up, and took her hand. The sun was going down and it was beginning to get dark as Tony led Dolly towards the trees.

Chapter 33

Hand in hand, Tony led Dolly through the trees. She didn't speak or put up any resistance. When he sat down on the ground, she sat beside him. She felt relaxed and happy – perhaps the drink had something to do with that.

'It's been such a wonderful day,' she said, looking at him.

'And we can make it even better.' Tony put his arm round her waist.

Dolly looked around; there wasn't anyone in sight. She nestled close to him. When she turned her head, he kissed her, and she responded. It had been a long while since she had been kissed passionately like this, and she was enjoying it.

They lay back and, very slowly, Tony's hand began to travel up her dress. When he began to finger her suspenders, she knew he would want to go further, and she wasn't going to stop him. Although she knew what he was going to do, the excitement of being made love to again thrilled her. It had been a long time since her feelings had been aroused like this.

Afterwards, Tony rolled onto his back and looked at Dolly. She propped herself up on her elbow and looked at him.

He quickly sat up. 'Dolly, I really do love you, but I'm sorry, I shouldn't have done that.'

She smiled. 'I didn't stop you.'

'I took advantage of you.'

'Only because I let you.'

'I do love you, Dolly. Please marry me.'

As Dolly stood up, Tony grabbed her hand and pulled her back down.

'Don't you have any feelings for me at all?'

'Yes, Tony, I do, but...'

'I know you're worried about us not having kids, but I can assure you, to me, that's not the be-all and end-all. Honestly, I just want to spend the rest of my life with you.' He ran his fingers through Dolly's hair. 'Besides, we could always adopt. There's plenty of kids whose parents were killed in the war.'

Dolly knew that Tony had genuinely meant what he had said about spending the rest of his life with her. It upset her because she knew she couldn't say yes. She began laughing, to try to make light of it.

'What's so funny?'

'You.'

'Why?'

'You've just made love to me, and proposed, and now you're talking about adopting. You don't waste time, Mr Marchant, to get your point over, do you?'

'That's because I love you and want you to marry me. I know we could be so happy together. So what do you say?'

Dolly scrambled to her feet and brushed herself down. Tony jumped up, and took hold of her shoulders.

'Tony, please don't.'

He quickly let her go.

'I think we both got carried away with the moment and all that's happened today,' said Dolly.

'I didn't. I meant every word. Don't you have any feelings for me?'

'Yes I do,' she said softly. 'I'm very fond of you, you know that.'

'But not enough to marry me? What is it that you've got against marrying me?'

Dolly didn't answer and began to walk away. 'Please don't spoil the lovely day.'

Tony walked beside her.

'I bet my hair looks a mess,' she said, fluffing up the back of her hair.

Tony didn't answer.

'Please Tony. Don't let us fall out over this. We've been friends for far too long.'

'I'm sorry, Doll, but ever since you came back from America, I've hoped that one day you'd change your mind and marry me. But now, as you've made it very clear that's not what you want...' he kicked a stone along the path, 'I think we'd better call it a day. If that's what you want.' When Dolly didn't reply, he said, 'I expect Mum's waiting to go home,' and hastened his step.

'Where have you two been?' asked Mrs Marchant when Dolly and Tony walked back into the ballroom. The band was still playing, and there were a few people on the dance floor.

'We went for a walk round the gardens,' said Dolly. 'They must have looked really lovely before the war, and before they were turned over for the "Dig for Victory" campaign.'

'You all right, Mum?' asked Tony. 'Do you want

341

to go?'

'Only when you're ready,' Mrs Marchant replied.

'It has been a long day,' said Dolly.

'Right,' said Tony. 'We'll say goodbye to Vera and John, and then we'll be off. Is that all right with you, Dolly?'

'That'll be fine.'

After all the hugs, kisses, and goodbyes, the three of them were on their way home.

'It's been such a wonderful day,' said Dolly, in the car. She sat beside Tony, and his mother sat in the back.

'I only hope Vera will be happy,' said Mrs Marchant.

'Course she will,' said Dolly.

'I don't think you've got any worries about Vera, Mum,' said Tony. 'She told me that she's never been happier.'

'That's good. Now all we've got to do is get you married – then, son, I'll be happy.'

Tony didn't reply as he glanced across at Dolly.

Dolly quickly turned her head away and looked out of the window. Her thoughts were in turmoil. What had she done? She liked Tony so much; she didn't want to hurt him, but she couldn't stop thinking about what he'd said earlier, about getting married and adopting.

'Will I see you tomorrow?' Dolly asked Tony when they had arrived back home and were getting out of the car.

'Dunno.'

'Dolly, do you wanna come in for a cuppa?'

342

asked Mrs Marchant.

'No, thanks all the same, but I'll be off. It's been a long, lovely, wonderful day. I'll come along sometime tomorrow and collect all me things.' She kissed Mrs Marchant's cheek. 'Goodnight.'

'Goodnight, love, and thank you for all you've done today.'

Tony stood at the front gate and let his mother pass. When she was out of earshot, he said, 'I've been thinking ... if you won't marry me then I think it's best if we just stopped seeing each other.'

Dolly went to speak, but he put up his hand to stop her.

'I don't know how many times I've told you I love you, but if you can't see your way to marry me, then we are both wasting our lives. We need to move on.'

Dolly stood, dumfounded. 'Tony, I'm so sorry.'

'You don't have to be sorry, and thank you.'

'What for?'

'For stating your case perfectly well.' He leant forward and kissed her cheek. 'Goodnight, Dolly.' He then turned and went indoors.

She stood and watched him as he closed the front door. She desperately wanted to run after him and tell him that she did love him. Instead, she slowly turned and walked along to her own house.

Her parents were sitting in the kitchen with all the doors and windows wide open. Her mother was knitting, and her father was reading.

'Hello, love,' said Grace when Dolly walked in. 'It's been a bit of a scorcher today. Did it all go off all right?'

'It went off lovely.'

'I must say you and Vera looked very nice. When you and Tony walked back down the aisle, I could have cried. You looked such a lovely couple.'

'I should have walked with the best man, but Tony took my arm before I could tell him what he should do, so don't go getting any ideas.'

Jim glanced over at Grace, and raised his eyebrows.

'As if I would,' Grace said quickly. 'Now, you must tell me all about the food. What was the cake like? Are his parents all right? I must say, his mother looked very smart. I think they must have a bob or two.'

Dolly smiled. 'I'll have a cup of tea first,' she said, going into the scullery. 'Do you want one, Dad?'

'No, thanks all the same. I've got a bottle of beer keeping cold in the bucket outside. You can bring that in if yer like.'

'What about you, Mum?'

'I'll have a cuppa. D'you want any help?'

'No, that's all right. I've been waited on all day.'

Dolly went out into the yard and picked up her father's beer. Back in the scullery, she opened the bottle and poured the beer into a glass. She stood for a while watching the bubbles, and then put the kettle on the gas before taking the beer into her father and to talk about today. It was a day that she wouldn't forget in a hurry as she had now sealed her fate with Tony.

'So how did the wedding reception go off?' asked

Penny the following morning. She was in her wheelchair sitting outside the front of the house, watching the world go by, although she always said not a lot happened in Wood Street, especially on a Sunday.

'Wonderful. And it's great to see you sitting out here,' said Dolly as she perched herself on the concrete windowsill that ran all the way round the front room window.

'It's nice to get a bit of fresh air. I must say you and Vera looked lovely.'

'Thank you. It was great to see you in church, and with Gail. She was so good.'

'I think she enjoyed eating that ribbon. I thought Mrs M looked really nice. It's a pity none of us don't get more of a reason to dress up now and again. It seems that weddings and funerals are our only reason. So, will you be next?'

'What for? Me wedding or funeral?'

'Ha ha, very funny. You know what I mean.'

'I don't think so.'

'I was hoping, that's all. The way Tony looked at you when you were both walking back down the aisle – I thought he would have got you to change your mind. I almost expected him to drop to his knees and propose there and then.'

'Well, thank God he didn't.'

'So are you off driving this afternoon?'

'No.'

'Don't tell me you've given up.'

'No.' Dolly crossed her fingers behind her back. 'It's just that I'm a bit worried about doing some damage to Tony's car.'

'You're not gonna ask that copper to teach you,

345

are you?'

Dolly didn't answer, but she thought that perhaps that was the best way to show Tony that she was moving on, as he'd suggested.

It wasn't till the following Tuesday that Harry phoned.

'Sorry I've not got in touch before, but we've been rather busy. How did the wedding go?'

'Very well, thank you.'

'I bet you looked very nice. Do you have any photos?'

She laughed. 'Now what would you want a photo of Vera's wedding for?'

'You never know. We could keep it in the rogues' gallery.'

'I just hope you're joking.'

'Of course I am. So how's your driving coming along?'

'It's not.'

'Oh dear, what's happened?'

'I'm worried about damaging Tony's car.'

'I'm sure you're not doing too much harm to it.'

'I don't know, but I do feel guilty when I crunch the gears.'

'How about you coming out with me?'

Dolly hesitated. 'But what about your car?'

'I can always get my car repaired at work. So, how about it?'

Dolly quickly gave this invite some thought. This could really prove to Tony that she couldn't marry him. 'All right. Just as long as you're OK about it.'

'It'll be fine. Look, I'll give you a ring in the week, and let you know when I'm off duty. Is that all right?'

'Only if you're sure.'

'I think you'll make a very caring and safe driver.'

'Thanks, Harry.'

'It'll be my pleasure.'

When Dolly put the phone down, she wondered if she was doing the right thing.

Harry had a big grin on his face when he replaced the receiver. He began whistling, and thinking – hoping that this could be the start of something big.

Chapter 34

Dolly was looking out of the office window waiting for Harry. It was almost five o'clock and he was picking her up from work to take her out for another driving lesson. As the evenings were light, Dolly had been out driving every time Harry was off duty. Sometimes, it would even be over the weekend, but neither her parents nor Penny were happy with this arrangement. When his car came into view, Dolly quickly locked the office door and went to meet him.

Harry got out of the car and gave Dolly a quick peck on the cheek. 'Are you ready?'

'Yes,' said Dolly, 'ready and waiting.' She handed him her L-plates.

'Good. I'll just put these on the car. Jump in and then we can be off.'

Very slowly, she drove out of the site and soon they were going along the road.

'You're getting on very well,' Harry said.

'Thank you.' Dolly didn't want to get into a conversation as she was busy concentrating.

After a while, Harry said, 'Turn left down here and stop the car.'

Dolly did as she was told. When they stopped, she asked. 'Have I done something wrong?'

Harry laughed. 'No. You're doing really well.'

'Should I put in for my test?'

'No, not yet. Has Tony seen how well you're doing? Has he been taking you out?'

'No.' Dolly had told Tony that she was worried about his car, and he had accepted that.

'Now you're getting better, I thought I might be ditched and you'd go off with him.'

Dolly laughed. 'No, course not. I'm very grateful that you've been helping me.'

She had to be on her guard, as she hadn't told Harry that she and Tony weren't an item. She wasn't sure why she hadn't mentioned it. Was it because deep down she was hoping to get back with Tony? Her mind was in turmoil. Harry did ask once if he could take her out, but that was before she and Tony parted. She had seen so little of Tony lately. He was rarely at Penny's these days, and when he was there, he was so indifferent towards Dolly. Was he really doing his own thing? Should she tell Harry?

'Right,' Harry interrupted her thoughts, 'I want you to reverse round this corner.'

'What, now?'

Harry laughed. 'Yes, now. Keep as close to the kerb as you can.'

Very slowly, Dolly did as she was told. When she stopped, Harry said, 'That was very good.'

Dolly felt very pleased with herself.

'Are you sure he only takes you out driving?' Penny asked, the following Saturday afternoon, when Dolly went in after being out with Harry again.

'Course he does. We don't sit in the car making love, if that's what you're worried about.'

'It ain't any of my business what you get up to, not that you'd tell me anyway if teaching you to drive wasn't his only motive.'

'It is, and if I say so meself, I'm beginning to get rather good at it.'

'Good for you. So he ain't asked you out again to see another show or something?'

Dolly wasn't going to tell Penny that Harry had asked her out again some time ago, and that she had turned him down because she didn't want to get involved in that way. She changed the subject. 'So, how about you try walking to the kitchen or something? Like you did the other day.'

Penny smiled. 'I'm getting on, ain't I?'

'I should say so. Now come on, best foot forward.'

'I ain't really got a best foot.'

'We shall see about that, but I tell you what, I think your shiny boots look lovely today.'

Penny looked down. 'They do look rather nice, don't they? Good old Reg, he says he enjoys keeping me boots looking nice.'

'Right. So let's get you using them, and hopefully making 'em nice and dirty.'

'Bully,' said Penny.

'That's all very well, but when are you going over to the Gregorys?'

Later, Penny was sitting on the bed with her legs sticking out. Dolly had put her callipers on, as she'd been doing for weeks now. Gradually, Penny was gaining the confidence to walk to the kitchen with just her sticks, and without Dolly or Ivy holding on to her.

'D'you know, as it's such a nice day, I'd like to have a go at going across the road.'

'Great! I'll help Ivy to get the mats up, and then we will stand either side of you.'

'Thanks, Dolly.'

Ivy removed all the mats from the passage, as she did whenever Penny wanted to venture from her room. The last thing they wanted was for Penny to slip. Then, with Ivy and Dolly either side of her, Penny slowly made her way to the front door. When Ivy opened it, Penny stood for quite a while just looking around.

'It's funny,' she said, 'but everything looks so different standing up to what it does in a wheelchair.'

'Well, me old mate, this is the view you got to get used to.' Dolly was finding it hard not to get too emotional at her friend's achievement. 'Just let us know when you're ready for your great adventure.'

Penny took a deep breath. 'I think I'm ready.'

With Dolly and Ivy close by, Penny slowly made her way to the edge of the pavement. 'How do I get down the kerb?' Panic filled her voice.

Getting up and down kerbs wasn't something they'd thought about, or Penny would have asked about it at the hospital.

'I would think you put one stick down, then when you've got your balance, you put that foot down then do the same with the other,' said Dolly. 'Let us know when you're ready and we will help you.'

Penny stood for quite a while at the edge of the kerb. There weren't any cars around to cause a problem.

Dolly could see both the Misses Gregory looking through the shop window. She was pleased they hadn't come out and called to Penny, as that would probably make her even more nervous.

After a while, Penny said, 'Right, I'm gonna have a go. Can you stand either side of me? Just in case.'

'Course,' said Ivy and Dolly together, and they moved in closer.

It took a few attempts before Penny tentatively put one stick in the road, then gradually she swung her foot next to it. With her stiff legs, she looked very awkward, but after a while, she got her balance. Feeling confident, she placed the other stick forward and moved into the road. 'I did it! I'm in the road.'

'Good for you!' said Dolly. 'Now, it's over to the shop.'

At the opposite kerb, Penny was a little more confident. As soon as she had stepped onto the pavement, the Misses Gregory came out of their shop and gave her a clap.

'You clever, clever girl,' said May. 'Come on in and have a seat.'

Ivy and Dolly stood and watched the happy scene, and they both smiled as they each wiped away a tear.

Inside the shop, the Misses Gregory were beaming.

'What a wonderful day,' said May. 'How long have you been walking?'

Ada said, 'Dolly has been telling us how much you've progressed these past few months, but we never thought you'd get this far so soon.'

Penny sat down on a bent wooden chair. 'She is a bit of a nag,' she said, grinning at her friend.

'All this is down to Dolly,' said Ivy.

Dolly looked away. She felt embarrassed at all this praise. After all, it was Penny who had done the hard work.

They stayed in the shop for a little while, and then Ivy left to make sure Gail was all right. Different people came in the shop. Some of whom Penny hadn't seen for years. Everyone sang her praises and told her how well she looked.

When Dolly could see that her friend looked tired, she managed to catch Penny's eye, and mouthed, 'Had enough?'

Penny nodded.

'I'll pop over and get Ivy, and then you can make your way back home.'

'Thanks, Dolly,' said Penny.

Penny sat in her wheelchair while Dolly removed her callipers and boots. 'Are you all right?' she asked.

'A bit wobbly, that's all.'

'Well, that was quite an achievement.'

'I know, and I can't wait to tell Reg. He'll be so pleased with me. Next time we go to the hospital, I'll be able to tell them what I've done.'

Dolly would have liked to tell Tony, but these days they hardly spoke. When they did, it was all very polite and formal. She was beginning to realise just how much she missed him being around.

'Are you out with your copper bloke tonight?' asked Penny when she was giving Gail her bottle.

'No. He's on duty tonight.'

'How's the driving going anyway?'

'Not bad. I don't crunch the gears so much now.'

'I bet he's pleased about that.'

'I don't know about him, but I'm certainly pleased about it. Every time I did it I'd wince for the car.'

'You daft apeth.'

'I know.'

'You'll have to tell Tony how you're getting on; he might take you out again.'

Dolly had told Penny that she wasn't seeing much of Tony now as she was worried about damaging his car. She wasn't sure if they believed her, but so far, nobody had queried it. It seemed that Tony had told Reg he wasn't happy with Dolly for letting a copper teach her to drive.

A couple of days later, Dolly had just got off the bus and was hurrying down the street when the heavens opened up. It had been threatening a thunderstorm all day, and Dolly was hoping to get home before it broke, but she was too late.

Tony drove up beside her, and winding down his window, shouted, 'Quick, get in.'

Dolly didn't hesitate. 'Thanks,' she said, getting in beside him. 'That was a bit of luck you coming along just then.'

Tony didn't reply.

As they drove along, hailstones bounced off the car's bonnet.

'Thanks, Tony, I would have got soaked. Look at this rain.'

'Well, I can't leave a lady in distress now, can I?'

'Thanks,' Dolly said again.

'How are you?' Tony asked. 'And how's the driving going?'

'Not too bad. I've been on the roads a few times, and in the traffic.'

'That's great. Have you put in for your test yet?'

'No. Harry don't think I'm ready just yet.'

I bet he don't, he wants to keep her around for as long as he can, Tony thought. 'I hear you got Penny to walk to the Gregorys' shop.'

'Yes, me and Ivy stood beside her while she stepped off the kerb.'

'So Reg said. He's dead chuffed about it.'

Once again they lapsed into silence, until Tony asked, 'So, how are you keeping these days?'

'I'm fine. How about you?'

'Mustn't grumble.'

To Dolly, this conversation was boring and pointless. 'How's Vera?' she asked.

'She's fine. She brought the photos over a week or so back.'

'Were they nice?'

'They were all right.'

'I would have liked to have seen them.'

'She took 'em back with her.'

'That's a pity.'

Tony wasn't going to tell her that his mother had bought some, or that he'd got a lovely one of him and Dolly together. Perhaps one day he'd tell her, and then perhaps she'd ask to see them.

'It's nice to see you again, Tony,' Dolly said when they arrived at her house, 'and thanks again for the lift.' She opened the car door and got out.

'It was my pleasure,' he began, 'and Doll...?' but she'd gone before he could finish the sentence, which was just as well, as he was going to ask her if she wanted a few more lessons, but then decided against it.

When Dolly closed the front door, she stood for a while thinking about Tony. She missed him so much. Was she being silly? After all, he had told her he loved her. Should she make the first move to see him again? Would he want to see her?

'Is that you, Dolly?' called her mother through the kitchen door. 'You must be like a drowned rat. Come on in and take those wet things off.'

'I'm not too bad,' she said, standing in the passage and removing her damp coat and hat. 'Tony gave me a lift.'

'That was nice of him.'

Her mother didn't say any more. Dolly had told them both, in no uncertain terms, that she and Tony had fallen out. They didn't know the real reason why, and the mood Dolly had been in since the wedding told them not to ask.

On Sunday, Dolly was just going into Penny's when Tony came walking along the street towards her. He was whistling.

'You sound happy,' said Dolly as they went through the front gate together.

'Yeh, I'm just off with Reg to look at a job.'

'What, on a Sunday?'

'Well, it's the only time we get now. As you can see by the work sheets, we're a bit busy these days.'

Dolly was very aware that Bert Edwards was putting a lot of work their way. 'So where you off to?' she asked Tony as she pushed open the front door. 'It's only me,' she shouted out, as they walked down the passage.

'I don't rightly know,' said Tony, as they went into the kitchen.

Tony bent down, kissed Penny, and then kissed his fingers and put them on Gail's cheek. 'And how's my little lovely, today?' he asked, tickling her chin, and making her smile.

'I'm lovely, thank you,' said a grinning Penny. 'So you're off with Reg then?'

'Looks like it. Is he ready?'

'I think so. Give him a shout, he's out back.'

'I'll wait till he comes in.'

Dolly had gone into the scullery. 'Everything all right, Ivy?' she asked.

'Everything's fine. Reg is getting quite excited about this new job they might be doing. I'm just making a few sandwiches for 'em and doing up a flask of tea, just in case there ain't anywhere for 'em to get something. From what he was saying, it's quite a new building job, out in the sticks somewhere.'

Just then, Reg walked in. 'Hello, Dolly,' he said, and kissed her cheek. 'Everything ready, Mum?'

'Here you are, love. I put an extra cup in for Tony.'

'Thanks, we won't be too late... Bye.' He kissed his mother's cheek. As he walked through the kitchen, Tony also called out, 'Bye', and they both left.

'Do you know where they're going?' asked Dolly.

'No,' said Penny, quickly.

Dolly was surprised at that answer. Penny and Reg never had secrets from each other, more so since his gambling. So what was all the secrecy about? She decided to wait till she was at work tomorrow. Perhaps she would be told then.

At work on Tuesday, Dolly had been busy. There had been a lot of invoices to sort out, and it was soon five o'clock. As she put on her coat, Harry drove into the yard in a police car. She locked up the office, and walked towards his car as he got out.

'Hi there, Dolly. I was hoping to catch you before you left.'

'Hello, Harry, is everything all right?'

'Not really. I'm sorry, but I can't take you out for the time being as I'm being sent away on a course.'

'Oh,' was all she managed to say at first. 'So where are you going?'

'Hendon. It's an advanced driving school. If I pass, I'll be in a squad car, and then I'll be racing round all over the place.'

Dolly could see by his face that he was very pleased at that prospect. 'So when are you off?'

'Tonight... I should be away for the rest of the week.'

'That'll be nice for you.'

'But don't worry. When I get back, we could see about you taking your test.'

'That'll be lovely. Thank you.'

'Right. I've got to be off. See you soon.' With that, Harry got into his police car and drove off.

Dolly watched him go. She felt so alone. She desperately wanted Tony to be there, but it was her own fault. She made up her mind that from now on, if he wanted, they could be together again, and not just to teach her to drive. But she had to convince him that she really did love him. She smiled to herself as she walked to the bus stop. Somehow, she knew that things could only get better.

Chapter 35

'So will you be asking Tony to take you out, now that your copper friend's going away?' asked Penny when Dolly told her about Harry going on a course at the Hendon driving school.

'I don't know.'

'I reckon he'll jump at the chance. He was a bit put out when you started going out with Harry.'

'I wasn't going out with him. I went to the

theatre one night. How many more times do I have to tell you?'

'All right. All right. Don't get aerated.'

'Sorry.'

'You seem a bit on edge. Anything wrong?' asked Penny.

'No. Has Tony been in lately?'

'No. We ain't seen him since yesterday, when he went with Reg to look at the new site. Have you seen him?'

'No.'

'Do you miss Tony taking you out driving?'

'Yes, I like his company.'

'Well, you know the answer to that, don't you?'

'I can't marry him, if that's what you're on about.'

'I don't know why not. After all, he knows the score.'

'I know. Did Reg say if they're going to be working away?' Dolly asked; anything to get off the subject of her love life.

'No.'

'I think Dad might be a bit concerned.'

'What about?'

'Well, he is getting on a bit. If there's a lot of travelling involved, he might not be up to it.'

'I'm sure Reg will sort all that out, if it comes to it.'

'So nothing's been sorted yet then?'

'Not as far as I know.'

'Is it one of Bert Edwards' jobs?'

'I don't know. You're asking a lot of questions, ain't you?'

'Well, it might be my job as well.'

'Well then, you wouldn't have anything to worry about, would you?'

Dolly decided to drop the subject. She thought Penny might remind her about going to work at Peek Freans. But she was surprised at Penny's attitude; she seemed very abrasive. Was there something she wasn't telling? After all, she always knew about all of Reg's jobs. Would Tony know more? Perhaps she could ask him about it – that could be her excuse.

On Wednesday, as Dolly was walking home, Meg Windsor called out to her.

'Hello, Dolly,' she said, breathless from running to catch up with her.

'Haven't seen you round this way for quite a while,' said Dolly. 'Where are you off to?'

'It's me old aunt, you know, the one who lives in Princes Street. Mum told me to pop in to see her as she ain't been all that well.'

'Oh, I'm sorry to hear that.'

'Mind you, she's been in and out of death's door ever since I can remember. Trouble is, now she's going a bit funny in the head. Mum reckons she won't be here for much longer.'

'Oh dear, I'm sorry to hear that,' repeated Dolly.

'Vera looked lovely at her wedding. She's got herself a real stunner there, ain't she?'

Sometimes, Dolly had a job to keep up with Meg. She always flitted from one subject to the other. 'He seems a very nice man and let's face it, she deserves some happiness.'

'Well, she is getting on a bit. I must say, you and

360

Tony looked very cosy walking back down the aisle together. What about you two? Will you be next? I'd have thought that Tony would have got you up the aisle before now. After all, you were engaged at one time.'

'That was a long time ago.'

'Yes, before the GIs came over. I tried to get meself one of them. Would have liked to have gone to America.'

'Unfortunately, it didn't work out for some of us.' Dolly was careful not to say too much.

'I was sorry when I found out that you wasn't going to be working at Peek Freans. It could have been great us working and going out together.'

'Well, it got a bit difficult when I was offered a lot more work.'

'You still working for Reg?'

'Yes. What about you?'

'Still in the same old job, but the money's not bad. So are you and Tony together these days?'

'Off and on.'

'How's the driving going?'

'That's also off and on.'

''Ere, by the way, who was that good-looking bloke I saw you with a couple of weeks ago? Was that your car?'

'No, course not.'

'Well, you was driving.'

'He's been teaching me.'

'Oh yes? And where did you find him? He looked a real dish.'

'He's just a friend.'

'Has he got a mate?' Meg gave Dolly a nudge.

'I don't go out with him.'

'More fool you, he looks a real man. So why was you out with him then?'

'I told you, he's just teaching me to drive.'

'Pity. I was hoping you'd left Tony, and he was free for me.'

Dolly was longing for Meg to get to her aunt's road. 'Been shopping lately?' she asked, to get off the subject of herself.

'Nah, but me and some of the girls went to the Palais a few weeks ago – you should come with us. We had a great time, and there was plenty of blokes looking round for female company. I got meself a fella. His name's Frank. I'm seeing him again next week. He's all right for a night out, but that's all.'

'I'm pleased for you, Meg.'

'He's not the real thing, but he's got a mate who's not bad. Right, here's me aunt's road. I tell you what, I'll get me mum to drop a note into your house when we go dancing again. You can come with us; we'll have a great time. Bye.'

'Bye,' said Dolly.

When Dolly turned into Wood Street, she could see Tony's car parked in the road and was very tempted to go and see him. Instead, she decided to go and see Penny after she'd had her dinner. Perhaps, with a bit of luck, Tony would be there.

'I saw Mrs Marchant this morning,' said her mother, as soon as Dolly walked in.

Dolly followed her mother into the scullery. 'That smells good.'

'It's only a bacon roll.'

Dolly always admired her mother. She could

362

make a delicious meal out of almost nothing. It was wrong that rationing was still in place after all these years. 'So what did she have to say?'

'She showed me the wedding photos.'

'Did she? I ain't seen 'em.'

'I didn't think you had. Otherwise, you would have told me. I'm surprised Tony hasn't shown you. There's a lovely one of you and him. And the cake looked smashing.'

'It was. I'll have to ask Tony to show 'em to me.' Dolly was a little annoyed that she hadn't seen them yet. What was Tony playing at?

After dinner, and when Dolly had helped her mother with the washing-up, she went to see Penny.

'Yoo-hoo,' she called out, 'it's only me.'

Ivy opened the kitchen door, and Dolly walked in.

Penny was sitting in the chair, nursing Gail, and Reg was sitting at the table studying some leaflets.

'Hi,' Dolly said casually as she sat down. 'Have you been out today, Pen?'

Since she'd walked across the road, her friend had been going out a bit more in her wheelchair, even if it was only to the Gregorys' shop. She said that while the weather was good, she liked to get out and talk to people.

'Well, it was a lovely day today, and it's such a shame to stay indoors, but we only went round the block. Ivy pushed Gail and I trundled along beside her. We bumped into Meg's mum. She was telling us about her sister – that's Meg's old aunt. Did you know she only lives a couple of streets away?'

'Yes. I've seen Meg a few times when she visits her. In fact, I saw her on me way home from work today. She said the poor old dear was losing her marbles and not going to be around for much longer.'

'I was telling Reg that, and he wants to know who the landlord is. They're quite nice houses round that way and didn't suffer too much with the bombing.'

'Why? You thinking of moving?'

'No, course not, but the place might want doing up, and he'd like to get his estimate in first.'

Dolly was a bit shocked at that statement. 'You might wait till the old dear's gone.'

'It's business,' said Penny.

It was just then that Tony walked in. 'Hello, all,' he said. 'How's things, Doll?'

Dolly was thrilled that he'd greeted her as normal. 'Fine. Did you have a good day on Sunday?'

Tony looked at Reg. 'It was interesting. I hear your copper's gone away.'

'He ain't my copper, but yes, he's gone to Hendon.'

'So he'll be racing about in a squad car next, then.'

'Don't know. Mum said she saw Vera's wedding photos today. I'd like to see them.'

'So would I,' said Penny. 'Ask your mum to pop 'em along sometime.'

'I'll do that,' said Tony.

'What about me?' asked Dolly. 'When do I get to see them?'

'They'll be in here, so you can see 'em then,' said Penny.

Dolly was a bit put out at that. Perhaps Tony didn't want to see her. Perhaps he had decided to make a clean break, after all.

They spent the rest of the evening talking about nothing in particular. When it was time to finish, Penny said, 'How about a game of cards on Friday, Doll, now that you won't be going out driving this week? Will that be all right with you, Tone?'

'Don't see why not.'

'Right, that's settled,' Penny said, grinning at Dolly.

Dolly waited for Tony to say that he was leaving, but he didn't make any moves. Then Penny said she was off to bed, so Dolly went over to Penny, and kissed her cheek. 'Thanks,' she whispered.

Tony still hadn't moved, and Dolly could see that Ivy was also waiting to go to bed. Her friend knew that she wanted to see Tony, but if she couldn't speak to him tonight, then Friday could give her the excuse she'd been waiting for. She did love him, but was he fed up with their on-off relationship?

'Night all,' Dolly called out.

As she walked home, she felt happier than she had since the night of Vera's wedding, when she and Tony had made love. She hung around outside her own house for a short while, but still Tony didn't come out of Penny's. He must have wanted to talk to Reg about something. She went indoors. When they were next on their own, she would tell him that she loved him and wanted to marry him.

The next evening, Tony drove into the yard just

as Dolly locked up. She was thrilled to see him.

'Hello,' she said, trying to sound casual, although her heart felt as if it was doing somersaults. She really did love him.

'Jump in,' he said. 'I've got something to tell you.'

Dolly got in the car next to him. 'And I've got something to tell you.'

Soon they were on their way home.

'So, what have you got to tell me?' Dolly asked.

'It's just that I might be working away.'

'Oh. Was this the job you and Reg were looking at?'

'Yeh, in a way.'

'Where is it?'

'That new town – Crawley.'

'Penny didn't say anything about that.'

'Penny don't know. So don't say anything to her.'

'Why not? Surely Reg would tell her if he was thinking of moving.'

'I don't think he is. It's just me that wants to work there. There's plenty of building work going on, and I might be able to get a house for me and Mum.'

'Oh.'

'I'm just telling you, for now, so don't say anything to your parents or Reg.'

'So why the big secret?'

'I've got to talk Mum into going.'

'Would she want to move?'

'She will when she sees those houses.'

'But she'll be leaving all her friends and neighbours that she's known ever since she moved here.'

'Everybody who moves there will be new, so they'll all be settling in together.'

'But why?'

'It's a good opportunity. I'd like to settle down and start me own business one day. Who knows, I might find a nice young lady to settle down with. Besides, one of these days, all these houses will be demolished and where will we all finish up then? I don't think me mum will fancy being in one of those tower blocks they're thinking of building. Can't say I like the idea meself.'

'You seemed to have made up your mind.'

'Yes I have. So what did you want to tell me?'

'It doesn't matter now.' How could she shatter his dreams?

'Look, if you'd like me to take you driving while your copper's away, that'll be fine.'

'Thanks, Tony. I'd like that.'

When they arrived in Wood Street, Dolly got out of the car, and Tony shouted, 'See you around.'

Dolly just waved back as he drove the short distance to his house. She stood at her gate and watched him for a minute or two, before he got out of his car. Once again things weren't going right for them. She wanted to cry – it was all her own fault.

Tony looked through the rear view mirror at Dolly standing at her gate.

'Dolly, I would give up everything for you, if only you could love me and want to marry me,' he said to himself as he opened the car door and got out. He looked back towards her house, but Dolly had gone inside.

'You going in to see Penny?' asked her mother, as Dolly put the clean crockery in the cupboard.

'Don't know.'

'You seem very down just lately, has anything been said to upset you?'

'No. It's just that sometimes I feel that my life's got into a rut.'

'My God, girl,' replied Grace as she dried her hands on the towel that hung on the back of the kitchen door. 'You ain't been back from America a year yet, and here you are moping around. Will you ever be satisfied? All our lives are in a rut.'

Dolly looked at her mother with surprise.

'You want to try thinking about Penny and her life, for a change, and not just about yourself. If anyone's life's in a rut, it's hers – poor cow.'

Dolly watched in amazement as her mother left the scullery. She had never known her to have such an outburst. *Is she right?* Dolly thought. *Will I ever be satisfied with my life?*

Chapter 36

On Friday evening, Dolly took extra care with her appearance. She looked in the mirror on her dressing table and gently pushed up the back of her hair. She was pleased with the results. She hoped that she and Tony would leave Penny's together. That way, when they were outside, she would ask him to take her driving on Saturday afternoon. Then, when they were in the car, she would tell him her true feelings, despite the fact he had been talking about moving away. She hoped she could change his mind. When they got married, they could find somewhere to live locally. All these thoughts were racing around inside her head. She did love Tony, and didn't want to lose him, but she wasn't even going to think about that.

At Penny's, Tony had sat opposite Dolly. Every time she looked up, he looked at her, and his face would break into a broad smile. She smiled back. Dolly also noticed Penny looking at them. Could this be the night when her life would change forever?

'Right, that's it,' said Tony. 'Look at the time.'

'It's only eleven o'clock,' said Reg. 'What's the rush?'

'Once again you've taken all me money,' said Tony, standing up. 'Don't forget, we've got that job to finish in the morning.'

'Well, it could go on all day,' said Reg. 'Think of the overtime you'll be getting.'

Dolly looked at Tony. Should she say something? 'That's a pity,' she blurted out. 'I was hoping you could take me out for a little drive tomorrow. I'm frightened I shall forget how.'

'It's a bit like riding a bike,' said Tony. 'Once you learn, you never forget.'

'Remember, I couldn't ride a bike,' Dolly said, grinning.

Tony laughed. 'You were pretty useless on two wheels, as I remember. The times I had to take your bike home after you fell off and buckled the front wheel.'

'I was pretty hopeless. In the end, Dad took it

369

away from me.' Dolly remembered those far-off days with affection.

'Well, let's hope you're better with four,' said Tony.

'You'll be pleased to hear that I have got better at changing gear.'

'Well that's something I suppose. I could pick you up when we finish work. I don't know what time that will be. Will that be all right? Your bloke won't mind, will he?'

Dolly knew that it was useless to keep denying that Harry was her boyfriend. 'That will be smashing. Thank you.' She wasn't going to tell them that Harry would be back on Sunday.

When Tony left, he gave Dolly a quick kiss on the cheek.

'See you tomorrow,' he said, leaving Dolly feeling lightheaded.

As Penny left the room, she gave Dolly a thumbs up. 'Come and say goodnight to Gail before you go.'

Dolly wondered what Penny was thinking of. Couldn't her friend see that she was in a hurry to talk to Tony? She couldn't refuse, and when she left the house, she hoped Tony would still be around, but looking up the road, she could see he'd gone.

'Looks like I'll have to tell him tomorrow,' she said to herself.

Dolly didn't have a lot to do in the office on Saturday morning, so she spent her time preparing what she would say to Tony. Suddenly, a thought struck her. *What if he's changed his mind and don't want to marry me?* Her mind had started to run around in circles, then Bert Edwards rang to say that he was bringing over some more invoices. She kept looking at her watch, and then out of the hut, wishing that Bert would come soon with the work. After that, she could go off home and get ready for Tony to come and pick her up.

It was half an hour later that Bert arrived with the invoices, and more orders. 'So sorry I'm late, but there's been a bit of a crisis at the site.'

'What's wrong?' asked Dolly, terrified that he would tell her there had been an accident.

'One of the upstairs pipes burst and that flooded the building. All the hard work those blokes have put in these weeks has been washed away.'

'Oh, I'm sorry. What happens now?'

'Fortunately, the owner is insured, so that's one good thing, but he wants the place cleaned up and the work to start again as soon as possible. He's got people waiting to move in and he's worried he's gonna lose 'em. With the rent he charges, that's quite a few bob. It'll mean a lot of overtime for the lads, but I don't suppose they'll mind that when they get their pay packet. So Reg said that when you go home, could you pop in and tell Penny, and Billy's mum. Also, can you let Tony's and your mum know that the lads may be very late tonight.'

'Course I will.'

'By the way, I shall want these early on Monday morning, especially those for the materials that need ordering, so can you get them done as soon as you get in?' He handed Dolly a file. 'Bye. Have a great weekend.' With that, he left.

371

'A fat lot of a good weekend I'll have now,' Dolly said to herself, as Bert Edwards drove away. She looked though the invoices; she could work on them on Monday.

As she locked up, Dolly looked to the heavens. 'I know me love life is me own fault, but can you give me a bit of help?'

That evening, Dolly had been next door to Penny's mother, to tell her that Billy would be home late. Then, she had gone along to Mrs Marchant, and after that, she had sat in with Penny, waiting for Reg to come home. When at ten o'clock he hadn't arrived, she decided to go home to wait with her mother, for her father.

They were sitting quietly listening to the wireless when they heard the front door shut.

Grace jumped up. 'I'll put the kettle on,' she said.

'No, you sit down and talk to Dad. I'll do it. Do you want a cup of tea too?'

Grace nodded, just as the kitchen door opened. 'My God,' she said, 'what's happened to you?'

'Been working, ain't I?' came Jim's reply.

'But you're covered with dust, and look at the bottom of your trousers, they're soaking wet. Don't sit on the chair like that,' Grace yelled. 'Go and get changed!'

'I'm cold, hungry, and bloody tired, and all you're worried about is the bloody chair!' Jim stormed off, slamming the door behind him.

'Oh dear,' said Grace when Dolly brought the tea in from the scullery. 'I think I've just upset yer dad.'

'Perhaps we can get him something to eat. What

have you got?'

'Well, his dinner was in the oven. I didn't think he'd be this late. I expect it's dried up, by now.'

'I'll go and see if I can rescue something.'

With that, Dolly went back into the scullery. When she heard her father return to the kitchen, she heard her mother saying she was sorry and the chink of the spoon stirring the tea. 'Here you go; Dolly's sorting out your dinner.'

'Reg did send out for some sandwiches and tea,' said Jim.

'So the place is in a bit of a mess then?'

'I should say so. We've been up to our ankles in water, and all the doors we put in are soaking wet. The water came from a burst pipe above, so all the ceilings that we put up have come down. It's a right mess. We're going in again tomorrow. By the way, Dolly...' her father called out. 'Tony said he's sorry, but it'll be a few days before he can take you out driving.'

Dolly sighed. 'Thanks, Dad,' she called back.

On Sunday morning, Dolly went into Penny's and suggested that she and Ivy take Penny for a walk. 'Mum said she'll take Gail to see her other granny. So, what do you say?'

'We could have a go,' said Penny. 'But I can't go too far.'

'I know.'

'Me mum didn't believe it when I told her I'd walked over to the Gregorys' shop. Perhaps yer mum could bring her back to see me do it.'

'I don't see why not.'

So that afternoon, Grace pushed Gail round to

Penny's mother, while Penny, Dolly, and Ivy prepared Penny for her great outdoor adventure.

There were lots of laughs as Penny stomped her way slowly along the road with her straight legs and two sticks. They were on their way to meet her mother.

'How you doing, love?' asked Ivy, who was concerned that her daughter-in-law was pushing herself too hard.

'I'm fine. But I can't look up yet. So can you tell me when Mum comes along?'

'Course I will.'

They had only taken a few more steps when Mrs Watts came out of her front door with Gail in the pram, and with Grace following behind. She had just started to push the pram along the road, when she spotted Penny. She let go and rushed along to her daughter. Grace smiled as she took hold of the pram's handles,

'My clever, clever girl,' Mrs Watts called out.

'Don't touch me, Mum, or else I might fall over,' shouted Penny, her voice full of alarm.

Dolly and Ivy were close at her side, ready for any mishaps.

Mrs Watts slowed down. When she reached her daughter, she gently touched her hand. Tears were streaming down her face. 'I've dreamed of this day.'

'Well, I did tell you I'd done it, didn't I?'

'I know, but it's different to actually see you walking. And I'm sure you've got taller.' She wiped away her tears with the back of her hand. 'I wish I didn't have to work such long hours, then I could see so much more of you and Gail.'

374

'I know that, Mum.'

'Let us know when you're ready to turn back,' said Dolly.

'I think we could go now.'

Everybody turned round, and with Gail sitting up in her pram and taking notice of all that was going on, they slowly made their way to Ivy's house.

'In years to come, you will be able to tell this lovely daughter of yours about the day you walked to meet your mum,' Mrs Watts said, still wiping her eyes.

Dolly noted that despite the wet cheeks, they were all grinning.

After Dolly had removed Penny's boots and callipers, they all sat in Ivy Smith's kitchen, drinking tea and laughing.

Penny said, 'I wish I could have me leg irons fitted to a pair of sandals. Those boots are a bit hot in this weather.'

'Could they do that?' asked Mrs Watts who was sitting and holding Gail.

'Course not, Mum.' Penny raised her eyes to the ceiling in frustration.

'What time will the boys be back?' asked Mrs Watts.

'Don't know,' said Penny. 'I think they want to make the most of the light evenings to try to get as much done as possible. Think of the extra money Billy will bring in.'

'I shan't take any extra from him. He's a good lad and gives me as much as he can.'

'I only wish we could help you out a bit more, Mum.'

'With me working, and the bit you and Billy give me, we manage all right. Besides, you've got to think of this little one; she'll be wanting clothes and toys as she gets older, won't you, my darling?'

Gail smiled up at her grandmother and Dolly looked over at her own mother. What wouldn't her parents give to have a grandchild to love and spoil?

'Who'd like another cup of tea?' asked Ivy.

'I'll give you a hand,' said Dolly as she followed Ivy into the scullery, carrying the tray with the dirty cups and saucers on it.

'It's a pity Penny's mum don't see more of Gail,' said Ivy when they were in the scullery. 'She thinks the world of that baby.'

'Don't we all,' said Dolly.

Soon, Dolly, Grace, and Mrs Watts left to go home and prepare their evening meals.

'It was lovely to see Penny's mum with Gail wasn't it?' Grace said to Dolly when they were in the kitchen preparing the vegetables.

'It was.' Dolly knew her mother felt the loss of her own baby almost as much as she did. 'And Penny did so well with her walking.'

'Well, she's made up her mind that she'll be the one that takes Gail to school.' Grace stopped what she was doing and looked at her daughter. 'I hope all this hasn't upset you too much, love.'

'It's something I have to live with, Mum. Besides, I do get to help Penny.'

Grace turned away. What wouldn't she give to make her daughter truly happy?

It was the middle of a very warm August, and

Dolly had been leaving her door open at the office. On Monday morning, she had just settled down to see to the orders and invoices that Bert Edwards had left, when Harry Jordan walked in. He took off his cap.

Dolly stood up. 'Harry, how are you?'

'I'm fine. Did you miss me?' He went up to Dolly and touched her shoulder.

She jumped back. 'A bit.' For a moment, she thought he was going to kiss her.

'How's the driving going? Have you been out with Tony?'

'No. He's been busy working.'

'That's a pity. You mustn't let it slip.'

'I know. How did your course go?'

'Wonderful. The thrill of driving a fast car round a skidpan was so exciting. I'll be able to teach you a few things. So when can I take you out again?'

'I don't know. Things are a bit up and down at the moment.'

'I'm sorry to hear that. Nothing serious, I hope.'

Dolly smiled. 'No, it's nothing to worry about.'

'I'll call in sometime next week, and perhaps we can arrange a driving lesson.'

'That would be nice,' Dolly said.

'Bye,' Harry said as he left.

Dolly went to the window and watched Harry drive away. Although she would have liked to go out driving with him again, she knew she had to put him off. She didn't want anything to cause any problems between her and Tony – not now.

'Hello, love,' said her mother when Dolly walked in. 'Had a good day?'

'Not bad, how about you?'

'Saw Meg's mum, this morning, at the market. She was telling me that her poor old sister – you know, Meg's aunt – ain't getting any better, and she's a bit worried about her. She said she'd like to have her move in with her, but her husband won't hear of it. That's such a shame – fancy not being wanted!'

'It's a good job Meg can pop in to see her now and again.'

Grace smiled. 'She said that she was proud of Meg doing that. It seems none of the old dear's other nieces have bothered. You going out to-night?'

'Only in to see Penny.'

In some ways, Dolly wished she had asked Harry to take her out, just for a driving lesson.

Later, Penny excitedly told Dolly about Reg's new plan. 'Now they're doing all this overtime, Reg is talking about getting a new van.'

'What? A brand new one?'

'No, he tried that, but it seems you have to put your name down, and he was told it could take years.'

'That's a shame.'

'But he's gonna try to get a good second-hand one. He's got a lot of people looking out for him.'

'That'll be lovely for you. Would he be able to put in a better ramp for you?'

Penny nodded. 'But if the doors open wide enough, I hope I can sit in the front.'

'Will there be enough room for you with your callipers?'

'I hope so. Reg reckons he could lift me into the

seat, and that we could even take Gail on me lap. That would be wonderful, all sitting up the front together, like a proper family, and not stuck in the back in the dark not being able to see anything.'

'Oh Penny, that would be wonderful.'

'That means I'll be able to go out with Reg and talk to him.'

'Let's hope he can get a van then,' said Dolly. Tony had told her that second-hand cars and vans were hard to get now that petrol was off ration.

'So,' said Penny. 'Could you ask your copper mate, that if he hears of anything going, perhaps he could let you know?'

'I'll ask him when I see him again.'

'Thanks.'

They sat and talked about things in general. Dolly happened to mention that her mother had seen Meg's mother, who had told her all about Meg's old aunt and how the rest of the family weren't helping.

'Reg is still trying to find out who the landlord is,' said Penny. 'You don't know, do you Doll?'

'No, I don't.' She was cross with Penny. They might at least wait till Meg's aunt had gone.

'Don't get on your high horse. It is only business, after all, and I bet someone else will get in there before the old dear goes. When you see Meg again, perhaps you could ask her.'

Dolly didn't answer.

Chapter 37

Although Dolly went into Penny's most evenings, she had been feeling restless lately, and wanted a change. On Thursday, she asked her mother if she fancied going to the pictures.

'What if your father gets home before we do?'

'We can leave him a note. Besides, we won't be that late.'

'I don't know. I like to be here when he's home, to give him his dinner.'

'All right, don't worry about it.'

'What's on, anyway?'

'Frank Sinatra, *On the Town*.'

'You like him, don't you?'

Dolly nodded.

'I'll ask your father tonight. Perhaps we could go tomorrow.'

'OK.'

'So will that be all right, Dad?' Dolly asked later.

'I dunno. Reg reckons we might be finished by then, but as I've had a few late nights, I'd like to get home and have me dinner at a reasonable time. Perhaps another time, love,' he said, getting back to his newspaper.

'That's all right.' Dolly was disappointed, but she was pleased the job was almost finished. Perhaps, now, she and Tony could get together.

On Friday morning, Dolly had just walked into the office when Reg came in. He handed her a sheet of paper as well as the wages sheets.

'As you can see, the lads have got plenty of overtime, so if you could let me know how much I've got to get out of the bank when I come back a bit later, I'll be able to pay 'em tonight.'

'So what's this sheet for?' Dolly held up the piece of paper.

'That's their bonus. The bloke who the building belongs to is very pleased with what they've done and how quick they finished it, that he's given them a bit extra. I think he got a nice bit of key money from the bloke who's moving in there. But don't add it to the wages sheets, cos that way they won't have to pay tax on it.'

'Will they be working all day tomorrow?'

'Not sure at the moment. It depends what time they finish up tonight.'

Dolly's mind was racing. She hadn't seen Tony all week. If he was off on Saturday afternoon, he might take her driving.

'Oh, by the way,' said Reg, 'have you found out who the landlord is on that property in Princes Street?'

'No.'

'Mum asked our landlord, but he don't know. So when you see that Meg again, perhaps you could find out for me? It could be a nice little number for us to do, getting it all up together again, cos I don't suppose much has been done to it all the while Meg's aunt's been living there.'

'I shouldn't think Meg would know,' said Dolly, who was getting angry at this request.

'They must pay the rent to someone. Anyway, see what you can find out.'

'Can't you wait till she's dead?' Dolly blurted out.

'No. If I leave it, then someone else will beat us to it.'

Dolly wasn't happy. She didn't reply as Reg left the office. This would be the last thing she would ask Meg, the next time she saw her.

She set about going through the wages sheets and was very surprised at what they all earned this last week. The extra would indeed be a bonus.

Saturday morning arrived, and Dolly hoped that Tony would come into the office when he finished work, but when she left at twelve o'clock, there was no sign of him. She was surprised to see his car outside his house when she walked along Wood Street.

'Hello, Dad,' she said as she went into the kitchen. 'Reg said you might be finishing early. What time did he let you go?'

'Just before twelve. We can finish the last bits on Monday. I think he was a bit surprised at the overtime we'd put in.'

'And the bonus was very nice as well.'

'Yeh... Can't say I like me daughter knowing what I earn, though.'

Dolly laughed. 'Don't worry, I won't tell Mum. I don't suppose Tony said what he was doing this afternoon, did he?'

'As a matter of fact he did. He said he was taking his mum out for a ride, although he didn't say where.'

Dolly suddenly felt sad. Why hadn't Tony asked her if she would like to go with them? Perhaps he was taking his mother to look at that new estate in Crawley, and wanted her approval. Other than going to his house to ask him, there wasn't a lot she could do about it. 'Have you got any more work now this job's nearly finished?' she asked her father.

'I think so. Reg seems to think that the bloke whose flat we've been doing up will ask Bert for us again.'

'That's good.' Dolly thought that was one thing in her favour. Tony would be around for a while yet.

Dolly didn't see Tony till Sunday, when she went in to see Penny. 'Dad said you took your mum out yesterday. Did you have a nice time?'

'Yeh, we went for a ride in the country.'

Penny looked up. 'What brought that on? You don't normally take your mum out.'

'Thought she needed a break.'

Dolly knew she had to say something. 'I would have liked to have gone with you.'

'Sorry, Doll, perhaps some other time,' was all he said.

After he left, Penny asked, 'What have you said to upset Tony?'

'Nothing really.'

'I thought things seemed to be a bit strained since the wedding.'

'I told him I thought he ought to go out a bit more and meet other people.'

'Why?'

'You know why.'

'You know you could be pushing him into someone else's arms – like Meg Windsor. How would you feel about that?'

'I would hate it. Oh, Pen, what have I done? I do love Tony.'

'Well, bloody well go up the road and tell him.'

'Shall I?'

'Go on, go!'

Dolly gave Penny a quick kiss on the cheek, and left, but her heart sank when she saw his car had gone. He wasn't at home. She turned round to go back to see Penny, and had only gone a few steps when she changed her mind. She would go and speak to Mrs Marchant, and find out if they went to look at the new houses.

She felt very nervous about knocking on the door. Supposing Tony had sworn her to secrecy. Perhaps he didn't want anyone to know till it was all signed and sealed.

'Hello, love,' said Mrs Marchant when she opened the door. 'Tony ain't in at the moment, but he shouldn't be long. He's only gone round the corner to see someone. D'you fancy a cuppa?'

Although Dolly had just been drinking tea with Penny, she said, 'Yes, please,' and followed Mrs Marchant along the passage and into the kitchen. She needed an excuse to be here, so asked, 'Is there any chance of me getting one of the wedding photos?'

'I thought you got some.'

'Only the little ones. I'd like a bigger one to put in a frame.'

'They do look nice standing on me mantel-piece.'

'Did you have a nice time yesterday?'

'We had a lovely afternoon. We went and looked at some lovely houses in Crawley. Tony said he'd like to move there, but I said I wouldn't. It's a bit out of the way for me. Mind you, I loved the houses. You should see the kitchen and the bathroom.'

'I have. I went with Reg and Tony a while back.'

'He said. So what did you think of 'em?'

'They are lovely, but as you said, a bit out of the way. What about a job? Would Tony be able to find work?'

'He reckons so, but I don't know how I'd manage without his money coming in – not if he has to pay rent. He couldn't afford to do both.'

That comment gave Dolly a bit of hope. 'How would you manage if he ever left to get married?'

'Gawd only knows...' She stopped and grinned. 'You ain't...? You know...? Him and you...?'

Dolly laughed. 'No, course not.'

'That's a pity. Always fancied the idea of you as me daughter-in-law.'

'I might have been if...'

Suddenly, the door burst open and Tony walked into the kitchen. 'Dolly! What you doing here?'

'She came in for a cuppa,' said his mother. 'D'you want one?'

'Yes, please.'

Mrs Marchant went into the scullery.

'I hope you don't mind, Tony,' Dolly began, 'but I thought I'd have a chat with your mum. I ain't seen a lot of her since the wedding. Besides,

I wanted to see the photos.'

'I showed them to you when you was with Penny.'

'I know, but I would like one of me own, so if Vera could get me one, I'll pay her, of course.'

'You should have said before, when we ordered ours.'

'Sorry, but I didn't think about it at the time. And now I don't see that much of you, I thought I'd better do it, just in case you move away.'

'What's Mum been saying?'

'Not a lot, just that you took her to see those new houses.'

'Yeh, that's right.'

'So are you thinking of moving?'

'Dunno yet. The job prospect is very good. But I don't know about getting Mum to move.'

Mrs Marchant came in with the tea tray. 'I heard that. I'm sorry love, but I don't wanna move. If you think you'll be happy moving away, well I won't stop you.'

Tony looked at Dolly.

'Don't look at me,' she said quickly. 'What you do is your business.'

'I'll get the photos,' said Mrs Marchant. 'They're in the front room.'

As she left the kitchen, Dolly said, 'Is there any chance of you taking me out driving this afternoon?'

'If you want. What about your copper friend?'

'He's busy.'

'I see. So I'm just a filler when he can't take you.'

'Don't get cross. Besides, I want to talk to you.'

386

'What about?'

'Just tell me what ones you want,' said Mrs Marchant as she walked back into the kitchen.

Dolly looked through the album. 'I'd like this one.'

Mrs Marchant smiled. 'That's a really nice one of you and Tony. You both look so happy.'

'It was a very happy day, and the evening was lovely as well...' She looked at Tony. 'Wasn't it?'

'Will two o'clock be all right?' he said, ignoring the fact he knew what Dolly was talking about.

'I shall be ready and waiting.'

As she walked back home, Dolly knew that today could be the day that changed her life forever. If Tony turned her down, she would be devastated and would have to rethink her life, but if he didn't, well, she'd be on cloud nine.

'All right, love?' asked her mother when Dolly walked in.

'I'm going out driving with Tony a bit later.'

'That's nice. Dinner will be ready at one. Will that be all right?'

'That'll be fine. Thanks, Mum.' Dolly went upstairs to get ready.

At two o'clock, Dolly walked nervously along to Tony's, carrying her L-plates.

He opened the front door before she'd had a chance to knock. Dolly thought that he must have been looking out of the window for her.

'Do you want to put these on now?' he asked, taking the L-plates from her.

'No. I'd rather wait till we are away from here.'

'You are daft.'

'It's just that I'm nervous and don't want to

look a fool.'

'Right. Jump in.'

'Can we go somewhere quiet?'

'If you like.'

As Tony drove, they were silent. Dolly was nervous. What if he turned her down? What would she do?

'Will this do?' he asked as they pulled into a quiet cul-de-sac.

'This will be fine.'

As Tony went to get out of the car, she put her hand out to stop him. 'Just a moment; I want to talk to you.'

'Oh dear, what have I done now?'

Dolly smiled. 'You haven't done anything.' She took a deep breath. 'Tony, I know I've mucked you about over the years, but I want you to know that I truly love you.'

'What's brought this on? Has me mum been on at you? I know she don't wanna move, but I never thought she'd ask you to try to talk me out of it.'

'No!' Dolly said, alarmed. 'She hasn't said anything. It's me. I love you and want to marry you.'

'Well, I'm glad to hear that you don't want me to move away, but I'm sorry, I can't stay here.'

'Why?'

'Cos I love you, Dolly. I always have, but over the years you've made it pretty plain that you don't want me, so as you said a while ago, we have to move on, and that's what I'm gonna do. But thanks for the offer. Now do you want to do some driving or not?'

Tears filled Dolly's eyes. 'I really do love you, Tony.'

'Is it home or a driving lesson?'

'I'd like to go home.'

'Please yourself.'

When Tony dropped Dolly off outside her house, she ran indoors and straight up to her bedroom.

When her mother knocked on the door and asked if she was all right, Dolly didn't answer. Grace opened the door and saw her daughter sitting on the bed, crying.

'Oh my God! What is it? Whatever's happened? Have you damaged Tony's car?'

Dolly shook her head.

'Well then, whatever is it?'

'He's moving away.'

'So why get this upset? I'm sure he'll come and see you sometimes.'

'I asked him to marry me and he said no.'

Grace sat down on the bed. 'Oh dear, did he give you a reason?'

'Just that he's fed up with me mucking him about.'

'I see. Well let's face it, Dolly, you have had him on a bit of string all these years, so you can't really blame him.'

Dolly stopped crying and stared at her mother. 'I thought you'd have a bit more sympathy.'

'Well, I think you've brought this on yourself. When's he moving away?'

'I don't know.'

'Come on, dry your eyes and come downstairs.'

'What good will that do?'

'I don't know. But you sitting up here feeling sorry for yourself won't do any good either.' Grace stood up and went to the bedroom door. 'Give him time to think about it. You never know, he might change his mind.'

Dolly was stunned. Her mother always took her side. Had she been such a cow that now everyone would feel sorry for Tony?

When she walked into the kitchen, her mother said, 'There's a cup of tea in the pot if you want it.'

'No, thanks.'

'So what new thing are you going to do now?'

'What d'you mean?'

'Let's face it, Dolly, you always seem to be looking for something new to do.'

'I'm frightened of making another mistake.'

'Tony would never be a mistake.'

'I know.'

'Well, you'll just have to wait and see if he stays. Is his mother going with him?'

'No. She reckons the houses are lovely, but that Crawley is too much out of the way for her. She'll miss all the people round here.'

'I've heard a few people say that. Some of the women at work went to Dagenham. They said it was all right at first, but it's really only for the young mums. They mix in well with other young mums, but the older ones couldn't seem to make friends. It's sad really, all those lovely houses. Pity they don't build some nice ones round here. There's enough empty spaces.'

This wasn't helping Dolly with her situation. 'I'm going to see Penny.'

'You look miserable,' said Penny when Dolly walked into her bedroom. 'Who's upset you?'

Dolly stood and watched Penny changing Gail. 'Tony.'

'What's the poor bugger done now?' Penny picked up Gail and placed her daughter over her shoulder.

'He don't wanna marry me.'

Penny burst out laughing, making Gail cry.

'What's so funny about that?'

'Here, take Gail and soothe her.' Penny passed the baby to Dolly. 'All these years, he's been pining for you, and now cos you've changed your mind, you expect him to fall at your feet. Good for him.'

'What?'

'Well, what did you expect?'

'I thought he might like the idea of marrying me.' Dolly suddenly felt very foolish, and she knew her friend was right. 'What can I do to win him back?'

'Don't ask me. Come on, let's go to the kitchen.' Penny wheeled herself out of the room and Dolly followed.

'Her bottle's all ready,' said Ivy.

'Thanks, Mum.'

'I'll do it,' said Dolly, and she sat in the chair to begin feeding Gail.

'You look a bit sad today,' said Ivy. 'Everything all right?'

Dolly gave her weak smile. 'I'm fine, thanks.'

Penny grinned at her. 'Dolly asked Tony to marry her and he's turned her down.'

Dolly knew she wasn't going to get any sympathy from her friend.

'Oh Dolly,' said Ivy, 'I am so sorry. I always

thought that you two would finish up together.'

Dolly looked at Penny, who was astounded. 'Let's face it, she's been mucking him about for years.'

'Penny, how can you be so unkind?' said Ivy, shocked at her daughter-in-law's comment.

'Why don't you go out in the street and tell all the neighbours?' said Dolly.

'I would,' Penny replied, 'if I could get me boots and leg irons on meself.'

Dolly stood up. She passed Gail, and the bottle, to Penny, and walked out of the kitchen to the front door.

Ivy went after her and stopped her from opening the front door. 'Dolly, just a minute, don't go.'

'I'm sorry, Ivy. I can't let her talk to me like that.'

Ivy put her arms round Dolly and hugged her. 'Penny can be very cruel at times, but she really don't mean any harm. I'm sure she's just as upset as you are.'

Dolly straightened up. 'She's got a funny way of showing it.'

'I know, but come back to the kitchen, and let's all talk nicely.'

Dolly knew that Ivy was such a kind person, but said, 'I'd rather not.'

Chapter 38

The following Sunday morning, Tony had been out with Reg to look at a van.

'So what was it like?' asked Penny when they came back home.

'It's a right rust bucket. D'you know, it's even worse than the one he's got,' said Tony as he settled himself down.

'Cheeky sod,' said Reg, 'I love my old van.'

'Well I don't,' said Penny.

'Don't worry; I'll still keep on trying,' said Reg. 'D'you think Dolly's copper might be able to help?'

'Dunno,' said Tony.

'You don't see that much of her now, do you?' said Penny.

'No.'

'That's a pity. It could have been useful,' said Reg. 'I'll have a word with her anyway.'

Although Penny knew the answer, she still had to ask. 'So what went wrong with the big romance then?'

'We just thought it best if we both went our own ways. That's all.'

'That's a shame; we all thought there might be a wedding one day.'

'What is it with women and weddings?' said Reg. 'So is her copper taking her out driving now then, Pen?'

'Dunno. Since he's been on the squad cars, he's been on different shifts, so she's hardly seen him.'

'That's a pity,' said Reg. 'So how was she doing then?'

'Pretty good. She said that Harry reckoned she could quite easily pass her test now.'

As Tony left, he thought about Dolly. *What's wrong with us? When I say yes, she says no. And when she says yes, I say no. I dearly want to marry her. But should I go cap in hand and plead?*

'It's only me,' he called out to his mother as he closed his own front door.

'Dinner's nearly ready, love,' called Mrs Marchant from the scullery. She walked into the kitchen, where Tony stood, looking thoughtful. 'You going out this afternoon?'

'No, I wasn't. Why? Did you want to go somewhere?'

'No. Now when do I want to go anywhere? If you've got nothing to do, you could pop along to see Dolly. I saw her mother in the Gregorys' this morning, and she said she was worried about her. She hasn't seen that copper since he's changed shifts, and she's a bit upset about letting her driving go. I thought you was taking her out?'

'I was, but we had a bit of a disagreement.'

'What over?'

'I can't remember.'

'I expect it was something silly. Anyway, go along and see her.'

'She might not want to see me.'

Mrs Marchant walked back into the scullery. 'Kids,' she said out loud.

Tony grinned. *We all need our mums to look after*

394

us, he thought.

That afternoon when Tony knocked on Dolly's door, he wasn't expecting her to be in, so was a bit surprised when she opened it. 'Oh, I thought you might be in with Penny.'

'I was just going,' she said. 'Do you want to see Dad?'

'No. It's just that Mum saw your mum this morning, and she said you was a bit down. Mum's sent me along to take you out for a driving lesson.'

Dolly laughed. 'Do you always do what your mum tells you?'

'Only if it's good advice. So, do you fancy going out?'

'Hang on, I'll just get me L-plates.' As Dolly went back into the kitchen, she said, 'Just going out with Tony.'

Grace smiled to herself. *It doesn't matter how old your children are,* she thought, *they still need their mums to give them a bit of help, and even a push, now and again.*

Tony drove along in silence till he stopped the car. 'Is this all right for you?'

'It's fine.'

'Penny was saying that your copper friend reckons you're ready to take your test.'

'He did say that.'

'Well, why don't you apply? I'll always take you.'

'Would you?'

'I said so, didn't I?'

'Only if you don't mind.'

'Of course I don't mind.'

'Thank you.'

'Now, let's see what you've been doing. Come on; sit here.'

They changed seats and Dolly was in charge.

After Tony had put her though her paces, he announced, 'Your copper was right; you are ready to take your test.'

'Thank you. Would you take me?'

'How many times d'you need telling?'

'Sorry. I'll book it in tomorrow. Are you sure you don't mind?'

'Course not. That's what friends are for.'

So, thought Dolly, *I'm still your friend.*

It was Monday 11 September. Finally, Dolly was on the way to take her driving test.

'Are you sure you don't want to drive there?' asked Tony.

'No. I'm too nervous.'

'Just relax and try not to think about it being a test.'

'It's all right for you to say, but I'm sure there's more traffic about today.'

He patted her hand. 'You'll be fine.'

Dolly was pleased that Tony had offered to take her. This was the first token of affection he'd shown her since her wedding proposal. Were things getting better between them?

Tony was eagerly waiting for Dolly to return to the depot. The smile on her face as she got out of the car clutching her sheet of paper told him that she had passed.

She rushed up to him and threw her arms round his neck. 'Thank you, thank you,' she said, and kissed his cheek. 'I could never have done it without you.'

'Let's go and get the paperwork sorted out.' He took her hand and they walked to the office together.

'I'm so happy,' she said as Tony drove home.

'All you've got to do now is get a car.'

'That will have to wait a little while yet.' Would this be the end of their friendship again? Had her excuse to see him now finished?

'I hope you don't think you can borrow mine,' he said, interrupting her thoughts.

'Course not. I wouldn't dream of even asking you. Dad might help me out, but I'll have to wait and see.' She thought this might be a good time to try to see him again. 'Could we go out for a drink tonight? Strictly as friends, just to celebrate my pass?'

'I don't see why not.'

'About seven then?'

'OK.'

Once again, Dolly eagerly waited for Tony. She wasn't going to mention anything about getting married or going out as a couple, but would wait and see how things were between them.

'You look nice,' he said when she opened the door.

'Thank you.'

'Where would you like to go?'

'I don't mind,' she said. 'You say.'

'As it's a nice evening, how about going up to Greenwich again?'

'That'll be nice. I like going there.'

'I know.'

As they strolled along the grassy bank up to the observatory, Tony said, 'I'm really pleased for you, for passing your test.'

'Thank you.'

'Did Penny tell you Reg was looking for a new van?'

'Yes, she was saying she would like to go out with him more when he gets one.'

'We went to look at one and it was terrible. Even worse than the one he's got.'

'I didn't think there could be one worse than that.'

'Anyway, he's still asking around. Would your copper friend have any idea where he might go to pick up something reasonable?'

'Dunno. I don't see a lot of him now he's driving squad cars.'

Tony smiled to himself. There was hope for him yet, so he had to make the most of tonight. 'Shall we sit down?'

'What about this drink I promised you?'

'That can wait.'

An elderly couple were sitting on the bench, and Tony hoped they would soon move away. He knew that this was the moment to ask Dolly to marry him.

'Lovely evening,' said the lady.

'It certainly is,' said Dolly.

'I love it up here,' she said. 'It looks like the whole world is at peace down there.'

'If only it was,' said the man.

'Don't take any notice of him. He's a bit of a misery at times. Are you married?' the lady asked.

'No,' said Dolly.

'Wait till you are,' said the man. 'Things won't be rosy all the time then. Come on, Flo, I need to stretch me legs.'

Slowly, they stood up. 'Take no notice of him...' she said, taking her husband's arm. 'Bye.'

'Bye,' said Dolly as the couple walked away.

As soon as they were out of earshot, Tony burst out laughing. 'I hope I don't get old and miserable like that.'

'I suppose a lot of that depends on who you marry.'

Tony turned to Dolly. 'I know who I want to marry.'

Despite the warm evening, Dolly felt a shiver of excitement. 'Now who would that be?' What was Tony going to say?

'Dolly, I know we've had a few ups and downs in our relationship, but I still think it would be right if we got married.'

'Is this a proposal?'

He laughed. 'Yes. I suppose I've gone about it in me own ham-fisted way. So, what d'you say?'

'Yes please, and thank you for making me very happy.'

They were in each other's arms, and kissing. Despite some children shouting out at them, they carried on.

Tony gently pulled away and said, 'I do love you Dolly Day Dream.'

'And I love you, Tony. I know, deep down, that I always have.'

They sat looking out at the view, both content with their lives.

'I shall never forget this day,' said Dolly. 'Today I passed me driving test and have been proposed to.'

Tony kissed her cheek. 'So what was the best?'

She smiled and put her finger to her cheek. 'Um, now let me think...'

Once again, Tony kissed her long and hard.

'I think a lot of people will be very happy about this,' said Dolly. She snuggled up to Tony who had his arm round her. 'But we must tell our parents first.'

'Shall we do that tonight?'

'Why not? But what about that drink I promised you?'

'We've got the rest of our lives to make up for that.'

Hand in hand, they walked back down to the car, stopping for kisses on the way.

'Who shall we tell first?' asked Dolly as Tony drove them home.

'It has to be your parents. At least I don't have to get your dad's permission.'

'I am over twenty-one now, but you do know it will have to be a registry office wedding, don't you?'

'I don't care. Can't say I go for all that dressing up lark.'

'Where will we live?'

'We could start looking now, I suppose.'

'You're not still thinking of moving away, are you?'

'Nah. I think that was only to find out if you'd miss me.'

'It might be hard to get a place.'

'There's no harm in looking. If we don't find anywhere, me mum would be thrilled to have you living there. She thinks the world of you, you know.'

'And I think the world of her. I suppose if we have to, that'll be all right for the time being.'

Tony touched Dolly's knee. 'Anywhere will be fine with me, just as long as you're happy, and we're together.'

'I do love you,' she said.

After lots of hugs, kisses, and handshaking at Dolly's, they popped along to Mrs Marchant and went through it all again.

'Right, next stop Penny's,' said Dolly.

'If you say so,' said Tony. 'I feel like a prize bull being paraded along the road.'

'Would you like it to be a secret then?'

'No, course not. Give us a kiss.'

'Mr Marchant control yourself.'

Laughing, and hand in hand, they went along to see Penny.

'It's only us,' Dolly called out as they made their way along the passage to the kitchen. Everyone was sitting round the kitchen table when Tony and Dolly walked in.

'You two are making a right old noise,' said Penny. 'Good job Gail is still wide awake.'

'Sorry,' said Dolly. 'But we've got something to tell you.'

'By the looks on your faces, I'd say it's about time as well.' Penny gave a great big smile. 'Come here, the both of you.' She held out her hands, and they both bent down for a hug.

Reg stood up, kissed Dolly on the cheek, and shook Tony's hand. 'Congrats to both of you.'

'How did you guess?' asked Dolly.

'Ivy saw your dad in the Gregorys' shop. He was grinning fit to burst, and he couldn't wait to tell her.'

'Sorry about that, Dolly.' Ivy also gave her a hug.

'We guessed we'd be next after Mrs M,' said Reg.

'We better had been, otherwise there would be a few feathers flying,' said Penny.

'Anyway, as I was saying.' Reg looked at Penny, and grinned. 'This is what happens when they've got you hooked. You can't get a word in edge-ways. We've got the drink out for a toast.'

Ivy came in from the scullery with a tray and glasses.

Reg picked up a bottle of sherry from behind the chair, filled the glasses and passed them round. 'To Dolly and Tony,' he said, raising his own glass.

'To Dolly and Tony,' said Penny and Ivy, lifting theirs in return.

'And about time too,' added Penny.

Dolly looked at Tony as she sipped her sherry. Her eyes filled with tears. She was so happy.

Chapter 39

Dolly was so happy when she and Tony went in to see Penny and Reg. She told them the date for their wedding would be Saturday 14 October.

Reg looked up from some papers he was working on. 'I suppose you'll both want that day off?'

Penny only looked at Reg, but the grin on her face said it all.

'No,' said Tony laughing. 'It's not till three o'clock, so we could both be there in the morning.'

Reg jumped up. 'I can't tell you how happy we are for the both of you. I could even drive you to the registry office in me new van.'

'You got a new van?' said Tony. 'When did you get that?'

'I was out this afternoon with Bert, and we went and had a look at it. It's not in bad shape. When the paperwork's all done, I'll be able to bring it home.'

'And I'll be able to go out with Reg,' said Penny. 'So it looks like good things are happening all round.'

'I'm so pleased for you,' said Dolly. 'But if you don't mind, I'd rather go to me wedding in a taxi.'

'She's so stuck up,' said Penny.

Dolly had been sad when her final divorce papers had come through, but despite all the ups and downs she'd had with Tony since returning home from America, she now knew that she had found true happiness, at last, with her first love.

Since they had set their wedding date, they decided to spend the following few weeks looking for somewhere to live, before they would have to settle down with Mrs Marchant.

The following Monday, on the bus home from work, Dolly's thoughts turned to house hunting. Tonight, once again, they were going to look at a place over Poplar way. Although Dolly knew that she would be happy living with Mrs Marchant, the idea reminded her of when she was married to Joe and living with his parents. She hadn't voiced her concerns about this to anyone. She knew how hurt Mrs Marchant would be if she knew Dolly's thoughts, but Dolly knew she couldn't have a nicer or more considerate mother-in-law.

As Dolly got off the bus, she saw Meg Windsor walking along.

'Hello, Meg,' Dolly said, meeting up with her. 'How's your aunt?'

'She's in hospital and very poorly. Me mum found her on the floor yesterday. They don't reckon it'll be long before she goes.'

'I'm sorry to hear that.'

'I'm just going to her place now to get her some nighties and clean drawers, and pick up a few bits for her. Mum said that you and Tony are getting married at last.'

'That's right. It's only a registry office, but you're more than welcome to come if you want.'

'I'll see. So it's no big do then?'

'No. Been there once.'

'Course. I very nearly forgot about that.'

'Well, it was a while ago.'

As they reached Princes Street, Meg stopped. 'I really do hope you and Tony will be happy,' she said, then walked away.

'Thank you, Meg,' Dolly said, but Meg's back was turned. She stood for a moment, and thought about the time she almost went to work with Meg. Would things be different today if she had? Would she have gone out with her to the Palais and met someone else? She shuddered. Thank goodness that hadn't happened, and everything had turned out for the best. She set off again.

'Dolly.'

Dolly stopped and turned round. Meg was calling her.

'Is there something wrong?' asked Dolly, quickly walking towards her. 'Do you want me to come with you?'

'Where you gonna live?' asked Meg.

'With Tony's mum if we can't find anywhere else. Why?'

'Well, it won't be long before Aunt Rene's house is empty, so the landlord will want someone to pay the rent. Why don't you ask him?'

For a few moments, Dolly just stood and looked at Meg. Then, when it had sunk in what Meg was saying, she threw her arms round her neck and hugged her.

Meg looked very surprised when Dolly let go. 'Well, I didn't expect that. But you'd better have a look at it first as it's in a right old state. Tony would really have his work cut out with clearing

405

it up and decorating. Come along with me now, if you like.'

When Meg unlocked the front door, there was a damp odour. 'She only lived in the one room downstairs. I expect the pot's still under the bed. If it wasn't for me and mum looking after her, she would have died months ago.'

'My mum said that your mum was really proud of you for keeping an eye on her.'

'Well, none of the other relations bothered. It's such a shame as she wasn't a bad old stick. Mind you, she could be a bit of an old cow when it suited her. Come upstairs. There's two bedrooms, but they ain't been used in years, and the paper's falling off the walls.'

When Dolly walked into the bedrooms, she could only see the potential. These rooms would be a picture, if the landlord would agree to them taking over the tenancy.

'Downstairs is the same as all the houses round here. Although, Aunt Rene was lucky; they didn't have a lot of damage during the bombing. And the old landlord did have the windows put back in.'

'I think that was because they got a grant from the government to do immediate repairs,' said Dolly.

'Oh yeh, I forgot you probably got to know about all that through working with Reg.'

'Most of the work had been done before I came back.'

As they walked back downstairs, Meg said, 'Mind how you go. The lino's a bit ropey. So how's it all going now with Reg? You gonna stay working there?'

Although Dolly's mind was in turmoil, she was trying to think rationally and answer Meg's questions. 'Yes. I'm a lot busier now he's working with someone else.'

'That's good.'

In the front room was Aunt Rene's bed. Meg began rummaging through a chest of drawers. 'Right, this is what I need,' she said, shoving some old-looking clothes into a bag. 'Me mum will take these in to her, tomorrow.'

'Meg, thank you.'

'What for? I ain't done nothing.'

'For telling me about the landlord. Hopefully, Tony can get in touch with him.'

'Oh, don't hold out any hopes. He might have someone in mind. You know what these blokes are like. They can't wait to put the old 'uns in their box and then push the rents up.'

That comment made Dolly feel a bit sad.

'I'll give you the rent book for his address. You can write to him and ask. That won't do any harm. You could always say that Tony will do all the repairs and decorating. That might help.'

'Thanks, Meg.'

'Well, it ain't no skin off my nose. Besides, if you get to live here, I'll always know where to come for a cuppa.'

That comment took Dolly by surprise, but she asked, 'You going now?'

'In a bit. I'll have another look round.'

'D'you want me stay with you?'

'No, thanks.'

'I'll drop the rent book back tomorrow.'

'Thanks.'

'I hope your aunt's all right.'

'I don't think she is, but thanks all the same.'

As Dolly left the house, she felt sad for Meg and her aunt. She could see that Meg had a real soft spot for the old lady, but if the house was going to be empty, it was an opportunity Dolly couldn't afford to miss. Most of the rents were way out of her and Tony's price range, and some places were little more than slums. Some landlords wanted a lot of money for handing over a key to just two poky rooms, and that was before the high rent would have to be paid. She almost ran the rest of the way home. Could this be her lucky day?

'Mum, Mum...' Dolly flew into the kitchen. 'You'll never guess...'

'My God, girl, whatever's the matter?'

'I've just seen Meg, and I've been to look at her aunt's house. Look, she's given me the landlord's address for Tony to write to him.' Dolly held out the rent book.

'Has the old lady died then?'

'No. Not yet.'

'Oh Dolly, how could you?'

'What d'you mean?' Suddenly, the excitement had left her.

'The poor woman's not even in her grave yet and you've been looking over her house.'

'Meg asked me to go with her. She don't think her aunt has long to live.'

'I know what you said.'

Dolly was filled with remorse. She remembered how cross she was with Penny and Reg when they had suggested finding out who the landlord was.

What would Tony say when she saw him later?

Over dinner that evening, Dolly had told her father about seeing Meg's aunt's house, and now Grace was telling Jim that she thought it was awful the way Dolly was so excited about it.

'Oh come off it, Grace,' he replied. 'You know how the two of 'em have been out night after night, and on the weekends, trying to find somewhere to live. Besides, as Dolly said, the landlord could have someone else lined up.'

'I know, but it's still not right. Next, people will be going to the undertakers and asking if they've got a funeral coming up and where is it.'

'Mum, that's not fair,' Dolly piped up. 'I told you it was Meg who said we should write to the landlord. That's all Tony's gonna do. We ain't throwing the old dear out.' Tears filled her eyes; she was upset about the way this conversation was going.

'I bet Tony's pleased about it,' said her father.

'He don't know yet,' Dolly said sadly. 'I'll be seeing him a bit later on. I thought I'd let him have his dinner first.'

Dolly knew what Tony's reaction would be, but they hadn't got the place yet. She looked over at her mother, knowing deep down that she would be as happy as everyone else would be if they were able to rent the house.

'Hello, Dolly, love. You all right?' asked Mrs Marchant.

'Hello, love,' said Tony, greeting Dolly with a kiss on the cheek. 'How's things?'

'Fine. You had a good day?'

'Not bad. Right, are you ready to go to the

outer reaches of Poplar? From what I can gather, this place is a bit of a dump.'

Dolly sat down. 'Tony, you know the house that Meg's aunt has been living in? The one Reg has been on to me about getting the landlord's address so he can get in first to do it up.'

Tony also sat down. 'Yeh.'

'Well, look, I saw Meg today. She showed me round, and I've got the rent book with the landlord's address.'

'Has the old lady died then, Dolly?' asked Mrs Marchant.'

'No, but Meg said she's in hospital and very ill. She asked if you would be willing to do it up, if the landlord agrees, so we could live there. She thinks he will, because then he won't have to pay to have it done. It's in a bit of a state. So what do you say? Mum thinks it's wrong.' The words all came out in a rush.

'What's wrong?' asked Mrs Marchant.

'Me getting excited when Meg's aunt isn't dead yet.'

'Oh Dolly, don't upset yourself,' said Mrs Marchant. 'I'm sure she didn't mean it. After all, the old dear's had her life. I'm sure if she knew you both she'd be more than pleased that you might have her house.'

Tony had been sitting with his mouth open. 'You've been in there?'

Dolly nodded. 'Well?'

He jumped up and grabbed hold of her, hugging her tight. 'You, my darling, are a little genius.'

'We haven't got it yet,' Dolly said as she tried to

get her breath back after Tony's hug.

'Let's have a walk round there and have a look.'

As they stood outside, looking at the house, Dolly said, '10 Princes Street. It sounds a lovely address.'

Tony, who had his arm round Dolly, kissed her cheek. 'Let's hope this will be our address one day.'

'I still feel very guilty about this.'

'I'll write a nice letter and explain everything. So don't upset yourself.'

'If we're lucky enough to be the new tenants, it will need a lot of work done to it.'

'Who cares? I'll enjoy doing it.'

'I'll help.'

'You just keep the tea coming.'

'We'll only have a few weeks before the wedding.'

'We can stay with mum till it's ready.'

'Here we are talking about moving into the house and poor old Aunt Rene's not even dead yet.'

'Oh Dolly, we'll wait till she is, if you like, but as you know, landlords don't like their property to be empty. I'll write a letter tonight and explain the situation. Perhaps I could arrange to meet him and have a word. What do you say to that? I'll be very discreet about it. In the meantime, perhaps, you could go and speak to Meg and her mum.'

'I'll do that. Anyway, I've got to take the rent book back. And thank you.'

Dolly turned to face Tony, and they kissed long and hard. *Could this really be a dream come true?* she thought.

'We won't be able to keep this from Penny and

411

Reg,' said Tony as they walked home.

'I know.'

'I wonder what he'll say.'

'Hopefully, he'll be pleased for us.'

'I worry about Penny, though. Will she think we've deliberately kept this to ourselves?'

'Course she won't. She'd be that pleased about it, and don't forget, we'll only be round the corner.' Dolly smiled. She did love Tony.

At the end of the week, Tony drove into the yard. He got out of his car, ran up to the office, and pushed open the door. 'Dolly, I've got an answer from the landlord,' he said, waving a letter around. He took her in his arms and kissed her.

'Well, I think it must be good news.'

'It is. Look, it says here he wants to see me. He's heard about the work Reg's done.'

'That's wonderful. When are you seeing him?'

'Well, he thinks we should wait to see if Miss Roberts is going back home.'

'Oh. Let's hope he don't change his mind before then.'

'I don't think he will. He said he's pleased that someone will do all the work for nothing.'

Dolly was singing as she set about washing the windows in the front room. She couldn't believe that she and Tony were getting married in two weeks' time. When they first decided to get married, Tony had wanted it to happen almost straight away, but Dolly said they had to try to find somewhere to live first, although she would have been prepared to live with her future mother-in-law if they could not find anywhere.

They had been so very lucky, and finally being able to rent the house had been like a dream. Sadly, Meg's aunt had died, and the landlord was keen to get another tenant into the house as quickly as possible. As Tony had already been to see him, they were in the right place at the right time. Dolly couldn't believe their luck. A whole house for just her and Tony. It wasn't until Tony had paid a month's rent in advance, and received a rent book with his name on it, that she was convinced it was really happening. Reg was a bit put out that he didn't get the contract, but that didn't stop him helping Tony. Along with Dolly's father, and even Penny's brother, Billy, they all helped with the decorating. Fortunately, the house was structurally sound, so all of the work was cosmetic.

Dolly knew her parents were disappointed that she wasn't able to get married in a church, as she was a divorcee. Tony said he wasn't a bit worried about it, as he didn't like a lot of fuss. It didn't matter that much to Dolly, either. She had walked down an aisle once before. This would be the one day that everybody looked forward to, and as soon as they were married, they were going to put their names down to adopt a baby, then their happiness would be complete.

Dolly's mother came into the room. 'That cooker's cleaned up a treat. You were lucky that the old dear didn't use it very much.'

Dolly stopped what she was doing and turned round. She was pleased her mother had overcome her outburst when she had first heard about the house. 'I'm only sorry I never got to meet her.'

413

'Yes. That was a shame. Have you put any money in the gas meter today?'

'No, not yet.'

'Well, if you've got a couple of shillings, I'll be able to make us a cuppa. I'm glad I brought me own kettle and teacups.'

'I hope we get something like that for a wedding present.'

'If not, most of us old married ones have got some extra crocks and things to help get you started.'

'Everybody's been so kind. D'you know, the other morning, Tony opened his front door and there was a box of plates on the step. We don't know where they came from.'

'Oh, that was from someone I meet round the market. She said she'd get her son to drop 'em round.'

Dolly wiped her damp hands down her pinny, and then kissed her mother's cheek.

'What was that for?'

'For being here.'

'You daft apeth. Where's your purse?'

Grace walked away and touched her cheek. She was so happy for her daughter, who she knew would be happy for the rest of her life with Tony. As she put the money in the gas meter, she realised that she had dreamed of this scene ever since Dolly had been a little girl playing with her doll's house. Now, her daughter was in her own house, and Grace was able to help her.

Dolly returned to her windows. It was lovely living just a few streets away from her parents and her very best friend. Penny was over the moon when she'd heard that Dolly and Tony could rent this house.

Her mother called from the kitchen to say that tea was ready. As Dolly walked along the bare boards to the kitchen, she wanted to run and jump for joy. The layout was the same as most of the houses in the area: with a scullery, kitchen, front room, and two bedrooms upstairs. She was marrying the man she loved and had a wonderful house. Once again, she couldn't believe her luck.

In the kitchen, Grace had set out a tea tray on a small table that Reg had found on a bomb site, along with a couple of old stools that Tony was going to fix up.

'This room will look so different when you get your furniture,' she said, looking around, holding her cup with both hands. 'Reg and the boys have made a good job of the decorating.'

'Tony said it was in a bit of a state when they first started. I'll be glad when the dockets come through for the furniture and carpets.'

'Well, take your time. Everything will come together eventually.'

'I know, Mum, but you know me; I want everything perfect now.'

'It'll come, love. It'll come.'

On Saturday 14 October, Dolly was once again changing her name, but she knew that this time it was for keeps. Today, she would become Mrs Marchant. As she sat in the taxi next to her father, she felt so happy. She had chosen a beige suit with matching tan gloves, shoes, and hat, and she carried a small bouquet of roses. Her father smiled at her as he gently patted the back of her hand. This was something Dolly knew he'd always wanted to do: give his daughter away to the man they all loved.

Dolly was surprised to see so many people in the registry office. Her mother, along with Penny who wore her callipers, sat in the front row. Next to Penny sat Reg, and then Ivy who held Gail. Gail was busy trying to look all around her. Mrs Marchant, who was smiling fit to burst, sat on Tony's side, along with his cousin, Vera, and her husband, John. There were also many other neighbours, including Penny's mother and brother, and Meg and her mother. Even the two Misses Gregory had closed the shop to be there. Dolly smiled at them all as she walked with her father to stand by Tony's side.

She and Tony had been surprised at the gifts they'd received, despite all the shortages. There had even been a cheque for twenty pounds from Bert Edwards. Everybody had rallied round to provide a simple wedding breakfast, which was going to be held in the couple's new house. All week, tables, chairs, and crockery had been deposited at number 10 Princes Street. Although the wedding breakfast would only be for immediate family and close friends, Dolly and Tony would make sure that it was as near to perfect as it could be. They even managed to get a two-tiered, iced wedding cake.

Photographs were taken outside the registry office, and after all the kisses and good wishes, those that had been invited made their way back to the house. When Tony and Dolly arrived, they stood for a moment, simply holding hands and looking at their new home.

Tony handed his mother the front door key, and sweeping up Dolly in his arms, said, 'This is all ours.' He followed his mother into the house, carrying Dolly over the threshold. When he put her down in the passage, her kissed her long and hard, then said, 'I love you Dolly Day Dream.'

'And I love you, Tony, so very much.'

'I'll put the kettle on for when the others get here,' said Mrs Marchant, and she quickly made her way to the scullery.

As Tony and Dolly made their way towards the kitchen, the front door opened behind them and the house filled up with happy laughing people.

Everybody commented on the fine spread. After the toast and speeches were finished, someone placed a record player on the table and everybody began dancing.

'This is like a real old-fashioned wedding,' said Mrs Marchant to Grace who sat next to her. She held up her glass. 'Don't like those fancy dos in hotels.'

'No, you can't beat those old-fashioned weddings, when we had nothing,' Grace said, raising her own glass. 'Cheers!'

'Cheers!' said Mrs Marchant. 'Let's hope they get what they both want.'

'I'll drink to that,' said Grace.

Everybody knew that Tony and Dolly wanted to adopt a baby.

Chapter 40

Two weeks later, Dolly was in the scullery, singing along to the wireless, when she heard Tony walk into the kitchen.

'Hello, love,' she called out. 'Everything all right? I managed to get Bert's invoices and orders finished early so I thought I'd get home before you. Dinner won't be long.' When Tony didn't answer, she went to the kitchen door. Tony looked as white as a ghost. 'What's wrong? What is it?'

'Dolly, come in here and sit down.'

She went and sat next to Tony. 'What is it? You're frightening me... Oh my God! It's Dad. Something's happened to Dad. How bad is he?' She put her hand to her mouth.

Tony put his arm around Dolly's shoulders. 'No ... it's not your dad, it's Reg ... he's had an accident...'

'How bad is he?'

Tony took Dolly's hand. 'I'm afraid he's dead.'

Dolly jumped up. 'No! No! He can't be! We must go and tell Penny. She don't need this.'

'Dolly, sit down,' Tony said forcefully.

She quickly did as she was told.

'We can't tell Penny; she was with him.'

For a moment, Dolly just silently stared at Tony. Then softly, she asked, 'Is she dead as well?'

'No, but she's very badly injured.'

'Oh my God! Was Gail with them?'

They all knew that Penny would often hold Gail on her lap when they went out.

'No, thank God.'

Once again Dolly jumped up. 'We must go and tell Ivy.'

'She knows.'

'She'll want someone to take care of Gail while she goes to the hospital. What about Penny's mum?'

'I've done all that. Your mum has got Gail, and Billy is at the hospital with his mum and Ivy.'

'When did this happen?'

'Early this afternoon. Just after lunchtime.'

'So why didn't you come and tell me?' Dolly said angrily.

'I was busy going round to their loved ones and then taking them to the hospital. I thought that was the right thing to do.'

The sound of something boiling over made Tony go into the scullery. When he came back, he said. 'I've turned the gas off.'

Dolly looked up at him with tears running down her face. 'Thanks, Tony, but how do you know all this?'

'Well, Bert Edwards was on his way to look at a new job, when he got stuck in a traffic jam. As it slowly moved along, he could see that a van had been involved in an accident with a coal truck. As he drove past, he realised it was Reg's van, but he couldn't see any sign of Reg or Penny, so he turned round and drove to the site instead. He told me what had happened, and as it sounded serious, I took Billy and we went to have a look. I spoke to the copper there, and when I said that

Billy was Penny's brother, he told us to go to the hospital. We found Penny – she's in a bad way. After that, I went to collect Ivy and Mrs Watts and took them to the hospital. Poor Ivy, having to identify Reg's body. I'm sorry, Doll, but with everything that was going on...' He took her in his arms, and she sobbed her heart out for several minutes.

When Dolly had composed herself, she asked, 'Can we go and see Penny?'

'We may not be allowed in.'

'But Ivy and Mrs Watts will be there. I need to find out more, and help if I can.'

'All right. But we'll go and tell your mum and dad where we're going first, just in case they get any news before we do. Then they'll know where to find us.'

'What about your dinner?'

'Sorry, Doll, but I can't think about having anything to eat.'

'I understand. I'll just get me coat.'

By the time Dolly had walked into her mother's kitchen, she was once again in floods of tears. The sight of her mother sitting at the table feeding Gail filled her with sorrow. Gail was perched on cushions and tied onto the back of the chair with a scarf. When Gail saw Dolly, she held out her little hands and smiled. 'Doll, Doll,' she said, not yet able to say 'Dolly'.

'Sit down, love,' said her father. 'This is a bad do. Do either of you want a cuppa?'

'No, thanks,' said Tony. 'We're just going to the hospital to see if there's any news.'

Grace wiped Gail's mouth with a clean tea towel. 'Dolly, could you let Ivy know that I'll be popping into the house for some nappies?'

'Yes, but I'm sure that will be fine. Ivy won't mind what you do.'

'Come on, love,' said Tony, taking hold of Dolly's arm. 'Let's be going.'

Dolly kissed Gail, hugged her parents, and then quickly left.

As they were driving to the hospital, Tony told Dolly what he could about how the accident had happened. They knew that Reg was taking Penny to the hospital that day as she was going to try to walk along the bars without her callipers. Dolly knew how excited Penny had been about that. She had been trying to stand alone at home, but couldn't move. It appeared that one of the van's tyres had blown out, and this would have caused Reg to swerve. It seemed he went right into the path of a fully-laden coal lorry coming in the opposite direction, and he was killed instantly. As Penny was wearing her callipers, she wasn't able to stop herself from being thrown forward and she smashed her head on the dashboard.

'If he'd kept his old van, then Penny would have been in the back, and perhaps not so badly hurt,' sobbed Dolly.

'I don't know,' was all Tony said.

When they arrived at the hospital, they quickly made their way to the room that Penny had been taken to. As they pushed open the door, a nurse came up to them.

'Are you here to see Penny Smith?'

Dolly only nodded.

'At the moment, her mother, brother, and

mother-in-law are with her, but I'm sure they would like a break.'

'How is she?' asked Dolly, dreading the answer.

The nurse gently touched Dolly's arm. 'Not that good, I'm afraid.'

Dolly suppressed a sob. She knew she had to try to be brave for all of them.

Tony took her hand and they slowly made their way into the darkened room. Dolly noticed it was small, and that there was only the one bed. Billy quickly got up from his seat and let Dolly sit next to his sister.

Penny was lying flat without a pillow. Her face was grey, and the top of her head had been heavily bandaged. Dolly thought this must have been where she had taken the full impact of the crash. She looked very peaceful.

Dolly gently took hold of her friend's hand, but there wasn't any flicker behind her closed eyelids. 'Now what have you been up to?' She tried to keep her voice as calm as possible as she let her tears fall.

Mrs Watts stood up and led Tony to the other side of the room. She dabbed at her red and swollen eyes. 'They don't hold out much hope, I'm afraid.'

Tony looked over at Dolly. He knew this news would shatter his beloved wife. He didn't want her to hear this. He also knew that if she could, she would pick up her friend and run away with her.

'She's got a fractured skull,' Mrs Watts continued, 'and they don't think she'll ever regain consciousness.'

Tony turned back to face her. 'What can we do?'

'I'm afraid there's nothing anyone can do. It's just a matter of time.'

Dolly glanced over at Mrs Watts and Tony. She knew that they were discussing Penny. Was there any hope? She then looked across at Ivy, who herself appeared as if she had been in an accident. She held Penny's other hand, looking dishevelled, with red puffy eyes that were full of disbelief.

Shortly after, the nurse and doctor arrived. Everyone was asked to wait outside. It was a very sad gathering.

'I'm so sorry about Reg,' said Dolly as she gathered Ivy in her arms.

'Thank you,' sobbed Ivy.

'Me and Tony will give you all the help you need. You know that, don't you?'

She nodded and wiped her nose. 'How's Gail?'

'Mum was just giving her dinner when we popped in. She said to let you know she would be going into your house to get some nappies.'

'That's fine. She can get anything she wants.'

'Tony will take anyone home who wants to go. I can stay here till you get back.'

'Thanks, but we're all right Dolly,' said Mrs Watts.

'I feel so helpless,' said Dolly. 'What did the doctor say? Will she get better?'

Ivy and Mrs Watts looked at each other.

'They don't hold out much hope,' said Billy.

Dolly sat down on a chair. She had never felt so sad. This was her best friend. They had laughed and cried together for all of their lives. They always thought they would grow old together.

Dolly woke with a start. Her neck was stiff, and her back ached. She had been in this chair for hours. She looked at Tony who sat next to her. He was awake.

'Are you all right?' he asked.

Dolly shook her head. 'Any news? Has Penny moved? Where is everyone?'

'No news. Ivy and Mrs Watts are in there now.'

'Where's Billy?'

'He's gone to look for some tea.'

'He's a good lad,' said Dolly, then, 'Tony,' she whispered, 'what about Ivy? She's got Reg's funeral to arrange.'

'We had a long talk about it. I'm going to take over and sort everything out for her. She don't need all that to worry about.'

Dolly gave him a watery smile. 'Thank you.'

'You ready to go back in?'

Dolly nodded, stood up, and stretched.

Mrs Watts sat on the opposite side of the bed. She stirred when Dolly and Tony entered the room.

'What's happened?' Dolly asked.

'Nothing, I'm afraid,' said Mrs Watts. 'She's still sleeping. They gave her a drug to make her more comfortable.' She looked lovingly at her daughter.

Dolly was about to take Mrs Watts' hand, when Penny made a strange sound.

'I'll go and get the nurse,' said Tony who hurriedly left the room.

Almost immediately, he returned with a doctor and everyone moved away from the bed.

The doctor listened for a heartbeat for a few moments and then stood up. 'I'm very sorry...' he said, and began to lift the sheet.

'I'll do that,' Mrs Watts said quickly, with tears streaming down her face. She bent down and gently kissed her daughter's cheek. 'I love you, my darling.'

Dolly also leant over and kissed Penny, but she couldn't speak, and turned away.

After Ivy and Tony had also kissed Penny, Mrs Watts slowly pulled the sheet over her daughter's peaceful face.

After the sad funeral service for both Reg and Penny, they were buried side by side. As hard as it was going to be, everybody knew that they would now have to try to get on with their lives. The following weekend, Dolly and Tony helped Ivy with all of the paperwork.

'This is all the stuff he had when he first started his business,' said Tony, looking through a folder. 'I don't suppose he made out a will.'

'I wouldn't have thought so,' said Ivy. 'He always said he didn't have anything to leave.'

'If you like, I'll take this lot home and go through it, just to make sure he don't owe any money to anyone... Well, I'm blowed...'

'What is it?' said Ivy.

'He did leave a will, of sorts. It says here that he took out an insurance policy just enough to cover his funeral. He asks Ivy to look after Gail and Penny.'

Dolly was busy going through Penny's things. 'And look, Penny has made out a kind of a will, too. It's only in this exercise book, but it says here, "If anything ever happens to me, my lovely daughter Gail must have all my jewellery...".' She turned to Ivy. 'Did she have much?'

'She had a nice bracelet, and there's her rings, of course.'

'I remember that bracelet,' began Dolly. 'Reg bought it for her when he was in the army. I think he got it when he was abroad.'

Tony looked up. 'Yes, he did, and I bought one as well, but you'd got married so I gave it to me mum.'

Dolly wanted to throw her arms round him. 'I'm sorry,' she whispered. Tony gave one of his smiles that always melted her.

'And if I remember right,' he continued, 'Penny sold her bracelet to give Reg the money to help him get his business started.'

'She did love him,' said Dolly, continuing to leaf through the book. 'Oh my God...'

'What is it?' asked Ivy. 'Is there something wrong?'

Dolly looked up as tears began to run down her face.

'What is it, love?' Tony reached over and took the exercise book from her. He looked at Ivy. 'It says here that if anything happens to Penny, she wants Dolly Taylor, only "Taylor" has been crossed out and replaced with "Walters", then crossed out and replaced with "Marchant"... So every time you've changed your name, she's kept this book up to date–'

'So what does she want Dolly to do?' asked Ivy.

'She wants me to adopt Gail legally,' sobbed Dolly.

Epilogue

Four Years Later

Holding Dolly's hand, Gail skipped along for her first day at school. Although Dolly felt happy, it was a day tinged with sadness. This was something Penny should have been able to do with her daughter, but it wasn't to be.

Gail was a happy, laughing child always full of questions. She looked up at Dolly and asked, 'Will my baby brother be home when I get there?'

'No. We can all go and collect him together on Saturday.'

That was the day they would collect their new baby boy from the hospital. Tony had been over the moon at the thought of having a son as well as a daughter.

Dolly couldn't believe how lucky she was. She was married to Tony, had Gail, and now they were going to adopt a baby boy, but she felt sad for the young unmarried girl who had to give up her baby. One thing she was sure of was that both children would have the best and happiest future that she and Tony could give them.

'Dolly...?' Gail's little voice broke into her thoughts.

'Yes, love?' They were now standing at the gate ready to go in. Dolly had told Gail that her real mother and father, Penny and Reg, were in heaven, and that Dolly and Tony were to look after her.

'Will you be waiting for me when I finish today? I don't think I will be able to find me own way home.'

Dolly bent down and hugged her daughter. 'Of course, I will. I'll always be here for you.'

'You won't ever leave me like my real mummy did, will you?'

Dolly swallowed hard. 'No, darling. But you know your mummy didn't want to leave you.'

'I know, but...'

'I promise I shall always be here.'

With that, Gail kissed Dolly's cheek and skipped away.

Tears streamed down Dolly's cheeks as she watched her daughter go, and when Gail turned to wave, it took all of Dolly's strength not to run after her and take her back home.

The publishers hope that this book has given you enjoyable reading. Large Print Books are especially designed to be as easy to see and hold as possible. If you wish a complete list of our books please ask at your local library or write directly to:

Magna Large Print Books
Magna House, Long Preston,
Skipton, North Yorkshire.
BD23 4ND

This Large Print Book for the partially sighted, who cannot read normal print, is published under the auspices of

THE ULVERSCROFT FOUNDATION